aftereffect

THE ORDER OF RAVENS AND WOLVES

T.L. HODEL

Author warning: This book is a dark romance and is intended for a mature audience. Reader discretion advised. This book contains but is not limited too, violence, profanity, references to abuse, alcohol and tabbaco use, nonconsensual and dubious consensual sexual scenes.

For Harley

Name pronunciations

Micha: Mike-ah
Riley: Rye-lee
Logan: Low-gan
Mason: Mase-on
Junior: June-your
Finn: Fin
Silas: Cy-liss
Preston: Press-ton
Parker: Park-er
Lana: La-nah
Harper: Harp-her
Louis: Lew-is
Derek: Dare-ick
Paisley: Pays-lee
Shelby: Shell-bee
Chase: Chase
Tanner: Tan-ner
Naomi: Nay-oh-me
Ryker: Rye-ker
Grier: gr-ear
Creswell: Cress-well
Kessler: Kes-ler
Whitley: Whit-lee
Hudson: Hud-sun

Playlist

"Carry On My Wayward Son" By Kanas
"Secrets" By One Republic
"Chills" By Mickey Valen
"Nevermind" By Dennis Lloyd
"Blow" By Ed Sheehan, Bruno Mars, Chris Stapleton
"Venom" By Eminem
"Enter Sandman" By Metallica
"Irresistible" By Fallout Boy ft. Demi Lovato
"Natural" By Imagine Dragons
"My Way" By Limp Bizkit
"Lie" By NF
"Teeth" By 5 Seconds Of Mars
"Girl" By Maren Morris
"Fall In Line" By Christina Aquilera, Demi Lovato
"Sober" By Pink
"U+ UR Hand" By Pink
"Bad Things" By Machine Gun Kelly, Camila Cabello
"Sit Still Look Pretty" By Daya
"You Don't Own Me" By Grace ft. G-Easy
"Boadicea" By Enya
"I Hate Myself For Loving You" By Joan Jett and the
Black hearts

10 YEARS AGO:

WHY WERE WE HERE?

I sneered at the kids running around the playground equipment. My little brother was one of those squealing brats. This was a good time for Mase, whereas I didn't play well with others. I thought our mother learned that after my last playdate. She said I overreacted, that Brandon didn't mean to hurt Mase.

My father got it. When Brandon's parents showed up complaining about their son's broken arm, he just told them to keep a closer eye on their kid before he slammed the door in their faces.

I eyed my father and the other four men who sat across the picnic table. How many times did he tell me that the Order had to remain nothing more than whispers in the dark? Secrecy was important.

So, why were the men who ran the Order sitting at a picnic table with an eight-year-old kid, looking like they were ready for a business meeting? Not exactly inconspicuous if you asked me. Especially with the armed guards surrounding us.

The Kings didn't get along. Unless it was Order business, they didn't get together. Not to mention that there were better places to meet than the park. I was reminded of the Order's oath every time they argued—an oath they seemed to forget:

> *The Ravens stand strong,*
> *Through credence and time,*
> *My brother is my bond,*
> *His family is mine.*

I looked over at Dr. Creswell, wondering if he was the reason we were here? His son, Silas, was being initiated tonight with Mase. Next to him was his brother, Sebastian. Sebastian's son, Finn, was only two, but the kid was stupidly smart—he literally remembered everything.

Preston, Ava, and Parker's father, Dean Whitley, sat on the other side of the table. Beside my father, looking as bored as I was, sat Ryker Hudson. He was my best friend Logan's father and the cause of current tension between the Kings.

"Dad! Dad! Look at me!" Mase yelled, waving his hands in the air while jumping up and down on the slide. "Watch how fast I can go!"

Should I tell him to stop? Could we leave if he fell?

Waving my little brother off, my father murmured, "That's great, Mase."

Taking a trip down the slide wasn't something our father considered worthy of his attention. My gaze narrowed on him. Why was he humoring Mase?

"Why are we here?"

My father's brow rose. "Is there something wrong with a father wanting to spend time with his boys?"

Yes! He didn't play catch with us, and we certainly didn't do trips to the park. Such activities were trivial, and trivial was for the mundane and unimportant.

"Alright. Should we build a sandcastle first?" I said, calling his bluff. "Or do you want to push me on the swings?"

He sighed and waved his hand through the air. "The park wasn't my first choice, but it will keep your brother occupied."

"Could've left him with Mom?"

"Your mother's behavior lately is... distressing."

I'd seen her cry a couple of times, but that's just what girls did. Pull on their hair once, and they go running off to cry to the first adult they see. Pfft! Crybabies.

"You should've let me bring my boy," Ryker interrupted.

"Your boy's not ready," my father argued.

"And yours is?"

"Yes."

"Logan's the same age-"

"Enough!" Dean Whitley piped in. "My boy's older than both of yours, and you don't hear me complaining."

Ryker's green eyes narrowed in on Dean. "My boy's-"

"Not the future leader," Dr. Creswell calmly pointed out.

I watched them bicker and groaned, "If you guys are going to be a while, let me know. I'll find something else to do."

There was a kid laughing on the monkey bars... I could push him off.

"Your boy's impatient," Ryker said. "Not a good quality for a leader to have."

I wasn't afraid of him, unlike the other kids who called Ryker "the boogieman." Logan started climbing through my bedroom window in the middle of the night. He wouldn't talk about it, but I saw the bruises.

"Tell me, Ryker, does your wife know where you were last night?" I smiled when his face lit up with anger. That's right, I saw you sneaking out of my mother's room. "It'd be a shame if she found out ..." And by she, I meant my father.

"Watch your tone, Micha!" my father scolded and slapped his hands on the table. "Ryker is a King, and you will respect him!"

My hands balled into fists. My father was just doing what he was supposed to do. No one disrespected a King. Ryker's smile still pissed me off though.

"Now, if we could get back to what brought us here." My father took a minute to straighten up and regain his composure. "Tell me, son, what did you think of last night?"

Tearing my gaze off Ryker, I shrugged and said, "It was okay."

"Did you feel sorry for that girl?"

She crossed the wrong people and paid the price. Nothing I hadn't seen before. The only difference was that they made me watch. I'd never forget the moment she sank to her knees, eyes still burning with hatred, and her fists balled.

"Why should I feel sorry for her?"

"Do you think you should feel sorry for her?"

I hated it when he did that shrink stuff. Answering a question with a question.

"Just tell me what you want me to do."

Ryker snorted. "Your boy's got an attitude problem."

"I can handle my son," my father growled.

Ryker shrugged in response.

Turning his attention back to me, my father sighed. "Alright, Micha, one day you'll be the king of Kings."

I rolled my eyes. Tell me something I don't know.

"And every king needs a queen," he said, sliding a black binder across the table.

I opened it up, forehead crinkling at the pictures of girls. They were all around my age, playing in a white room. I knew the room well. It was the same place our initiations took place. Being the eldest Kessler and next in line for the throne, I had to attend every initiation. I was only four at Preston's.

Looking up at my father, I asked, "Did they do something?"

"No," he stated flatly. "I want you to pick one."

"For what?"

"To keep."

My lip curled. "Why would I want to keep one? What am I going to do with a girl?"

Ryker chuckled. "Trust me, boy, there's plenty you can do with a girl."

I knew what men did with women. I just didn't understand it. My father said I would when I was older, but I couldn't see that happening. The only girl I spent time with was Ava, and I'd rather punch her than kiss her.

"Will she be like the girls at Malum?"

My father shook his head. "The girls at Malum are for everyone to use. This one you'll marry. She'll bear your children and do whatever else you'd like. If you choose to share her, that's your prerogative. But she'll belong to you and you alone. Do you understand?"

I didn't, but I nodded anyway. Was owning a person like having a pet?

"What if she doesn't listen?"

"Well, son," a slow smile spread across his face, "Then you make her."

I liked making people do things. Billy Johnson wouldn't get off the swing so Mase could have a turn... now he didn't go on the swings at all. Returning my attention to the pictures, I scanned through the images.

A blonde in a pink party dress. A girl building a block house, and another coloring. Page after page of smiles and happiness, just like this stupid park.

"Whatcha looking at?" Mason asked, peering over my shoulder.

I sighed. "Go back to the park, Mase."

"Will you come with me?" he pleaded, hope shining in his green eyes.

I scanned his jeans and red shirt, crinkling my nose at the dirt and grass covering it. "No."

"Come on," Mase frowned. "Look, we can kick over that guy's sandcastle, and then build our own."

The kid in the sandbox had his tongue out, completely focused on what he was doing. Bet he'd cry if I destroyed it.

"Go away," I grumbled, angry that I was stuck looking at stupid girls. "I'm busy."

"Doing what?"

"Your brother's looking for his future bride," my father answered.

"Why? Girls are gross."

My father snickered. "You won't always feel that way."

I ignored them and continued flipping through the binder, uninterested.

"Wait." Mase pressed his grubby finger on a picture of a red-haired girl. "I like her freckles. Can I have that one?"

This girl was too small and thin. Why would Mase want her?

"If you want," my father nodded. "But you don't have to choose now."

I closed the book. "Do I?"

"No. Ryker didn't pick Paisley until later, but her family wasn't cooperative and there were a few casualties. Paisley didn't take it well."

"She's fine now," Ryker argued.

"But at what cost?" My father let out a puff of air and waved his hand over the binder. "These girls won't be a problem."

I was getting ready to reopen the binder when a small voice interrupted me.

"S'cuse me…"

Annoyed, I turned around, glaring at the girl in a yellow dress. She was small, with pale skin and black hair.

"I lost my puppy. He's this big." Her hands motioned a size far too small for any dog. "His ear goes like this," she said, cupping a hand on the top of her head, "And he has a tail."

A dog with a tail and ears. Idiot! I watched her pigtails sway in the breeze and smirked at the worry that shone in her deep blue eyes. Maybe this day wouldn't be so bad after all.

Mason jumped up before I could say anything. "I can help look. If we find him, will you help me build a sandcastle? But we have to wreck his first," he added, pointing at the sandbox.

"Why do we haveta do that? We sit side him and make a bigger one."

I snorted. She couldn't even talk properly. What was she, five?

"Huh." Mase looked up, confused why that thought never occurred to him. And it shouldn't have. Why should he share the sandbox with anybody? If he wanted it, then he should take it!

"Okay!" Mase agreed, and grabbed the girl's hand. "Let's find your dog."

My arm shot out, stopping them. "I don't think you should." I wasn't going to let some girl make my brother soft.

The girl's head cocked to the side. "How come?"

"He's probably dead."

Shock pulled at her features. "Nuh uh, he runned away. That's all."

"Nope." I shook my head. "He's dead."

Mase's eyes popped open. "Do you really think he's dead?"

I shrugged.

"Cool," he exclaimed and ran off. "I'm gonna see if I can find the body!"

Based on her expression, my brother just added fuel to the fire.

Her face twisted in anger. "You're not very nice."

"Why should I be nice? You're the one who came up to me, looking for your dead dog."

"He's not dead!" she shrieked, stomping her foot.

"No one cares about your dog," Ryker sighed, waving his hand dismissively. "Now run along before you annoy me."

Most kids shied away from Ryker, but not this girl. She huffed, straightened her back, and stared him right in the eyes. "My daddy says that I don't have to listen to you." Her gaze swept over the Kings as she added, "That you're bad men."

Ryker's brow wasn't the only one that rose.

My father leaned forward, his elbows braced on the table. "What's your name, child?"

"Riley Marie Adams," she stated proudly.

The Kings exchanged a sideways glance, but it was Ryker who spoke. "Your daddy's the deputy sheriff, isn't he?"

She nodded sharply. "Yes, he is."

The Kings had had some problems with the new deputy sheriff. He wouldn't get 'in line', as my father called it, and kept poking his nose in places it didn't belong. They'd discussed what to do with him during last night's lesson.

Dr. Creswell leaned in closer to my father. "How did we not know about this?" he asked, nodding at the girl.

"It seems our new deputy is very astute," he answered, eyes stuck on Riley. "I didn't expect him to be hiding a family."

Dean's brow rose. "He's not stupid. Family is a weakness."

"One we can exploit." Ryker tilted his head and smirked. "Do you like games, little one?"

Riley eyed him for a second, unsure, but then slowly nodded.

"What are you doing?" Sebastian whispered.

"What none of you have the balls to do," Ryker murmured, keeping his focus on the girl watching us. "Would you like to play a game with me, little one?"

Before she could respond, a woman with black hair ran up.

"Riley!" she called out, crouching down and grabbing her shoulders. "Ay dios mio! Don't run off like that!"

"But Mommy!" Riley whined. "I was looking for Charlie."

"I don't care! You don't run away like that!" The woman stood and turned our way. "I'm sorry if she bothered you."

"No bother," Ryker said, his green eyes glimmering.

My gaze locked on Riley, who was standing there with a scowl on her face. When she looked back at me, I mouthed, "He's dead."

"He's not! You butthead!" she spat out confidently.

"Riley!" her mother gasped, shocked. "What did I tell you about calling people names?"

"But Mommy —"

"Don't 'but Mommy' me, missy! Now apologize!"

I had to hold back a smile when she frowned and huffed, "I'm sorry."

"Is that how we apologize, young lady?"

I understood the frustration shining in her eyes. It came with being a kid, when adults wouldn't listen to you.

Riley sighed, wandered over, and hugged me. "I'm sorry."

"It's okay," I smiled, and added in a whisper only she could hear, "Dog killer."

She pushed me away and yelled, "I hate you!"

"Riley–" Her mother started to scold her, but I held up my hand.

"It's okay," I said, placing a sad expression on my face. "Some kids just aren't that nice."

Riley reared back, her mouth open in shock.

"Oh, you poor boy." Her mother hugged me, then glanced over her shoulder at Riley. "You and I are going to have a talk with your father when he gets home."

Riley said nothing, just stared in disbelief. It was amazing how quickly an adult would side with a sad child. Like cheering them up would somehow make their pathetic existence better.

"You know how your father and I feel about bullying," her mother said, shaking her finger.

"I only offered to help find her dog." I gave Riley a smile while her mother's back was turned, and mouthed 'dog killer.' "Then she started calling me names."

"You're a whore!" Riley screamed, before she slapped me and took off.

My fingers dug into my flesh as I cupped my stinging cheek. She hit me! She actually hit me!

"Riley Marie Adams! Get your butt back here right now!" her mother called out.

"No, I hate him!" she yelled and ran across the playground.

"I'm so sorry. I don't know what's gotten into her," her mother apologized and rushed away.

The Kings burst out laughing, stinging me more than the bite from her strike. I watched Riley run around, dodging her mother, and balled my fists. She thought she could make a fool out of me?

I was Micha William Kessler, next in line to lead the Order of

Ravens and Wolves. My family owned this town, and who was she? A nobody, worth less than nothing.

"Can I pick any girl I want?"

"Yes," my father nodded, still chuckling at my humiliation.

I gritted my teeth and hissed, "I want her."

Chapter 1
Micha

My lip curled at the scent of fish in the air. The Docks in Ashen Springs was a shit neighborhood. Last week someone was shot a block away, and there was a string of break-ins a block down from that. But on this street, my street, I could hear water softly lapping off the docks. Two days. That's all it took to clean this street up.

Not many people dared to go against me. Compassion and mercy weren't things I was known for. I killed my first man when I was ten, and eleven for a woman. Did I feel bad about it? No. Only the weak had a conscience. Guilt could drive a person mad—my mother taught me that.

I walked up to the run-down brown and white apartment building. It was the only structure on this street I gave a fuck about. On the third floor—in apartment 3c—was the pigtailed little brat that slapped me in the park, Riley Adams.

My little mouse was a stubborn thing. For years I taunted her, humiliating her every chance I got, but she refused to back down. Even with tears sparkling in her sapphire eyes, she fought back. Maybe I would've lost interest if she had broken?

Despite all the bravado, Riley was an easy target. The poor girl from the Docks, with an alcoholic mother. But it wasn't her tears I wanted; it was her hatred. That rage burning deep in her eyes, that was my crack.

I needed it. Craved the sting of her wrath almost as much as the satisfaction of her humiliation. Our roles were simple–predator and prey. A mouse for me to toy with when I was bored. But then things got... complicated.

I entered the apartment and headed up the stairs as I thought about that night. I was on my way back to my Jeep after a late-night meeting with Jim Severson, when movement in the alley caught my eye.

Jim had his uses, but he was constantly pissing me off with his better-than-you attitude. Fucker owned a chain of department stores, stores that we helped become successful. He wasn't the goddamned president! Which was why I decided to sit back and watch the figure dressed in black rob his store.

Except the figure didn't grab a crowbar or lockpicks out of their backpack. They pulled out cans of spray paint. Ashen Springs had been struck by a string of graffiti recently. Personally, I thought what was considered vandalism improved the place.

The public school had a better mascot. City Hall was decorated with a beachside mural, and the billboard downtown now actually looked like the geysers outside of town.

When the vandal hit my father's office, painting a regal king sitting on a throne of people, I couldn't help but admire the fucker. It took balls to stand up to my father.

My intrigue only grew when I realized it was a girl. When I saw her eyes, I smiled. I'd recognize the rage and anger twinkling in those deep pools of blue anywhere. My little mouse was Ashen Springs' mystery vandal.

This was too good to pass up.

Squaring my shoulders, I prepared to march over there and make Riley regret her decisions. Then she lifted her arms and I froze, my eyes pouring over the exposed curve of her waist.

The more I looked, the more I saw; toned legs, perky little tits which would fill my hands nicely, and her ass! Damn! That was the first time Riley Adams got my dick hard. Naturally, I turned her in.

I'd never forget the look on Riley's face. It was almost as good as Bryce's. I thought he was going to pass out when he slapped cuffs on his boss's daughter.

I played the concerned citizen. Stepping out of the shadows, I said, "Took you guys long enough."

Riley groaned and rolled her eyes. "I should've known."

"I hope you haven't been drinking." I tilted my head and gave her a small grin, "Isn't the old saying, like mother like daughter?"

I smirked and tapped the lopsided number three hanging on her door, watching it swing back and forth on the one nail holding it in place. How pissed would Riley be if she knew my father owned this place? I made him buy it, which he wasn't too happy about.

The place was in shambles. Worn out carpets, broken elevator, and it smelled like fish—everything this close to the docks did. My guess was that he'd tear it down the second Riley moved. He'd already started handing out eviction notices.

Logan's house would be a big upgrade. Most girls would consider themselves lucky if their father married Paisley Hudson. Not Riley. She'd rather die, cold in a box on the street, than move into my neighborhood. But she didn't have a choice. Her mother died three days ago in a car accident, probably drunk again. Riley was better off.

Stepping around the boxes littering the floor, I made my way to the bedroom on the right. I was tempted to throw the bottle of sleeping pills on her dresser into the trash. She'd been taking them since her mother died.

I didn't see what she was so broken up about. If anything, Riley was the parent in that relationship. She took care of the house, and made sure the bills were paid.

Her father wasn't much better. He should've taken her away years ago, and I never understood why he didn't. The sheriff didn't miss visits and attended school meetings. Yet, for some reason, he kept his daughter at a distance.

No wonder no one knew what she was up to in her spare time. Riley had absolutely no supervision. That was about to change. One more week, then she'd be sixteen and mine.

I cocked my head down at my sleeping mouse, sprawled across the mattress. Even on her tiny bed, she looked small, leg haphazardly thrown over the blanket. She wasn't going to like living by my rules, but she would, or face the consequences.

My hand ran through her long black hair, twisting the silky strands around my fingers. And oh, how I was going to enjoy doling out those consequences.

Her purple Minnie Mouse pajamas caused me to smirk. My tough girl had a thing for the cartoon character. Her smiling face was all over–stuffed animals, figurines, and pictures.

There were even images drawn in her sketchbook. The drawings I really liked were in the back of her diary. Minnie scantily clad in lace, kneeling at Mickey's feet. Her diary also held another secret, one she definitely didn't want me knowing.

The bed creaked as I sat on the edge and lifted Riley's foot.

"My innocent little mouse," I said, trailing my finger over her tiny toes. They were painted the same deep blue as her eyes.

"You think your secret fantasies are dirty?" I sighed and

smoothed my palm over the soft skin of her calf. "You have no idea what dirty is."

Riley mumbled out a groan and reached out to hug her Minnie Mouse pillow. I dropped her foot and gritted my teeth. I'd always been somewhat possessive of her. I liked picking on her, therefore, no one else could. But now stupid little things were pissing me off, like that pillow.

I hated that fucking thing! Minnie smiling at me night after night from her spot nestled between Riley's breasts. I wanted to tear it apart and laugh manically as I ground the stuffing under the heel of my boot.

Fuck you, you cartoon bitch!

My jaw ticked. If she wanted to hug that thing, fine! I reached back and pulled my shirt over my head. The air conditioning brushing across my bare skin did nothing to cool my anger.

After carefully prying Riley's arms away, I tucked my shirt around Minnie's face and stepped back. She nuzzled in and released a contented sigh, making me smile.

That's right, little mouse. Soak it in.

My eyes poured over her hair, to her closed eyes, and rosy cheeks. Fuck, she was beautiful. How did I not see it? I climbed on the bed and slid my hands up her smooth legs to grab handfuls of her firm butt.

"How did I miss this ass?"

Riley didn't dress like other girls. I was pretty sure her entire wardrobe consisted of jeans and hoodies. Didn't stop fuckers from noticing her, though.

Just last week, Logan and I paid a visit to some asshole from the skatepark. He was getting a little too close for my comfort. If Riley started dressing like other chicks, I might kill a motherfucker.

I crawled over Riley's prone form, smirking at her sweaty forehead and heavy breaths. "Are you dreaming about me again, Mouse?" I whispered in her ear.

Her diary was very descriptive. I knew every dirty little thought she had about me, and how much she hated herself for it.

Riley grumbled and wriggled under me. I groaned and readjusted myself. It was getting harder to keep my hands off her. Seeing her like this made it damn near impossible. One more week, that's all I had to wait. She'd go to Mexico, bury her mother, and when she got back, Riley would be mine.

"Who do you belong to?" I whispered in her ear.

"You," she whispered back.

It took months of nightly visits and hushed coaxes to get her to respond properly. Getting her to say it when she was awake… now, that would be a harder task.

"That's right, Mouse," I said, pressing my lips to her forehead. "Be a good girl in Mexico. Remember, I'll be watching. I'm always watching."

With that, I stood, retrieved my shirt, and slipped out of the room. I almost made it to the door before my phone went off.

"What," I softly snarled, while checking to make sure Riley's uncle, who was sleeping in the next room, hadn't woken up.

Logan's voice rang out, "Where the fuck are you?"

He'd just won a race and there was a party at his house. I came to Riley's, not only to see my mouse, but to kill time. Logan's parties were epic, but I didn't feel like being surrounded by a bunch of drunken idiots.

"Nowhere," I growled, closing the apartment door and locking it.

"Uh huh," Logan sang with a chuckle. "How's my little sis doing tonight?"

My obsession was my friend's latest source of amusement. Logan used the sister angle to tease me.

"She's not your sister," I growled.

"I beg to differ. Her dad is married to my mom," he argued, "Ergo, she's my sister."

I sighed and stepped out into the cool night air.

"Don't tell me he's with that trash?" a voice called out in the background.

Naomi. Of course she was fucking there. Everywhere I looked, there she was, with her fake fucking smile. "Naomi better watch her fucking mouth."

"Someone's frustrated," Logan snickered. "She still got that pillow?"

"Fuck off."

He openly laughed. "It's safe to come over. Everyone's gone… well, except for Naomi and some blonde chick your brother's been eye-fucking all night."

"Better than fighting," I grumbled.

"Yeah, but she won't give him the time of day."

I couldn't help but snicker. Ashen Springs' biggest heartbreaker couldn't seal the deal?

Naomi's voice was louder this time. "Let's see how great he thinks his little dockside whore is when she gets to Ashworth."

And there goes my good mood.

I climbed into my Jeep and said, "Put me on speaker."

"Should've kept your mouth shut," Logan tsked and did as I said.

"Are you deaf or just fucking stupid?" I barked out. "Didn't I tell you to stay the fuck away from her?"

"Yeah, yeah," she sighed, making me arch my brow.

I did not like being dismissed, especially by a spoiled princess like Naomi.

"Oh relax," Naomi sang when I growled impatiently. "It's not like I'm going to tell her something you don't want her to know."

Did she just fucking threaten me?

"I'm not in the mood for your shit, Naomi."

"You have nothing to worry about," she sang in that annoying tone I hated. "I'm sure her mother told her all about your conversation."

One night, I cornered Maria Adams at work and called her out on her bad parenting. I may have also reminded her that the contract her ex-husband signed was coming due. Two days later, she was dead. I'd done a lot of shit to Riley, but that... she'd never forgive me for, even if she was better off without her mother.

"I'll be there in ten," I said, my finger hovering over my phone. "And Logan, do me a favor? Make sure that bitch can't say anything else fucking stupid." I ended the call and pulled away from the curb.

Chapter 2
Riley

Every town or city has four different types of social classes. On the bottom was the lower class, made up of people who worked tirelessly at thankless jobs—cleaning toilets and serving food—in hopes that they'd make enough to pay their bills. Sometimes, the best they could hope for was a decent-sized box on a quiet street corner.

Just above them was the middle class, made up of nurses, mechanics, and other skilled laborers. They had to save up for a family vacation, but they could still take a vacation. The upper class consisted of doctors, lawyers, and business owners. They had big houses, and a car for every member of their family.

And finally, there were *those* people. The ones who lived in fully staffed estates. The law didn't apply to those people, and everyone was quick to bow down to their demands. Generally speaking, those people didn't associate with the lower class.

This wasn't the case in Ashen Springs, though. If it were, my life would've been a lot easier. There were four families who controlled my hometown. My trouble came from the eldest son of the most prominent one, the Kesslers.

I was six years old when I first met Micha Kessler, and I can honestly say that despite what people think, the last thing anyone wants is to be noticed by those people. Because when one of the elite decides to destroy you, no one will help.

My own dad, who was the sheriff, said bullying wasn't a police matter. And that was after Micha pushed me off the swings and I broke my arm. Mom offered some support when it came to my outcast status; that is, when she wasn't drowning her sorrows in a bottle.

But she was gone now.

She decided that a bottle of vodka–that was her drink of choice– was more important, and left me alone, which made my current situation that much worse.

"Don't you have any pants without holes in them?"

I scowled at the shiny sheriff's badge proudly displayed on my dad's chest. Who didn't like being picked up in an airport full of people by a cop?

"I could've worn my Gucci dress, but thought it might clash with your uniform."

My dad's brow rose. "Gucci?"

What? I watched red carpet shows. Shelby made me; the one downside of having an uber-girly best friend.

"How old is that shirt?"

"Who cares?" I shrugged. "It's comfortable."

I was a bit surprised when he took his eyes off the road to scan my outfit. Driving lessons were a nightmare. God forbid I take my hands off ten and two!

"Get rid of it," he grumbled. "I can see your bra."

The blue might be a bit faded with age, but I could hardly see my bra. Maybe the outline?

"Oh my God! Not my bra!" I gasped and threw my hand over my mouth. "Can you imagine the scandal!"

"I'm serious, Riley. Teenage boys get enough ideas on their own. You don't need to be giving them any more."

"Trust me," I muttered and slumped back, "I'm not giving anybody ideas."

I thought once that Lance Peterson was winking at me, which was kind of flattering, considering he was the quarterback, and the guy every girl in school wanted. It turned out he just had something in his eye.

Can't say I blamed him. I was hardly the Barbie bimbo type guys went for. While I did get Mom's thick black hair and shapely figure, my boobs barely filled out a B cup.

Besides, the rumors Micha Kessler had started about me and Mr. Loggings, who owned the book store, weren't doing me any favors. FYI, I only helped him take inventory when he broke his leg.

I'd lost count of how many times some snooty bitch, or jock prick, asked me if I'd read any good books lately. Apparently, originality was dead.

"Did you get the flowers Bryce sent?"

"Yeah, I got them." *And promptly threw them out.*

"Did you thank him?"

"What exactly am I supposed to thank him for? Slapping me in handcuffs? Or locking me in a cell?"

The smug look on Micha's face that night still pissed me off.

"Criminals go to jail, Riley." My dad rolled his eyes my way, "If you don't want to get locked up, then don't break the law."

Geez, you paint a couple of buildings and suddenly you're a criminal!

"It's not like I sold drugs," I argued, with my own eye roll.

"Do you have any idea how long it took Severson to remove that circus you painted on the side of his store?"

Last time Shelby and I were at Severson's, she tripped and knocked over a display. It wasn't our fault, but that didn't matter. To the owner, we were just some kids from the wrong side of the tracks dirtying up his establishment. He said if we wanted to horse around, we should go to the circus. So, I gave him one.

"I don't know," I smirked, "But it took me over an hour to put it there. You know, as a father, you should be seriously concerned about the law enforcement in this place. I didn't see any cops when I was out 'breaking the law,'" I said, with finger quotes. "I mean, what if I was getting raped or something?"

"Well, you wouldn't have to worry about that if you were home, where you should've been, now would you? God knows who your mother's been letting you run around with."

"Mom didn't *let* me do anything!"

"Exactly my point!"

I wanted to say something, defend Mom, but there was nothing to say. Being known as the sheriff's daughter came in handy in my neighborhood. Most people didn't mess with me, and I was more than capable of dealing with the ones who did.

On the other side, I was also known as the drunk's daughter. At the age of sixteen I'd probably been in more bars than most adults, and was on a first name basis with the three owners of the ones closest to our apartment.

I turned away before my dad saw the tear roll down my cheek. Mom had promised this time would be different. That she'd go through the program and stay sober.

When things got better, I actually believed her. And then she crashed her car in the middle of the night, on an empty street. My thumb brushed over my shirt, tracing the scar on the right side of my abdomen.

At least no one was with her this time.

"Things are going to change. This year you're going to Ashworth Academy."

"What's wrong with my school?"

Ashworth was where all the silver spooned assholes went. Not exactly a place where someone who knew it cost nine cents to flush the toilet belonged.

"You need friends who can teach you better values."

I snorted. *Yeah right, like the value of designer labels and a good manicure.*

"Over eighty percent of Ashworth's students get into Ivy League schools."

"Right, cause I'm *so* Ivy League material," I muttered, picking at the flaky blue polish on my nails. "Chase wouldn't make me go there."

"Chase isn't your father! I am."

I met Chase the night my parents told me they were getting divorced. The news crushed me, and I ran down to the bluffs to hide. Chase was standing there at the edge of the cliff with a bottle in one hand.

He looked so lost, and all I wanted to do was help him. So I walked over, grabbed his hand, and told him it would be okay. I'd help him find his way home.

Ever since then, he'd always been there for me. Coming to school functions, and helping me around the house. Chase was the one who taught me how to ride my bike without training wheels. He helped me with homework, and nurtured my artistic interest.

Unlike my dad, who expected me to be the upstanding beacon of mortality that fit his picture-perfect image.

"Chase wouldn't throw me in jail for having a little artistic vision."

"Graffiti isn't art, Riley!" my dad scolded. "You need to let go of these childish dreams and grow the fuck up. My daughter will not waste her life as a starving artist!"

"Who said anything about starving? I hear the prostitution racket is pretty lucrative."

His face blanched. "You're not having… I mean… are you?"

Of course that's the only thing he'd take from that.

I sighed and flopped my head back on the smooth leather seat of his cruiser. "Don't worry, Dad. My virginity remains intact." And I doubted that would change anytime soon.

"Keep it that way," he reiterated, with a finger point.

I threw my hands up in the air. "Well, there goes my weekend plans."

"I know you just lost your mother, but that doesn't give you the right to be an asshole," he said, turning the cruiser down a long driveway lined with lilac bushes. "Drop the attitude. We're here."

I grumbled under my breath and watched the flowery bushes pass by. Maybe I was being rude? He hadn't done anything to me. If anything, my dad was kind of supportive. He didn't argue about me going to Mexico. He even let Chase go with me, though he could only stay for the funeral.

I kind of expected my dad to insist I come back with Chase, but he let me stay for a week. Which was kind of shocking, considering how overprotective he was. At least that was something I could always count on.

As soon as I saw the house, I no longer cared whether I was being rude or not. I'd like to say it wasn't impressive, but that would be a lie.

The perfectly cut sheets of green grass stretched on for what seemed like forever, surrounding a building that, in my opinion, was way too clean to be lived in. I scanned a pair of white pillars framing a large blue door, almost afraid that I'd dirty them just by walking by.

A couple of men worked in a garden to the left, while a woman in a black and white uniform dusted the banister on the porch. In the middle of the driveway, a cute little cherub stood on a marble leaf pedestal, pouring water from a tulip-shaped jug, filling my ears with a soft trickle.

It even sounded better up here. The nicest thing we had down by the docks was *Shelly's Chicken Shack*.

I don't know why this pissed me off. You were supposed to be happy for your loved ones when they did well, right? My dad worked hard all his life, and though he was strict, he usually did the right thing. Even if it made people mad.

I respected that about him. Maybe it was more about who owned this house? There was a time I thought my parents might work things out, and then Paisley Hudson came into the picture. The queen of Ashen Springs. My dad went off to live his life with her, and Mom turned back to drinking.

"Only one fountain." I stepped out of the cruiser, unable to keep from sneering at the stone cherub. "What will the ladies at my next garden party say?"

"Stop it!" my dad ordered. "Paisley's been looking forward to meeting you. Don't be an asshole."

"Whatever," I grumbled.

Don't know why he thought I wanted to have anything to do with her now. I didn't even go to the wedding. Looking up at the house, I sighed. Guess I didn't have much of a choice.

My expression soured further when a blonde woman burst out of the house, waving at us. Her bright eyes sparkled in the sunlight as she rushed over.

"You sure you want her to be my role model?" I asked, staring at her red summer dress–which probably cost more than Mom's car. "She doesn't wear much, and I'd hate to give boys any ideas."

"Very funny."

I thought it was.

"Be nice," my dad quietly scolded.

"Oh, Riley!" Paisley cried out, pulling me in for a tight hug. "I'm so glad you're here."

Who hugs someone they just met?

"Riley, this is Paisley," my dad said, stating the obvious.

Paisley took a step back, but kept her hands on my shoulders. *Really?*

"You look so much like your mother," she said, tucking a lock of hair behind my ear. "Such a pretty girl."

"Not as pretty as you," I sang with my best fake smile. "Look at that dress."

"Oh, this old thing." She giggled and waved her hand through the air. "Once you're settled, I'll have to take you shopping. I know this fabulous boutique…"

I arched my brow at my dad. *Seriously?*

He arched his brow in response.

"Anyway, we can discuss that later. I want you to feel at home here, so if there's anything you need, just let me know."

"Do you have a bar?"

"Um, yes," Paisley said, a bit unsure.

My dad glanced down at me and growled, "Riley!"

"What? She wants me to feel at home," I said, looking up at him. "How can I do that if I'm not scraping someone off a bar floor?"

Paisley's face dropped into that same pitiful look everyone gave me.

"Riley," my dad sighed, "Your mother had her problems, but she–"

"She what?" I interrupted, brows raised in question. "Loved me? Would never leave me alone? Or how about, I was the one thing that gave her the strength to get better?" I snorted out a snicker. "That was a good one."

My dad placed his hand on my shoulder, which I promptly shrugged off. I didn't need his sympathy, and most importantly, I didn't want it.

"You can't think like that. Your mother was sick."

"Sure," I muttered, snatching my bag off the backseat of the cruiser and marching towards the house. "Heard that before, too."

"Riley!" my dad called after me.

"Let her go," I heard Paisley say.

The phrase *"Toto, we're not in Kanas anymore"* came to mind the second I stepped through the door. If I didn't know any better, I'd think I just walked into a scene from *Gone With the Wind*. I looked up, following a wide staircase to a balcony overlooking the entryway.

Well, I would call it a balcony, but I'm sure there was some rich person name for it. There were tiny bits of useless furniture everywhere. A table big enough to hold some weird plant, a wooden chair that a doll might fit in, and various other things.

Mom and I had to put a book under our table to stop it from rocking, and none of our chairs matched. Here they had tables and chairs for decoration.

The dark hardwood floors gleamed in the sunlight, and to the left, on the other side of a large archway, I could see the shiny appliances of a kitchen. I stood there, staring at the set of glass French doors on the other side of the kitchen, and the pool beyond. I was so flabbergasted by my surroundings that I didn't hear Paisley come in.

"Riley?"

I squeaked and sprang forward, clutching my chest.

"I'm sorry, I didn't mean to scare you."

"It's okay," I said, settling my beating heart.

Paisley smiled. "Would you like me to show you around?"

I shrugged, "Sure." Probably need a guide in this place anyway.

Paisley pointed out each room as we passed. By the time we finished the tour of the second floor, I was more than ready to escape to the confines of my room–which I would probably need a map to find if I ever left. She opened the door and I walked in, stopping after a few steps.

Is this a bedroom, or an apartment?

In the middle of the room, on the plushest beige carpet I'd ever walked on, sat a large four poster bed. There was a set of bedside tables and a dresser made of the same light wood. Much like me, my Minnie Mouse pillow looked out of place among the frilly, lace-lined pillows stacked against the headboard.

Down a couple steps–yes steps–was a navy couch, flat screen TV, and small coffee table. Because every teenager needed their own living room. In the corner by a big bay window, complete with cushioned bench seat, was a desk.

On top of the desk sat a brand new laptop and various writing implements. Other than my boxes of crap, this room looked like it came right off the page of a magazine.

I spotted a cluster of six original cels of Minnie Mouse hung on the wall. I dropped my bag and walked over, gingerly tracing the wooden frame.

"Do you like it?" Paisley asked from the doorway. "They're drawings from Disney."

I rolled my eyes. *No shit!*

"And this," she continued, strolling over to a framed brown leather jacket hung up by a door, "Is something someone named Ripley wore in some movie."

I staggered, staring at the signed picture of Sigourney Weaver in the corner by the jacket. *Aliens* was my favorite movie. Did my dad know me after all? My eyes narrowed. Was he trying to buy me?

"This is your closet," Paisley explained, opening the door beside Ripley's jacket.

I will not be bought by material things.

The closet was as big as my last bedroom, and filled with clothes that weren't mine. At least, not any I already had. There was even a place for a large vanity table amongst the rows of shelves and hangers, something completely wasted on me.

Other than mascara and the occasional lip gloss, makeup was a foreign concept. What did catch my eye was an easel stacked in the corner with all the art supplies I could possibly need.

"A little bird told me you liked to paint."

Crinkling my nose, I stared at the art supplies. "My dad told you to get that?" What happened to 'no daughter of mine will be a starving artist'?

"No," she said, spinning around to walk over to another door. "Here," she explained, opening the door to show me a beautiful black bathroom, "Is your bathroom. That's Logan's room," she pointed at the adjoining door.

Oh right. I forgot about that. My new stepbrother was Logan Hudson, best friend to the Antichrist himself. Mom didn't just leave me alone, she tossed me into the ninth plane of Hell.

"You two have to share. I hope that's okay?"

I sighed, eyeing the four-claw bathtub and stand-alone shower. "That's fine." Bathrooms were communal space, after all.

"Logan's not here right now, but I'm sure you'll meet him later."

"We've met," I grumbled. "If you don't mind, I've had a long flight…"

"Of course," Paisley nodded and sauntered out the door. "If you need anything, let me know."

"Sure," I muttered, resisting the urge to slam the door in her face.

Seconds after Paisley left, *R.E.M's 'Shiny Happy People'* blared loudly from my pocket. The song brought a smile to my lips. It was my way of poking fun at my overly bubbly best friend.

"Hey," I said, answering the call.

"Are you back?" Shelby's sweet voice rang out. "What am I saying, of course you are. If you were still on the plane, you wouldn't answer your phone. Though I could see a miserable bitch like you dragging a plane full of people to hell."

"Only if you were on the plane with me, whore."

"Hey, it's not my fault I'm utterly irresistible."

We both giggled.

"How'd it go with your dad?"

I groaned and rolled my eyes. "He's sending me to Ashworth."

"Oh my God! I hate you! You'll be eating gourmet food while I'm choking down the cafeteria's soggy ass pizza."

I wondered what Shelby would say if she saw this room? Would she look at me differently? Would they all look at me differently?

"You like that soggy ass pizza."

"Yeah, but maybe I'd like escargot and caviar better?"

My lips curled. "Of course *you* would try caviar."

"Can't be any worse than Maggie's peanut butter pancakes."

I gagged, remembering the day Shelby's little sister decided to make us breakfast.

"Have you met Paisley yet? Marnie said she saw her working at the church fair. She was all smiles, handing out cookies and stuff."

Paisley seemed like the cookie giving type.

"She hugged me," I explained with a groan.

"And she's still alive?"

I shrugged. "Didn't have anything to stab her with."

"Well, look on the bright side… you get to live in the lap of luxury while the rest of us pretend to be excited for the neighbor-hood BBQ."

Shelby wasn't poor. Her mom was a nurse, and her dad was a lawyer. Not a very good one, especially since his practice was barely holding on, but he was a lawyer nevertheless. They had a modest house, and enough money for Shelby to get her own car.

"At least you're not trapped in Stepford."

"Oh, come on. It can't be that bad. What's your room like?"

I flopped back on the bed, hating my dad and his happy wife, with their picture-perfect house. I could keep this bed though. Wow! It felt like I was lying on a cloud.

"It's…" I paused, searching my brain for the right word, "Big?"

"Damn it," Shelby groaned. "Maggie hid Dad's keys again."

"Check the cookie jar. That's where she hides her money."

"You know, it's not fair that you know more about my little sister than I do."

"What can I say, the squirt loves me."

"Ugh! I'm coming! I gotta go. Stay strong! Don't let those Stepford bitches turn you into a mindless drone. Call me tomorrow."

"I will," I promised.

"Kisses," Shelby sang, and hung up.

I tossed my phone on the mattress and searched my bag for Mom's brown sweater. I could still smell her as I inhaled the fading flowery scent and dropped back on the bed. It flooded my mind with her bright smile and sparkling eyes. Images that now caused an aching, hollow void in my chest.

I'd never hear her voice again. Never feel her warm embrace, or smell the sweet scent of her perfume. It was all gone. Taken away by one selfish decision.

My whole world was ripped apart because the one person I loved most, couldn't love me back.

Chapter 3
Riley

My growling stomach woke me up. It had been a while since I had a decent meal. Not for lack of my aunt trying. Every time I turned around, she was shoving food in my face. Even showed up at the airport with muffins.

Apparently, my family's way of dealing with pain was to eat. While my uncle and Chase were more than happy with the all-you-can-eat food supply—the only thing they could cook came from a can—all I wanted to do was lie in bed and forget about the world. Which is exactly what I would've done, if Chase hadn't dragged me out every morning.

I rubbed my tired eyes and glanced around the room, half expecting my aunt to be standing there with a plate of *pan de muerto*. One look around the moonlit room and I remembered I wasn't in Mexico anymore. I kind of wished I was.

I groaned and slapped the mattress in search of my phone. "Really? It's midnight?"

My stomach rumbled in response.

"Fine. You win." I dropped my phone and rolled out of bed.

My search for the exit wasn't a pleasant one. I stood in the closet for a bit before my brain registered the hanging clothes. I smacked my knee off the vanity, stubbed my toe on the couch, and tripped up the step behind it.

By the time I made it out into the hall, I was pretty sure the house itself had it out for me.

It didn't help that this house was so big. The vast space held an eerie ambience in the night. My footsteps echoed as I tiptoed past shadows whose forms stretched unnaturally in the moonlight.

The dark wasn't something I was afraid of. Even as a child, I'd embraced it. The darkness didn't tell my secrets. It didn't judge, or make me feel inferior. It cloaked me in the shadows, sheltering me from my harsh reality.

But this was enemy territory, and Micha had a thing for popping up when I least expected. I searched every shadow twice as I slowly made my way down the stairs toward the kitchen.

Though it was only dimly lit by the patio lights, it seemed like a beacon, shining brightly in the middle of a dark abyss. One I readily rushed into.

My first instinct was to turn on the light, but I paused with my finger just below the light switch.

Did I really want to turn it on? My dad would be less than happy if I was up this late, and what if Logan was home? Or worse, what if he wasn't alone?

I dropped my arm, deciding it was better not to draw attention to myself.

This house was overwhelming. They had everything. Literally! From an espresso machine with far too many buttons, to a separate ice dispenser–because apparently cracking ice out of a tray was too much work.

I knew my way around a stove. My grandma insisted I learn how to cook. I think that went with my family's motto of *'feed them and everything will be fine.'* She and I used to have cooking parties. We'd blare the radio and dance our way through meal prep.

I could make anything from mac and cheese, to a full on turkey dinner, and I didn't even know what half this crap was. What the hell do you use a springy looking, long spoon thingy for? I wasn't sure I wanted to know.

I ended up settling on a bowl of strawberries. It was a simple snack to prepare, just rinse and pull the tops off. Plus, fresh fruit, most of the time, was a luxury we couldn't afford.

I sat on one of the stools at the island and took a bite out of a berry. The juices flowing over my tongue were bitter-sweet. Here I was, eating one of Mom's favorite fruits, while she was rotting in a grave. Not very hungry anymore, I tossed the berry back into the bowl.

I kept going over that night in my mind, searching for something I had missed. A clue, or some kind of sign. We'd just finished watching a movie, and I was getting ready for bed, when Mom announced she was running out for milk.

Apparently, she wanted to make pancakes in the morning. The last time Mom cooked was my birthday the year before… And what did I do?

I went to bed, foolishly believing that things were fine. I knew something was wrong when Chase woke me up.

The rest of the night was a blur. My body went through the motions, but it was like I wasn't there. An empty shell, sitting on the hard hospital chair. My dad, Chase, and Shelby tried to comfort me. I
could see their tears and feel their embraces. But all that was

drowned out by the damn deafening *tick, tick, tick* of the clock on the wall. The sound thundered in my ears and filled my head, until I heard those inevitable words… *"I'm sorry Miss Adams, we did everything we could."*

Instead of streamers and balloons, my birthday was filled with dirt and tears. How's that for a sweet sixteen? While packing up the apartment, I found a present hidden in Mom's closet. Wrapped up in pretty pink paper, with a note that said: *'To my precious daughter.'*

It was currently upstairs packed in a box, unopened. I swept away the tear burning down my cheek and turned my attention to the glass doors.

Moonlight bounced off the clean edge of the pool. Water had this way of reflecting things, almost like there was a secret world hidden just beneath the surface. The same as this one, just a little different.

Much like the reflected world I painted on City Hall. A beach-side mural of peace and happiness. Where no one turned to alcohol, the little girl's parents were still happy, and the little boy wiped away her tears instead of causing them.

My dad said it was a waste of my time and the town's money. But Ashen Springs had yet to remove my painting. It was still there, months later, for all to see.

My head tilted as I scanned the outer wall and smirked. Surely painting the place you lived in couldn't be considered vandalism? People did it all the time, right? And Paisley did get me all those art supplies.

It'd be a shame to let them go to waste. I knew how much my dad hated waste. Slipping off the stool, I crept closer to the glass doors, eager to see my next possible canvas.

The room was suddenly flooded with light.

"Shit," I grumbled, throwing my arm up to shield my eyes. *Busted!* "I was just going to bed."

Hopefully my dad would buy my excuse and I could leave without getting a lecture. Except it wasn't my dad who answered…

"Last time I checked, the bedrooms were upstairs."

Logan.

"Why is a little mouse scampering around in the dark?"

My fists immediately balled. Little mouse… that's what Micha called me.

"To avoid assholes," I snarled, and spun around.

Thankfully, Logan stood alone in the archway. He didn't say anything, just leaned against the frame with that stupid smirk on his face. Running into any of the Knights wasn't a good thing.

That's what people called Micha and his friends–which was the worst gang name ever, if you asked me. If I had to pick one Knight to have a run-in with, it'd be Logan. The asshole was kind of charming. So much so, it almost made it hard to hate him.

Almost.

"You know, it's rude to stare."

I huffed and crossed my arms. "I wasn't staring."

"It's okay," he said, giving me a wink. "I know I'm pretty."

I rolled my eyes. "What do you want?"

As much as it pained me to admit, he was right. There was a reason girls fawned over the great Logan Hudson. He was tall and cut, with blond hair that was tousled in a messy, yet styled way. If it wasn't for the ink covering his neck and arms, Logan would fit the pretty boy persona perfectly.

"If I didn't know any better, I'd say you weren't happy to see me."

"Your powers of observation are astounding." I sighed and plopped back onto the stool. "Don't you have a puppy to kick somewhere?"

His jade eyes twinkled as a smirk tugged at the corner of his mouth. "Is that any way to talk to your brother?"

"Don't remind me," I grumbled.

My dad couldn't have married that nice receptionist down at the station. No, he had to marry Paisley Hudson.

Logan pushed off the doorframe, meandered over, and plucked a strawberry out of my bowl. He flashed me his perfect white teeth and popped it into his mouth.

"Help yourself," I muttered, hoping he'd choke on it.

"Don't mind if I do."

I sat back, watching him eat *my* strawberries, which I suddenly wanted, and tried to figure out what his game was. Logan didn't just casually talk to me–not unless he was trying to lull me into a false sense of security–and I wasn't about to fall for that trick.

"Careful with the eye-fucking, sis. I wouldn't want you getting any ideas."

"The only ideas I get when it comes to you involve an axe and a lot of jail time."

"Sounds kinky," he sang, and shot me a playful wink.

I openly groaned and rolled my eyes. "I don't see your usual parade of skanks. Don't tell me you're playing solo tonight?"

Logan barked out a laugh. "Oh, sweetheart, I *never* play solo."

"My mistake," I said, sweeping my hand through the air. "Don't know how I missed the line-up of girls waiting to bask in your masculine glory."

At that moment, a scantily clad blonde in a red dress decided to join us. She carried herself with an aura of arrogance, and why shouldn't she?

This girl would make a potato sack look great. Long, shapely legs, perfectly manicured nails, and hair that shone like spun gold. Girls like her looked down on girls like me—the ones who didn't spend an hour in front of the mirror.

"What's taking so long?" she mewled, wrapping her arms around Logan's neck. "Amy and I are getting bored."

"I'll be right there," Logan said, giving me a smug smirk.

Well played, Karma. Well played.

Though I knew the girl was the mayor's daughter, I didn't know her name. The only time I'd seen her was when her family made appearances at town functions, like the annual seaside festival.

And by appearances, I mean they spent ten, maybe fifteen minutes, talking to a couple of people and taking pictures for the paper. Marnie called it good publicity. I called it bullshit.

Keeping his gaze locked on me, Logan reached around and squeezed her ass. "Why don't you two start without me."

Pause for inward eye roll.

I knew something about fake. Hell, most of my childhood was spent watching Mom hide her pain behind a smile. And though this girl was staring at Logan with a dreamy gleam in her eyes, it was nothing more than a mask. And that mask dropped the instant she noticed me.

"Shouldn't you be cleaning something?"

My brow rose. Guess looks didn't account for personality.

"And what makes you think I'm a maid? Maybe I'm round one, and you're about to get my sloppy seconds." Just because I wasn't some cookie cutter Barbie cutout didn't mean I was any less than her.

"Round one, hey?" Logan chuckled, making me regret my choice of words. "I'm game if you are, sis?"

"You couldn't handle me," I growled, glaring at the twinkle in his eye.

The bastard laughed! Full-on belly chuckled, like I'd just said the funniest thing he'd ever heard.

"Have you even seen a cock?"

I huffed and crossed my arms. "Course I have."

"Porn doesn't count."

"It wasn't porn." I read a lot of art books, and the male form happened to be very popular.

"Uh huh," Logan snickered. "I'm sure you have a closet full of slutty lingerie."

"Maybe I do."

He bent down, resting his forearms on the counter. "What do you think, Naomi?" he said, amusement and challenge sparking in his bright eyes. "Is she wearing a lacy thong, or white cotton panties?"

They happen to be blue, thank you very much.

The curl in Naomi's lip deepened. "I think she smells like cheap cleaner."

Snapping my glare her way, I snarled, "At least I don't smell like a baby prostitute."

She reared back, shocked. "Who the hell do you think you are?"

"Naomi, this is Riley," Logan waved his hand between us. "Riley, Naomi."

Don't get me wrong, I wasn't expecting a warm welcome. Wasn't a big deal. I'd put up with Micha and his minions all my life, none of which were the regular brand of bully.

Besides, being the sheriff's daughter wasn't exactly a great qualifying aspect for popularity. What I didn't expect was the deep scowl on Naomi's face when she heard my name. She *really* hated me.

"Daddy may have married up, but you'll never be anything more than a piece of docksider trash."

Docksider trash wasn't the worst thing I'd been called, and that was today.

"So, no slumber party then?" I said, giving her a fake frown. "How about ice cream?"

She flicked her hair over her shoulder and rolled her eyes.

"Okay, not an ice cream fan?" I tsked, "How about pie? Everybody likes pie."

"Do you think you're funny?"

I shrugged. "I have my moments."

She leaned in, bending over the island, and said in a low tone, "From what I hear, so did your mother."

The smile instantly fell off my face.

"I hear yours gets around." I lifted my brows in suggestion. I'd seen the mayor's wife sneaking out of Tanner's apartment, above Chase's tattoo parlor. "Guess her daughter's just as cheap," I added, dragging my gaze over the scrap of red fabric she wore.

"Did you just call me cheap?"

"Hmm, let's see," I said, scrunching my face up in contemplation. "Slumber party. Ice cream. Pie. Cheap." I nodded and pursed my lips, "It appears I did. My bad." I touched the center of my chest and widened my eyes. "I meant to say fake."

"I am not fake," she called out, insulted.

"When's the last time that smile on your face was real?"

"It's called keeping up appearances. Something I'm sure you know nothing about." Her gaze fell down to my faded navy shirt. "I stopped wearing Minnie Mouse when I was five."

I frowned. I liked this shirt. "At least I'm not afraid to show the world who I am."

"Honey, no one cares who you are," she sang, and waltzed away, heels clicking on the tiled floor behind her.

I cleared my throat and brushed away the twang in my chest. Because Naomi was right. No one did care. It was better this way.

Logan chuckled. "And Ma thought you'd have problems fitting in."

"Oh yeah, I'm sure we'll be braiding each other's hair in no time."

"No one's called Naomi on her shit before," he said, tossing the last strawberry in his mouth. "That was kind of awesome."

My eyes narrowed suspiciously. Since when was anything I did awesome? Maybe Naomi was just the warm up round. Wouldn't be the first time they enlisted someone to help torment me. Micha once sweet-talked the girl at the ice cream parlor into *accidently* dumping a milkshake on my head.

"Is she your girlfriend or something?"

"I don't do girlfriends."

"So then, why is she here?"

"I wanted to fuck Amy, and Amy wanted to fuck her. So…" He twirled his hand in the air.

I grimaced. "Gross."

"You asked."

"My mistake."

Why was Logan being so… nice? Adrenaline coursed through me as my gaze shifted to the shadowy entryway. Was Naomi the only one here?

There was no figure looming in the dark, but that didn't mean he wasn't out there. I glanced at the stairs, wondering if I could make it to my room in time.

The click of a lighter pulled my attention back to Logan. He puffed on the end of a cigarette, making the ember glow brighter, and eyed me. "You expecting someone?"

"Should I be?"

"Maybe?" He exhaled a cloud of smoke and nodded out of the room. "Why don't you go find out?"

I glared at him and batted away the cloud of smoke, filling my nostrils with the rich scent of tobacco. "And risk running into your skank again? I'll pass." We both knew Naomi wasn't who I was worried about running into. "I'm just going to go to bed."

"You do that." Logan butt his cigarette out in the strawberry bowl and waltzed away, pausing in the entryway. "Your door does have a lock on it, right?"

Chapter 4
Micha

My mouse came back today. I should be at Logan's playing with her, instead of waiting for the Order's thieving accountant to show his face.

Fucking Jack!

But Order business came first. As future King of Kings, I had to show I was committed, no matter how small I thought the job was. Didn't mean I was happy about it.

When you waited years to get your hands on the prize, another day felt like an eternity. I could toy with Jack for a bit before ending his miserable life. Might amuse me some . . . Fucker owed me that, at least.

I cocked my head at the guy getting mugged down the alley and the two hookers strolling that way. I was a bit surprised when the younger one's face dropped. For a second, I thought she might try and help.

That would be something new in this lawless cesspool. New Haven. The name itself was mocking. There was no haven here, just addicts and criminals only concerned about themselves. A fact proven when the older hooker steered the younger one back to the front of the motel.

I'd been watching them for a while now. Not because I was bored. They interested me. The younger one clearly wasn't from around here. If I had to guess, I'd say she was sixteen, if that, and was clearly new at this. She shied away from Johns when they pawed at her.

Better get used to it, sweetheart.

If she thought this was bad, wait till some sick fuck got her alone. I'd pay to see that shit. My lips pursed as I pulled my eyes up the girl's bare legs. Maybe I wouldn't have to pay . . . Since the auction last week, there were a few spots open at Malum.

My phone went off, buzzing quietly in my pocket, drawing my attention away from the hookers.

"What?"

"Well, hello to you too." Logan chuckled. "You finished with Jack yet?"

"Does it sound like I'm fucking finished," I growled, glaring at the motel. "Fucker's still hiding in his room."

"So go in and get him."

"It's cleaner if we do it on the street."

Most people around here would look the other way. But you never knew who was staying in a hotel, craphole or not. There was always some prick out there looking to play the hero, which meant more loose ends, payouts, and time wasted.

"She there?"

"I assume you're referring to my newly acquired little sister?"

"Your parents have been married for a year, asshole."

"Ah," he sang, "But technically, little sis just joined the family."

I groaned. There was no way in hell Logan would claim the sheriff as family, but he sure as shit had no problem with Riley. "So, she is there?"

"Yup," he exclaimed with a pop. "Just went to bed."

I looked at my watch and frowned. "What the fuck was she doing up so late?"

"Calm down, Romeo," Logan chuckled. "She wasn't sneaking off for a late-night meeting."

She fucking better not have been!

"She was eating strawberries."

Strawberries. I'd have to remember that.

"Your girl's got quite the mouth on her."

"Why do you say that?"

"She told Naomi she smelled like a baby prostitute," Logan chuckled.

Naomi did smell like a baby prostitute.

I cocked my head and watched a figure come out of the alley and lean against the motel. He had the demeanor of a dealer, slumped in the shadows looking shady as fuck.

"I told Naomi to stay the fuck away from her," I said, as the man typed something into his phone. A few seconds later, Jack slipped out of the motel.

Fucking finally.

"You didn't really think she'd listen, did you?"

Yes, I fucking did!

Jack nervously shuffled down the sidewalk with his shirt half tucked into his dirty jeans, wearing a pair of mismatched shoes. His habit may have led him to steal from us, but he wasn't stupid. He knew we were coming.

Logan groaned, "Bitch acts like you're her boyfriend or some shit."

Naomi was nothing more than a warm hole, a convenient way to get off. I never gave her any reason to think otherwise, but that was a problem to address later. Right now, I had other things to deal with.

Jack met up with his dealer and said something. The hooded figure didn't look happy. Guess he already blew through the money he took from us. I better get this shit done, before the dealer decided to cut his losses.

"Gotta go," I said, hanging up on Logan and snatching the walkie off my passenger seat. "Move in."

Four squad cars rolled in immediately, lighting up the dark sky with their red and blues. It was amazing how quickly a couple of cops could change the scene. The bums hanging out on the corner disappeared, while the hookers straightened up and attempted to act nonchalant.

Jack and his dealer spun on their heels and rushed down the alley. Tires squealed against asphalt as the squad cars screeched to a stop. Two cops jumped out and ran down the alley after Jack. Everything seemed to be going fine until gunfire echoed through the air.

"For fuck sakes," I grumbled, as the rest of the cops took cover behind their car doors with weapons drawn.

A voice finally crackled over the walkie. "Subject secured."

"Hold him," I ordered, as I tossed the walkie and stepped out of my Jeep. I took a second to stretch my tired limbs before sauntering over to the cluster of squad cars. "Who the fuck fired?"

One of the cops, Alex, or Allen I thought, answered, "Wendel. One of them pulled a gun."

Probably the dealer. Jack wasn't dressed to conceal weapons. Not to mention the fucker was too much of a coward to take a shot at a cop.

"You want me to do something about that?" Alex or Allen asked, tipping his chin behind me.

I turned to find the younger hooker openly staring at us, curiosity shining in her bright eyes. The other one knew this wasn't a regular shake down. She was slapping her arm, trying to draw her attention away.

"Take her to Malum."

Alex or Allen cocked his head and eyed the older hooker. "I'm not sure the other one will let us take her."

He wasn't wrong. I'd watched her protect the girl all night, steering her away from questionable Johns, and sheltering her from druggies walking the street. Strange, considering the shithole they resided in.

"Then take her, too," I murmured, and headed down the alley. Nothing wrong with more pussy. Besides, the younger one might be more cooperative with her protector there.

The closer I got to Jack's whiny fucking voice, the more it clawed at the back of my brain, slowly picking at what was left of my nerves. I'd been trying to track him down for three days now and knew more about the asshole than I wanted to.

"Come on, guys," Jack pleaded, on his knees with the barrel of a Glock pressed to the back of his head. "We can work something out. You want to take down Goncho? I can help! I know who his clients are."

"Thief not enough for you, Jack?" I tsk-ed, stepping out of the shadows. "You turning snitch now too?"

The color drained from his face as he quietly muttered, "Shit."

Yeah shit, asshole!

I walked over to the dealer, who was groaning on the ground, blood oozing out of a bullet wound in his calf. He was young. Early twenties maybe. Too bad he wouldn't see his next birthday.

"Goncho's one of our clients," I said, holding my hand out for Wendel's gun, which he promptly gave me. "But I don't need to tell you that, now do I, Jack?"

"I-I wasn't serious."

I glanced down at the dealer. "How much of our money did you give this piece of shit?"

"The name's Don, dick," the dealer growled up at me. "And that prick owes me ten grand."

"Well, let me help you with that," I said, pulling the slide back and popping a bullet in the chamber.

"No wait . . ." Don pleaded, throwing his arm up.

I squeezed the trigger, sending a bullet through his head before he could finish. A loud bang echoed through the air as blood sprayed the ground, and Don's arm flopped onto the street beside a growing pool of red.

Jack hunched over and hurled.

Pussy.

"You should be thanking me, Jack," I frowned at the blood on my boots. *I liked these boots.* "I just wiped your debt clean."

"Jesus, Micha," Jack wiped his mouth with the back of his arm, "You could've paid him off."

"Don't you think you've cost us enough already?" I asked, passing Wendel back his gun.

"Your father —"

"I'm not my father."

He'd be lucky to deal with my father. From the quiver in Jack's chin, I guessed he knew that.

"I didn't do anything."

"Mind explaining to me why I found our accountant two towns over in a shitty motel then?"

"I was visiting my sister."

I knew for a fact Jack didn't have family. He only had a wife, who was currently working off his debt at my father's club.

In my experience, there were certain phases people went

through when they knew they were fucked. The first was usually some sort of lie to get out of the situation.

Whatever. I'd play along.

"What's her name?"

"Tanya."

"What does she do?"

"She a waitress."

"Where?"

"*Buffalo Jim's.*"

"Uh huh," I said, eyeing Jack. He'd obviously thought this out. "Maybe we should go pay your sister Angie a visit?"

"Go ahead. It's just down the street."

I smirked. "Thought you said her name was Tanya?"

"I-I-I . . ." Jack hung his head and sighed.

Ah, the sweet sound of defeat.

"What are you going to do?"

I furrowed my brow at him. "What do you think?"

That's when it hit him—how completely and utterly fucked he was. Fear settled in Jack's features as he looked up at me with desperation in his dark eyes.

Why couldn't people die with a little dignity? Accept the fate of their choices, instead of giving me that pathetic look. Did they honestly think I'd take pity on them?

"Micha, please," Jack pleaded, in a shaky voice. "I'll pay you back. I swear."

"And how are you going to do that? With the sixty-three cents in your bank account, or the house that's about to be foreclosed on?"

"I have a friend. He can get his hands on a '67 Shelby. Logan likes cars."

Ah, bargaining. Phase two.

"If Logan wanted a '67 Shelby, he'd buy one. Why would he want a stolen car?"

"I can get him a good deal."

"So," I huffed, already bored, "You expect us to wipe your debt clean, and Logan still has to pay for it? I thought you were an accountant, Jack. How's that good business sense?"

"Killing someone before they pay you back isn't good business sense, either."

"Sure it is," I argued. "I doubt your replacement will make the same mistake when he hears what happened to you."

"What about my wife? You can have her . . . just let me go."

I sighed. "We already have your wife."

"She has sisters. One of them is only fifteen. Young and fresh, easy to train."

"Training takes time. Not to mention the cost of paying off family members and the authorities. It takes a lot to make someone disappear." I looked down at Jack and said, "I've seen your wife, and I don't think her sister's worth it."

Jack's wife wasn't ugly, but she wasn't exactly pretty either. Lucky for her, some guys were into the plain thing.

"But–"

I waved my hand, cutting him off, and tipped my head at Wendel. "Take him."

"Wait!" Jack called out. "You don't want to do this, Micha . . . I know things. Things you don't want people to know!"

Threatening. Phase three.

"Is that right? Who are you going to tell those things to? The cops? Well, here they are." My arms swung through the air, arcing over the uniformed men on our payroll. "Go ahead. *Talk.* See who they side with. A sniveling little weasel like you, or the men who line their pockets and pay their kids' tuition."

Jack knew how far our reach went. Information was everything, and the dirt we had on people could not only ruin their careers, but their lives. On the off chance that someone didn't care, they were simply removed.

"What about Riley Adams?"

My eyes narrowed. My mouse was none of his fucking business! Just hearing her name on his fucking lips pissed me off.

"Does she know what you guys did to her mother?"

Technically, we didn't do anything to Maria. That was all Ryker. If Derek had just signed the contract, then Ryker wouldn't have been sent in at all.

The Order had rituals. Before we could take a wife, we needed the male head of house's permission, and then the girl was branded.

I gave Riley hers when she was seven. Three small triangles, just under the hairline at the back of her neck. Even drugged out of her mind, she fought. My mouse was a fiery little thing. I wondered if she remembered that.

Jack sneered and continued his threat. "I think someone should tell her."

I barked out a laugh. "And who's going to do that, Jack? *You?* Haven't you heard?" the smile dropped off my face, "Dead men don't talk."

"You know, you really shouldn't record stuff like that. You never know who'll see it," he explained. "I am curious though . . . I heard the sheriff shot Ryker, but he was tied to a chair when the gun went off . . ."

Only four people knew that tape existed. Not even my father knew about it. How the fuck did scum like Jack find out?

"Which one of you was it?" he asked, tilting his head. "My money's on Preston. He's never been right in the head. It couldn't have been Logan, but . . ."

My eyes rolled his way, and he smiled.

"That's it, isn't it? Little bastard finally stood up to daddy?"

I was going to make it quick and easy. A bullet between the eyes, done. Now he'd thoroughly tested my patience.

I took a deep breath, rolled my neck, and squatted to his level. "You really are stupid, Jack. If such a tape *did* exist, and Preston *was* in it, what do you think he'd do to the person who had it? As you said, he's never been right in the head."

That was an understatement. Preston wasn't just wrong in the head, he was completely fucked up. Other than his sister and the other Knights, he didn't give a shit about anything, or anyone, including his parents. And it wasn't some rebellious urge or loner tendencies.

My father—a psychologist—diagnosed Preston as a sociopath. He literally couldn't feel things like guilt and compassion. There was no conscience speaking up in the back of his head, which made him one scary motherfucker.

I smirked and slapped Jack's cheek. "I guess you'll find out just how true that statement is."

With that, I nodded at the officer behind him, who immediately dragged Jack away, kicking and screaming.

"What do you want me to with this?" Wendel asked, kicking the dead dealer.

I had things on my mind other than wondering what to do with a dead piece of shit. *Like finding that fucking tape . . .* But the last thing I needed was one of these idiots telling my father I was more concerned with something Jack said, than cleaning up.

No one could know what Logan did. Killing a King—even a sick fuck like Ryker—was forbidden. It wouldn't matter that he did it to save Mase.

I slapped my hand on Wendel's shoulder. "You took down a drug dealer. Good job making the streets safer, Officer Wendel." Furthering someone's career went a long way in ensuring loyalty. "I look forward to reading about your commendation."

With that, I left, shooting Logan and Preston a text. I told them to meet me at the basement where the Order did the messier jobs. An underground chamber, hidden in the last place anyone would look—under Ashen Springs police station.

I wasn't looking forward to watching Preston and Logan work over Jack. One was bad enough, but when you combined a sociopath and sadist, things got . . . messy. Tonight was a clusterfuck, but tomorrow my little mouse officially became mine, and I got to play.

I turned the ignition on my Jeep, and pulled away from the curb. Riley had no idea what was coming for her. Would she fight it? My dick hardened at the thought.

I hoped she did.

Chapter 5
Riley

Paisley came bursting into my room at some ungodly hour, all happy and chipper. On a good day, I barley tolerated morning people. And that was after a good night's sleep. Which, thanks to Logan, was pretty much impossible.

I kept waking up, expecting to see Micha standing at the foot of my bed. The last place anyone would find Micha Kessler was in my bedroom. Unless he was shoving me away, because God forbid I taint his space; the guy couldn't even stand to touch me.

Worked for me.

The prick was on the top of my "stay the fuck away from me" list. A list Paisley was quickly becoming part of. Her over-the-top bubbly personality was beyond annoying. Apparently, we were spending the day setting up my room.

Yay. And then we were going to the spa. *Double yay.*

Next, she'd be dragging me to garden parties and tea with the ladies. The fact that she managed to make it out of my room unscathed was nothing short of a miracle.

"Up and at 'em sleepyhead," Paisley called from out in the hall. "We've got a busy day."

If I stayed under the blanket and pretended to be dead, would she leave me alone?

"Ugh!" I groaned, throwing the blanket off my head and slapping my arms down on the bed. Who was I kidding? She was probably waiting out there with a plate of cookies and milk.

Grumbling, I rolled over to snatch the elastic off my bed, and threw my uncontrollable morning hair into a messy ponytail. After which, I proceeded to pad barefoot out of the room in search of caffeine.

My morning continued to get better when I met my dad at the bottom of the stairs. He clipped his holster around the waist of his uniform and gave me a quick scan.

"Don't you think you should put some clothes on?"

I was wearing purple pajama shorts and a tank top. It wasn't like I was walking around in my underwear. "I slept great, Dad, thanks for asking."

He sighed and fixed the cuff of his shirt. "Paisley's looking forward to today. Don't be an asshole."

I rolled my eyes and muttered, "She's the only one."

"I mean it, Riley."

I gave him a big fake smile and said, "I'll be on my best behavior," while stretching my arms over my head.

By the time I realized my mistake, it was too late. My shirt had already ridden up, and my dad's eyes zeroed in on my belly button piercing.

"What the hell is that?!"

I quickly tugged the shirt back down. "Nothing."

"Did Chase let you get that?"

Chase was the one who did it. He thought it might make me look at the jagged scar on my abdomen differently. Spoiler alert: It didn't. The crooked line on the left side of my belly would always be a reminder of Mom's need for alcohol. I almost died, and she still couldn't stop.

"No," I lied.

His brow rose. "You expect me to believe that?"

My dad could always tell when I was lying. I guess having a tendency to speak your mind makes one a shitty liar. So, rather than risk busting myself–or Chase, for that matter–I glanced over his shoulder and focused on the purple plant by the door.

"I'm late." He sighed and headed for the door. "We'll talk about this when I get home."

"Can't wait," I muttered as I watched him leave. Then, with a sigh, I floated towards the kitchen.

He was probably calling Chase this very minute. I couldn't worry about that right now, because someone was cooking bacon.

Mmm, bacon.

The feel of a warm hand pressing on my shoulder made me realize I was walking around with my eyes closed. Instead of my obnoxiously happy stepmom, I was met with the kind smile of an older woman with greying black hair.

"Good morning *querido*. Can I get you something?"

"Coffee," I muttered, planting my butt on one of the island stools and hating that it wasn't my fluffy bed.

The kitchen, like everything else in this house, was magazine quality. Sunlight bounced off the stainless-steel appliances and dark marble countertops, which matched the tiles.

The walls were painted a light tan, and little knick-knacks decorated the room. Paisley seemed to favor sunflowers. They were everywhere, accenting the walls and cupboards.

I looked at the painting hung next to the fridge. It was pretty, well done, with the right blend of colors, and completely mundane. It was of a girl in a yellow dress, walking through a field of sunflowers.

An image that had absolutely no meaning and had been done a hundred times before. I'd take a finger painting by a two-year-old on a sugar high over that.

Just as I was contemplating going upstairs to get my supplies, a mug of steaming goodness appeared. I cradled the cup and thanked the coffee gods for this glorious nectar, practically moaning when the hot, bitter liquid touched my tongue. The coffee was followed by a plate of food.

"Eat."

I eyed the woman's time-worn face. "Who are you supposed to be? The cook?"

How anybody got an ounce of privacy in this place baffled me. Every time I turned around, someone else was asking if they could do something for me. I half expected someone to offer to wipe my ass. I even took a bat to the bathroom, just in case.

"You can call me Rosy. Now eat," she said, nodding at the plate.

I used to get mad when people asked if my Mexican mother was a maid, but seeing Rosy's obvious Latino features, along with the Saint Christopher medallion hanging on her neck, I couldn't help but buy into the stereotype.

She seemed nice enough, though. She gave me coffee, and a generous helping of bacon, which gave her extra points in my books. I smiled and popped a piece into my mouth.

Seemingly satisfied, Rosy turned and worked on the dishes in the sink. I'd never get used to that–sitting back while someone else did all the work. It felt wrong.

I tried to help the girl who came to clean my bathroom, but she stared at me like I had two heads. My cheek flopped in my palm and I sighed. Even here, in my dad's house, I was an outcast.

I never felt out of place with Mom. Despite her problems, we had fun. Like the day I taught her how to paint. It took days for us to get all the paint out of our hair.

I cherished those moments. When, for just a few minutes, I had my mom again. There was no alcohol or tears. Just us, and our shitty apartment. A shitty apartment I'd never see again.

I couldn't even go back and visit Mrs. Greenway, who we had breakfast with every Sunday before church. The building was bought by Mr. Kessler, and he had kicked everyone out.

Mrs. Greenway had to move in with her daughter halfway across the country. But that's how it went. The rich got everything handed to them, while the poor struggled to keep what little they had. I felt like a traitor, sitting in this big house, having my food cooked for me.

"It was nice to meet you, Miss Riley," Rosy said, pulling me out of my thoughts.

"You too," I said, managing to give her a meager smile.

"I know it seems like the end of the world now," Rosy smiled and placed her hand on mine, "But you still have your father, and Mrs. Paisley is a kind lady. She'll be there for you, if you let her."

I rolled my eyes. Why did everyone think Paisley was so nice? Where was she when her and my dad got married? I didn't see her trying to include me, and now I was just supposed to accept her? Yeah, I don't think so.

Rosy released a disgruntled sigh. "A week before you came here, she sat us all down and told us you should be our first priority."

My brows furrowed. "Why would she do that?"

"She wanted to make sure you were comfortable."

She should've told them to stay away then. All this attention was driving me crazy.

"Mrs. Paisley hasn't had an easy time," she continued. "Her first husband wasn't a good man. Give her a chance."

Just then, Logan sauntered in. It was sickening how good everyone here looked in the morning. I kind of wanted to walk over there and mess up his hair, but it would probably just make him look better. Bastard!

"Hey, Rosy." He nodded at her, and smirked at me. "Love that morning look you've got going on, sis."

I rolled my eyes and grumbled, "Let me guess. I should give him a chance, too?"

She glanced over at Logan, who was pouring himself a cup of coffee. "Like I said, Mrs. Paisley's first husband wasn't a good man." She gave my hand a reassuring squeeze and left.

Logan took a sip of his coffee and leaned back, crossing his ankles. What did Rosy mean by 'not a good man?' Was she talking about Logan's dad? Now that I thought about it, I hadn't seen any pictures of his dad, and Paisley had a lot of photos on display. There were even a couple of pictures of my mom, so why none of him?

"You have a closet full of new clothes, you know? Not that I'm complaining about your current outfit of choice." His jade eyes rolled slowly over my PJs. "It shows off your assets."

For a second, I seriously contemplated murder. Besides his army of shanks, who would really miss him? I'd be doing the world a favor.

I grabbed my dishes and slipped off the stool. "Stop looking at my assets."

"Sorry, sis, I was tasked with your new wardrobe." A large smile spread across his face. "Your assets are kind of my business."

A closet full of slut gear, fantastic.

I turned on the faucet, letting warm water cascade over my fingers. "Guess your mom was too busy to do it herself?"

"I have better fashion sense." Logan cocked his head and gave me a strange look. "You don't have to do that … we have people to clean up."

I was well aware of how many *people* they had to do stuff here. "There's nothing wrong with cleaning up after yourself. You should try it sometime."

"I clean up after myself."

"Hosing down your latest plaything doesn't count."

"Why would I hose them down?" He flashed me his perfect white teeth. "My job's done when the mess is complete."

What a gentleman.

"Speaking of playthings, isn't Naomi looking for you?" I wasn't Bitchy Barbie's biggest fan, but she had her uses. She was good at distracting pricks like Logan.

"Aw, you miss her already?"

"Well," I drawled, "I was going to go trip a couple of orphans later. Thought she'd like to join the fun."

"Sorry, sis," he barked out a laugh, "You'll have to see your new best friend another day. I don't do sleepovers."

Of course he didn't. Guys like Logan never did. Yet girls still swooned. It was disgusting, really. And that had nothing to do with how Tucker Monroe pretended to be interested in me last year, only to humiliate me in front of his friends.

"Do you treat all women with this much respect, or is Bitchy Barbie special?"

Logan shrugged. "She knows the deal. Why? Jealous?"

"Hardly. And if you keep looking at me like that," I lifted my arms to display a fork in my wet hand, "I'll gouge your eyes out with this fork."

"You hear that, bro?" He chuckled over my shoulder. "She threatened me with a fork."

I pushed back urge to take a peek. He got to me once, and I wasn't about to let it happen again. "Ha, ha, very funny. I didn't fall for it last night, and I'm not falling for it now."

All he gave for a response was a small shrug, which didn't help settle my nerves any. Maybe I should look? No! Home was the one safe place I had, and no one was going to take that from me.

"You know what? I hope Micha is here," I growled, shutting off the water. "Then I can shove this fork–"

The threat died on my tongue when I spun for the dishwasher and jarred to a stop. Not more than an inch from my face was a broad chest covered in expensive red fabric.

The dishes slipped through my wet fingers, crashing to the floor. My brain barely registered the sound of breaking ceramic, or the feeling of the tiny pieces bouncing off my feet. I knew who it was before he spoke.

"Hello, Mouse."

Micha Kessler.

This was an inevitability. There was no escaping Micha in this house. I knew that. Still, I was completely blindsided. I closed my eyes like I did when I was a child and there was monster under my bed. But when I opened them, that penetrating gaze was still glaring down at me.

Micha tilted his head, shifting his gaze to the floor. "You dropped your fork." Hatred dripped off him like venom as his chocolate eyes rolled back up to mine. "Where were you going to shove that?"

"Give me a second to grab another and I'll show you."

I swear it was some unwritten rule that the bigger the asshole, the better they looked. And Micha was the biggest asshole I knew. If his tall body and well-built physique wasn't enough to make people want to look at him, then his angular jaw coated with the right amount of dark stubble, thick lips, and molten chocolate eyes drew them in.

"There's one right there," Micha tipped his chin, causing a lock of dark chestnut hair to flop over his forehead. "Pick it up."

I swallowed my nerves and struggled to calm my fluttering heart. Even now, after years of torment, his beauty was disarming.

My eyes narrowed, meeting his challenging gaze. "I prefer to stand. That way I can see you coming."

His brow arched. "Did that sound like a fucking request? Pick. Up. The fork."

"Sorry, I don't take orders from assholes."

"Is that right?" Micha sighed, and clicked his tongue. He was getting impatient. "Tell me something, Mouse, when exactly did you think it was okay to prance around with your ass on display?"

I opened my mouth, but no words came out, stunned by the way his eyes drifted down my body, pausing on the swell of my breast. I swallowed nervously and took a cautious step back, narrowly avoiding the pieces of ceramic littering the floor.

"I-I-I'm not …" This was all wrong. I needed to get out of there. "No one's looking at my ass."

Micha followed, causing my heart to tighten in my chest with the sound of ceramic crunching under his booted foot.

"Logan is."

If someone was staring at my ass, it sure as hell wouldn't be Logan. They were constantly reminding me of how pathetic I was. Besides, why would Micha care? I quickened my steps, not liking the dark glint in his eyes.

"No, he isn't," I argued, tugging down on the shorts I suddenly found too short.

My retreat came to a crashing halt as I backed into a wall of muscle and Logan's voice wafted in my ear. "Yes, I am, sis."

Micha stepped in before I could move away. My heart stopped dead in my chest. Either that, or it was beating so fast I couldn't feel it anymore. I never thought I'd want the cruel pranks, or hurtful taunts, but I did.

Humiliation was easy. But this … being sandwiched between two hard bodies while Micha stared down at me like he was starving and I was his next meal. I didn't know how to fight that.

"I like you nervous, Mouse," Micha purred, and reached out to twist a loose strand of my hair between his fingers.

Logan rested his chin on my shoulder and looked up at me with those deep green eyes. "You're not nervous, are you?"

Of course I was nervous. I was downright terrified, and they knew it. Hell, they got off on it. Micha and Logan's brand of unhinged didn't just border on the immoral; it crossed right over into the dark abyss of debauchery.

"Stop it," I said, shying away from one, only to press into the other.

Micha lifted his hand and watched his finger graze a trail over my collarbone and down to the swell of my breasts. "Or what?"

I jutted my chin upward. "I'll scream."

"Go ahead. We like it when they scream."

Logan smirked and brushed his thumb over my cheek. "We like it even better when they cry."

"She doesn't cry," Micha said, continuing to swirl his finger. "Do you, Mouse?"

I did cry, I just didn't let him see it. Micha Kessler had done many things to me, but I swore no matter what, he'd never get my pain. I'd hold my tears back until I was alone, which was becoming increasingly hard to do, with his touch burning a trail of goose-bumps across my skin.

"What do you want?" I asked, hoping to bring this to an end.

"Coy doesn't suit you, Mouse." Micha gripped my chin, forcing me to look at him. "You know what I want."

I didn't know what his game was, but I knew I was done playing it. Twisting my head, I ripped out of his grip and snarled, "I have shit to do, so if you don't mind getting to the—"

My wide eyes snapped back up. It looked like he was … hard!

"Now's she's getting it," Logan snickered in my ear.

"I'm only going to say this once, so listen up." Micha's features hardened as he leaned back and gave me a quick scan. "I own your ass. Every thought you have, breath you take, and decisions made are mine. Be good, do what I say when I say it, and maybe I'll only take your body."

My fists balled. This shit was simply another way to humiliate me. It was the same old song and dance, just a different tune.

"And why would I ever agree to something like that?"

"Because if you don't," Micha leaned in to growl in my ear, "I'll take everything."

The joke was on him. I didn't have anything left to take. What remained of my broken soul left when Mom died.

"I'm not afraid of you."

"Is that what you tell yourself at night?" The corner of his mouth lifted. "When you're dreaming about me."

"Pfft, you wish."

"I read your diary."

I faltered. He had to be bluffing. It was my dirty little secret, one I hated myself for. Not even Shelby knew. I could do nothing but stare wide eyed at his smug expression. Couldn't even move when he brushed his thumb over my bottom lip.

"Do you think about me when you touch yourself?" He tugged on my lips and smirked, "I bet that pussy's wet right now."

I watched everything in slow motion. My arm swinging through the air. His head twisting to the side, and my hand rise for another strike.

Micha grabbed my wrist, twisted my arm behind my back, and folded me over, lifting my feet off the ground, as my cheek was pressed into the hard marble counter top.

"Let me go!" I snarled, fighting to push myself up, despite his heavy hand on my back.

"Fight me if you want." I yelped when his heavy hand landed on my butt. "There's nothing your mousy little claws can do." Another smack, this time hard enough to make me jump. "Your pretty little ass is mine!"

My ass stung, I was out of breath, and thoroughly humiliated. I'd had about enough of this shit! Without even thinking, I swung my foot back, bringing my heel up into his groin.

Micha sucked in a large breath, cooling my face with the sudden intake of air, and then he doubled over with a curse.

Free from his hold, I righted myself and sneered down at his face, twisted in agony.

"How's that for mousy?" I snidely spat, and stepped over his crumpled form to storm out.

Chapter 6
Micha

MOTHERFUCKER!

I groaned at the ache in my balls and pulled myself off the floor. She got me good. Knew it, too. Strutting out of here with her chin up, all proud. Fucking adorable.

If I'd have pulled that shit on any other chick, they'd be begging to suck my dick. Not my mouse. What did she do when I had her cornered? She shot me the sweetest fucking smile and then kicked me in the nuts!

Game on, Mouse. Game on.

"That was great," Logan choked out, doubled over in laughter. "*How's that for mousy.*"

"You done?" I grumbled, unamused.

"Is this going to be a regular thing?" he asked, fighting to control his amusement. "Cause I'd hate to miss the next show."

I hoped he fell over and smacked his face on the floor.

Logan's laughter subsided for a second, but then picked right up when he looked over at me.

"Big bad Micha Kessler," he cried out, clutching his side, "Taken down by a little girl."

Laugh it up, asshole!

"A little girl who is currently upstairs with your mom," I pointed out. "Alone."

That shut him up. All amusement dropped from Logan's face, as he twisted his neck and stared at the stairs.

"Shit, Micha!" He threw his hands up in the air. "What'd you have to go and get her all worked up for?"

"Don't put this all on me. You were there too, asshole."

"Well yeah, but ..." Logan shot another worried glance out into the hall.

I loved my best friend, but when it came to his mom, he was a giant pussy. Couldn't blame him. Ryker made their lives a nightmare. The only people they'd had in this house were each other.

"Well, we're not going anywhere now. Tell Mase to go without us."

I shrugged and headed for the stairs, grabbing my bag on the way. It didn't matter to me where we swam, as long as we got some good laps in. I was too preoccupied this summer with watching my mouse, and Coach was going to kick my ass tomorrow when school started.

Logan grumbled and followed. "Could be at the beach surrounded by chicks in bikinis, but *no*. You had to go and piss off the hellcat."

"If you're going to whine all day," I sighed, "Let me know, so I can put some earplugs in."

His green eyes narrowed. "You planned that shit, didn't you?"

I didn't, but smirked regardless. Sometimes shit just worked out.

"Isn't there some bro-code shit about your friend's sister being off limits?"

My brow rose. "You fucked Silas's mom." Silas's mother was a famous actress and hot as hell. I'd have fucked her too. "Besides, Riley's your *stepsister*."

I wouldn't point my dick in the same direction of a chick that shared Logan's bloodline. She'd be crazier than Ava, which was a truly terrifying thought.

"That's right," Logan grinned, "We're not blood related."

My eyes narrowed. I knew that look. "Touch her, and I'll break your fucking jaw!"

"I don't know … Might be worth it."

I glared at him, hands balled and ready to swing.

"Relax, Romeo," he chuckled, holding his hands up. "I make it a rule to stay far away from chicks that go for the balls."

"What about Amy?"

"What about her?"

"Didn't she kick you in the balls last month?"

He shrugged. "That's different."

"How is that different?"

The corner of his mouth tipped up. "She likes it when I'm mad."

Of course she does, misogynistic bitch.

We were all fucked up, but Logan ... At fourteen, as part of our initiation into the Order, we were taken to Malum and given a girl we could do anything we wanted with. No one liked to talk about what happened to Logan's.

"If she didn't prefer pussy," I said, rounding the corner at the top of the stairs, "I'd say you found your perfect match. She's just as twisted as you."

"Nah. She's fun to fuck, but boring as hell."

I couldn't argue. Amy was that hot, slutty, librarian-type guys dreamed about. Proper and dull during the day, but a wildcat in the sack.

"Besides, I'm not the one who got off on getting kicked in the nuts," Logan shook his head. "That's fucked up, bro."

What can I say? I did get off on that shit. The cute way her face scrunched up, along with the storm raging in those sapphire orbs. I got hard just thinking about it. Speaking of my mouse …

The door to her room was ajar. I could see Riley sitting on the floor with her legs crossed, her long hair flowing down her back like black silk. Unsurprisingly, she'd left the new clothes in her closet alone, and was wearing a pair of jean shorts and a yellow shirt, both faded with age, not style.

I leaned against the wall and watched her pick her nails as Paisley described the finer points of decorating. Occasionally, she'd snort out an annoyed sigh, but that didn't deter Paisley. She kept rambling on with a smile on her face.

Some people thought she was fake, but as sickening as it was, Logan's mother really was that nice. I figured it was her way of making up for all the evil shit her husband did. Shortly after she married Riley's dad, she paid a visit to her mother.

She wanted to help with finances and be involved in her step-daughter's life. Maria Adams was less than happy. Can't say I blamed her, considering what Ryker did to her. Honestly, I don't know what Paisley was thinking. People didn't forget the person who destroyed their life.

Riley's brows furrowed in confusion. "You want me to organize my underwear by color?"

"Yes," Paisley nodded. "Then it's easier to match them to your outfit."

"Match them to my outfit?" Riley gave her an 'are you stupid' look. "What the hell for? They're underwear. They go under my clothes. No one's going to see them."

I will, little mouse.

I think Paisley was just happy to have another girl around. Only, Riley wasn't like the girls she was used to. She painted buildings in the dark, watched old movies, and couldn't care less about makeup or fashion.

"How long do think it'll be before she's had enough?" Logan whispered, peeking over my shoulder.

His question was answered when Riley huffed, walked over to a box, and dumped it out on the floor.

"This one's unpacked," she sang with a smile on her face.

She was such a brat. I gave it a week before I had a reason to punish her–something I very much looked forward to.

"Maybe we should go in there?"

I groaned and tugged Logan down the hall to his room. "Riley's not going to do anything."

As much as she didn't like her new stepmom, Paisley was innocent, and Riley knew it. Hurting her would be like slapping a baby. Riley was more likely to attack the person who did something to Paisley, than she was to attack Paisley herself.

We walked into Logan's room, where he kissed his hand and placed it on the picture of a cherry-red Porsche 916 hung on his wall. "One day, baby."

It was a ritual I'd seen countless times before. "Haven't found one yet?"

He frowned. "No."

There was no one better suited to take over *Hudson Avionics* than Logan. His room was full of cars, planes, and other various things.

I wouldn't be surprised if he could take an engine apart and put it back together blindfolded. But that car . . . that was his unicorn. There were only eleven made, meaning it was out of reach, even for a man with his money and resources.

"Did you go through Jack's phone?" Logan asked, while pulling out a pair of swim trunks from his dresser.

"Yeah." I grimaced at the memories of Preston and Logan's methods of information extraction. People said I was cold. Those assholes ate burgers while tossing what was left of Jack into the incinerator. "Didn't find much."

"Are you sure he even has the tape? Could've been bullshitting us."

My brow rose. "Pretty sure he would've spilled anything he was holding back when you stuck that hot poker in his nut sack."

Logan looked up and smiled. "Yeah, he didn't like that much."

I shook my head, pulled my shirt off, and dropped my bag on the bed. "Whoever Jack's friend is, he was careful. Only made contact through texts with a burner phone and called himself 'The Piper.'"

Logan's back stiffened.

"What?"

"Nothing," he said, shaking it off. "Just something *he* used to say."

By *he,* he meant his father. Logan had scars all over his body from that bastard. Couldn't even look himself in the mirror until he covered them with a shitload of ink. We didn't talk about Ryker. Didn't so much as say his name. He was dead, rotting in the ocean we threw him in.

"It's time to pay the piper, boy," Logan said, with a far off look in his green eyes.

"You okay?"

"Yeah," he growled, marching out the door. "I'm fine."

* * *

We swam for most of the day. Logan started to complain after about an hour, but he'd thank me after practice tomorrow. Coach was one of the few people who didn't give a fuck who our fathers were. If you wanted to be on his team, you'd have to work for it–something I respected him for.

Logan tried the "it was summer break" excuse last year. Coach's response was *We live ten minutes from the ocean, and you couldn't find time to swim?* Then, just to prove a point, practice was held at the docks for the next two weeks.

I showered, threw on a pair of jeans and shirt, and headed down-stairs to get something to eat. Logan took his sweet ass time getting ready, and my father was due any minute.

Any minute turned out to be twenty. I was halfway through a plate of Rosy's lasagna when he finally waltzed in.

"Son," he said, tipping his head in my direction. "Dressed casually, I see."

He'd been trying to get me in a suit for years. "Dressing for your position" he called it. When he retired and I took over, then I'd wear the Armani three-piece.

"You're late," I said, glancing at my watch.

"I know." He walked farther into the room, waving his hand over his shoulder.

Marco, the head of our security, entered, followed by four others, two of which were dragging the sheriff. His hair was disheveled and a deep purple bruise marked the left side of his jaw.

"The sheriff here," My father indicated Derek, as he was dropped in the chair opposite me, "Wasn't particularly cooperative."

"Fuck you, Louis!" Derek snarled and spat at my father's feet.

"Now Derek," my father slapped his hands down on the sher-iff's shoulders and gave them a squeeze, "I thought we were past this?"

I watched anger swirl in the sheriff's eyes. While they were the same color as my mouse, the wrathful storm raging within was different, not as intense. She may have gotten the color from her father, but her eyes were far more expressive.

"Why don't we settle this man to man? Or are you worried you'll get your suit dirty?"

Ah, same defiant tone, though.

My father arched a brow down at the sheriff, then tipped his head at Marco, who promptly marched over and smacked Derek across the face.

He was a big guy, well over six and a half feet. and a former Army Ranger. The force of his strike knocked Derek clean out of his chair. The sheriff hit the ground with an "oof" and lay there grumbling a string of curses. Stubbornness must be an Adams' trait.

"There's nothing to settle," my father said, smoothing his suit jacket before stepping over Derek's prone form to take a seat. "The contract's signed. It's done."

Marco fisted Derek's collar and tossed him back into the chair, causing the legs to screech against the tile floor.

"You can't do this!" Derek yelled, slamming his fists against the table. "I only signed that fucking thing to save my wife!"

Most people could be bought or blackmailed—both were tried to get the sheriff's co-operation. But he wouldn't give. That's when Ryker decided to take care of it. The things he did to Riley's mother were so deranged that Derek not only helped us get rid of his body, but took the blame for shooting him.

To the rest of the world, Ryker Hudson was missing and declared dead a year ago, but the Order needed an explanation.

I stopped and studied Derek. Could he be Jack's friend? He was the one who hid the tape and had access to it. No, he wouldn't risk Riley finding out what had happened to her mother. It would destroy her.

"You still signed it," my father stated flatly.

"God damn it, Louis! This shit isn't right!"

"I suggest you calm down."

"Fuck you!" Derek snarled and stood. "My daughter's not going to be any part of this!"

The click of a gun froze him in his tracks.

"This is getting tiresome," my father sighed, waving the sheriff's own gun at him. "Now sit down before I decide it's easier to dispose of you and have Logan sign the contract."

Derek's suspicious gaze studied my father. "Logan can't sign shit."

"He's her brother now," my father explained, "Making him next in line to decide your daughter's fate."

The sheriff took his seat with a smug smile. "Actually, Chase is."

It was my father's turn to eye the sheriff. "Chase Mathers has no relation to your daughter."

"He's her uncle. His wife was my sister. So, go ahead and kill me. Good luck getting him to sign shit."

"If he's her uncle, then why doesn't Riley know?" I asked, not sure if I believed him. I'd never heard her refer to him as anything other than a friend.

"Samantha and I stopped talking when Riley was a baby. She doesn't remember her."

My father sat back, looking casual, but I knew differently. He'd just stored that in his mind to add to his book he called the "King's Ledger." It was the place he kept all things he thought might be useful one day.

No one other than me knew it existed, not even the other Kings, who he had information on as well. I had to hand it to him, I don't know how he did it, but my father was thorough. I was so drunk when I fucked Marcy Granger that I didn't even know her name until I read it in his book.

"Well, thank you for that little tidbit of information, Sheriff." My father sighed. "But I'm sorry to inform you that brother trumps uncle."

Derek's face slipped back into anger. He knew he was losing, but still wouldn't give up. At least I knew where my mouse got it from.

"You won't get away with this!"

"I don't know what you're so worried about," I growled. "She'll be well taken care of."

I kept my end of the bargain. Riley would be safe and provided for. I'd even take her comfort into account. Hell, I already did. I filled her room with furniture from her uncle's shop in Mexico. Even went so far as to track down all the jewelry her mother had sold over the years, and some of it wasn't easy to find.

"You really think she's going to go along with this shit?" Derek sneered, with a smug glint in his eyes.

I shrugged. "She won't have a choice."

"She hates you. You know that, don't you?"

My brow arched. "Not as much as she'll hate you, when she finds out you gave her away."

Derek's face paled as his eyes went wide with realization, and for the first time since he got here, the sheriff was quiet.

Chapter 7
Riley

It turned out I was one of those girls who didn't want the window down because it might mess up my hair. But in my defense, I didn't know hair could be this soft, or skin, for that matter.

Okay, so the spa wasn't that bad. Well, except for the whole Brazilian thing. When I was asked if I wanted the works, I just shrugged, figuring when in Rome. *Big mistake.*

I should've known something was up when they asked me to remove my underwear. I just thought they wanted to be thorough and get my entire leg. I mean, I was wearing boyshorts, so it made sense.

After I hit the first lady, they called in back-up. I had to hand it to *Asher's Spa and Boutique*, they had some tough girls working there.

Paisley giggled from the driver's seat. "How many times are you going to smell yourself?"

"That depends," I said, dropping my arm away from my nose. "How long am I going to smell like strawberries?"

"You have the same lotion in your bag."

I eyed the black bag at my feet, wondering which of the many bottles it was. *Wait a minute . . . Did I switch bodies with Shelby?*

The smile dropped off Paisley's face when we turned down the driveway. She slowed to a stop, and stared at a sleek black town car parked in front of the house.

"Are you okay?"

She didn't get a chance to answer before my door was thrown open by Logan.

"Damn, sis," he said, giving me a once over. "I'd definitely fuck you now."

"I think I'll pass," I grumbled, and pushed my way past him. No way was I getting caught in another situation like this morning. Sure, having Paisley there offered some comfort, but not much. He was her son, after all.

"Hey," Logan called out after me. "Your dad wants to talk to you. He's in the kitchen."

"Great," I muttered, opening the door and stepping inside.

I kind of hoped he'd forget about the whole piercing thing. Could I avoid the whole thing? Go hide in my room and pretend I was pissed at him? No. There was no stopping one of his lectures. Sighing, I dropped my bag and headed for the kitchen.

"Look, I know you don't approve, but–"

I froze two steps into the kitchen. Five large men, all wearing black suits, turned to look at me. Each one stood stiffly with their arms neatly clasped behind their backs. The only one who moved was the guy who stepped in front of the archway, blocking the entrance I just came in.

"Good evening, Riley."

My attention was drawn to the table in the back, where Micha sat with both of our fathers. If Louis Kessler sitting in my kitchen dressed like he was at a business meeting wasn't enough to tell me something was wrong, then the bruises on my dad's face and the blood on his shirt was.

Mr. Kessler nodded at Micha. "I believe you've met my son."

"Yeah," I said, eyeing his perfectly tailored suit. He looked like his son. Same olive complexion, dark eyes, and chestnut hair, though his had a few strands of silver. "We've met."

If that's what you want to call it.

My gaze shifted back to my dad, eyes traveling over the swollen purple flesh marring his jaw. My dad wasn't a small guy. He held his own against the guys he arrested. Seeing him like this, with his head hung, and a broken look in his eyes, was unnerving.

"What's going on?" I asked, an uneasy feeling settling in the pit of my stomach.

"Please," Mr. Kessler waved at the chair across from him, "Have a seat."

I was pretty sure I'd seen this in a horror movie before. Some guy, sitting in a house, talking in a polite manner. Then *bam*! You wake up strapped to a slab about to be dismembered!

"I'm good right here."

Micha released an impatient sigh. "Sit down, Mouse."

Crossing my arms, I straightened my back and lifted my chin. I wasn't going anywhere near him.

"She's a stubborn little thing, isn't she?" Mr. Kessler said, giving his son a quick glance.

Micha's nostrils flared and I smirked.

That's right, asshole. Fuck you.

"Sit down!" he ordered, an angry grumble in his tone.

"No."

Micha arched his brow, silently saying, "You sure you want to do this?"

My eyes narrowed. *Bring it, bitch.*

One nod, that's all it took. My elbow was seized by the guy standing behind me, and I was dragged across the room.

"Hey!" I shrieked, slapping the goon's arm.

My resistance was useless. Next thing I knew, my ass was slammed down in the chair.

I rubbed my sore butt and glared at Micha. "Having your cronies manhandle me now?"

"There's repercussions for being disobedient, Mouse."

"I suggest you start listening to my son," Mr. Kessler piped in, "Otherwise your life is about to become very difficult."

"My life's already difficult," I grumbled, looking over at my dad.

I'd heard rumors. Quiet whispers about the dark things the founding families did. Small-town gossip, that's all I thought it was. They weren't sacrificing people under the full moon. But I had to admit, sitting here in the commanding presence of Mr. Kessler, I couldn't help but wonder if some of those rumors might be true.

"Did you do that to my dad?"

"Yes," Mr. Kessler answered flatly.

"Why?"

For some reason, he seemed intrigued by my question. I wasn't sure what intrigued him. My dad was hurt. It was only normal to wonder why. Mom came home all the time with mysterious bruises and scrapes. I learned long ago not to jump to conclusions. For all I knew, my dad had a gambling problem like Shelby's.

"Your father was," he studied me for a second, rubbing the dark hair coating his chin, before saying, "Uncooperative."

"Are you in the mob or something?" Some bookie broke Shelby's dad's arm last year.

"No. I'm a psychiatrist."

"For who?" My brow arched at the men strategically placed in the room, "Charles Manson?"

"I see many people. Your mother was one of them."

Mom saw a shrink?

"She was?"

He nodded. "We have a well renowned addiction program."

Wasn't that great.

Mom still crashed her car into a telephone pole.

"I'm sorry for your loss," Mr. Kessler said, sitting back and folding his hands on his crossed legs. "Your mother was a very troubled woman."

"Be glad she didn't take you with her," Micha added in a grumble.

Anger burned through me as I snapped my gaze his way. "Did I ask for your opinion?"

"No, but you're going to get it." Though his face dropped in a blank expression, I could see anger tugging at his features. "Your mother was a useless piece of shit, who'd rather drink than take care of her child. You're better off without her."

My fists balled, fingernails digging into my palm. "You don't know anything!"

"I know she almost killed you four years ago. Didn't stop her from drinking though, did it?"

I looked away, swallowing the lump in my throat. The doctors said they weren't sure I was going to make it. I died three times, and sometimes still got pain in my abdomen where the chunk of metal skewered me.

"I've been meaning to ask you, how are your balls?" I growled through clenched teeth. Micha, of all people, had no right to talk about Mom! He was constantly berating me about her problems, and now thought he could use her death? Don't think so. "Cause if they're still sore, I can get you some ice."

Not even a twitch.

"Huh? Guess, I'll have to do better next time."

Next thing I knew, my chair was screeching across the tiled floor as Micha dragged me closer. He braced his elbow on the table and leaned in. Sandalwood with a hint of citrus assailed my nostrils, pissing me off that on top of everything else, the bastard also smelled good.

"Don't get too close," I hissed, glaring straight into his swirling chocolate eyes. "I might use my mousy little claws again."

"Careful, Mouse," the corner of his mouth tipped up, and suddenly egging him on didn't seem like such a good idea anymore, "If you keep running that smart mouth, I'm liable to take you over my knee and spank you right here, in front of daddy."

I gulped. Not because I was scared, but because I believed him. Thankfully, my dad chose that moment to speak up.

"Get your hands off my daughter!"

Micha's dark eyes snapped up, and he glared over my shoulder. "I'm not touching her. I could…" he challenged, sliding his warm palm up my thigh to toy with the hemline of my shorts.

Appalled by the sparks shooting across my skin, I slapped his hand away. A black look took over Micha's face, darkening his glare as he seized a fistful of my hair.

"Push me away again," he growled, yanking my head back and making me cry out, "And I'll make daddy watch me defile his baby girl."

I often wondered if something was wrong with me. Why else would I dream about the person I hated most in this world? Now I knew there was something wrong with me.

The last thing I should be feeling is heat tingling low in my belly. I clamped my thighs together and closed my eyes, hoping to shut out my body's response.

"This is turning you on, isn't it?" Micha's hot breath wafted over my ear, turning my traitorous body even more against me. "Dirty little mouse. Not so innocent after all, are you?"

I don't know if it was the sound of my dad yelling, or the soft click of what I thought might be a gun, but either way, I managed to snap out of it.

"Get away from me!" I snarled, slapping Micha. "I don't want any part of your sick games!"

His fingers tightened in my hair, as he forced me to go nose to nose with him. "Then why are those little virgin panties sticking to your skin?" he growled, then tossed me back, like I disgusted him.

That was fine with me. I liked it better this way–him hating me, and me hating him. I didn't have time to stew in my anger because when I turned around, the first thing I saw was a gun.

I recognized the gold engraving in the handle. It was the same gun Mom had given my dad on their tenth anniversary. Except this time, it wasn't in my dad's holster. It sat on the table in front of Mr. Kessler with the barrel pointed at my dad.

"Are we ready to proceed?" Mr. Kessler asked.

My eyes were stuck on the black Glock. "Can you put that away first?"

"You needn't concern yourself with that, my dear," Micha's dad said, dropping a briefcase on the table and popping it open. "Isn't that right, Derek?"

"Fuck you," my dad grumbled.

His curse was immediately followed by a harsh slap across his already bruised face from the goon standing behind him. I cringed at the drop of blood sliding down his now split lip.

"You see, I have other ways of dealing with your father's impetuous nature. The gun is simply to remind you that your father's safety is entirely dependent on you."

My wide eyes flew up just in time to see Mr. Kessler pull a file out of his briefcase.

"This, my dear," he said slapping it down on the table, "Is a contract signed by your father and myself."

I glanced warily at the manila folder, wondering what my dad got himself into. "What's the contract for?"

"*You*, my dear."

I didn't think it was possible for someone's heart to stop with a single word, but it did. Stopped dead in my chest.

"W-What do you mean, me?"

"Your father agreed to give you to my son when you turned sixteen. And I do believe you recently had a birthday."

I did. Turned sixteen the day before I buried Mom.

"I-I don't understand . . ." I stuttered, staring dumbfounded.

"It's quite simple," Mr. Kessler stated like he was ordering a cup of coffee. "You now belong to Micha."

I couldn't breathe. Where did all the air go? My chest heaved, but my lungs remained empty. It couldn't be true! My dad wouldn't do that. He wouldn't!

"Dad?" I questioned in a shaky voice.

My heart dropped when he hung his head and muttered, "I'm sorry."

This wasn't happening. I closed my eyes and held my breath. As if that simple act would make this all disappear.

"I told you," Micha whispered in my ear. "I own you, Mouse."

I lost count of how many times I'd heard him say those exact words. I never expected this! Thought it was just another one of his ego trips, like when he enlisted other people to humiliate me, or laughed when I used to try to get help.

I quickly learned help would never come. Most people in this town wouldn't so much as look wrong in the Kessler's direction. Guess my dad could be added to that list.

He was just sitting there, guilt written all over his face.

"Is that why Mom left you?" I snarled, with angry tears brimming in my eyes. "Because you gave her daughter away?"

"What!? No!" He actually had the gall to look insulted. "Riley, you don't understand . . . I didn't have a choice. They were –"

"Shut up! All the shit you say about Chase…" I released a stuttered sigh, "He would never do this to me."

Chase threatened to rip the ears of a boy who tried to kiss me in the fifth grade. He helped me get caught up when I fell behind in math, and even came with me to Mexico to bury Mom. He would never hand me over to the enemy.

"Ah yes, Chase Mathers," Mr. Kessler said, dropping a picture of Chase on top of the folder.

"Former president of the Lost Souls motorcycle club. Did you know his brother had his wife and child killed? All so he could take over the club. Sad, really." He shook his head. "It's a good thing he thinks Chase died with them. I'd hate to think of what would happen if he learned otherwise."

A tear rolled down my cheek when the next picture was dropped.

"Shelby Grace. Junior at Ashen Springs High. Based on the numerous tickets she's gotten, I'd assume she has a preference for speed. It'd be a shame if her brakes failed." He flipped to the next picture. "Trina and Marnie Dupire. They'd make me a decent sum, working in my club. Twins are always big sellers. Shall I go on?"

I swallowed the lump in my throat and shook my head. The threat was clear.

Mr. Kessler nodded and clipped the briefcase closed. "Marco, Levi, clean the sheriff up and take him to his wife. I'm sure she's worried about him."

My dad didn't fight. He looked as defeated as I felt, as he was dragged out of the room. I sat there with my jaw clenched, digging my fingernails into my thighs. I wanted to lunge at Micha. Maybe grab the gun and shoot Mr. Kessler, but I'd probably just end up getting someone I cared about hurt.

"Come on, son," Mr. Kessler stood and smoothed his suit jacket. "We'll give Riley the night to consider her options. Choose wisely, my dear . . . Your loved ones are counting on you."

"Not so brave now, are you?" Micha said, sweeping my hair over my shoulder.

"I don't know how, but I will bring you down," I promised, glaring all my hatred at him, "And then we'll see just how brave you are when you're on your knees!"

He chuckled and kissed me on the forehead. "I look forward to it."

His dad's cold eyes narrowed in on me. "I don't need to tell you what will happen if you run, do I?"

I shook my head. "No."

"I'm glad we understand each other. You should be honored. One day, you'll be a Kessler." He frowned at the tears streaming down my face. "I suggest you learn to act like one."

Chapter 8
Riley

Take the night to consider my options. Was that some kind of cruel irony? What options did I really have? Refuse and risk putting someone I cared about in danger. Didn't seem like much of an option to me.

If Louis Kessler was anything like his son, there was no doubt in my mind that he'd carry through with the threat. There was only one plausible way out of this situation.

I had to gain the upper hand. Find something to use against Micha. Even the devil had a weakness, but try as I might, I couldn't think of one.

I'd been at war with the bastard for years, and not once had I seen a crack in that icy exterior. It looked like I was well and truly fucked, a claustrophobic feeling that was only increased by the goon left to stand vigil outside my bedroom door.

Thankfully, he stopped coming in to check on me, and I was

eventually able to fall asleep. Besides, I was running out of stuff to throw at him.

I hadn't seen my dad. He tried to come and talk to me in the morning, but I told him I was getting ready for school. I wasn't ready to face him. Didn't know if I ever would be. It hurt just to hear his voice.

Fathers were supposed to protect you from shit like this. They were the one man a girl could always rely on. Guess I shouldn't be surprised; Mom left me. Why should he be any different?

The black Escalade I was practically thrown into pulled through the gates to Ashworth. On any other day, I might've found the big brick building beautiful. Shelby and I used to try to peek through the oak trees bordering the property, hoping to get a view of the elusive school. But right now, all Ashworth looked like was a fancy prison, complete with iron gates and pretty little stone walkways.

Even the students, walking around in their uniforms, seemed like inmates. Perfectly put together inmates, but inmates nonetheless.

I scowled at the red plaid skirt around my waist, mad that the boys got to wear black slacks. I think I was around eight the last time I wore a dress or skirt. Shelby would get a kick out of this. She'd been trying to get me to girl things up for years.

I was kind of tempted to text her, but texts led to phone calls. And the second she heard my voice, she'd know something was wrong. I was pretty sure the whole, "don't tell anybody about this, or else," thing went without saying. Not that anybody in this town would care.

"Don't try anything funny." The goon, who was apparently my new shadow, said. "I'll be right outside."

"Don't worry, I'm not going to run off and get one of my friends killed," I snarled, and hopped out of the Escalade.

"Oh, they won't be killed," the goon said, giving me a sideways glance. "Dead men don't make good leverage."

I swallowed and closed the door. *Well, that's comforting.*

The Escalade drove away, and I was left standing in front of Ashworth. I looked up, scanning the many windows. Each one was pristine and spotless. The prettiest thing Ashworth High had was the back wall of graffiti–a wall I proudly started two years ago.

I doubted any of the students here would appreciate something like that. Sighing, I told myself I could do this, and walked through the doors.

* * *

It turned out some things were the same in rich kid school as public. Take the office, for example; large white room by the main entrance, full of middle-aged staff who looked tired and bored, completed by the two misfit kids sitting outside the principal's office, and the crotchety white-haired receptionist.

I looked at Mrs. Green from my seat on a big plush chair–okay, so not everything was the same… Her hair was pulled so tightly back that it stretched her face over her bones, making her lips look thin and angry. She looked at me over her square-framed glasses. "We have certain standards at Ashworth, Miss Adams."

"So, no orgies then?" I gave her a thumbs up. "Got it."

She stared at me, unimpressed.

"Not a joker, huh? Guess I'll return the camel."

"Your former school warned us that you might be a problem."

"Yeah, they didn't like the camel either."

She sighed and wrote something down on a note pad. "That's three demerits for an improper uniform."

"What! I'm wearing the stupid uniform! See," I argued, waving my hands over the crisp white shirt and skirt.

"You're missing the tie," she explained, with a point of the pen in her hand.

My mouth dropped open. The stupid thing was impossible to figure out. I gave up trying to tie the tie, and tossed it on my bed.

"You can't be serious?"

When her steel-gray eyes fixed on me, I reared back. Suddenly, I felt like a complete asshole for knocking over Tommy Gunderson's block tower in the first grade.

"Here's your schedule." Mrs. Green held out a piece of paper, which I quickly took. "I hope you're not prone to tardiness?"

"No ma'am." I shook my head, not wanting to initiate another look into my soul.

One of the misfits burst out laughing, and all it took to silence him was one glare. Should I slip out while she was mentally dissecting someone else? Or would she come looking for me? I wasn't sure which would be worse. Thankfully, a small girl with deep red hair walked in, taking the soul sucking attention of the receptionist.

"You wanted to see me, Mrs. Grier?"

Okay, so it's Grier, not Green. Thanks, little redheaded chick.

"Harper, this is Logan Hudson's stepsister." Mrs. Grier absently waved in my direction. "I want you to show her around."

I rolled my eyes. *I have a name, people!*

"Hi…" I paused to give Mrs. Grier a sideways glance. She was staring at me again! "I'm Riley."

"Harper," the redhead replied.

Harper reminded me of a doll. Not those crappy plastic ones I played with as a kid, but the perfect porcelain ones Shelby collected. She had the same long eyelashes, big doe eyes, spattering of freckles, and full bouncy curls.

I guess Harper wasn't a fan of being under Mrs. Grier's stare either, because the next thing I knew, she was spinning on her heels and heading out the door. I tried to follow. Tried being the operative word. For a small thing, she was fast.

Moving through the hall with her head down, she somehow didn't crash into a single person. I bumped into at least three, and I could see where I was going. F.Y.I Ashworth students were just as snobby as I had expected. One girl glared at me like I dirtied her up, because I brushed her arm.

When we reached my locker, Harper stepped back and pressed her back against the wall. Her brown eyes bounced around like she expected a monster to jump out of the shadows. Maybe one would? This was Micha's school, after all.

"Are you okay?" I asked, opening my locker, which was surprisingly easy to do. My old locker I had to hit the top hinge, kick the bottom, and lift the door to get in.

"I'm fine," Harper muttered, ducking behind her hair.

"Are you sure?" I closed and opened my locker again, utterly fascinated by the properly functioning door. "You seem kind of jumpy."

She murmured something, but spoke so softly that I wasn't sure she said anything at all. Maybe Harper was just nervous? Not everyone was a social butterfly like Shelby. I was with Harper. People sucked!

"We both have Mr. Walker for homeroom," she announced, staring at my schedule.

"Great," I smiled. "We can sit together."

Her face dropped, full of shock. Or was that terror? Who knew with this chick.

"Why would you want to sit with me?"

"Why wouldn't I?" I asked, crinkling my nose.

"I-I'm not . . . someone y-you want to be seen with."

"I'm pretty sure the same goes for me." I rolled my eyes and sighed. "I fit in here about as well as cheese digests in a lactose intolerant stomach."

Except for the uniform, I was nothing like the princesses walking the halls. Even Harper, with her terrified eyes and trembling body, was more put together than me. I paused and cocked my head.

Harper wasn't just trembling; she was full on shaking. All the color had drained from her face, and her eyes were wide with panic.

"Run," she whispered.

But it was too late. Before either of us could move, I was slammed back into a locker with Micha glowering down at me. "Hello, Mouse. Did you consider your options?"

Logan smirked and leaned against the wall, while a guy I knew to be Micha's little brother, Mason, cut Harper off. Though little wasn't the word I'd use for Mason. Except for the green eyes, Mason looked just like Micha, right down to the brick wall build he had going on. Though Mason was a little bigger.

"Don't really have a choice, now do I?" I snarled at Micha, angry that even this stupid uniform looked good on him.

"Sure you do. You could choose not to abide by the contract."

"Right. And then you hurt the people I love."

He shrugged. "Still a choice." When I didn't respond, he sighed and added, "Look at it this way, you'll actually get what all those girls out there dream about."

"And what's that?"

"To marry the guy who popped their cherry and live happily ever after. It may not be happy," his lips curled in a malicious smirk, "But it'll be ever after. Till death do us part, baby."

It didn't really hit me until that second. Standing there with Micha staring down at me, I felt the walls closing in. Micha wasn't just going to play with me for a bit . . . he was going to keep me!

"Why are you doing this?" I muttered, trying desperately to hold back the tears burning in my eyes.

Micha leaned in and whispered, "Because I can."

"Do you hate me that much?"

Though he didn't answer, I could see the anger swirling in those deep chocolate pools. When I couldn't take his penetrating gaze anymore, I moved to leave. Should've known it wouldn't be that easy; nothing with Micha ever was.

His arm shot out, blocking my path. "Did I say you could go?"

I didn't like the glimmer in his eyes.

"You need to ask."

I could argue. Duck under his arm and tell him to go fuck himself. Which is what I really wanted to do. Instead, I stamped down my anger and said, "Can I go?"

"Sir."

My brows furrowed. "What?"

"Can I go, Sir," he explained.

My jaw dropped. He couldn't be serious!

"Uh huh," he tsk-ed. "Before you think about running that smart mouth of yours, ask yourself if you want to be punished in front of all these people?"

I gulped and glanced around the busy hallway. He wouldn't do anything in school, right? The possibility that he might carry through with his threat wasn't what scared me. It was the little voice in the back of my head that whispered, "Do it."

"Maybe you do?" Micha stepped in, pressing his hard body against mine.

His masculine scent washed over me—sandalwood with a hint of citrus—I found myself staring at the hands I had pressed against his chest, intending to shove him away.

God, he's firm!

"I had no idea you were into voyeurism, Mouse," Micha purred in my ear, while dragging his fingers up my thigh. "I'm game if you are."

What the hell was wrong with me? I had to get out of there!

"Can I go? Sir," I hissed.

Micha's victorious smile made me hate myself a little more.

"Of course you can, Mouse." He stepped back and said, "But first, you'll be needing this."

My brows pinched together at the red silk in his hand. "A tie?"

"You're not wearing one, and I wouldn't want you getting in trouble."

Why did I feel like there was an ulterior motive here? Maybe I was overreacting. Really, what harm could a tie do? And I'd already gotten in trouble once.

"Fine," I sighed, and let him fasten it around my neck. "We done?"

Micha shrugged and waved his hands for me to pass.

I warily watched him as I walked away, and said, "Come on, Harper."

But Harper couldn't move. She was frozen with a look of dread on her face. Standing in front of her, with his forearm on the wall above, was Mason. Harper jumped back, banging her back off a locker, when he bent down and ran his nose over the top of her head. After which he leaned back and glared at her terrified face.

"You still smell like shit."

What the fuck?

I marched over there and yanked Harper behind my back. "Don't talk to her like that!"

"She knows her place." Mason crossed his arms and shot me a cocky grin. "Do you?"

I poked him hard in the chest, "Yeah! It's right between you and her!"

His green eyes twinkled with amusement. "Sounds like a fun

time. What do you say, freckles?" He glanced over my shoulder at Harper. "Maybe you'll get lucky, and I'll let you suck my dick after I fuck your friend."

Harper squeaked and buried her face in my back.

There was no hesitation. My palm rose, smacking him across the face.

"Come near her again, and I'll rip your balls off!" I growled, and pulled Harper down the hall.

Fuck Micha, and fuck his brother! The whole Kessler family could kiss my ass!

Chapter 9
Micha

I stood in the hall watching Riley storm away with a firm grip on Harper's wrist. She glanced back, glaring at me with a storm raging in those deep sapphire eyes. She continued her march with her chin lifted proudly. Fucking adorable. I bet calling me Sir hurt like a bitch.

"She slapped me!" Mase whined, cupping his cheek.

Yes, she did. My eyes rolled over Riley's uniform. I thought she looked hot as hell in those tight jeans, but damn! I made a quick adjustment, relieving some of the strain on my dick, and made a mental note to fuck her in that skirt.

"I told you," Logan snickered.

"You said she was a firecracker, not that she was violent. Damn!" Mase cocked his head and walked up next to me. "I like her."

I slapped the back of his head.

"Ouch!" he cried out. "What the hell was that for?"

I cocked my brow. "When I'm done fucking your friend?"

"What? So I can't even say anything about her now?"

"Just do what I do . . . imagine it," Logan piped in with a chuckle. "The things that girl does in my head."

My hands balled into fists as I stemmed down the urge to hit my best friend.

That grumpy growl was unmistakable. "What the hell is he staring at?"

"Only the finest ass in Ashworth," Logan snickered.

That's it!

I spun around, fist raised. The only thing that stopped me was Silas's raised brow. Instead, I scrubbed a hand down my face. *What the fuck is wrong with me?*

"He okay?" Silas asked Mase.

Logan was the one to answer. "He has an issue with us checking out his girl."

"Well, I can't blame him," Silas huffed, folding his arms across his chest. "I wouldn't want either of you looking at mine, either."

"What did we do?" Logan and Mase said in unison.

"Half the girls in this school."

It was true. Pussy was a hobby for them, and my brother was worse.

Mase rolled his eyes. "I wouldn't say half the girls–"

"No, no," Logan cut him off, "He's right. We're sluts. Own that shit."

"Alright, fine." Mase conceded. "But my brother doesn't need to worry. His little mouse isn't my type."

"Girl is your type," Silas argued.

Logan chuckled. "Mase is just mad because she slapped him."

"So have most of the chicks in this school."

Unlike Logan, who somehow convinced girls that a one-night stand was their idea, my brother preferred the fuck and chuck method. Mase broke hearts so often, I was starting to think he got off on it.

"Why's everyone hating on me today?" Mason sang with a frown. "I happen to think I'm a very pleasant person."

"Tell that to Tamara," Silas huffed. "I thought she was going to rip your balls off last night. What the fuck did you do to her?"

Mason smirked. "Her best friend."

"Chicks are crazy." Silas shook his head. "And I had to drop my course to watch one."

He might be pissed, but in reality, I was doing him a favor. The only reason Silas signed up for that damn course was because he was told to.

His family was in the limelight–famous actress for a mother, and his grandpa was Governor–they kept a tight leash on him. Which was probably why he was so damn angry all the time. What he had in common with my jackass brother, I never understood.

"You can take it next semester," I said, meeting his scowl.

His light eyes narrowed, deepening the frown on his face.

Mason sauntered over and slapped him on the back. "Cheer up, buddy. It's a new year, and we have fresh pussy to plunder."

He sighed and gave my brother an unimpressed glare.

All those guys out there wishing they had bigger dicks should talk to Silas. He was hung like a horse, and it wasn't a blessing. Girls took one look at the anaconda in his pants and ran the other way.

Even Naomi stayed away from that shit. It wasn't like he was a virgin; in fact, he was far from it. But everyone he'd been with was well used. Not exactly the good girl his family was pushing for.

"I told you, bro, take them from behind," Mason explained,

grabbing onto the air as if there was a girl bent over in front of him. "Then they can't see your shit until it's already in."

Logan got that far-off look he always did when he was deep in thought. "You think Finn's got it, too?"

At only eleven, Finn was the youngest of us. Kid was smart as fuck–genius IQ and eidetic memory. Unlike his grumpy cousin, Finn was always smiling and pumped to take on the world.

We all tried to keep it that way, hiding the darker parts of the Order from him. But that could only last so long. Sooner or later he'd be pulled in, and his dark side would show itself. His father was already fighting for him to be more involved. The only reason it hadn't happened yet was because he spent most of the year away at a school for geniuses.

"I don't know," Mase said. "He is Long Don's cousin."

Silas grumbled out a sigh. "Can we stop talking about my cousin's dick?"

"Someone should give the little man lessons," Logan said. "He's got to learn how to use that shit."

"That's true. There's probably a lot of hard up girls in that school of his," Mase nodded in agreement. "All pent up and frustrated."

"We are not talking about this," Silas groaned, shook his head, and walked away. "I'm going to class."

"Hey, what about me?" Mason called out, running after him. "Where's the love, bro?"

"Go fuck yourself!" Silas grumbled.

Mase's response was to wrap his arms around Silas and kiss his cheek.

"Fucker's going to get hit one day," I grumbled.

Would serve him right too.

"One day?" Logan cocked a brow. "Silas cold-cocked him last week."

Once again, I wondered what that grumpy asshole had in common with my idiot brother.

"Everything go good last night?" Logan asked, nudging me with his elbow.

"Yes." I knew he was referring to the talk I had with the sheriff. "He's going to look into his people."

We needed to find out who got the tape out of evidence lock up. Because it sure as hell wasn't Jack. And while the sheriff didn't want me anywhere near his baby girl, he also didn't want Riley seeing what was on that tape.

"Jack's gone... maybe his friend gave up?"

"Not this guy." I sighed and passed him the note and newspaper clipping that said, *Officer Wendel Morris gunned down during routine traffic stop.* "Found this taped to my Jeep this morning."

I'd read the note so many times, I had it memorized.

Jack wasn't nimble,
Jack wasn't quick,
Jack thought he was a little too slick,
Singing my song,
Before knight took out pawn,
But you left your rook open wide.

"You didn't tell me Wendel was shot?"

"He was fine when I left." The date on the article was the same night we took care of Jack. That was the bothersome part. The Order had enemies, but to take out a cop on our payroll . . . That was bold. I stuffed the note in my pocket and walked down the hall.

Logan followed. "Who the fuck is this guy?"

"I'm working on it." Called Preston this morning with the new info. If someone saw who shot Wendel, Preston would find out.

"We need to tell your pops."

"Can't."

"Why not?" Logan argued. "My dad was a sick bastard. No one's going to cry over him, and if anyone can understand why we did, it would be your pops."

"Okay, say we tell my dad and he helps us find this fucker." I paused and glanced over at him. "How long before Mase starts asking questions?"

Logan's face blanched. Our mother's death almost destroyed Mase. He didn't remember what she did. As far as he was concerned, she was a fluffy Brady Bunch mom who, one day, decided to kill herself. If he found out that not only was Ryker his father, but that it was his threat to take him away that pushed her over the edge…

There was a reason my father chose not to tell him. Biological or not, Mason was his son. We saw betrayal destroy him once, and none of us wanted that again.

"I don't want to answer them." My brow rose at Logan. "Do you?"

He released a defeated sigh, and shook his head. "No, I don't."

"We'll just have to find this asshole on our own. Sooner or later, he'll fuck up and we'll take him out."

"Alright," he said, slapping a hand on my shoulder. "Tell Preston if he needs anything, to let me know."

"Don't worry, that fucker has never been shy about enlisting you in his sick shit."

Logan smiled and ducked in his homeroom. "We understand each other."

"You're both fucked in the head, is what you are," I grumbled and continued down the hall.

My mind immediately went back to my mouse. She asked me if I hated her that much, and I didn't answer. Truth was, I didn't know what to say. Did I hate her? I used to think so. I wanted her pain. Craved it like a drug. But lately, all I could picture was licking those tears off her face as I had her pinned beneath me.

I got hard just imagining what she would taste like. Was she as sweet as she smelled? Would she scream my name when I made her come? Fuck, I needed to screw my head back on and stop thinking about her.

The solution to my problem seemed to present itself when I turned the corner and saw Naomi standing outside the classroom door.

"Oh, Micha," she called out, plastering that fucking fake smile on her face, "I was hoping I'd run into you. Jasmine and Mark are going to the bluffs after school…"

I crossed my arms, and let my eyes wander. Naomi was annoying as fuck, but she had a decent body–long legs, good size tits, and lips like a porn star. Her uniform was trashed up a bit with a tighter shirt and shorter skirt. Most of the girls did that shit, though. I didn't see why.

My mouse looked hotter than any of them, and the only skin I could see was the gap between the knee-high socks and skirt. What kind of panties did she have on under that skirt? I bet they had Minnie Mouse on them.

Fuck. I was fucking hard again. My eyes zeroed in on Naomi's mouth. What the fuck was she yammering on about? Had she been talking this whole fucking time? Maybe I should shut her up? I wouldn't argue a little relief. But the last time I went there, she started acting like I was her boyfriend or some shit.

Is she still fucking talking?

I crossed my arms and leaned back, trying to pay attention to what was spewing out of her mouth. But my mind kept going back to Riley in that Goddamn skirt.

Fuck it!

I grabbed Naomi's hand and pulled her into a nearby closet. I'd deal with the clingy shit later.

Chapter 10
Riley

Apparently the teachers at Ashworth thought public school meant stupid. Either that, or my dad had complained about my solid B average. In every class, the teachers were constantly looking over my shoulder and asking if I understood the material.

I was tempted to tell them off, but I didn't want to end up in the principal's office the first day. Mostly because I wanted to avoid Mrs. Grier. I could still feel her stare dissecting me.

Thankfully, Micha was a senior, so I didn't have to put up with him. His brother, however, had pretty much the same schedule as me. Every class I went in, there was Mason, with a stupid smile on his face.

If that wasn't bad enough, some guy in English spent the entire time scowling at me, creeping me out with the look of death every time I turned around. Aside from those two, everyone else seemed to go out of their way to avoid me. *Literally*.

Crowds parted when I walked by. Mind you, half the time I was standing around like an idiot. The map they gave me sucked!

Not everyone here was a complete asshole. Brandon, a guy I was paired up with in art, talked my ear off. He was big Monet fan, claiming that he revolutionized the art industry. I argued that while Monet was the driving force behind impressionism, artists like Tavar Zawacki would rather send a message than paint a pretty picture.

The guy who helped me find my chem class, Sean, was the biggest flirt I'd ever met–and that was saying something considering the fact that I lived with Logan. Sean wouldn't let up. He walked me right into class and kissed the back of my hand. Based on the look Mason gave him, I guessed those two weren't exactly friends.

By the time lunch came, I was more than ready for some normalcy. After all, cafeterias were all the same, right? *Wrong*. I stood there, gaze shifting back to the map in my hands. Was this the right place?

My map said it was, but that couldn't be right. Cafeterias were run-down dingy rooms, full of loud teenagers and overflowing trashcans. They didn't have garden views and pretty tables with fresh flowers.

Where was all the tension that came with forcing different cliques to occupy the same space? What happened to the guys picking a fight in the back, or the couple making out in the corner? Well, okay, there was a couple making out in the corner, but the rest was missing. Maybe I really was in Stepford?

Warily, I flowed into the line of students, wondering how one was supposed to act in this environment. Was there some kind of protocol? Or was it just a "be yourself" type of thing? I snickered. The last thing Ashworth wanted was for me to be myself. That was pretty clear when they kept referring to me as Logan's stepsister.

The displayed menu posed another problem. Half this crap I couldn't pronounce, let alone consider eating. Maybe Shelby could help? I pulled out my phone and texted her.

Me: *What the hell is a Larb salad and Fergburger?*

Shelby's text came nearly immediately.

Shelby: *Are you watching some weird alien movie again?*

Me: *No, it's on the menu at Ashworth.*

Shelby: *Trina says they might have fish eggs and snails in them. I say try it. Maybe you'll start putting on dresses and wearing makeup. You know, like a girl.*

I scoffed. If only she knew.

Me: *I'm wearing a skirt right now, thank you very much.*

Shelby: *What! No way. Let me see!*

Me: *Yeah right, and give you blackmail material, don't think so.*

Shelby: *I would never!*

I cocked my brow at the phone.

Me: *Who do you think you're talking to.*

Shelby: *Oh come on, let me see. I'm not going to stop until you do.*

Me: *Well I guess it's a good thing I can turn off my phone then.*

The last thing that Shelby texted before I hit the power button was, **bitch**! I'd pay for that later. She'd be calling nonstop after school. Eventually, I'd cave and send her a pic. But only because I didn't want Shelby showing up here. I needed to keep her out of danger and away from Micha.

I ended up settling on a chicken salad sandwich–simple, tasty, and absolutely no chance of fish eggs. With tray in hand–which was shiny and silver, not plastic and crappy–I exhaled and scanned the crowd. A group of cheerleaders sat in the middle, next to the tables of jocks, followed by the typical cliques of misfits, smart kids, and so on.

I almost cried out in relief when I spotted Harper, sitting alone in the back. Her head was down, and she jumped when I dropped my tray on the table. The girl spent so much time staring at the floor that she could probably identify people by their shoes.

"Of all the gin joints in all the worlds, you had to walk into mine."

Her big doe eyes rolled up and stared blankly.

"Casablanca?"

Still nothing.

"Humphrey Bogart and Ingrid Bergman?" I shook my head and sat down. Didn't anybody watch movies anymore?

"What are you doing?"

"Eating," I replied, taking a bite out of a carrot stick.

"Here?"

"Sure." I shrugged, and then paused to shoot her a worried glance. "Why? There aren't any Teletubbies around, are there?"

Her brow rose.

"What? Those things freak me out." They really did. Dancing around all happy and shit. It wasn't natural.

"You're strange." She ducked her head, but not before I saw a small smile tugging at the corner of her mouth.

I can live with strange. If that's what it took to get her to lighten up for a few seconds then I'd be strange all damn day.

Most of our lives, Shelby and I had been the weird girls. Even when we were kids, Shelby was in a different league. Everybody wanted her attention. Why she chose to give it me, I never understood.

Besides being a little meek, Harper was a more likely choice for Shelby's friend. Anyone could see she was beautiful. Why wasn't she sitting at the table with the other beautiful girls?

"Oh my God, Harper," a tall girl with caramel-colored skin squealed as she bounded toward us. "Why didn't you tell me someone slapped Mason!"

Her dark hair bounced off her back as she cocked her hip and waggled her head.

"I was with you all morning, and you didn't say a thing!" Her tray dropped on the table with a resounding bang. "Was it really Logan's stepsister? What's she like?"

She plopped down next to me, curiosity shining in her bright hazel eyes. "Is she a tight-ass like her old man?"

Harper's worried eyes shifted over at me.

Would she still think my dad was a tight-ass if she knew he had sold me into human slavery?

"I didn't know Sheriff Adams had a kid, did you?" the girl continued. "I mean, where's she been all this time? And who's her mother? I can't imagine him with a wife and kid. Yeah, okay, he's hot, but he married Paisley Hudson. *Paisley!*"

She pointed a forkful of salad at Harper. "There's seriously something wrong with that woman. She comes to church every Sunday with a big smile and a plate of homemade cookies."

She waved her fork in the air, flinging salad everywhere. "And I know she didn't bake those cookies. No one looks that good and bakes."

Harper shifted in her chair. "Um . . . Lana?"

"Oh, don't give me that look," Lana groaned. "You've heard the rumors about Logan's dad. They have to be somewhat true. Logan's clearly crazy, and his mother acts like she just finished hosting a children's show."

She stabbed her fork in the salad and shoved it into her mouth. "I wouldn't be surprised if she was a robot."

Huh? This chick might not be so bad.

Lana's eyes went wide, and she placed her palms flat on the table. "Maybe the stepsister is just as crazy as they are?"

"Lana!" Harper called out in frustration.

"Oh, come on! She hit Mason. Mason! Mess with one Kessler and you mess with them all, everyone knows that." Her forehead crinkled and her lips pursed. "Come to think of it, Stacy Kroner said Micha hit some guy for saying something about some girl named Riley. Who the hell is Riley?"

My brow rose. *He did what?*

"Lana!" Harper yelled.

"I know!" Lana proclaimed, sounding amazed. "I wouldn't want to be on Micha's radar, either. I mean, they're all dicks, but Micha is downright scary. I wonder what she did?"

Harper looked at me and said, "Maybe she didn't do anything?"

Lana sat back and twisted the cap off a bottle of water. "She *had* to have done something."

"Maybe Micha's just an asshole," I interjected, unable to maintain my silence anymore.

Lana turned my way, shocked to see someone else sitting at the table. Well, if she stopped talking long enough to take a breath, she might notice things around her. Shelby did the same thing. Once she spent three hours with me before she noticed Marnie was there too.

"Who are you?"

"Um, Lana this is–"

"The infamous stepsister," I finished for Harper.

Lana's jaw dropped. "*You're* Sheriff Adams' daughter?"

"According to my mom," I shrugged, "But I'm still holding out hope for a secret love child scenario."

"But you're so . . ." she paused and rolled her hand, "Hot?"

"According to you, so is my dad," I snickered, kind of flattered. I'd always considered myself average at best.

Lana hid her face in her palms and groaned, "Harper! Why didn't you stop me?"

"Seriously?" Harper grumbled. "I *tried* to stop you, but like always, you wouldn't shut up."

"I don't talk *that* much," Lana huffed.

I just met this chick and couldn't help but snort in disagreement.

"You suffer from a chronic case of verbal diarrhea," Harper muttered.

Lana rolled her eyes and turned to me, "Hi, I'm Lana."

"Riley," I replied, happy that someone in this place didn't automatically assume my name was Logan's stepsister.

"Riley, huh?" Lana sat back and eyed me. "What does Micha Kessler want with you?"

I shrugged, because what was I supposed to say? *Oh, my dad signed a contract, and now I'm basically engaged to someone I hate?* Yeah, that didn't make me sound crazy at all.

Lana tilted her head to the side. "You've heard of the Knights, right?"

"Of course." Who in this town hadn't? "And before you say it," I added when her mouth opened, ready to spew more words, "I've heard the rumors too. Secret societies and dark rituals, blah, blah, blah. They're just rumors."

Marnie spent all last year researching the Order of Ravens and Wolves. She thought it would be this huge article for the school paper. Guess what she found?

Nothing. Nada. Zip. Not even so much as a mention in any of the town's history. Though now I couldn't help but wonder if there might be some truth to the town gossip.

"So you don't believe any of it?"

"Nope," I said, following Harper's lead and concentrating on my food.

One bite of my sandwich and I was lost in flavor overload.

Jesus, even the chicken salad was better here! How could something so simple taste so good?

"Okay," Lana said in a hushed tone, and pointed. "Then explain that."

I turned around just in time to see Micha and his friends saunter into the cafeteria. The atmosphere instantly changed. Loud chatter dulled to quiet whispers. The air felt thicker, and eyes around the room tried to avoid direct contact.

It was like when a crowded restaurant pretended they weren't paying attention to the couple arguing in the corner.

Logan and Mason followed Micha. Behind them was the English class creeper, who Lana introduced as Silas Creswell. Aside from his obvious anger issues, Silas was just as good-looking as the rest of them. He was tall, with black hair, and light crystal blue eyes.

The last and tallest was Parker Whitley. I only knew him because of the stories of his cold-hearted brother, Preston. Lana seemed to like him, though. Her voice went all high and squeaky when she pointed him out.

He was okay, I guess, if you were into the whole surfer look. His sandy hair hung loosely to his shoulders and he carried himself in a carefree manner.

While they were all stunningly handsome–I was starting to wonder if they put something in the water here–my eyes were drawn to Micha. Even among these gods of teenage boys, he stood out, radiating power and confidence. He didn't have to wait in line or tell people to clear a table. He'd simply look their way, and they scurried away like he was the devil himself.

"Oh, girl," Lana sang, when Micha's eyes rolled up and locked on me, "You're in trouble."

Tell me about it.

Though I could feel him watching me, I tried to ignore him and went back to eating, which was fruitless. My sandwich didn't taste so good anymore. Sighing, I dropped it back onto the tray.

"Whose tie is that?"

"It's Micha's," Harper quietly answered.

Lana's eyes went wide.

"I couldn't figure mine out," I explained with a shrug.

"Don't you know what wearing a guy's tie means?"

"No," I sighed, "But I'm sure you'll tell me."

"Ivy's wearing Duncan's tie." She nodded at a blonde, before turning my attention to another table. "That's Julie, she has Neil's." Her hand swung over to the group of cheerleaders. "And over there is Pam and Carter. They've been together for two years. Guess whose tie she's wearing?"

"So, what you're saying is–"

"Honey, you've been claimed."

I looked down at the tie around my neck, and then at Micha.

Son of a bitch!

I knew something was up! Well, if he thought he could get away with shit, he was wrong! I glared at Micha and grabbed the tie, pulling the knot loose. Micha tilted his head and cocked his brow in warning when I slipped the silk over my head.

"Don't," Lana warned in a hushed whisper. "You don't know what he's capable of."

"I don't care." And I really didn't. I was so far beyond giving a fuck, it wasn't funny.

Standing up, I strolled across the cafeteria and held the tie up, making sure to look at Micha as I dangled it over the trash. His eyes darkened with warning as he shook his head.

You think you can own me, Micha Kessler?

I dropped the tie, and skipped out of the cafeteria with a smile on my face.

Own that, asshole!

Chapter 11
Riley

Expecting retribution, I hid in the back corner of the library with my sketchbook. But retribution never came, and I soon got lost in the phoenix I was drawing. Why a phoenix? I don't know. That's just what came out. By the time the bell rang, I was already feeling better, hopeful even. Maybe I did have a chance after all?

Should've known better.

As I was rounding the corner for my locker, someone grabbed my arm. I squealed and threw my elbow back, but all that got me was a soft "oomph."

"Let go of me!" I demanded, fighting to stay in the hall. But my struggles were in vain. I was yanked into a dark room, away from witnesses, and slammed up against the wall.

"Did you think that shit was cute?"

Despite my current predicament, it was somewhat comforting to hear a familiar voice.

I twisted my neck and peeked over my shoulder at Micha. The shadowy room deepened the scowl on his face, bringing out the anger burning in his eyes–which of course, made me smile.

"A little," I sang, looking around the room. Not that I could see much, as the only light that filtered in was from under the door. A faint hint of dust hung in the air, and a couple shelves with a few items on them lined the wall to my right. Some kind of storage room, maybe?

"I've been lenient with you." Irritation dripped from his every word. "But my good will only goes so far."

Pfft, lenient!

If this is what Micha called being nice, then he was in serious need of a dictionary.

"Do you think I like to share my shit, Mouse?"

That made me snort. I once saw him push a kid off the swings because he looked at the sandcastle Micha was building. I kicked it over after that, by the way.

"My brother tells me you've been getting a bunch of unwanted attention."

"How's that my fault?" I snapped, and then smirked. "Besides, who says it's unwanted?"

Much like the sandcastle incident, it didn't take me long to regret my actions. Micha stepped in, flattening his front against my back, and my body instantly went into traitorous mode. Warming up as his hot breath fanned over the shell of my ear.

"Stay away from Callaghan."

Who the hell is Callaghan?

"You don't get to dictate who I spend my time with!"

"The fuck I don't!" Micha roared, slamming his fist against the wall.

I squeaked and pressed my forehead into the wall. I'd seen Micha angry–hell, I'd intentionally pissed him off–but he always kept his stone-cold exterior. I couldn't help but be afraid. Was this when my tormentor took things over the line of humiliation to violence? Not too far of a jump, considering Micha hated me.

"Leave me alone."

"I'm sorry," Micha said, tilting his head so his ear was next to my face. "What was that?"

"Leave."

My teeth gritted. *I will not be intimidated!*

"Me."

Fists balled. *I will stay strong!*

"Alone!"

Micha jerked back from my shrill tone, and I jumped. I ducked under his arm and made a break for the door, but I didn't make it far. My hand reached out, barely managed to touch the knob, before I was grabbed and slammed back against the wall. This time with enough force to knock the wind out of my lungs.

"Where the fuck do you think you're going!" he ground out, pressing his heavy hand between my shoulder blades to hold me in place.

I coughed, fighting to pull air back into my chest. "On my way to church."

"Gonna go confess your sins, little mouse?" His deep rumble poured through me, making my head swim.

How did he do that? Make a simple statement sound like the dirtiest porn on the planet?

"I figured an exorcism was in order," I said, closing my eyes and concentrating on the cool feel of the stone wall. Anything but Micha's clean masculine scent. "You know, since I'm being stalked by the Antichrist."

"Don't get cute with me!"

Maybe an exorcism wasn't a bad idea? There was clearly something wrong with me.

"I thought boys liked cute?"

Why does he have to smell so damn good?

Micha stilled behind me, dragging the silence on for what seemed like forever. I stood there, fighting to keep my shivering body from giving me away.

When he did speak, I could feel the triumph in his tone. "You're shaking, Mouse."

"It's cold in here."

"Are you afraid of me?" He dragged his finger down my spine, causing me to openly shiver. "Or are you afraid of how much you like it when I touch you?"

Both!

"I hate it when you touch me," I grumbled, cursing my stupid teenage hormones.

"Is that so?" His hand slid up my leg, over my skirt, and around my hip.

I clamped my thighs together and closed my eyes. His fingers splayed out, covering most of my abdomen with his large hand. And heaven help me, I loved the weight of his warm palm.

He leaned in and whispered, "I bet you're wet right now."

I whimpered and pressed into the wall, praying for some higher power to grant me the ability to meld into the stone surface. Because he was right. The only thing stopping my arousal from seeping through my damp panties was how tightly I had my thighs squeezed together.

"Fuck," he growled, releasing a low throaty groan. "I can't wait to find out if you taste as sweet as you smell."

My brain checked out–packed up and left the building. Micha Kessler wanted to taste me! My heart pounded wildly, as I took shallow breaths. This all had to be a dream, some sick way of fucking with my head. It couldn't be real! It just couldn't!

"If you had any idea of the shit I'm going to do to you, you'd run and never look back."

Yes! Running! That sounded like a fantastic idea! Problem was, I couldn't make my feet move.

"Not so brave now, are you?" His soft lips touched my neck, blazing a hot trail up to my ear. "I should fuck you right here, right now."

Panic shot through my veins, kicking me into fight mode. I threw my heel back and raked my nails down his arm.

"Fuck!" Micha snarled, snatching my wrists and slamming them on the wall above my head. His knees clamped my legs together, effectively taking away my chance of fighting. Still, I struggled.

"I'll scratch your eyes out!" I screamed, using all my strength to wriggle against his hold.

"You want to play, baby?" My heart stopped when his voice dropped an octave. "Okay. Let's play."

My mouth apparently had a mind of it's own. The words came out before I could stop them. "I'd play with Logan before I'd play with you!"

Micha went stiff, and I'd never been more scared in my life.

Now you've done it, Riley! Couldn't keep your big mouth shut!

While expected something, I didn't expect what happened. I felt it before I heard it. Pain bloomed across my ass, spreading a sharp sting up my back and down my thighs. Micha's arm rose, swinging back for another strike.

"Stop it!" I demanded when his heavy hand landed on my other cheek.

But he didn't even slow down. Micha continued his onslaught, and I couldn't do anything but hug the wall and pray it would be over soon.

This wasn't the playful spankings in the books Shelby read. This was meant to punish and break my will, and it was working. My backside was on fire, hips aching from banging into the wall, as my chin quivered and tears openly poured down my face.

"Please stop."

I didn't handle pain well. I started wearing shoes in the house after I stubbed my toe, and I threw out all my Legos after I stepped on one. Honestly, I was surprised I didn't freak out when Chase pierced my bellybutton.

"Keep testing me, Mouse." *Smack!* "And you won't be able to sit down for a week." *Smack!*

"I'm sorry."

And I was. Micha's wrath wasn't worth a few seconds of satisfaction.

"You haven't even begun to be sorry…" he grumbled in a tone that sent a cold spike of fear down my spine, "But you will."

"I'll be good." It was the only thing I could think to say. "I promise."

His hands flattened on the wall by my head. "You'll be a good girl, will you?"

Feeling weak and humiliated, I pressed my face into the cool stone and nodded. He hadn't even broken a sweat, while my chest heaved and loose strands of hair stuck to my forehead.

"Alright," Micha purred in my ear. "Let's see how long you can keep up the good girl act."

I held my breath waiting for the next strike and was overcome with relief when it didn't come. Instead, he slid his palms up my thighs and under my skirt. This was a test; I knew Micha well enough to know that. I swallowed my pride and willed my body to remain still.

"The next time you decide to get friendly with some guy, I'll fuck you in front of him. I don't share my shit, Riley."

I managed to bite my tongue when Micha palmed my sore flesh. But when his thumbs hooked in my panties, my fragile control slipped. I bolted.

He was expecting it.

He wrapped his arm around my waist and lifted me off the ground before I could take another step.

"Fuck you!" I screamed, striking his arm with my fists. "I hate you!"

"There's my tough girl."

I flailed wildly, kicking my dangling feet, and slapping the vise-like grip around my waist. I'd have had better luck taking on a Mack truck. Micha didn't even flinch. He held me up with one arm like I weighed nothing.

"Hey boss."

That's when I noticed the phone in his hand.

"Can't handle me yourself, gotta call in back up now?" I snarled and swung my arm back, narrowly missing his face. "Good! I'll kick his ass too."

Micha's voice was calm, eerily so. "You got her?"

"She's practicing with the track team."

I froze, heart stopping with my struggle.

Shelby was on the track team.

Micha's dark eyes locked on mine. "I want you and the guys to run a train on her."

"No!" I screamed. I couldn't let them hurt Shelby.

The voice on the phone chuckled. "Levi will be happy. He's been dying to get a piece of that."

I reached out, grabbing Micha's hand before he could hang up.

"No! Don't." I went limp and quietly said, "I'll do whatever you want. Just, please, don't hurt Shelby."

Micha watched me for a second, his eyes narrowed in contemplation. "Kneel," he ordered, dropping me back on my feet.

What could I do? I hung my head in defeat and slowly sank to my knees.

"I'll call you back," Micha said and stuffed his phone in his pocket.

I sat there under his oppressive gaze, blinking the tears out of my eyes, as he slowly stalked around me, circling his prey.

He tugged my ponytail free, letting my hair cascade down my back, and stroked my head like some kind of pet. Tears of frustration rolled down my cheeks.

"I know you hate me right now…"

I did. More than before, if that was even possible.

My fists balled, and I swallowed my anger. I couldn't afford to lose my temper right now. "Why are you doing this? You don't even like me."

"I don't hate you, Mouse. Never did. I actually have a lot of respect for you."

Sure, you do.

I sucked in a shuddered breath and angrily wiped the tears off my face. "I hate you."

"I know." Micha tipped my chin up, forcing me to meet his gaze. "I just don't care."

I shivered at the way his gaze darkened. What made it worse was how my body reacted. Part of me wanted him to hold me down and take what he wanted.

"Does this get you off, you sick fuck?" I snarled, not sure if I was talking to him or myself. "Forcing girls to do what you want?"

"Yes." The corner of his mouth curled. "But don't kid yourself, Mouse . . . it gets you off too."

"No, it doesn't."

If I said it enough, would it make it true?

"I might believe that," he lowered himself down, squatting to my eye level, "If you weren't squeezing your thighs together so tight."

I dropped my gaze and swallowed, not wanting him to see the truth. Why couldn't I be normal? Normal people went on walks on the beach. They had dates, and white picket fences with two-point-three kids. Normal people ran from the devil . . . they didn't dance with him.

"Don't worry, baby, I'm not going to let you hide who you are." He brushed my hair back and placed a gentle kiss on my forehead. "I'm going to make you fucking embrace it."

Chapter 12
Micha

"ALL YOU DID WAS SPANK HER?" LOGAN TOSSED HIS BAG INTO HIS locker and shook his head. "She's fucking lucky she's not mine."

Any chick should consider themselves lucky they weren't Logan's. My best friend wore the charming playboy vibe well, but underneath . . .? Underneath was a monster who fed off the pain and suffering of others. The louder a chick screamed, the harder he came.

"And what would you have done?" I asked, opening the door and letting the clean smell of chlorine fill the locker room.

"Probably backhanded her," he shrugged and followed me around the edge of the pool. "But I can guarantee you," he added while winking at a group of girls who were eye-fucking us from the bleachers, "She sure as hell wouldn't do it again."

"Kessler! Hudson!" Coach yelled and clapped his hands, ushering us along. "Get the lead out of your asses!"

"She won't do it again," I said as I climbed up on my block.

I missed this. Not the girls–I could give a fuck about them. It was the smooth feel of tiles under my feet and the humidity in the air. That rush of adrenaline pumping through my veins.

Every time I won a competition, I was a little closer to conquering the demons of my past. Fear was a weakness, and I was Micha Kessler. Future King of Kings. I didn't do weaknesses.

"I don't get you," Logan tsk-ed taking his position next to me. "All that prime pussy just screaming to be used, and you never partake."

My brow rose, as I cocked my head his way. "How many of them have you fucked?"

Bastard just smirked in response.

Shaking my head, I stared at the clear water and gripped the edge of the block. My back twitched, muscles tensing as my fingers dug into the hard surface. A slow reaction time could cost the race, and I didn't lose. I almost did, once…

Nine years ago:

"This tastes funny," Mason whined, kicking his red sneakers off the back of our mom's seat.

She sighed and started the car. "Just drink it, honey."

Mason was so excited when he heard we were getting ice cream and a milkshake. Now, he didn't even like it. I couldn't argue, though. It did taste bad. Strawberries were supposed to be sweet. I took another sip, smacking my lips at the bitterness.

We spent an hour at a little fair a town over, and another at the petting zoo Mase loved. Mom even took us to the go-cart track–one of the few places I liked. She wouldn't let Logan come, though.

Mason bumped my shoulder. "Let me try yours," he said, his greedy hand reaching out.

I passed my cup to him, and grumbled, "Have it."

He quickly grabbed it. Dangling feet swung happily as he sucked on the straw.

"Like it?"

He smiled and nodded his head.

"Good." Letting my heavy head fall back, I closed my eyes. We should be home soon.

Drip, drip, drip.

What was that?

Drip, drip, drip.

Why was it so dark? It was the middle of the day.

Drip, drip, drip.

I sat up, yawned, and rubbed my eyes. Mase was asleep beside me. Head back, mouth wide open, and chest heaving with deep breaths. His arms hung at his sides, one hand still holding my shake, haphazardly spilling the contents on the seat.

Drip, drip, drip.

"Mason," I yawned, closing my eyes, "You're spilling."

Drip, drip, drip.

"Mason!" I tried again, this time slapping his arm.

The cup flew out of his grip, splattering the contents on the back of the seat. I stared at the pink cloud sliding down the fabric, blinking the sleep out of my eyes. Why didn't that wake him up?

I sat up and tried again, shaking Mase and calling his name.

"Mom," I called out, worried, "Mase isn't waking up."

"It's okay, honey," she said, staring at the lake through the windshield. "We'll all be asleep soon."

.   .   .

The shrill sound of Coach's whistle cut through the air, spurring me into action. I launched my body and sliced into the cool water with the grace it took years to master.

At the end of the pool, I flipped around, kicked off the wall, and swam back. I pushed my limbs to work harder and move faster, always faster.

The light was right there. I had to get Mase to the light.

The erratic beat of my pulse echoed in my ears, while icy claws reached out, threatening to suck me into a dark abyss of pain and misery.

"Come on, Mase, breathe!"

"I was having a good day until I realized I was coaching a bunch of girls!" Coach yelled. "What were you pussies doing all summer? Having slumber parties and painting your nails? PICK UP THE PACE!"

I was the first to finish. There was a reason I was captain, and it had nothing to do with who my father was. Holding on to the edge of the pool, I pushed my goggles to the top of my head and swept the water off my face. Only then did I allow myself to release a satisfied breath.

"Congratulations, Kessler, you're two-point-four seconds slower than last year," Coach chastised before turning his attention back to the pool. "Come on, Hudson, stop thinking about pussy . . . with time like this, you ain't getting any."

I swore under my breath. If I'd been two seconds slower that day, Mason might not be here. Riley had consumed my summer. I might've become slightly obsessed with the raven-haired beauty. I could give her a permanent spot on the bleachers as my own personal cheerleader. I liked the sound of that.

Logan's head popped up in the next lane. "Sorry Coach," he apologized, while waving at a giggly blonde. "I was distracted."

"When you're in my pool, I own your ass," Coach stated, unimpressed. "Chase pussy on your own time."

"But you're always telling us to not be tense." Logan scanned Coach's stiff form and propped his elbows on the ledge. "You know, a good hard fuck might help remove that stick from your ass. If Mrs. Bantam isn't up for the job, I could set you up."

Snickers filled the air, bringing a satisfied smirk to Logan's face. Fucker was asking for it.

Coach returned Logan's smug expression. "Congratulations, guys, Hudson here just bought you ten laps."

That wiped the grin off Logan's face. He was constantly pushing Coach's buttons. Like most of us, he had a problem with authority, which kind of came with the territory.

Each one of us grew up being tested and prepared for a future decided before we were born. To say our childhoods weren't normal was an understatement, though Logan's was a nightmare.

"Come on, Coach," Logan pleaded. "Don't punish us because your dick's not getting any attention."

I shook my head. He just didn't know when to quit.

Coach's stern face met Logan's mocking grin. "Make that twenty laps."

I didn't mind the extra work. The rest of the team, however, groaned in protest. Logan released a long breath and popped his goggles back in place.

"That's it," Logan said as the shrill sound of a whistle cut through the air, "I'm fucking his wife tonight."

Chuckling, I took off, doing my laps without argument.

After practice, I showered and walked up to my locker with a towel wrapped around my waist. Logan was already rifling through shit when I got there. I shook my head as a couple of bottles fell out and clinked on the floor.

"It's the first day," I said, opening my locker. "How much shit do you have in there?"

"Hey, it takes work to look this good."

"You're worse than a fucking girl."

"Says the guy who sent me shopping for his girl."

I shrugged. "What can I say, you know what looks good."

"Yeah, right," he snorted. "You wanted her to have a closet full of lingerie."

Nothing wrong with that.

Parker and the rest of the football team funneled into their side of the locker room, causing Logan to groan. "Here comes Callaghan."

"Hey, Kessler," Callaghan called out. "Met your girl today. She's a tasty little piece."

My fists clenched. Mason told me all about that shit. Kissing her hand like he was fucking Prince Charming. My mouse and I would have words about that.

"Yeah, she made friends with your sister," I said, turning around to smirk at Callaghan. "Guess she'll be spending a lot more time with us."

That wiped the smile off his face. He knew by "us," I meant Mase. The shit I did to Riley was nothing compared to what Mase does to Harper. She brought it on herself.

"Keep your fucking brother away from my sister," Callaghan growled.

I arched my brow. "Or what?"

He took a breath and squared his shoulders. "Your little girl-friend won't be hanging around my sister for long."

That's one of the things I admired about Sean. Not many people could keep their composure when I was pushing their buttons, but he always managed to reel it in before he blew.

The only other person I knew with that kind of control, besides me, was my father. It made him a formidable foe. He had the downside of a conscience though.

"I thought you'd be the last person to deny your sister a friend," I tsk-ed and returned my attention to getting dressed. "But hey, I'm sure she's good with the one she has."

He sighed, knowing I was right. Harper didn't have anyone but Lana, mainly thanks to Mason.

"Bye-bye now," Logan sang, shooting Sean a wink.

"You know what, you're right. My sister does need more friends." Sean smirked and sauntered to his side of the locker room. "She should have a slumber party…"

I dropped my bag and glared over my shoulder. "What the fuck did he just say?"

"Not you, too," Parker sighed and rested his arm on the wall. "Maybe I should quit?"

Parker was a damn good running back and he loved the game. It was hard for any of us to find something we truly enjoyed. I wasn't going to take that away from him.

"Don't let Mase's feud affect your game. It's not your problem."

"Whitley!" Sean called from the other side of the room. "Consort with the enemy on your own time!"

Parker's brows knitted together. "You sure?"

Last year wasn't so bad. Sean was just another guy on the team. This year he was quarterback and captain, which Mason didn't like. He wanted Parker to quit.

"Yeah. Go," I said, throwing my chin in the football team's direction. "I got Mase."

"Okay." Parker nodded. "Let me know if he needs to be taught a lesson. I'm sure with a few drinks and Jasmine's help, I could get him on his knees."

I snickered. Parker's bat swung both ways, but he got a thrill out of fucking straight guys. And Jasmine, that sick bitch, liked helping him do it.

"Whitley!" Sean yelled again, making Parker walk away with a roll of his eyes.

"Speaking of little bro…" Logan slapped my arm and pointed at Mason strutting through the doors. "Looks like he had fun."

"Fuck sake," I muttered, seeing the blood on his knuckles. "When's he going to learn there are better ways to solve problems?"

Logan rested his back against the locker and said, "I'm telling you we should start an underground fighting ring. It'll give him a place to blow off some steam."

"Maybe you're right."

It wasn't a bad idea. There were plenty of assholes in this town who liked to beat the crap out of each other. Why not turn a profit?

"Mase is lethal," he pointed out. "He'd be our prize fighter."

"Damn right I would," Mason agreed, joining us.

"Whose face did you fuck up now?" I asked, pulling my jeans over my hips.

"Silas's."

Silas was usually the one pulling Mase off someone, not throwing punches with him. "Since when do you pick fights with your best friend?"

His green eyes rolled. "I might have laughed a little too hard when Riley crushed his balls and told him to stop staring at her or she'd rip them off."

Logan doubled over in laughter while I scowled and slammed my locker shut. Why the fuck did she have her hands on another guys' junk?

"You should've seen it," Mase snickered. "She walked right up to him, grabbed his nuts, and squeezed. Silas dropped like a sack of potatoes. Funniest shit I've ever seen!"

"Oh man," Logan cried, wiping the tears off his face. "I'd pay to see that shit."

"Why the fuck didn't Silas stop her?"

"Hey, this is all your fault," Mason pointed an accusing finger at me. "You're the one who ordered us to stalk her like a couple of creeps."

"Look at it this way," Logan said, fighting to control his laughter, "Anyone who saw that shit go down will stay the fuck away from her. If you think about it, she did you a favor."

That was true. Word would spread quickly, and no guy would approach her for fear of losing their balls. I could handle that.

"Though I'd think twice before letting her anywhere near your package," he added.

I snorted. "I'd like to see her try some shit like that with me."

She'd do it once.

Mase and Logan followed me outside into the sunny parking lot.

"Ah shit," I said, realizing what time it was. "Can you take Mase home?"

I was late to pick up Junior. He needed some school supplies, and his crack whore mother wasn't going to help. I had to get Peyton to pay her a visit twice before she'd stop selling him for her next fix.

"No problem," Logan nodded. "Come on kid, looks like you're riding with me."

My brother's face twisted at the word kid. "I'm only a year younger than you, asshole."

Logan threw his arm around Mase's shoulders. "That kind of attitude isn't going to get you ice cream," he said, ruffling his hair playfully.

"Fuck off," Mason growled, and shoved him away.

They walked off as I climbed into my Jeep and pulled out of the parking lot. I made my way to Junior's apartment, which made the shit hole Riley had lived in look like a palace. The kid had it rough.

I pulled him out of the lake a couple of years ago when some other kids pushed him in. He didn't know how to swim, which pissed me the fuck off. Until I met his mother.

I took him home with the intent to give his parents a piece of my mind. But after I saw the conditions he was living in, I couldn't leave him there. All the kid had in his room was a bare mattress on a dirty floor.

Junior, however, refused to leave his mother and said he needed to protect her. A fucking eight-year-old kid! I never got that. Why kids like Junior and Riley were so loyal to parents who didn't deserve it was beyond me. Three years later, and Junior was still doing it.

I knew something was wrong the second I saw Junior sitting outside kicking a rock. Normally he'd wait for me in his apartment. I didn't like him playing around in this neighborhood. Wanna-be thugs and dealers hung out on every corner.

Junior wasn't the most popular kid in school. He got in more fights than Mase. I might've thought he just had a bad day, if he wasn't wearing only one goddamn shoe!

"Hey," I said, pulling up beside him. "Where the fuck is your shoe?"

He opened the door and plopped down in the passenger seat. "Lost it."

What was he hiding?

I tipped my head and scanned his torn shirt. "How the hell do you lose a shoe?"

"I don't know," he yelled, throwing his arms up and turning my way. "I just lost it, okay!"

I just about lost it when I saw the bruise forming under his brown eye. "Who the fuck did that to you?"

"It's my fault." He scowled and dropped his head. "Mom said she had someone coming over."

Oh, hell no!

I threw open my door and jumped out of the Jeep.

"Micha —"

"You stay right there!" I said, and stormed into the apartment. Junior knew better than to follow.

All I could see walking up the stairs was red. This fucking bitch! I told her to keep her fucking tricks away from the kid! There was no pause when I reached Junior's door. I lifted my foot and kicked it open.

A couple of kids who were sitting in the hall took note, and stood to get a better look. My rage grew when I saw Junior's mother in the middle of the apartment, with a hairy ass between her legs. She didn't even have the decency to go in another room.

I was across the room before the guy could react. I hauled him off Junior's mother by his greasy hair and threw my fist at his jaw. He flew back, breaking an old rickety coffee table.

"You like to hit kids?" I growled, kicking him in the ribs twice. "Let's see how fucking tough you are now, asshole!"

Junior's mother shrieked, "Micha! Stop it!"

"You're fucking next, bitch," I said, throwing my finger in her direction.

Eyes wide, she shrunk back down on the couch and covered herself with a blanket.

I looked down at the groaning asshole on the ground. He was in a sad state, naked and hunched over, with a trickle of blood coming out of his mouth. The left side of his face was starting to bruise, and I was pretty sure I broke a couple ribs. I might've left, and let him stick his tiny cock back in Julia, if he hadn't opened his fucking mouth.

"Little prick deserved it."

I stepped forward and pressed my foot down on his cock. I'd have to burn these shoes later, but his scream was worth it.

"If I see you around here again," I pressed more weight down and twisted my foot, "I'll put a fucking bullet between your eyes. You got that?"

"Yes!" He screamed, face twisted in agony. "I got it!"

"Good," I said, giving one more twist before I released him. "Now get the fuck out of here."

Pussy didn't argue. He just grabbed his clothes and scurried away, still naked. Julia tried to call out, but he didn't listen.

She huffed and glared at me. "He was a good client."

I really wanted to hit her and knock some sense in that head, but for some reason, Junior loved his mother.

"Shut the fuck up," I growled, still considering punching her. "Go find Junior's shoe."

Chapter 13
Riley

I REREAD THE TEXT I GOT THIS MORNING.

Unknown: *Does the mouse want to escape her cage?*

Someone knew! But who? There was only one person who called me mouse, and Micha wasn't the kind of guy who would hide behind anonymity.

Then again, two days ago I thought I knew what he was capable of. I had no doubt he would've hurt Shelby. What if this was some kind of test? Or a trap? My eyes wandered back to the phone in my hand.

But what if it wasn't?

Who is this? I texted back.

Unknown: *A friend. You can call me The Piper.*

Me: *How do I know this isn't some kind of trick?*

The Piper: *You don't.*

Me: *What's in it for you?*

The Piper: *Does it matter?*

No. Not really.

Me: *Why should I trust you?*

The Piper: *What other choice do you have?*

I didn't have another choice. Try as I might, I couldn't think of a way out of this, at least not without someone getting hurt. I'd suffer a thousand deaths before ever putting someone else in danger, and Micha knew it.

While hiding in my room last night, I resigned myself to the fact that I was trapped. Looking at my phone, I wondered if I wanted to risk it. Did I want to let myself feel hopeful, only to have it crushed?

"Riley," my dad said, pulling the cruiser through Ashworth's gates. "Please talk to me."

Tucking my phone into my backpack, I turned to stare out the window. My eyes started to well up at the sound of his voice. I couldn't look at him.

"Come on, sweetpea, give me a chance to explain."

I grimaced at his use of my childhood nickname. He spent an hour outside my room last night, begging me to open the door. I wouldn't. Which was probably why he insisted on driving me this morning. Didn't mean I'd talk to him. Why should I care what he had to say?

"I know you hate me, but you don't know the full story."

Did it really matter? He gave me away. Signed a contract like I was something to be traded. Fathers were supposed to protect their daughters. Guess I shouldn't be surprised. Mom didn't care enough to stick around either. I sniffed and blinked back my tears.

"Sweatpea, if I had any idea that they'd actually use the fucking thing… I never wanted you in this position."

He never wanted me in this position!? He put me in this position!

"So why sign it, then?" I snarled.

So much for the silent treatment.

"I didn't have a choice."

"Right," I snorted, "Keep telling yourself that."

"God damn it! You don't know what he was doing, I couldn't watch… Your mother–" He sighed and hung his head. "I promise you, I never wanted any of this."

For the first time in days, I took in my dad's appearance. There were dark circles under his eyes, and it looked like he hadn't brushed his hair in days. He looked destroyed. I wanted desperately to believe him, but they were just words, and words didn't mean anything. Mom made promises, too.

"Did Mom know?"

The look on his face was all the answer I needed.

"Great," I huffed and grabbed my backpack. "Sorry I was such a burden on you guys."

My dad reached out and grabbed my arm before I could open the door.

"Your mother would've rather died than let me sign that thing. She almost… It doesn't matter." He shook his head, and stared deep into my eyes. "You're my daughter, and I will find a way out of this."

"No, I'm not. You gave me away, remember?" I said, and rushed into the school before the dam holding my tears back burst.

I wove through the hall filled with students, feeling like everyone was staring at me, mocking my heartache. It made me long for the days of simple bullying. They'd get a few laughs, and I could still hold my head up because name calling and stupid pranks didn't bare my soul.

No one saw my pain. They couldn't feel the heaviness in my heart, or the walls closing in on me. I'd never felt more exposed in my life.

Wanting to get away from their prying eyes, I ducked into the closest bathroom.

"Look, girls, I think she's going to cry."

Oh great . . . Naomi. Just what I need.

I almost turned around and walked out, until I heard another voice say, "Are you going to cry, Harper?"

I stopped. *Harper?*

No longer concerned with my own troubles, my feet carried me around the bend. At the back corner of the bathroom stood Naomi, and three other girls, two brunettes and a blonde. Each one had manicured nails and perfectly styled hair. I almost snorted outright at their uniforms.

Of course they were cheerleaders.

Harper was barely visible through the group. She sat on the floor with her back against the wall, hugging her knees. Though her face was hidden behind her deep red hair, I recognized the shudder of a sob.

"Oh look, it's Barbie and the slut squad," I said, dropping my backpack loudly onto the floor.

It worked. The four girls took their attention off Harper and turned to glare at me. The scowl on Naomi's face deepened as she took a step closer.

"Move along, this is our bathroom." She waved her hand through the air, "You can use the one in the basement . . . with the rest of the *help*."

The slut squad snickered behind her.

"I know you're not the sharpest tool in the shed, Barbie, so let me explain something to you… Bathrooms are communal space." I smirked when their jaws dropped. "But you're probably right, we shouldn't share a bathroom. I'd hate to catch herpes or something."

The slut squad gasped. The blonde one even threw her hand up over her mouth.

Oh, please.

Naomi straightened up and marched over, her heels clicking against the tiled floor. "We should be the ones worried. God knows what's on those thrift store clothes."

"Don't worry, I get my clothes off the bodies of dead cheerleaders," I sang and paused to roll my eyes over her red and black uniform. "What size are you?"

Naomi snickered. "Your fat ass wouldn't fit in any of my clothes."

Hey! My ass wasn't fat, not even a little.

"Oh, it's not for me. I saw this dog down by the homeless shelter and those pumps would look great on him."

"Of course you would know where the homeless shelter was." She snapped her fingers in the air. "Come on, girls. Let the *help* pick up the *trash.*"

Like obedient pets, the slut squad followed behind, each one giving me a snarky grimace as they passed.

I rolled my eyes and hurried over to Harper. "Are you okay?"

She lifted her tear-streaked face and that's when I saw the wet stain on her shirt. It looked like coffee or something. So much for Ashworth being dignified. The only difference between the assholes here and other schools was the size of their bank accounts.

I sighed and helped Harper off the floor. She didn't argue, didn't so much as make a peep as I guided her over to the sink and wet a paper towel. My heart went out to her. I recognized the shame on her face.

"Don't worry about them." I gave her a small smile while trying to clean her shirt. "Their brains are probably fried from all those nail polish fumes."

It was small, but Harper giggled, and it was the best sound I'd heard all day. I got the feeling she didn't laugh much, if at all. The girl was always terrified. Even now, with just us in here, she was stiff and jumpy.

I sighed and said, "You shouldn't let them push you around like that."

Guilt flashed across her big doe eyes, as she muttered, "I deserve it."

"No one deserves that."

"I do."

It was when she hung her head in defeat that I decided someone needed to take a stand. Show pricks like Micha and Naomi that just because they had money, the world wouldn't bend down for them. I would bring them down for all the Harpers of the world. I pulled out my phone and texted The Piper.

Me: *I'm in.*

* * *

My mystery ally said he'd be in touch, and in the meantime, for me to work on gaining Micha's trust. How in the hell was that supposed to help? Not to mention, that would take too long.

God knows what would happen between now and then. I needed to get out of this now, before someone got hurt. I sighed and picked at my sandwich. It was hopeless.

On the upside, I hadn't seen Micha this morning, so there was that. My brief moment of reprieve was crushed when Logan sauntered over, pushed Lana's chair aside, and sat between us. I swear the universe was trying to mock me.

"That was rude," I said, looking over at Lana, whose mouth was hanging open in shock.

His jade eyes twinkled as he flashed me his perfect white teeth. "I wouldn't want you two fighting over me."

We both rolled our eyes in response.

Logan crinkled his nose at my tray. "You know they have better things than chicken salad," he said, snatching half my sandwich.

I liked the chicken salad.

"I guess that means you can find your own lunch then," I said, pinching his arm.

He didn't even flinch. Just smiled as he ate half my sandwich in one bite.

Dick!

Next thing I knew, our table was taken over by boys. Mason sat beside Harper, which caused her to whimper and duck behind her hair. English class creeper took the other side, dwarfing poor Harper between their large frames.

Parker sat next to Lana, and I swear, the tomato in her salad was less red than she was. If I didn't think they were all assholes, I might've found her reaction cute. In the short time I'd known her, I'd never seen the girl speechless.

And then, the bane of my existence, Micha, took the chair next to me.

"Hello, Mouse," he said. "I trust you've been good this morning?"

"Well, I haven't fucked anyone, if that's what you mean," I snarled.

His brow rose. "How's your ass?"

I couldn't hold back the flush of hot embarrassment.

Say it a little louder, why don't you?

When I didn't respond, Micha turned his attention to his lunch, and took a bite of some bread stuff in a bowl. Rich people ate weird crap.

My lips curled. "What the hell are you eating?"

"Panzanella salad."

"That is not a salad," I said, watching him take another bite. "Where's the lettuce?"

"Not all salads have lettuce, Mouse." His dark eyes landed on my tray and the half sandwich Logan hadn't stolen.

"Here," he held up a forkful, "Try it."

I shook my head, eyeing the strange food.

"What's the matter? Afraid you'll like it?"

"I know I won't like it," I insisted, completely secure in my statement.

"Suit yourself."

He was giving up way too easy. "What's that supposed to mean?"

"Nothing." He shrugged. "Just didn't take you for the type afraid to try something new."

"I am not afraid."

He raised a challenging brow. "Then what's the harm in trying it?"

"Fine! I'll try your stupid salad," I huffed and crossed my arms. "But I won't like it."

"Alright, I'll make you a deal. If you don't like it, I'll leave you alone for the rest of the week."

My eyes narrowed. "What's the catch?"

"If you do," I saw the hint of smile curl his lips, "Then I get to spend the week in your bed."

I snorted. "No way!"

"It's up to you. You can take the bet and possibly win yourself a week of freedom. Or refuse, and I'll be in your bed anyway."

I'd sleep outside before sleeping in the same bed as him… and maybe burn the mattress.

"Well, you'll be alone in my bed."

"Not if you're tied to it."

"You wouldn't."

His brow rose. "You know I would."

My hands balled as I eyed the forkful he held out. If, by some small miracle, I actually did like that crap, I could always pretend I didn't. Sighing, I parted my lips so Micha could slide the fork into my mouth.

Oh my God! The flavors exploding on my tongue were out of this world. I don't know what those little cubes of bread were, but they were delicious. I didn't even care that Logan stole the rest of my sandwich.

It wasn't until Micha bent over and whispered in my ear that I realized what had happened. "See you tonight, Mouse."

My eyes zeroed in on the empty bowl.

Fuck you, Panzanella salad!

After practice, I took Junior out for something to eat. Someone had to feed the kid, because his mother sure wouldn't. She was worse than Riley's mother. At least Maria Adams never sold her daughter to fuel her habit.

That shit stopped when I sent Ava to have a chat with Junior's mother. There was something about being taught a lesson by the pretty little blond with an innocent smile. Plus, I wanted to make sure that prick from yesterday got the message.

After that, I headed over to Riley's. Not only did I want to get my hands on her—feeding her was one of the most erotic moments of my life—but Jack's friend left me another note.

An eye for an eye,
A dime for a dime,
I'll take what's yours,

If you take what's mine.

It wasn't the stupid little rhymes that had me concerned, it was the picture of Riley attached to it. If this fucker wanted to take a round with the master player, fine. But no one, and I mean no one, threatened what was mine! I didn't care if it was my Jeep, my shoe, or my mouse. This asshole was going to pay.

In the meantime, I'd have to have Riley protected, and since Marco wasn't overly anxious for another security detail–last time Riley asked him if all guys liked to lick ass–that left the job up to Preston. I'd like to see her try to make that fucker uncomfortable.

I turned down Logan's driveway and grimaced at the gaudy fountain. We'd tried to destroy that thing so many times, but Paisley had some weird attachment to it. The last time we cut the angel's head off, she cried. Logan put a stop to it after that. Always the momma's boy.

Stepping out of the Jeep, I took a minute to enjoy the fresh air. There was a big difference between the salty fish ridden ocean air where Junior lived and here. I don't know how the kid put up with it.

He wasn't very impressed when I told him about Riley, though I couldn't blame him. The only females in his life were his mother, and the useless social worker who stopped by once a month.

The gravel crunched under my feet as I made my way to the house. Riley should be home by now. She worked at Chase Mathers' tattoo parlor, and I still didn't feel any better about the guy. Okay so he was her uncle, but why didn't he tell her? What was he hiding?

The Order had dealings with a few motorcycle clubs, and they were some shady fuckers. Chase may have left the club behind, but he still ran the Lost Souls MC for a couple years. Nobody gave up that kind of power without a reason.

Paisley was rearranging a plant when I stepped inside.

"Micha," she asked, eyeing me curiously. "Logan's not here?"

If Paisley knew what was going on, the first thing she'd do is run to my father. "I'm here to see Riley."

"Oh?" She knew the drill; she had a contract herself. All the wives did. Paisley couldn't look Logan in the eye after the contract reading. He acted like it didn't bother him, but I knew better. "She's in her room."

I had some time before Preston got here. Time I intended to spend playing with my mouse.

"You won't hurt her, will you?"

I stopped halfway up the stairs and spun around. "Don't confuse me with your former husband. I might be hard on her, but I'd never beat on her for fun."

Paisley winced. "I'm sorry. I just–"

"I know." I shouldn't snap at her. Paisley had been through enough, and I didn't want to make her relive those memories.

"Derek should be home soon. I'll make sure he doesn't bother you."

And by that, she meant she'd keep Derek from pissing me off. Considering he was just as stubborn as his daughter, that was probably a good idea.

"You do that," I said, and continued up the stairs.

I sauntered into Riley's room and looked around, taking in the changes she'd made. Above the bed was a poster of her favorite movie, *Aliens*. On one of the bedside tables were two pictures of her mother, and various figurines and stuffed toys of Minnie Mouse lined a shelf on the far wall. In the corner of the room was a stack of art supplies and an easel.

My eyes followed the lines of a black dragon's wings, spread wide in flight, as his neck twisted and snarled a ball of blue flame. The eyes were what caught my attention. Deep green orbs, glistening with unshed tears. Somehow Riley had made this grand majestic beast look sad. It was beautiful.

Riley's voice wafted out of the bathroom, drawing my attention from the painting. I walked over and smirked. She was singing in the shower, and not very well. Pressing my palm on the wooden door, I listened to her out-of-tune voice, imagining the vision on the other side. A naked, wet, raven-haired beauty.

I could kick the door down and take what was rightfully mine. My dick sure liked the idea. Instead, I shrugged off my coat, dropped my bag, and walked over to the bed.

Laid out at the foot of the mattress was a set of Minnie Mouse pajamas–a tank top and navy shorts that would make her eyes pop. God, I loved her eyes, especially when she was pissed. The rage through those deep still water blues racked up a storm.

Crashing waves against rocky shores, popping white-hot sparks of hatred like fireworks. Fireworks that were just for me. My dick got hard just thinking about it. The simple pair of white cotton panties caused me to smirk.

How very virgin of her.

I sat down on the bed and picked up a picture of Riley's mother. All I wanted to do was crush the small wooden frame. What kind of mother was she? Drinking while her daughter took care of everything.

I didn't get Riley's weird attachment to her. What the hell did Maria Adams ever do to deserve her daughter's undying love?

I sighed and set the picture back on the bedside table. If Riley wanted to think of her mother as a paragon of virtue, I'd let her. Hell, it worked for Mase.

My attention was drawn back to the bathroom when I heard the shower cut off. I smiled, kicked my feet up, and linked my fingers behind my head.

Show time!

A few minutes later, Riley sauntered out, completely oblivious to my presence. I licked my lips watching water drip off her hair, glide over her smooth skin, and disappear under the towel wrapped around her chest. Fuck, I wanted to rip that shit off her. My heart pumped excitedly when those eyes rolled up.

"Jesus Christ!" Riley shrieked, jumping back.

"You shouldn't use the Lord's name in vain." I tsk-ed. "Good little church girl like you knows that."

The rage started burning as she narrowed her eyes. I loved this shit.

"Fuck you, and fuck God! You can both kiss my ass!"

Fuck me! I almost came right then and there.

"Is that an invitation?" I drawled, lifting my brow.

She clutched the towel tighter to her chest, as if that would save her, and pointed at the door. "Get out!"

"No."

"You can't just come in here!" she said, stomping her foot.

It was so fucking adorable when she acted all tough like that.

"I believe I can. Or did you forget about our little deal?"

"Well, I'm reneging on it."

The corner of my mouth lifted. "And that's why I brought rope."

She was pissed, her eyes narrowed and nose all scrunched up. I wanted to keep pushing her, watch her slip past the point of control and snap. Maybe she'd slap me again? That was fucking hot. Or maybe she'd lunge at me. Swing her fists and fight me with all her strength.

That's what I wanted; to fight with her until she broke in my hands and watch defeat slip into her eyes. Then, and only then, would I have the control I craved.

"I hate you."

"So you keep saying," I stated, turning my attention to her buzzing phone.

Shelby wanted to know how her day was.

Oh, it's about to get real good.

"Give me that."

"Come and get it," I dared, knowing there was no way she'd take me up on it.

Riley chewed her lip and shifted nervously on her feet. Her gaze shot from me, to the clothes laid out, undecided which to go for. If she went for her phone, I'd have that towel off in two seconds, and she knew it.

Slowly, with wide, alert eyes, Riley crept closer to the bed. Though my heart pumped with wild anticipation, outwardly I remained calm, scrolling through her phone, while keeping myself primed and ready to pounce.

Come on, little mouse, just a few steps closer.

I sighed inwardly when her hand shot out, quickly snatching up her clothes.

"It's password protected," Riley spat as she backed up.

"I know," I replied, setting her phone back on the bedside table. "You really shouldn't use your birthday."

There were those sparks again. *Pop, pop, pop.*

"Your towel is starting to slip," I pointed out, smirking when she cleared her throat and nervously readjusted.

"Why don't you go find Naomi?" she said, glancing over her shoulder at the bathroom.

Silly girl, do you honestly think I'm going to let you hide?

"From what I hear, you two have a lot of fun together."

People talked too much. I only fucked Naomi a couple of times, but if you listened to the rumors floating around Ashworth, we were a couple. I suspected Naomi had something to do with that.

"Jealous?"

"Pfft! As if."

I smirked and rose from the bed.

She was.

"Maybe I should call Naomi over here?" For every step I took, Riley took two back. Her eyes were locked on me, slowly prowling closer, and hadn't noticed she'd veered off course. The bathroom was to her left. "You want to watch Naomi suck my cock?"

I could practically hear her teeth grind. Normally, I didn't do the jealousy thing. The first time some chick got snarky over someone else, they were gone, but with Riley I wanted her seething at the mere thought of me being with someone else. Because I was. Christ, I almost punched my best friend for staring at her ass.

"Or maybe you want to watch me fuck her?" Riley's back hit the wall and I moved in. Caging her in my arms, I leaned in and whispered, "Hear her scream my name?"

She glared up at me and I almost stumbled. She was fucking aroused. Pupils dilated, with a flushed face. Fuck me. This chick really was made for me. If my mouse wanted to watch, I could arrange that. Let's see how far down the rabbit hole I could drag her.

"Have sex with who you want," she insisted. "I don't care."

"I don't have sex…" I chuckled at her innocence, "I fuck."

Her cheeks flushed a deeper shade, as she swallowed hard.

"Don't worry, Mouse." I traced the delicate angle of her jawline, reveling in the pink tint that flooded her cheeks. "I'll show you the difference."

She released a ragged breath. "Don't touch me."

I grazed my knuckles down her arm, watching a trail of goosebumps rise. "You like it."

"No, I don't." Riley quickly clamped her legs shut when I smoothed my palm up her thigh.

I bent over, running my nose up her neck, taking in her sweet scent. I never cared for coconuts before, but now I couldn't get enough of them.

"I can feel the heat coming off your pussy."

She gulped and hugged her clothes tightly to her chest, like they would somehow shield her from me. There was nothing on God's green earth that could keep me from her. All she did by trying to hide was make me want to rip her out in the open.

Stupid, Mouse, you shouldn't tempt the cat.

"Why don't you come back later? You know, when I'm less naked and have a free hand to slap you with?"

Always the stubborn one, my mouse. Refusing to back down, even when she was scared shitless. But she wasn't prepared to play this game.

I tilted my head and looked down at her. "You want to get dressed?"

"No." Her lips curled in a sneer, "I want to stay in this damp towel all damn day! What the hell do you think?"

I leaned back, slowly pulling my gaze up her legs, over the curve of her hip, and up to her chest. Soft mounds pressing against the towel with her heavy breaths. It would be so easy to take her right now. I bet that tight little virgin pussy was dripping.

"Go ahead, get dressed," I said, still contemplating whether or not I was going to take her right here and now. "Don't let me stop you."

"Do you mind?" Riley huffed.

A gentleman would've let her go in the bathroom, or at least turned around. But nobody said I was a gentleman.

"Not at all."

She tilted her head to the side and gave me a dirty look. "Kind of hard to get dressed when you're all up in my space."

"I could help you," I suggested, dragging my finger down her chest, enjoying the warmth of her soft skin.

I'd help her alright. Slide those white cotton panties right up her trembling thighs. Next would be the shirt. I pictured it fluttering over her head to caress her breasts. The soft fabric of her shorts wrapping around her thighs and over her ass. Fuck, I wanted to dress her every damn day.

"You could at least back up?" Riley said breathlessly.

One finger. That's all it took to steal her breath.

"I could," I said, dropping my hand and arching my brow.

She gave a derisive little snort and rolled her eyes.

What happened next caught me completely off guard.

Riley's features went hard as she ripped the towel off her body. I was too stunned to do anything. I just stood there like a fucking idiot while she furiously tore her clothes on, covering herself in record time, and denying me the chance to appreciate those perfect rosebud nipples.

"Satisfied?" she sang, with a little smile on her face.

My reaction was instant. Fisting her hair, I slammed her back against the wall and growled, "You're playing with fire, baby."

"Really? Because it looks to me like you're the one who just got burned?"

Oh, she wants to play, does she?

"Careful, Mouse," I purred, running my palm up her leg. "I'm two seconds away from giving you a proper introduction to my cock."

"Try it!" Riley snarled, raking her claws down my arm.

My fingers dug into her waist the same time she released the cutest little growl and swung her fist. I grabbed her wrist, flipped her around, and twisted her arm behind her back.

Riley cried out and threw her other arm blindly behind her. She was already out of breath, snarling and baring her teeth like a cornered kitten.

"You guys are having fun."

We both stopped and looked over at Logan, who was leaning against the doorframe.

"Where were you?" I asked, slapping Riley's ass when she swung at me again.

"Coach's house."

"How's his wife?"

A sly smirk slowly spread across his face. "Satisfied."

"Good. Now fuck off!" I picked Riley up by the waist, turned us around, and started to frog walk her to the bed. "We're busy."

"I can see that," he chuckled.

"Come on in, we're not busy at all," Riley snarled, and stomped the heel of her foot down on mine.

I barely felt the impact through my shoe.

"Gotta try harder than that, Mouse," I purred softly in her ear.

"Don't worry," she spat, while throwing her elbow back into my gut. "I'm just getting started."

Fuck! That strike actually pushed a grunt past my lips. God, that was hot. Her arm swung back, making a play for my nuts, but I dodged it. If I'd learned anything about my mouse, it was to keep a close eye on my boys.

"If you want to play with my balls, baby, all you have to do is ask."

That really got her going. Riley growled loudly, twisting her body and flailing her legs. My heart raced, pumping adrenaline through my veins. She was such a shitty fighter. I wanted to fight with her every day.

"Have fun, sis," Logan sang and waltzed out, closing the door behind him.

"You better sleep with one eye open asshole!" Riley yelled and threw her heel back in my shin.

"Fuck," I grunted and entwined my fingers in her long, silky locks, yanking her head back. "Keep fighting. You're making my dick hard."

I pressed my hips forward, so she could feel the steel rod in my pants.

Riley gasped and struggled harder. "If you come near me with that thing," she growled, once again throwing her elbow back. "I'll bite it off, I swear."

To reiterate this she chomped down on the air, teeth clacking.

"That's it, baby…" I folded her in half and smashed her face into the mattress. "Hurt me, scratch me, bite me… Get yours before I get mine." I snatched her wrists and held them with one hand against the small of her back. "And I *will* get mine."

Leaning back, I trailed my eyes down the curve of her spine. "I could take you right now," I breathed, caressing her presented ass with my gaze, "And there's not a damn thing you could do to stop me."

Riley went silent, focusing solely on her struggle. I craved the sting from her angry words almost as much as I craved her surrender. I needed to choke the resistance out of her until she went compliant in my hands.

"Give it up, Mouse. You can't win. The sooner you realize that, the easier things will be."

I felt her body go stiff as she mumbled something into the blankets.

"What was that?" I asked, releasing my hold on her hair enough for her to twist her face.

"You disgust me."

And just like that, my resistance snapped.

Chapter 15
Riley

I KNEW I'D FUCKED UP THE INSTANT THE WORDS LEFT MY LIPS, BUT I was powerless to stop it. Like word vomit, the insult spewed forth. "You disgust me!"

Me and my big mouth!

Micha went tense behind me, and I could feel the anger roll off him in waves. I just had to go and poke the beast. Now he was coming out to play.

His fingers tensed around my wrists and silence hung in the air like a heavy curtain as I waited for retribution. Could Micha feel my trepidation? Did he sense my anxiety? Maybe it made him feel powerful to have me like this? Weak, and too afraid to steal a glance at his face.

Did he get off on it?

Did I?

Was that why I kept pushing him? Because some sick and

twisted part of me liked this? Wanted to be overpowered and completely at his mercy. No! That was crazy talk. Micha was the enemy.

"I disgust you, do I?" Micha's voice was calm, too calm.

The pulse whooshing loudly in my ears told me that I had pushed him too far. This Micha wasn't the one I was used to. This one was an entirely different monster, one that scared the hell out of me.

"I'm sorry," I muttered, hating how pathetic I sounded.

He folded over me and softly growled in my ear, "You will be."

There was no telling what he'd do, and I wasn't about to stick around and find out. The second my wrists were released, I jumped. Clawing at the blankets and scrambling to pull myself across the bed.

Hope swelled in my chest as my knees sunk into the mattress. I told myself to keep going. Get enough distance to regain my bearings and kick him right in the balls. I could do it!

I was wrong.

Like some cruel mockery, Micha allowed me enough time to climb halfway across the bed before he followed. He crawled over me and pressed down, squashing my hopes and pinning me to the mattress with the heaviness of his body. I kicked and screamed, flailing my arms in a desperate attempt to wriggle out from under him, but it was no use.

"That's right, Mouse," he growled, pulling my arms over my head and transferring both my wrists to one hand. "Fight me."

My feet kicked, striking him in the calf. But he took those away too when he twisted my hip off the bed while wrapping his stronger legs around mine.

There were plenty of things someone in this position should do. Be repulsed and fight while screaming for help, or, at the very least, beg for mercy. I did none of that. My body fought my mind, soaking every twitch of his firm muscles.

"Get off me, you sick bastard!" I snarled, more to myself than him. Because only a sick bastard would react this way.

"You keep calling me names, Mouse. Is that because you hate me," his hand skimmed under my shirt and down my stomach to toy with the waistband of my shorts, "Or yourself?"

"W-what are you d-doing?" I nervously stuttered when his fingers dipped into my shorts.

Micha released my wrists and wrapped his hand around my neck, holding me back against his chest. "Where's my tough girl now?"

I swallowed, the action making me very aware of the grip he had on my throat. It wasn't enough to cut off my oxygen supply, but firm enough to let me know he could. And then, my big mouth struck again, spewing word vomit. "You get off on this, don't you? You sick fuck!"

"We've already established I'm a sick fuck. But if you need more proof…" Micha pressed his hips in, letting me feel how hard he was.

I cursed him, but cursed myself more. I hated how his hand warmed my skin, how that tingle low in my belly grew every time his finger swiped lower, moving closer and closer to a place I had yet to explore myself. Most of all, I hated that part of me that liked this.

"You're disgusting," I growled, not sure which one of us I was talking to.

His fingers tensed around my neck, as he pressed his cheek against my temple and whispered, "Let's see just how much I disgust you, shall we?"

All I could do was close my eyes in mortification when Micha shoved his hand down. Because as much as I tried to will my body to stop, it didn't. I could feel the dampness down there, and now he would, too.

Out of desperation, I grabbed his forearm and pulled with all my might, but I couldn't stop him. The firmness of his muscle barely flexed as he pushed his hand down and slid his finger through my slick folds. If someone could die from mortification, I would've dropped right then and there.

"Why are you wet, Riley?" The headiness in his voice made more dampness seep through my folds.

He pressed down on my clit. I gasped as sparks of pleasure shot through my body. I shook my head, trying to deny it. "Please stop…"

"Not a chance, baby," he growled in a low, throaty, tone, and repeated the action.

It took everything I had to hold the moan back. That small part of my body now controlled everything–my labored breathing, my thundering heart, and even my mind. With every swipe of his finger, it was getting harder to remember that I hated him.

That blasted finger swirled lower, pressing into my opening, and despite the slight burn from being breeched in a place formerly untouched, my entire body lit on fire.

"Fuck, that's a tight fit," Micha groaned, his hot breath heating up my already feverish skin. "You're going to squeeze the shit out of my dick."

"Never," I ground out, clenching my teeth against the pleasure he was forcing on me.

"Who says I need your permission?"

My body betrayed me again and clenched around the finger inside me.

"Oh, you like that, do you?"

His finger pumped in and out of me, stroking some sensitive spot inside, while his thumb continued to work my clit. I bit down on my lip so hard I could taste the metallic tinge of blood. No matter how I fought against it, I couldn't stop my mind from wondering what other parts of him felt like.

"You want me to hold you down." Even the deep tone of his voice set me off, flooding his hand with my arousal, "Force my way between your thighs, and take that sweet little virgin pussy?"

Not only could I feel how wet I was, I could hear it. This felt so much better than any dream, or fantasy I had. I was losing myself, giving in to his touch. I wanted to give, feel more.

No! I squeezed my eyes shut tighter and shook my head. I couldn't be that girl. I was normal. I had to be.

"That's it, baby," Micha purred, and dipped his head to pull his hot tongue up the side of my face. "Give in."

I don't know what was more humiliating. The messed-up way I was responding, or that he could feel said response? I couldn't let this happen. I had to do something!

Pushing through the cloud of haze in my head, I once again pulled on his arm and growled, "You might want to sleep with one eye open, because if you don't stop touching me, I'll stab you in your sleep."

"I can't wait to fuck that smart mouth." The corded muscles of Micha's arm tensed under my fingers, letting me feel the power held within. He swiped over that small bundle of nerves my traitorous body was so focused on, and damn it, I moaned. "Maybe I'll let Logan watch. I bet you'd like that."

I gritted my teeth through the pleasure and hissed, "Careful, I still have teeth."

"Yeah," Micha groaned, grazing his lips across my cheek. "You going to bite me, baby?"

Ready to scratch his eyes out, I reached over my shoulders. Micha was prepared for that though. He quickly ducked his head, taking his face out of my reach. So I did the only thing I could and grabbed fistfuls of his hair.

"I'll do a lot more than bite you," I promised, while yanking on his soft chestnut locks. He released a long throaty groan, and damn if it wasn't the sexiest thing I'd heard.

"Give it up, little mouse," he said, pinching my clit, sending a sudden spark of pleasure rocketing through my system. "You can't win this fight."

His fingers twisted and rotated, skillfully manipulating that small bundle of nerves. It felt soooo good.

"God, I hate you," I growled, yanking on the hair I had in my fists.

"You don't want to like it, but you do," he purred, continuing to build me higher, coiling a tense feeling deep inside.

Suddenly, I was holding onto his hair for an entirely different reason. My body won. My fight melted away as I moaned and arched my back, greedily seeking more. More of what? I didn't know. Just that I needed it.

A deep possessive growl vibrated from Micha's chest. "I saw you in that church. Watched you every Sunday. And do you know what I did while you were in there playing good girl on your knees?"

Maybe I should've been concerned with the fact that he'd been watching me? But nothing else mattered, except that edge he was slowly pushing me toward.

"I jerked off," he continued. "Fisted my cock and imagined it was your perfect little hands. While you were praying to your God, I was spraying my cum on the wall."

His filthy words sent me over the edge. Plummeting me into nirvana as a wave of white-hot bliss bowed my back.

"That's it, Mouse, scream for me."

I didn't realize I was screaming until he said so. My muscles had seized from the tiny fireworks erupting throughout my body. After my body had relaxed from the aftershocks, Micha shoved his fingers into my mouth.

"Taste how much I disgust you."

My cheeks heated as the sweet, yet salty taste exploded on my tongue. I could do nothing but collapse onto the bed, spent and oddly satisfied. That's when my mind started to come back, and I realized what had just happened. My first orgasm, and it came from him.

Micha put his hands on me, and I did nothing to stop it. I was pathetic. Mortified, I buried my face in the blanket, and tried not to cry.

I didn't move. Not when I felt Micha's weight lift off me. Not when I heard him walk away. I wanted to stay here with my face hidden in the soft blanket, smelling of lavender. As long as I was here, I wouldn't have to face what happened. What I allowed to happen.

I could stay in the dark and pretend I was somewhere else. That this was all happening to another person, and I was at home watching a movie with Mom.

We were sitting on our old scratchy couch in our pjs with a big bowl of popcorn between us. Mom wanted to watch the latest romance, but I argued for a sci-fi flick. Eventually, we settled on a comedy, and spent the rest of the night laughing. There was no alcohol or monsters hiding in the dark. It was just us and our shitty apartment.

Something dropped onto the bed, shattering my beautiful fantasy.

"Are you going to stay there sulking all night?"

My cheek brushed along the soft blanket, as I turned away from Micha's voice.

"I don't know what you're so upset about?"

The sound of a zipper and something falling on the bed surrounded me.

"You came, didn't you?"

Was he serious?

"It's not like–" I stopped, my eyes narrowing on the black bag and gray sweats sitting beside it. "What are you doing?"

"You didn't think I was going to stay in my clothes all night, did you?" he explained, lifting his shirt over his head.

My mouth was open, but nothing came out. I knew Micha was built, but holy hell! I lay there stunned, eyes rolling over his washboard abs, to the perfect V that disappeared in his dark jeans.

"Like what you see?"

I rolled my eyes at the smirk on his face, and snorted, "You wish."

Though I still couldn't stop staring at those sculpted lines under smooth tan skin.

Wait . . .

It dawned on me then. Micha planned to sleep here. In my room. With me. No friggin' way!

"You are not sleeping here!" I shrieked, sitting up.

Micha sighed, like my objection was nothing more than a passing nuisance. "I don't trust your father."

"So?"

"So," he unbuckled his belt and dropped his jeans, making me turn away, "Where you sleep, I sleep."

"Go sleep in another room," I demanded, angry that he was invading my space. I may not have wanted this house, or this room, but it was still mine.

"No."

I was so mad that I completely forgot Micha was getting dressed. Thankfully, when I turned around, he was donning the gray sweats. The fact that they hung low on his hips, giving me a better view of that cut V, only pissed me off more.

"Why not?" I asked. "I'm sure there's like twenty to choose from."

Stupid, big ass house!

"What part of 'where you sleep, I sleep,' didn't you understand?"

I glared at him.

He glared at me.

"Fine!" I huffed, jumping off the bed and marching towards the door. "I'll go find another room!"

"If you take one step out of this room, I'll drag your ass back in here and tie you to the fucking bed."

He wouldn't…

The nod he made, drawing my attention to a coil of thin black rope sitting on the end of the bed, told me that yes, he would.

"Well, aren't you prepared," I sneered.

"That's right, Mouse." Micha crossed his arms and gave me a stern stare. "I'm a regular fucking boy scout."

I thought about telling him to go fuck himself, and fight his demand, but then I remembered it didn't end so well last time. My throat ran dry as my eyes once again poured over the firm lines of his torso.

"Can you at least put something on?"

"I usually sleep naked." His brow arched. "Would you prefer that?"

I gulped. *No, no I wouldn't.*

"Now are you going to get your ass in this bed, or am I going to have to drag you?"

Being tied up and left to Micha's mercy was about as safe as diving head first into a pit of piranhas. And he *would* tie me up.

Out of any other options, I growled, stomped my foot, and

stormed back. After shooting him a dirty look, I slipped under the covers. The mattress dipped as he climbed in, and I quickly raised my arm, karate chopping the blankets behind me.

"Just make sure you stay on your side."

Micha chuckled, but made no move to crush my barrier.

"Goodnight, Mouse," he said, clicking off the lamp. "Sweet dreams."

"Fuck you, asshole."

"Not tonight, Mouse, I'm too tired." He yawned and shifted a little. "Maybe I'll fuck you tomorrow…"

I wasn't sure if my shiver was out of fear, or anticipation. And for that reason alone, I had to find a way to escape him.

I COULDN'T REMEMBER THE LAST TIME I HAD SLEPT FOR MORE THAN a couple of hours. When I closed my eyes, the sandman didn't whisk me off to a beautiful dreamland filled with flowers and cupcakes.

My slumber was filled with blood and darkness, haunting memories that jarred me awake. So when I woke up covered by a raven-haired beauty instead of my typical cold sweat, I was a little surprised. Somehow, I'd slept through the night.

It was adorable how she drew an imaginary line in the sand. Chopping down the blankets, as if that would stop me. I gave it to her, though, not out of some sense of morality, but because if I touched her, I knew I wouldn't stop. Holding back was not only a good way to fuck with her, but a test for myself. Now that I had her, how long could I maintain control?

I looked down at her small hand resting on my chest by her face and smirked. My hand twitched on her thigh, which was thrown over my hip. Even when we were sleeping, I won.

So much for your Berlin wall, Mouse.

I never understood Mase's attraction to Harper. She was so tiny. While my mouse wasn't much bigger, I could get used to this. Her soft body folded perfectly into mine, like she was made for me.

The heat from her pussy, burning through her shorts onto my thigh, had my heart pumping. But what really got it going was the anticipation of seeing her face when she woke up.

Riley didn't just hate me, she fucking loathed me. I could see it burning in those sapphire orbs–bright, beautiful hatred. Something else glimmered under all her rage. Something her innocent little mind didn't yet comprehend… but I did. I knew that beast all too well. He was made of pure lust and unbridled hunger.

Riley's alarm went off, shrieking loudly through the air, making my ears hurt. I frowned at the black clock, irritation growing with each piercing beep.

How loud does she have that fucking thing?

She grumbled and swung her arm out, blindly slapping the air for the snooze button, I assumed. She groaned, not finding it, and lifted her head. Her eyes fluttered open and began blinking in her surroundings.

That's it, Mouse, focus. See who you're wrapped around.

Those beautiful blue orbs ran across my chest and up to my face. She cocked her head, brows furrowed, and stared at me for a second. I waited as her confused gaze shifted to the hand she had resting on my chest. Then the moment I'd been waiting for… Her mouth dropped open in shock and eyes widened with realization.

"Oh my God!" Riley shrieked, springing back. "I told you to stay on your side."

My brow lifted at her accusatory tone. "I'm not the one who crossed the forbidden barrier."

Her eyes narrowed, swirling with that storm that got my heart pumping and made my dick hard. An intoxicating mix of anger, with two parts fear, and a hint of self hatred. If her alarm wasn't grating on my nerves, I might've kissed her.

No. I'm going to make her ask for that.

"Can you turn that thing off?" I asked, unable to take it anymore. "Why the fuck do you have it so loud?"

"Well, obviously," she growled, heavily slapping her alarm, "I'm a deep sleeper."

She had no idea just how much of a deep sleeper she was. How many times had I snuck in her room? And not once did she wake up. But what if someone else wanted to sneak into her room? My hands fisted at the thought. She better not take those fucking sleeping pills anymore.

"Why the fuck you have to sleep so deep?" I barked out, pissed off at her lack of self-preservation. "Do you have any idea what I could've done to you?"

Riley's eyes narrowed and her face scrunched up. "What, do sleeping girls not have enough fight for you, you sick fuck?"

She had no idea how true her statement was. I was on her side in two seconds. Crawling over her as she gulped and fell back against the mattress.

"Such a mouthy little mouse," I tsk-ed, and swept my finger down her cheek. Her fair complexion stood out against my tanned skin. Did her ass have my marks on it? The thought made me hard.

Riley glanced over at a pencil on the bedside table, lips pursing in contemplation.

Do it.

My dick jumped when her arm moved, her hand inching closer to the bedside table.

That's it, Mouse...

She wanted to do it–it was written all over her face–and I wanted her to. But to my dismay, her hand stilled.

"Do you mind?" she said in that snarky little demanding tone. "I need to get ready for school, or is the great Micha Kessler too good for school?"

As much as I would like to break my punctuality rule and play with her, Riley was right. School was important, and I didn't do late.

Besides, whoever left that note might be watching Ashworth, something Preston was counting on. If I showed up late, which I never was, then he might change his tactics, and we may miss our chance.

I sighed disappointedly and crawled off the bed to grab my bag. "I'm going for a shower."

Riley's face flushed bright red, and she quickly adverted her gaze from the tent in my pants.

"Care to join me?" I smirked.

"Thanks, but I prefer to keep my distance."

"Is that why you threw yourself over me last night?" I cocked my head and looked over my shoulder at her. "Because you wanted to keep your distance?"

"Careful in there," she growled, "I wouldn't want you to slip and break your neck."

"Don't worry about me, Mouse," I said, sauntering in the bathroom, "I always land on my feet."

She muttered something under her breath, probably cursing me out. Smirking, I closed the door. I dropped my bag onto the counter, turned on the shower, and stepped under the warm spray.

Would I find another note today? Who the fuck was this guy? He called himself The Piper, knew where the tape was, and since I found the last note in my locker, he'd somehow gotten into Ashworth.

Ashworth had decent security for a school. Considering who the student body was, they had to. Still, we weren't sure how he disabled the alarm. This guy was a professional, and he wanted us to know it too.

Fucker looked right at the camera before he walked in. Even with his face hidden by a hood, he seemed familiar. I'd seen it before, the little skip in his walk, and the cocky way he carried himself. I just couldn't remember where.

Preston thought it might not be about me. Maybe this guy, whoever he was, was after my father. After all, what better way to get to the King of Kings, than through his son? My father didn't have many weaknesses. He didn't even care about his wife.

My mother was simply a business arrangement; a way for him to have an heir and nothing more. The only woman I'd heard him talk about with any affection was the mysterious blonde he spent a night with in college. So it would make sense for someone to come after his sons. But if that was the case, Mase was the easier target.

And then there was Riley. She was pretty squeaky clean. Chase Mathers, on the other hand, wasn't. It wasn't unheard of for MC's to spill blood over turf and product. The president of the Lost Souls, one of the biggest MC's in this state, would have some pretty powerful enemies. Question was, did anyone know he was alive?

Of course, there was the possibility that Riley's dad was the target. He was the sheriff, and law enforcement wasn't exactly a favorite in some circles. He hadn't arrested any major players here, but he did start his career in Miami, where Riley was born.

Even though they moved here when she was a baby, my little mouse acted like a city girl, with her sharp attitude and snarky comments. That didn't help her last night, though. She tried so hard to hold back her orgasm. My dick hardened as I thought about how badly I wanted to lick the tears of frustration off her face. Nothing tasted sweeter than victory.

I pressed my palm against the tile wall, letting the warm water spray over my head and shoulders, and fisted my cock, stroking from root to tip. I wanted her bent over the bed, blue eyes filled with rage. She'd try to hate what I did to her. She'd try to make me stop, while her body pleaded for more.

"Fuck," I grunted, tightening my grip and pumping faster.

She'd beg me to stop; bite me, scratch me. But I wouldn't. I'd hold her down, force my cock inside her tight little pussy, and steal her innocence. I'd fuck her hard. Show my mouse that the same rage lived inside me. And she'd love every minute of it.

My fingers tightened on the tiled wall, as my balls pulled up and I came.

"Shit," I huffed, resting my forehead on the wall.

My knees were a little shaky. If Riley made me cum that hard jerking off, what would it be like when I fucked her? I couldn't wait to find out.

Once I caught my breath, I grabbed Logan's shampoo and shook my head at the vanilla scent. I'd have to make a pit stop at home after school and grab mine.

I squeezed some shampoo into my palm and muttered, "Fucking girl," and lathered up my hair.

* * *

I met Logan in the kitchen for breakfast.

He smiled at me. "Sounds like you had fun last night?"

"Not as much as I'd like," I grumbled, grabbing myself a plate and joining him at the table. "She been down yet?"

"Yep," Logan nodded. "Came and grabbed an apple, told me to fuck myself, and went back upstairs."

I chuckled. Guess she's still pissed. Unfortunately, I didn't have time to give her an attitude adjustment. Riley wouldn't see me until tonight. Jack's friend was becoming a thorn in my side, and I needed to figure this shit out. Maybe there was something in the King's ledger.

It was a book my father kept, full of information on the Kings, the heirs, and anyone else he thought might be important. I don't know what he did with it, but I'd like to know how he got it.

That was something I'd have to do alone though. The only reason I knew it existed was because I was next in line to lead the Order. When my father showed it to me, he said the King of Kings can't afford to trust those under him. People will stab each other in the back to be on top, and information was power. No one wanted their secrets out.

"Hey," Logan said, calling me out of my thoughts. "So, I've been thinking. What about Nash?"

"What about him?"

"Maybe your admirer is him?"

Fuck, why didn't I think of that? Nash was the former sheriff, and one of Ryker's friends. Or at least as close to a friend as someone like Logan's father could have. They were both twisted fucks who used to have parties with Logan and the other kids. Nash was the reason Ava couldn't have children. It made sense–he knew about us and the Order.

I swallowed my last bite of eggs and looked up at Logan. "Where is Nash these days?"

"It's not Nash," Preston stated, waltzing into the room.

"What are you doing here?" Logan asked.

Preston plucked an apple out of the bowl on the counter and took a bite. "Security detail, remember?"

Logan nodded and gave him a sideways glance. "Wait, so you're just going to follow her around?"

"Yep."

"Oh man, she's not going to like that."

"Too bad."

I eyed Preston's denim jacket. He had some weird attachment to that thing. It wasn't special, I could probably find a dozen more just like it in any department store. Then again, Preston never was much for primping.

I wouldn't be surprised if all he did in the morning was shower and run his fingers through his sandy hair. Don't get me wrong, I wasn't like Logan–who spent hours getting ready, like a fucking girl–but I did like the designer clothes.

"How do you know it's not Nash?" I asked, tipping my chin in question.

"Cause he's dead," Preston stated flatly. "Took care of him three years ago."

"Jesus Christ, Preston!" I growled. "You can't just go knocking people off."

He just shrugged. I got why he did it. Ava was his sister, and Parker, who was also victim to Nash and Ryker's sick games, was his brother. If Preston was capable of caring about anyone, it was his siblings. And that didn't include the shit Nash and Ryker did to him. But he couldn't just do this shit on his own.

There were ways to handle this kind of thing–people to pay, clean-up to be done. We had our way so no one would come looking.

"Nash had a family," I pointed out.

"Don't worry," Preston said so calmly that I wanted to punch him in the face, "No one made it out of the fire."

Logan got up and deposited his plate in the sink. "Wasn't his son, like, fifteen?"

"Seventeen," Preston corrected.

I sighed and scrubbed a hand down my face. I could hear my father's voice. *Preston's your responsibility. Why didn't you know about this? You should have better control of your people.* "I don't need this shit right now."

"If it makes you feel any better, he was dead before I burned the house down."

It didn't.

Logan shook his head. "You're one cold son of a bitch."

Preston cocked a brow at Logan. "Weren't you the one who fed Jack his own balls?"

The last thing I wanted was to be reminded of that night. I got up and walked my plate over to the sink. "Could you assholes not talk about that shit? I'd like to keep my food down."

My attention was drawn out of the room when Preston whistled and jutted his chin. "That your girl?"

I looked at Riley, who was standing by the door with a scowl on her face, and her foot tapping impatiently.

"Yeah, that's her," I said, eyes rolling over her uniform. God, she looked hot in that. I was half tempted to push her skirt up and fuck her against the wall.

"She doesn't look too impressed with you."

My lips curled at Preston's comment. She'd probably be even less impressed by the end of the day.

"Well, are you just going to stand there and stare at me all day?" Riley waggled her head and cocked her hip, "Or are one of you assholes going to take me to school?"

Logan snickered, while Preston arched his brow. I should've reconsidered putting Preston on security detail–he wasn't one to take lip, especially from a girl. But despite being a cold son of a bitch, he respected the order of things and fell in line when told to.

Besides, all I could think about was if her pert little ass had my marks on it under that red skirt. I was ready to march over there and find out.

"You know," Logan called out, loud enough for her to hear, "Girls are supposed to be less bitchy after they come."

I couldn't help but smirk when her eyes rolled his way.

If looks could kill.

"I'll be waiting outside," she said, and promptly marched out the door.

"Is she always like that?" Preston asked.

"Yes," Logan and I said in unison.

He hummed and cocked his hip against the counter. "Can I hit her?"

"Only if you want me to hit you back," I murmured, giving him a sideways glance.

He crossed his arms and eyed me. Fucker was actually considering it.

I scrubbed a hand down my face and headed for the door. "Touch her and I'll rip your fucking balls off."

Chapter 17
Riley

I DIDN'T KNOW WHO THE NEW GUY WAS, BUT THERE WAS SOMETHING seriously wrong with him. At first glance he seemed normal, hand-some even. His eyes though… A shiver ran up my spine just thinking about that steel gray glare.

There was nothing in it—no shine, glimmer, or sparkle. No emotion whatsoever. Something told me that this guy wouldn't have a problem putting a bullet in someone. I think he might even enjoy it.

I was a bit relieved when he didn't join Micha and I in the Jeep. He looked too old to be a high school student, but then again, who really knew? Micha didn't look like any of the boys in my old school, either—all tall and firm, with a deep domineering voice.

Maybe they put something in the water in this part of town? My hopes of escaping Death's scrutinizing glare evaporated when his red BMW started following us.

"Who is that guy?" I asked Micha. Maybe he was just going the same way?

"That's Preston. He'll be keeping an eye on you."

Followed around by some creepy guy? Yeah, no thanks.

"I don't need a babysitter."

"I didn't ask for your opinion."

I glared at Micha, who stared blankly out at the road, as if what I wanted didn't matter. Why was I surprised? Micha Kessler didn't ask permission, he just did.

Like last night.

My eyes fell to his large hand controlling the steering wheel. My face warmed thinking about what those fingers did. How he played my body like an instrument. Strumming me perfectly until I sang the song he wanted me to. And that's when it hit me. I had my first orgasm, and it came from Micha fucking Kessler.

How could I let him do that to me? I should've fought harder. It was my body, damn it! I could've held myself back, instead of liking it. And boy, did I like it. My eyes raked over him, drinking in the sight of Micha in his uniform. *Asshole.*

Who the fuck does he think he is, looking all good and smelling even better? Oh, right; he's Micha fucking Kessler. King of everything.

He could at least spare me a courtesy glance.

"All you have to do is ask, Mouse."

Oh, so now you acknowledge me?

"Ask for what?" If I tilted my head, I could almost see his abs through that shirt.

Micha took his eyes off the road long enough to roll his hungry gaze down my body. "Just say the word, Mouse. I'll pull over right fucking now, bury my face between your thighs, and fuck you with my tongue."

My jaw dropped. He wouldn't?

Micha licked his lips.

Oh my God, he would!

Would his mouth feel better than his fingers? His lips were all soft and warm, and tasted sweet and masculine, like sin-flavored candy. With my eyes still locked on his lips, I leaned over the center console, closer to his warmth. *Damn, I really wanted some candy right now...*

Thankfully, my ringing phone brought me back to reality.

Get a grip, Riley!

My heart picked up for an entirely different reason when I saw Shelby's name light up my screen. I chewed my lip and stared blankly down at my phone. I had to keep her far away from Micha. But if I kept dodging her, she'd eventually show up with questions. Questions I didn't know how to answer.

"You gonna answer that?"

I wanted to, I really did. I missed Shelby so much it hurt.

Sighing, I slipped my phone back into my bag and flopped my head back against the leather seat. "No."

Micha's brows knit together. "Wasn't that your best friend?"

"Yes."

"So why don't you want to talk to her."

"What the hell am I supposed to say?" I snarled. It was his fault I couldn't talk to her. "*'This is my house, don't mind the looming, asshole, I'm under contract to be his girlfriend or some shit?'* That'll go over well."

"Tell her I'm your boyfriend."

"I'm not gonna lie to Shelby." That would be worse than dodging her.

"It's not a lie, Mouse." Micha turned his upper body and slung his arm over the back of the seat. "Whether you're willing to accept it or not, you're mine. If you need to put a label on that to talk to your friend, then so be it."

"Great," I huffed out a snort. "I can join the ranks of the hundred other girls who once called you boyfriend."

Micha released an exasperated sigh. "Do you know how many girls I've slept with?"

"Please, enlighten me," I sang with a snarky head shake.

If he was anything like Logan or his brother, it was probably somewhere around a thousand.

"None."

"I think Naomi would argue." I may not have been part of the popular crowd, or in the inner circle of this town, but I wasn't stupid.

Micha arched his brow. "I said *slept* with, Mouse."

"Oh please," I scoffed and rolled my eyes. "You're not a . . ."

Oh . . .

My eyes widened in realization. Did he seriously expect me to believe that he'd never spent the night with a girl? Then again, why would he lie? Micha never had a problem telling me what he thought. Out of everyone in my life, he was probably the only one who'd never lied to me. How sad was that?

"I'm not trying to isolate you, Mouse," Micha sighed. "Call your friend."

"Why, so you can use her against me?" If he thought I was going to hand Shelby over on a silver platter, he was wrong. "No thanks."

"Why do you have to be so fucking difficult," he grumbled, while pinching the bridge of his nose.

"Oh, I'm sorry," I cried out, giving him an evil glare. "Feel free to find someone more compliant to put under contract."

Micha pulled out his phone and muttered under his breath as he dialed a number.

I recognized the voice that answered as the same man Micha told to run a train on Shelby.

"Hi boss."

Oh shit, I've done it now. I'm sorry Shelby.

"Hi, Marco. You can report back to my father."

My brows knit together. What was his game?

Marco sounded just as confused as me. "And the girl?"

"She's no longer an asset," Micha said, and ended the call.

What was his motive? Because let's face it, there had to be one. This was Micha Kessler after all. My eyes narrowed suspiciously. "I don't know what you're planning–"

I was cut off when his hand shot out and wrapped around my neck.

"Don't mock my generosity." He slammed me back in the seat. "Not many people get it."

Like the sucker for punishment I was, word vomit spewed out, and I screamed, "Fuck your generosity!" My hand swung through the air, striking Micha in the face.

I swear time slowed down. Micha turned his head back to face me and my pulse burst, erratically beating loudly in my ears. I could hear every hard thump as his eyes darkened to an almost black.

"Hit me again, Mouse," he growled, tightening his grip on my neck until all I could take was small, shallow breaths, "I dare you."

"Going to hurt Shelby now?" I growled right back in a squeaky tone. "That's how this works, right?"

Shut up, Riley!

"Who would it hurt more to lose?" Micha chuckled and pulled me across the center console, forcing me to meet his callous glare. "Chase, or Daddy?"

I felt all the blood drain from my face as I went still in his hold.

"That's what I thought." His fingers twitched around my neck. "I don't need your friend, Mouse. Heroes always have someone to lose." He leaned in, his cheek against mine, and damn it, I shivered.

"Now get the fuck to class, before I decide to teach you a real lesson."

With that, Micha let me go, thrusting me back into my seat. I didn't yell or fight. I just opened the door and jumped out of the Jeep, scurrying away as fast as I could.

* * *

Knowing Shelby wasn't being followed was a huge weight lifted off my shoulders. It still didn't let me relax much though. For all I knew, Micha called his guy back right after I left.

It wasn't like he hadn't changed his mind before. Look where I was now. He was supposed to hate me, not want me. Who knows, maybe he did hate me?

According to Shelby, who was surprisingly accepting of the whole boyfriend lie, I hated Micha because I was attracted to him. I guess she wasn't wrong. I did hate Micha before all this, I just hated him more now. On the upside, I wouldn't have to be nice to him, because by Shelby logic, the more I yelled at him, the more I liked him. So, I had that going for me.

"Oh my God," Lana said as she followed me down the hall to my locker. "Did you hear about Suzie Walker…"

She reminded me so much of Shelby, it was scary. They both talked so much their voices became background noise. Our math teacher spent more time telling her to be quiet than actually teaching.

One big shocker was Lana's nan, who was known around town as crazy old Greta. The adults whispered about her, and the kids dared each other to go knock on her door. Marnie was the only one of us who was brave enough to do it.

"Is that Preston?" Lana asked as I opened my locker.

I didn't have to look to see him. I could feel his death glare boring into my skull. "You know him?"

She nodded. "That's Parker's brother. He graduated two years ago, so what the heck is he doing here?"

That's why Lana knew him. I learned more about Parker from Lana than I could've being locked in a room with him for months. The girl had it bad.

"Apparently, babysitting me," I muttered.

Lana's lip curled in confusion. "What?"

I looked up, realizing my mistake. Though it was never stated, I kind of assumed the whole "don't tell anyone or else," was implied.

Crap, crap, crap.

"So um," I paused, scouring my brain. "Parker's kind of cute."

Lana immediately ducked her head and blushed. "He's okay…"

I closed my locker and let out a silent breath of relief.

"Why don't you ask him out?" Lana was beautiful with her dark complexion and thick curly hair. I couldn't see Parker refusing.

"Ask who out?" Mason asked, popping out of nowhere.

Lana's face flushed as the football team walked past. "No one."

I shook my head. Lana was not discreet. Anyone with a pair of eyes could tell which one of the players she was ogling.

"Lana Banana," Mason smirked and nudged her with his elbow. "Do you have a little crush on Parker?"

"No," she cried out, her eyes wide.

I rolled my eyes at Mason. "Leave her alone."

"What?" he said, throwing his hand over his chest, like he was all innocent. "I'm just trying to help a girl out."

"No, you're being an asshole."

"I'm hurt. Now what kind of friend would I be if I didn't let Parker know there was a cute, maybe a bit frumpy, girl interested?" He stopped and eyed Lana. "You know how to suck dick, right?"

Oh my God.

"See, asshole," I pointed out, while checking my phone for the text that just dinged.

The Piper: *Second floor bathroom, behind the third stall toilet.*

My feet stopped moving. I'd completely forgotten about my mystery ally.

"Everything okay?" Lana asked, stopping beside me.

"Yeah," I nodded and quickly pocketed my phone. "I'll meet you in the cafeteria."

"Come on, Lana Banana," Mason said, leading a reluctant Lana down the hall. "Let's go find you a strapping young football player!"

I considered going to her aid, but really, what was the worst that could happen? Parker said he wasn't interested, and then Lana could move on. Besides, I could always crush Mason's balls later.

Preston's death glare narrowed on me as I spun on my heels and headed for the stairs. I managed to make it all the way to the second floor without glancing over my shoulder. That would look suspicious.

Thankfully, the second floor wasn't as big as the main. It only took a couple of minutes to find the bathroom. I didn't see why Ashworth needed this much space. It was a friggin' high school for Christ's sake.

I pushed through the door into the clean white bathroom. My lip curled at the beige couch in the corner and the pretty little tray of perfumes on the counter. The only furniture in the bathroom at my old school was the stool Stacy Trent brought in so she could smoke by the window.

Hell, half the stall doors didn't even close properly–if they were there at all. This place was like the Plaza. I had yet to wipe a single toilet seat. It was kind of weird not picking a stall based on how much it made me gag.

I heard the door open, followed by clicking heels, and quickly ducked into the third stall.

"She shouldn't even be here."

Ugh, Naomi.

There didn't seem to be anything out of place. Toilet, garbage can, and a fresh roll of toilet paper. I moved closer to the wall and bent over to look behind the tank.

"Daddy pays good money for me to come here, and now they're just letting anyone in."

I quietly snorted at Naomi's use of daddy. What was she, five?

There was something back there. I could just see it stuck between the wall and the tank. I needed a better angle to grab it though. Climbing off the toilet, I sat on the floor and squished my body closer to the wall.

"I think her mother was my maid," another girl said. "She used to come to work drunk all the time. Mom was going to fire her, but . . . well, you know."

My arm froze between the cold wall and hard ceramic, and I stared at the door.

"Yeah," Naomi snickered. "She should've done us all a favor and taken Riley with her."

I swallowed the ache in my chest. Why should Ashworth be any different? I'd always be known in this town as the drunk's daughter.

"What do you have against Riley?" a third girl said. "Micha seems to like her."

"Oh really," Naomi sang, in a snotty tone. "Then why did he come to me the other day?"

Micha was with Naomi? When? And why did I care?

"Because you're easy."

"Shut up, Amy!" Naomi bit back. "You don't know anything."

"I know he slept in her bed last night. Has he ever slept in yours?"

"Whose side are you on, Amy?" the girl whose name I had yet to hear asked.

"I kind of like the girl. She's refreshing. And honestly, you bitches are starting to get on my nerves."

The other two gasped in shock.

"Well, fine," Naomi hissed.

"Yeah," the other added. "Enjoy your new friend."

I sat there listening to the click of heels fade away, wondering if that just happened? Did one of Naomi's minions defect? *Well, shit.*

My elbow bumped against the ceramic tank, pulling me back to the task at hand. I managed to wiggle my arm in enough to pull out a black box. My nose crinkled when I opened it. It was filled with putty or something.

What the hell is this for? I texted The Piper.

The Piper: *To take an impression of a key.*

Me: *What key?*

The Piper: *The one Micha wears around his neck.*

Micha wears a key around his neck. Shit, shows how much I pay attention.

Me: *How in the hell am I supposed to get that?*

The Piper: *Get him to take it off.*

Me: *Like naked! No way!*

The Piper: *Do you want out of the contract or not?*

Me: *Well yeah. But that's a lot to ask.*

The Piper: *Did you think it would be easy?*

I sighed. No. I knew it wouldn't be.

The Piper: *I also need a fingerprint. Collect a glass he used and put it in a Ziplock bag.*

What the hell was he planning to do? Break into some-super secret spy lair? I laughed at that. Micha the spy. He was more likely to kick down the enemy's door than sneak around in black suits, stealing secrets.

Me: *You didn't tell me what it's for.*

The Piper: *It doesn't matter.*

I huffed out an angry sigh. Why did everyone keep ordering me around? I was tired of it.

Me: *Listen buddy, you came to me. Not the other way around.*

The Piper: *You want to play the game with me, is that it, little one?*

Did I?

Me: *Maybe?*

The Piper: *Get me what I asked for and we'll talk.*

This guy could be some creeper pervert for all I knew. I really didn't know anything about him. Was he even a him?

Me: *In person?*

The Piper: *Don't worry, you'll meet me very soon.*

Chapter 18
Micha

My little mouse liked to get under my skin. Running her mouth like a brat when I asked her what she was doing in the second-floor bathroom. That bathroom was reserved for the cheerleaders, and last I checked, Riley wasn't waving pom-poms in the air.

She seemed to forget I knew her every move. Preston texted me before she left the damn bathroom. Still pulled attitude though. If she wanted to play this game, that was fine. She was still a beginner. I was a motherfucking master.

It wasn't hard to get a rise out of my mouse, but there were three things that really got to her. Her drunk mother, threatening or picking on other people, and the third, anything sexual. Which I employed by hauling her ass onto my lap and making her spend the lunch hour with my hand up her skirt.

Riley was the kind of girl who would rather throat punch you than kiss you. She thought she was immune to the powers of lust, but no one could fight that beast. I'd been trying to do it since the night I caught her painting *Severson's*.

As far as I was concerned, I had the patience of a goddamned saint. Sitting there with my fingers inches from her hot pussy. I'd been dreaming about that shit for months. I didn't go for it though.

No matter how much Riley wanted it. And she wanted it, told me as much every time her thighs clenched together. Her poor little mind didn't stay so clean. I whispered so much filth in her ear, she walked out of that cafeteria red as a tomato. Fucking adorable.

"Why do you drive a Jeep?"

I cocked my head at Junior. "What's wrong with my jeep?"

"Nothing," he said. "You have buckets of money, I figured you'd drive like a Ferrari or something."

I chuckled a little. "Cars are Logan's department. My Jeep gets me from point A to point B. That works just fine for me."

"Mason has a Corvette."

"Mase has a Corvette because chicks like it, not because he does."

I was surprised he could drive the fucking thing. Logan damn near blew a gasket when he bought it. Made Mase take driving lessons with him for a week before he'd give him the keys back.

"Doesn't your brother have enough girls?"

"There's only one girl he wants."

Junior's brow furrowed up at me. "So, why isn't he with her?"

How did I explain the inner workings of Harper and Mase's fucked-up relationship to an eleven-year-old? "Because she betrayed him."

That seemed to be a good enough answer for Junior, because he nodded and pushed through the doors to the Y. I sighed and followed. Why he insisted on coming here was beyond me.

Half the building was stuck in the seventies, with mustard-colored tiles and shag carpet, while the other half was so white and sterile it reminded me of a hospital. I hated that fucking chemically clean disinfectant smell.

"You know I have a pool at my house, right?" I said, shrugging off the shiver that ran up my spine.

Junior's face twisted. "That maid lady keeps pinching my cheeks."

He was talking about Paulina, who worked in my father's wing. Normally I couldn't be bothered to learn her name, but it was kind of disturbing the way she followed Junior around with this lost look on her face.

When I complained, my father told me to give her a break. She lost her son in a boating accident when he was around Junior's age. Personally, I think my father's fucking her, because no one on his staff gets special treatment.

"Besides," Junior said, heading over to the donation center, "I need a coat."

"What the fuck happened to the one I bought you?"

He shrugged. "Got a bit ripped."

Knowing Junior, it got ripped in a fight. His school was full of a rough bunch of fuckers. I'd enroll him in Westend, Ashworth's elementary school, but he didn't want to be seen in a uniform. Couldn't blame him. Walking around in his neighborhood wearing that preppy crap would just put a target on his back, and Junior had enough troubles.

I sighed as he dug through a box. "I'll buy you another one."

"This one's fine," he said, shrugging on a jean jacket that looked far too much like Preston's for my liking.

Unfortunately, there was no point in arguing with him. If I did buy Junior another jacket, he'd just wear that one anyway. Stubborn little fuck, he'd rather suffer than accept help. I learned that the night we met.

. . .

Three years ago:

I sat on the dock with my bottle in hand, glaring out at the lake. Moonlight glinted off the rippling water like it was a sea of diamonds. I snorted, and took another swig of whiskey. Just another example of what beauty can hide. Nothing in this world was truly beautiful. It may look pretty, but underneath it was just a twisted cesspool of pain and misery.

"Fuck you," I growled, spitting in the clear water.

Mother is God in the eyes of a child. Yeah, right! Whoever said that never met my mother. This was the third night this week that I sat at Cherry Lake getting drunk and cursing her name. Last time, Logan had to drag my ass home.

Why the fuck did I go to the carnival? I knew it was a bad idea, but Logan insisted on dragging me along. Seeing Riley and her mother just put me in a worse mood. What the fuck did she have to be so happy about? She just got out of the hospital, and there she was, laughing with the person that near killed her.

Maria Adams couldn't stop drinking, even after being faced with her daughter's mortality. She was stumbling around the carnival like an idiot. What did Riley do? She helped her useless mother walk around, like nothing was fucking wrong! Wasn't so happy when I pushed her in the mud though.

I smirked and tipped the bottle to my lips. "Should watch where you're going, Mouse."

My attention was drawn away from the lake when a group of kids broke through the tree line. It looked like they were arguing or fighting. There was one kid in the middle, with five or six around him. Couldn't be sure, my vision was starting to blur.

"How was your dinner tonight, Junior?" One kid laughed, pushing the scrawny fuck in the middle. Little bastard couldn't

weigh more than fifty pounds. "My mom threw out some extra cat food, just for you."

"Sorry, Trevor, all I found was a bunch of used condoms," Junior replied with a smile. "Isn't your dad out of town?"

Kid had balls. Too bad for him he was outnumbered, and the other boys seemed to be on Trevor's side. I sat back watching the swarm inch closer to the water's edge. It was a full-on fight now. Fists flying in a ball of fury. Still, Junior refused to go down. He fought back, knocking two of the kids back with a punch to the jaw.

"You give it to them, kid," I mumbled, polishing off the rest of my bottle.

Splash.

I looked back just into time to see Junior fall in the water. The other kids took off like their lives depended on it. Guess Junior lost that one. Too bad, I was rooting for the kid. I sighed and shook the empty bottle. I knew I should've brought two. Guess it's time to head back. I pulled myself off the ground and eyed the water.

Why hasn't he come up yet?

I stood there waiting for the kid to break the surface.

Nothing.

Fuck!

I'd never sobered up quicker than I did diving into that water. By the time I found him and flopped his body onto shore, all the alcohol had left my system. My heart wouldn't calm the fuck down. Time stood still as I sat there hunched over the kid, dripping wet, waiting for him to breathe. Finally, he rolled over, coughing out mouthfuls of water.

"Jesus Christ, kid," I said, falling back with a loud exhale. "You damn near gave me a heart attack."

"Who the hell are you?"

I sat up and cocked a brow at him. "I'm the guy who just pulled your ass out of the lake."

"Yeah, well," he said, glaring at me, "I didn't ask for your help."

I laughed outright. If Junior wasn't so fucking skinny, the kid would've reminded me of myself. He had the same dark hair, olive skin, and hard expression to match his fucking attitude.

"You were doing a real good job of pulling your own ass out of the water."

Junior pushed himself off the ground. "I was getting there."

"How? Sprout wings and fly the fuck away?" I tilted my head. "Why the fuck can't you swim?"

This town was ocean side. Add in the lake and hot springs, and it was just plain irresponsible not to teach your kid to swim. Even fucking Riley could swim, and her mother was a useless drunk. What kind of fucking parents did this kid have?

"I'd have figured it out." Junior shrugged. "How hard can it be?"

I looked at the water, and then back at him. "You do realize you damn near died?"

"I'm fine."

"Because I pulled your ass out of the water!"

He shrugged and started walking away.

Who the fuck was this kid?

"Where the fuck are you going?"

"Home."

I watched him take a couple of steps and waver. "You sure you're okay, kid?"

He tripped over his feet and crouched. "I'm fine."

"You don't look fine."

"Well, I am."

I pushed myself off the ground and sighed. "Look, kid, I didn't save you from drowning to watch you keel over."

"I told you," Junior growled, "I don't need your help."

Which was when he hunched over and violently heaved his stomach's contents onto the ground.

I ended up taking Junior home that night and hadn't left since. Someone needed to take care of him—his mother sure as fuck wasn't. So, I took it upon myself. Little fucker made it hard though. He didn't tell me when shit was going on, I had to find out myself. Like right now… My eyes narrowed on an angry red welt on Junior's back.

"What the fuck is that?"

Junior sighed. "I told you I didn't want to go swimming today."

"That's not a fucking answer, Junior. Did that prick come back?"

"No," He said, trying to slip past me.

I grabbed his arm and stopped him. "Who the fuck did that?"

"No one."

"Don't bullshit me, Junior."

He rolled his eyes and shook his head. "I fell, okay?"

There were a few things I'd learned from Logan, like how much pain the human body was capable of enduring. What it looked like when someone was fucking whipped, and when someone was making up excuses.

I fell.

I tripped.

I walked into a door.

Those were all things I'd heard Logan say over and over again. Not because he was trying to protect his asshole father, but because he didn't want anyone to know. Logan did it out of shame. Junior was doing it out of fear, and there was only one reason for that.

"Did your fucking mother do this?"

His dark eyes went wide as he quickly explained. "It wasn't her fault; I hid her stash."

Fucking Julia! Guess Ava's last visit didn't teach her enough. I was going to have to give her a lesson myself… a lesson of what it felt like to be buried six feet fucking under.

"Please don't hurt her, Micha," Junior pleaded. He knew what I was capable of. He helped me get rid of the body of the first fucker I caught pounding on him. "She needs me."

Like fuck she does!

"The only thing she needs is her next fix."

"Which is why she needs me." He hung his head and whispered, "I have to save her."

I felt for the kid, I really did. But his mother wasn't worth the effort.

"Some people can't be saved, Junior."

"I have to try."

"No, you don't." I scrubbed a hand down my face, growling out my frustration. "She should be taking care of you."

Junior hung his head and quietly said, "She loves me."

She loved him so much she was tricking him out for her next fix. It was a miracle the kid survived his infant stage. She couldn't even be bothered to give him a proper name. Junior got his name because the bracelet they put on him when he was born said, "Alverez Jr." The damn hospital named him because his mother couldn't be bothered.

"Please," Junior begged, drawing out the word while giving me those big, sad fucking eyes. "Don't hurt her. She won't do it again."

Yes, she fucking would. I knew that, and so did he.

"Fine," I begrudgingly agreed. As much as I wanted to slit Julia's goddamn throat, it would break Junior's heart. "But if she touches you again, that's fucking it."

I don't know who was worse, Junior, or Riley? Maria tried to kill her daughter, while Julia used her son to buy drugs. Yet they were both loyal to a fucking fault. Like a dog that just got kicked by his owner, but came running when he called. It made me want to strangle them both.

"Do me a favor," I said, walking out of the locker room to the pool. "Leave your mother's stash alone. You don't want that shit in your system."

Junior nodded. "Okay, but Tony got locked up, so she hasn't been able to get smack for a while. It's mostly just crack now."

Just smoking crack now. Fan-fucking-tastic. Like that was any better.

The fact that an eleven-year-old was on a first name basis with his mother's dealer and knew the street name for heroin was bad enough. I sighed and shook my head. What the fuck was I going to do with this kid?

Chapter 19
Riley

I was informed that Preston would be taking me home after school because Micha had something to do. Ever try to refuse Death? Yeah, it doesn't go over well. When I told Preston to go to hell, that I wasn't getting in a car with him, he simply picked me up and tossed me in.

Surprisingly, my savior was Logan. He told Preston he'd take over watchdog duty if Preston wanted to take a break. As happy as I was to lose Death for a bit, I was incredibly insulted that Micha appointed me a babysitter in the first place.

I didn't expect Preston to so easily agree, or for Logan to offer in the first place. And I definitely didn't expect him to pull into the Y.

"What are we doing here?" I asked, brows furrowed at the brown building.

Not that I had anything against the Y. I spent a lot of my child-hood years here. It was the only place I could take art lessons, lessons that we could afford, anyway. The question was, why was Logan here? Call me crazy, but I was pretty sure he could afford a top-notch coach in whatever sport or lesson he wanted.

"Ma wanted me to drop some stuff off," Logan explained, scooping up a couple of black bags in the backseat. "Personally, I don't know why she wastes her time. She should just throw this shit out. Nothing wrong with more naked people in the world."

I rolled my eyes. "How charming of you."

"Isn't it," he said, flashing me his perfect white teeth, before opening the door of his Mustang. "You can wait here if you want."

Logan's car was nice. Like, really nice. White stitching on the black leather interior stuck out in an artistic way. It smelled like Creamsicles and was so clean I was afraid to touch anything.

The paint job was just as pretty. A deep midnight blue with shades of aqua and teal. It glittered like a gemstone in the sunlight. But I didn't want to get caught sitting in this thing outside the Y. This car, in this neighborhood, screamed one thing—I have money, please rob me.

"I'll come in," I said, grabbing the last bag on the seat. "Besides, it looks like you might need some help."

"Come on then." Logan nodded and headed for the building.

I looked back. "Aren't you worried about your car?"

"No one will touch my car."

I grew up in this neighborhood and knew the kind of scum hanging around. People got mugged for their shoes for Christ's sake.

"You sound awfully sure of that."

"I am."

Whatever. If Logan wanted to risk his car, who was I to argue? He probably had three more just like it anyway.

I dropped my bag at the donation desk and left Logan to deal with the paperwork. The lady there seemed to know him. She was all smiles when he walked through the door. I saw his charming smile every day. Not to mention, I didn't think I could take any more of his flirting.

It was sickening how girls swooned over him, and apparently with age did not come wisdom. Because the girl handling donations was at least thirty, and she had the same awe-inspired sparkle in her eye as the girls at school. His smile made girls stupid; I'd stumbled over my own words a few times. It was sickening.

I walked over to the run-down furniture by the window overlooking the pool and ran my hand along the edge of the couch. When Mom had to work late, I'd curl up in the corner of the couch and draw the people swimming in the pool. That was when my admiration of the water began. Watching the way it shimmered and flowed was mesmerizing.

There weren't many people in the pool today. An older couple off to the side, and a dark-haired boy swimming with a man I was pretty sure the Greek gods themselves created.

Perfect olive-tinted skin stretched over muscles that flexed as he gracefully moved through the water. On his back was a large tattoo of a tree. Oak, I think? The trunk traveled up his spine, with the leafy branches spanning across his shoulder blades. It was beautiful. He was beautiful.

Wait . . . Why does that tattoo seem familiar?

My stomach flipped and I quickly ducked under the window. Micha? What the hell was he doing here? And who was that kid? I peeked over the edge, eyes zeroing in on the kid. He looked like a mini Micha. Even had the same bored expression. Did Micha have a kid?

Micha picked the boy up and tossed him back into the water. The boy laughed and splashed Micha, making my heart flutter when a large smile spread across his face. Not one of those evil smirks I was used to seeing, but a genuine smile, and it lit him up. Shining joy in his eyes, and for just a second, I was jealous. I wanted Micha to smile at me like that.

"Riley Adams, is that you?"

I jumped back, banging my head loudly off the window.

So much for my career as a spy. Pretty sure the whole building heard that.

An older, portly woman I knew as Mary-Lou giggled. "Don't hurt yourself now."

"Hi, Mary-Lou," I grumbled, rubbing the sore spot on the back of my head while peeling myself off the floor.

I was surprised to see her here. When I was a kid, she was a senior staff member. That was like five years ago. Thought she would've moved on to better things by now.

Mary-Lou wrapped her arms around me and pulled me in for a tight hug. At one point, this woman was a second mother to me. She read me stories, talked to me, and brought me soup when I was sick. So, I didn't mind her being friendly. Besides, it was nothing new. The first day I met her, she hugged me. She was just one of those people.

"Look at you, all grown-up," she said, stepping back to take me in. "I bet you have all the boys chasing you."

"Just one actually," I muttered.

Though he wasn't really the chase type, more like hunt and slaughter.

"I'm so glad to see you, sweetie, it's been too long." She pulled me in for another hug. "I hope you aren't here for classes, though. We don't have an art program anymore."

"I came with my stepbrother. He had to drop some . . . Wait . . . Why don't you have an art program?"

"Sasha got married and left." Mary-Lou frowned. "We didn't have anyone to replace her."

What about all those kids who couldn't afford classes? Where would they go to learn shading techniques? Or what brushes to use? It wasn't fair. The Y was one of the few opportunities us poor kids had.

"I'll teach it." The words left my mouth before I had a chance to think about it.

"Oh, that would be great!" Mary-Lou declared, clapping her hands.

Running my own art class and molding young minds, I could handle that. Hell, I was looking forward to it. Finally, something good in this crap-hole I called life. Should've known that wouldn't last.

There was a tap on the window next to us. I really didn't want to look over there, but it was like I had no control. My body turned as I told myself not to do it. Standing on the other side of the window was a very wet, half-naked Micha.

My eyes followed drops of water as they carved a path over his chest, down his washboard abs, and into the waist band of his dark blue swim trunks. It took me a second to notice that his mouth was moving. I couldn't hear what he was saying, but if that scowl on his face was any indication, then I probably didn't want to.

Kudos on the soundproofing, Ashen Springs YMCA.

I smiled and shrugged my shoulders, while pointing at my ear and shaking my head. He did not like that. Micha's face darkened, and he raised his voice to a point that I could almost hear him through the thick glass. This was too much fun! I furrowed my brow and cupped my hand behind my ear, infuriating him further.

Mary-Lou waved at Micha and whispered, "Do you know that young man?"

"Unfortunately." I shook my head and shrugged my shoulders when he once again tried to say something.

"Such a nice young man," Mary-Lou said, making me roll my eyes.

Yeah, sure. Rainbows and sunshine come out of his ass.

"I don't know where Junior would be without him."

"Who's Junior?" I asked, opting for the smile and wave technique when Micha once again tried to say something.

I could practically hear his teeth grinding when he slammed his fist on the glass.

"That's Junior." Mary-Lou pointed at the boy in the pool. "Poor thing used to come in here hungry and dirty. And then this young man showed up."

What? That made no sense? Why would Micha help some random kid?

Micha, who huffed and pointed to the left.

"Must be a cousin or something?" I said.

Mary-Lou shook her head. "Junior met him a couple of years ago, when Micha saved his life."

My eyes snapped to Mary-Lou. "He saved his life?"

I said it, but still couldn't believe it.

"That man is that little boy's hero. You should hear how Junior talks about him."

Next thing I knew, I was being ushered toward a door on the left.

"There's some paperwork you have to fill out. I'll go get it ready," Mary-Lou said. "You talk to your friend."

"What? No, no, no," I argued shaking my head as she unlocked it and pushed me through.

"It's okay, dear." She winked and added, "He's a fine young man. Good choice." Then she pulled the door shut.

I stood there with my mouth open.

What the hell just happened?

Micha cleared his throat and this time, I could hear it.

"Mind telling me what you're doing here?"

I sighed and rolled my eyes up to the roof. Seriously? Did someone up there hate me? Did I wrong the universe in some horrible way?

"I hear they have a great support group here for the victims of human slavery, so I thought I'd check it out," I said, chanting the words *'don't look at him'* in my head.

"There's that mouth again," Micha tsked. "Do you not remember what happened the last time you got mouthy with me?"

Oh, I remembered. Stupid Preston ratting me out. Not that I'd ever say that to him. I was pretty sure he had a direct line to the underworld. Now I had the memory of how firm Micha's thighs felt under me permanently seared into my skull. My cheeks flamed just thinking about it.

Don't look at him, don't look at him, don't look at him.

"Do you like being punished, Mouse, is that it? You want me to spank that perky little ass?"

Don't look at him.

"Or maybe you want something more . . . something like what I did last night?"

Butterflies erupted in my stomach and my core clenched. His fingers felt *so good.*

Don't look. Don't do it.

"I wonder how loud you'll scream when I put my mouth on your pussy."

I shivered thinking about his lips on me. Would they be as soft as they looked?

No, no, look at the wall. Stare at that tile. It's white, with underlying hints of white, and more thick lips, curved in that sexy smirk.

I could feel his hot breath on the back of my neck as he softly growled, "Next time you come, Mouse, it'll be on my cock."

"Never gonna happen!" I snarled, spinning around.

Ah crap. I looked.

Without the glass as a barrier, I could see every defined dip in his torso. The curve of his muscles as they flexed, and that perfect V dipping into his swim-shorts. I could feel his heat from here, smell his intoxicating scent, which was somehow more potent mixed with the chlorine. I watched his chest rise and fall and my fingers twitched, as my hand rose.

Just one touch couldn't hurt . . .

"Looking at me like that is a good way to get fucked, Mouse."

What? Oh shit.

I quickly dropped my hand and tore my eyes off his chest. "I'm not looking at you."

"It's okay, Mouse. Look all you want." Micha smirked. "You can even touch."

I swallowed down my gasp. His swim trunks were starting to tent.

"In fact," Micha reached his hand down his shorts and adjusted himself, making absolutely no attempt to hide it from me. "I want you to touch."

Holy hell! I couldn't breathe. I couldn't look away either. He still had his hand on his dick. Lightly stroking himself under his shorts.

"How about it, Mouse?" He slid his fingers through my hair, up the back of my head and pulled me closer. Bringing his lips next to my ear, he murmured, "You want to jerk me until I shoot my load all over those perfect tits?"

Thank God the kid Micha was swimming with came sauntering up, because I honestly don't know what I would've done. A big part of me wanted to do exactly what he said.

"Micha," the kid called, making Micha yank his hand out of his shorts and take a step back. "Why are you up here? Talking to a girl?"

Aw, he was so cute with his dark hair and freckles. I wanted to pinch his dimples.

"Junior," Micha sighed, and waved at me, "This is Riley."

Junior scanned me with a grimace on his face. "Thought you said she was pretty?"

Well, fuck you too, kid!

"She is pretty." I had the brief thought of *Oh my God, Micha thinks I'm pretty* before I mentally slapped myself. "She just needs to learn how to dress."

"Hey!" I huffed. "This uniform was not my idea!"

"The only problem I have with the uniform is how much I want to fuck you in it," Micha stated with a blank expression. "It's your other clothes that are the issue."

What was wrong with jeans and a shirt? Everyone else wore them, including Mr. High-and-mighty. Just because I was a girl, didn't mean I had to wear dresses and skirts. Yeah, like that was going to happen.

"Um, Micha," I said softly, "There's a kid here. You probably shouldn't say stuff like that."

Junior's brows knit as his eyes rolled over me. "I've seen more dick than you."

I wasn't sure how to respond to that. I hoped he was talking about his own dick, because the implications of the other was not something I wanted to think about.

"Bet you haven't even see Micha's dick yet. You kinda seem like a prude."

"Hey! What dicks I have or have not seen are none of your business," I growled, pointing at Junior. "Besides, you're what, like, eight? Shouldn't you be playing with a ball or something?"

"I'm old enough to know girls wear makeup. You should try it sometime."

My face dropped. Micha and this kid totally deserved each other.

"Well, I'll let you and the future leader of the 'Assholes of America' get back to it," I sneered at Junior, and then turned to pull on the door handle.

Locked! God damn it, Mary-Lou!

"She's not very smart, either."

"Alright!" I spun around and shook my finger at the kid. "You listen to me, you little prick–"

"What?" Junior snarled, "It's not my fault you look like a boy. Shouldn't girls have boobs?"

I crossed my arms over my chest and shrieked, "Stop looking at my boobs."

"Can't look at something that's not there."

"Despite what this one told you," I threw my thumb in Micha's direction, "The whole asshole thing doesn't work on girls."

"Seems to work for you," Junior sang. "You were drooling over Micha a second ago."

That's it! I was going to slap the hell out of this little prick!

Micha burst out laughing, stopping me in my tracks. If I wasn't so pissed at this little twerp, I might've enjoyed the deep baritone of his laugh.

Instead, I scowled at him. "What's so funny?"

"You're arguing with an eleven-year-old."

"He started it," I huffed.

"Not my fault Micha's had better girls than you." He looked at Micha. "What happened to that blonde? She was pretty."

Assuming he was talking about Naomi, I narrowed my glare and shot back, "Yeah, well, I've had better guys, too."

Micha's laughter instantly ceased. "Junior, go do some laps. I'll be there in a minute."

Junior stuck his tongue out and stomped down to the pool. I stuck mine right back out at him.

Oh shit!

There was a black look on Micha's face, one that didn't bode very well for me, or for my churning stomach.

"That last statement better be a lie, Mouse."

The closest thing I had to any kind of relationship—other than my first and only kiss, which was sloppy as hell—was when Scotty Miller fell on me during soccer practice. We were ten, and I nut-punched him for it.

"Just wait a second," I said, holding my palms out in front of me. "Nothing happened."

"Who the fuck touched you?" he yelled, muscles tense and ready to pounce.

Everyone swimming stopped and looked up at us.

"No one touched me," I whispered, pretty sure that Micha was about to murder Scotty Miller.

His fist slammed down on the door, making me jump. "Don't fuck with me, Mouse!"

"No one touched me, okay?" I yelled. "I've only been kissed once, and that wasn't very good."

I could hear Junior laugh at my statement.

Prick!

"Besides," I said, toning my volume down, "I'm not the one with a kid."

"Junior's eleven, Riley." Micha cocked an incredulous brow down at me. "My balls hadn't dropped yet when he was born."

Well, that was graphic.

Micha sighed and reached past me. Instinctively, I jumped out of the way. That was when I realized he was unlocking the door.

"Go home, Riley," Micha said, holding the door open for me.

I ducked under his arm and cautiously slipped past him. Micha still looked mad, and I didn't want someone to get hurt because he thought something had happened. "Seriously, no one touched me."

"I know. If they had, they'd already be dead," he said before he shut the door.

Chapter 20
Riley

Why was it so dark? I didn't like the dark. That's where the boogeyman lived. I needed to get to Mommy and Daddy's room. I tried to get up, but my hands and feet were tied.

Dread rocketed through my heart. Did the boogeyman get me? I wasn't in my room. The bed I was laying on was too hard, and it smelled like Grandma's flowerpots.

I tried twisting around to see where I was, but everything was so dark. I needed my night light.

"Mommy?" I cried out.

She didn't answer. Why didn't she answer? Mommy always came when I called.

"Mommy! Mommy, where are you?"

I turned my head, searching for the comforting shine of Minnie Mouse. Nothing. Hot tears rolled down my cool skin, making me shiver.

"Mommy?" I tried again. "Daddy? I'm scared."

Were they mad at me? I didn't mean for Charlie to get hurt. I tried to hold onto his leash. He was just so fast.

"MOMMY! MOMMY! I'm sorry. I didn't mean it!"

A man's voice cut through the air, silencing my screams. "Calm down, girl."

My heart settled a bit when a soft glow lit up part of the room. I sniffed and watched a man in purple robes light more torches along the wall. At least the boogeyman can't get me now.

"Who are you?"

"I'm Louis, child," he answered, lighting the last torch. "We met at the park the other day."

"We did?" I asked, searching for something familiar. There was nothing. Not in the man, and not in the room. Just gray stone walls and the soft echo of water dripping. Rope was around my wrists and ankles, tying me to a stone bed. Why would anyone want a stone bed? It was hard and uncomfortable.

"Where are we?" I asked, my nose crinkling at the musty earth smell in the air.

"The basement."

This place looked more like a dungeon than a basement, like the ones in the princess stories Mommy read to me. I shivered at the shrill whistle the wind made tunneling down the stairs. If this was what it was like to be a princess, I didn't want to be one anymore. I didn't need the pretty dresses. I just needed Mommy and Daddy.

"Where's my Mommy?"

Louis walked over to a table draped in purple cloth. "She's not here."

"Where is she?"

"At home, asleep in her bed." He pulled the cloth off the table, making things clatter together. I really wished I could see what was on it. "She doesn't even know you're gone."

"Liar!" I yelled.

Mommy always knew where I was. She had eyes in the back of her head. Told me so when she caught me in the cookie jar.

"Where is she, then?"

"I don't know." I frowned. Where was she?

"You see," he said, "She's not here, so you can stop screaming. Maybe she's mad at you?"

Was she mad at me? Daddy told me bad men lied to little girls, and I shouldn't listen to strangers.

"My daddy will arrest you!" I insisted. "He's a policeman, and you're a bad man. He puts bad men in jail."

"He can try," Louis chuckled, and waved at me over his shoulder. "Now be quiet."

I refused, screaming my head off.

The sound pierced the air as I thrashed about, fighting against my binds. Mommy didn't like it when I acted like this. She called it "throwing a tantrum," but she wasn't here and I wanted to go home.

"Enough!" Louis's stern voice stilled my movements. Huffing, he turned around and crossed his arms. "You're a stubborn little thing, aren't you?"

"I'm not little. I'm a big girl."

He arched his brow. "Do big girls cry like babies?"

"No," I agreed quietly.

"Good," he said, turning his attention back to the table. "Now stop acting out and be quiet."

My heart pounded loudly as he shuffled around, filling the air with tiny clinks. What was he doing?

"I'm cold," I whined, not sure if I was shivering from the temperature, or out of fright.

Mommy put on my warm jammies. I shouldn't be cold. But when I craned my head to look, I saw a white nightgown instead of

Minnie Mouse's smile. Grandma bought me those jammies. I felt safe in them. I didn't want this nightgown.

"Where are my jammies? I want my jammies!"

Louis released a long sigh and spun around. "You see this?" he said holding up a needle. I nodded and silently watched the light glint off the sharp pointy end. "If you don't stop throwing a fit, I'm going to stick you with it and make you go to sleep. Do you want that?"

I didn't like needles and shook my head. He seemed satisfied with my silence and went back to what he was doing.

It seemed like we were there forever before my ears twitched, picking up the distant sounds of footsteps. Relief washed over me. Mommy was coming.

"Mommy! Mommy, I'm here!" I called out.

Instead of Mommy, four more robed men came into the room, followed by a little boy. Hoods cloaked their faces, allowing me to only see their eyes. Two pairs of blue, a green, and a brown. Each set focused on me. Out of all of them, it was the boy who sent a shiver up my spine. There was a meanness in his stare that I didn't like.

"Where's my mommy? I want my mommy . . ."

"Where's my mommy?" the boy mocked, climbing up and crawling over my flailing body. He sat down on my hips and brought his face inches from mine. "Your mommy's not coming."

"Yes, she is."

She had to.

"No, she isn't," he said with an evil smirk. "You're mine now."

"No, I'm not! I want my mommy. I hate you!" I screamed in his face.

"Alright, that's enough!" Louis said, in a scolding tone. He pushed my head back down on the hard surface. "Do you want to see your mommy again?"

I sniffed and rolled my eyes to meet him. "Yes."

"Then be a good girl, and I'll take you back to your mommy."

Shifting my gaze between him and the boy, I warily said, "Promise?"

"Yes." He nodded and ran his fingers through my long hair. "I promise."

I wanted to see Mommy, so I tried to be good and stay quiet as the other robed men circled around us. But when one of them held up a scary silver tube, my bottom lip trembled. I whimpered, shuffling away from the glowing blue end.

"Shh," Louis hushed, continuing to stroke my hair. "Be still now. My son needs to mark you."

"Why?" I croaked.

He tilted his head down at me. "So everyone knows you belong to him."

"I don't belong to him," I cried, kicking my bound legs. "I hate you! I hate all of you! Get away from me!"

I was silenced by a harsh slap jerking my head to the side.

"Stop it!" Louis barked down at me. "You should be honored that my son chose you. Now apologize!"

Tears slid down my face, cooling my burning cheek. I didn't want to get hit again, so I whispered, "I'm sorry."

Louis's face softened. "That's it. Be a big girl now."

I didn't feel like a big girl.

"Are you going to hurt me?"

"Yes," the boy answered matter-of-factly.

I whimpered when he took the silver tube from one of the men. He scanned me, then looked up at Louis. "Where do I put it?"

"Wherever you like, son. I'm partial to the back of the neck, just under the hairline. It's easily concealed."

"Is that where you put it on Mom?" the boy asked.

Louis nodded.

"Maybe I should put the mark somewhere people can see it?" the boy growled, sliding his gaze to the green-eyed man. *"I wouldn't want someone getting ideas."*

"You want to talk about that now, boy?" Green Eyes asked. "Or do you want to mark your woman? If she's anything like her mother, you're in for a treat."

My brows furrowed. "Did you hurt my mommy?"

He smirked and leaned down, his green eyes gleaming mischievously. "If your daddy doesn't start listening, then I'm going to play a game with your mommy." I shrunk back when his knuckles grazed my burning cheek. "Do you want to play with us, little one?"

I shook my head. No, no I didn't.

"Ryker!" Louis roared. "That's enough!"

Green Eyes rolled his eyes. "Relax," he sighed, straightening his back, "I was only having fun with the child."

"She's not yours to have fun with."

Ryker grumbled and glared at him so hard I thought he might hit Louis. I was so caught up in their friction that I forgot about the boy. That is, until my head was twisted to the side. Instead of screaming, like I wanted to, I rolled my eyes back up to Louis.

"Be very still now." He smiled while brushing his thumbs over my forehead. Despite feeling the boy's fingers on my skin, I listened.

If I was good, I could go home. That's what he said.

"You have to be strong now, can you do that for me?"

I nodded.

"That's a good girl."

Ryker snorted. "You shouldn't coddle her."

"Feel free to handle it however you wish when it's your son," Louis replied.

"Which one?"

Hatred flooded Louis's eyes. He looked up at the other man and growled, "I can't stop you from playing your sick games with your son, but you're not getting mine!"

"But he's not yours, is he?"

One of the blue-eyed men cleared his throat. "Can we do this and get this child back to her parents before they wake up and notice she's gone?"

"We have time. I gave them a heavy dose," Louis said. "Are you ready, Doctor?"

The other blue-eyed man nodded and held up a needle. "She won't remember a thing."

I didn't have time to contemplate the needle because the boy pressed the tube against my neck and searing pain rocketed through my system...

I bolted up, covered in a fine coat of sweat and out of breath. It took me a second to register that I was in my room, not some underground torture chamber. My heart hammered as I swept my hair off my forehead. It was just a stupid dream. I must've fallen asleep. My sketchbook was laying open on the bed beside me.

Moonlight poured in through my window, casting my room in a soft light. Couch, bed, desk, and Ripley's jacket. All familiar things. Even Micha's bag sitting on the floor gave me some sense of security.

Speaking of Micha...

Where was he? What happened to *'where you sleep, I sleep?'* I shook my head. Was I really wondering why the bane of my existence wasn't here? Either I was a sucker for punishment, or that dream really got to me.

I looked down at the eyes of the phoenix staring up at me and shivered.

"Do you want to play with us, little one?"

I slammed my sketchbook shut, blocking out the sinister voice.

"Get a grip, Riley. It was just a dream. You've had them before."

Maybe a hot shower would help.

I got off the bed and walked into the bathroom, comforted a little more when I flicked on the light. I don't think I'd ever get used to the opulence in this house. Here I was, plain old boring me, in a bathroom fit for royalty.

The shower itself had four heads, which made it feel like I was standing under a warm rainstorm. The shower in mine and Mom's apartment had two settings: a slow trickle, and peel-the-skin-off-your-bones, and I never knew which I was going to get. I kind of missed the game of chance I played every morning.

I peeled my clothes off and stepped into the shower. The hot water rained on me, seeping warmth into my tense muscles, while rinsing the cold sweat of my nightmare down the drain. I couldn't chase away the chill in my bones though. A thick cloud of steam was filling the air, and I still shivered. I couldn't shake my eerie sense of familiarity.

The way the stone slab felt on my skin, the musty smell, and the sting from Louis's slap. It all felt so real. But that was crazy, right? Who, in this day and age, wore ceremonial robes? This wasn't medieval times. People weren't tortured in underground chambers by some secret sect of the stonecutters. Still…

I brushed my hair over my shoulder and felt around the back of my neck. No bumps or anything that I could feel, just smooth skin. Why was I still not convinced?

"You're losing it, Riley." My cheeks puffed out with an exhale. "Micha didn't brand you."

The thought was laughable, so much so that I might've chuckled a little at my paranoia. Except, I heard the shower door click closed and Micha say, "Yes, I did," followed by the feel of his skin on mine.

"What the hell do you think you're doing?" I shrieked, throwing my arms up to cover myself.

He pressed in closer and my blood turned to ice. Micha was behind me, naked, and very hard.

Everywhere!

"Having a shower," Micha stated, and lifted his arm to grab something above me.

I didn't know what it was. At this point, I didn't care. If I looked, then I might see more than I wanted to.

"Get out!" I demanded, my voice sounding stronger than I felt. "This shower's occupied."

"I don't mind."

"Well, I do!"

"You sure about that, Mouse?" Micha snickered in a mocking tone. "You were eye-fucking me pretty hard today."

That was beside the point. Wasn't my fault he had those eye-catching abs. Didn't mean I liked looking at him.

"You're such an—" I stopped and cocked my head in contemplation. "Did you say that you did brand me?"

The sweet scent of my coconut body wash filled the air as Micha spoke. "If it makes you feel any better, you weren't supposed to remember."

"How is that supposed to make me feel better?" And why did it give me a thrill to know he was using my body wash?

"I said *if,* Mouse."

He was so infuriating, and now he smelled like me. This gorgeous god of a man smelled like me. What did he look like all sudsy and slick? I couldn't think like this, all wet and naked with Micha fucking Kessler.

I let my forehead fall to the tile wall and closed my eyes to try to get some clarity. It grew quiet, too quiet. I almost looked behind me to see if Micha was still there. I could feel him watching me, but I couldn't hear him.

Only the spray of the shower and my own breathing. I was so tense that when his hand slowly swept something soft down my back, I shot forward, hugging my body to the wall.

"Calm down, Mouse," Micha said, pulling me back to him and dragging the soapy loofa down my back and over my butt cheek. "I'm not going to hurt you."

"Yet," I whispered.

"What?"

My body started to openly quake when his hand slid around my hip and over my stomach.

I cleared my throat and clarified, "You're not going to hurt me, yet."

"I guess that all depends on you, Mouse. Though I do have to say," he leaned forward and ran his tongue up my cheek, scooping up the solitary tear that rolled out of my eye. My clit throbbed when he released a low throaty groan. "Nothing tastes quite as sweet as your tears."

I sucked in a shuddered breath. Micha always hurt me. The things he said and did left scars. Even now I was in pain. My skin tingled, nipples pebbled, and I was achingly wet between my thighs.

It was only a matter of time before he wore me down, I knew that. I could fight it, but in the end, he would win. My body would give in, and that was what hurt the most of all.

"Fuck you," I growled, refusing to give in to my unwanted desires.

Micha dropped the loofa, splayed his hand on my stomach, and pressed me back into him.

"You're not ready to play that game, Mouse," he breathed in my ear. "But if you want to give it a go…"

He thrust his hips and I gulped. His erection pressed into my back, soft yet hard, like a steel rod wrapped in silk. It terrified me and excited me at the same time.

"Don't touch me," I snarled, slapping his hand. I was losing myself and needed to get away from him.

Micha growled, moved his hand to my neck, twisted me around, and slammed my back against the wall. "The next time you say no or don't to me, your mouth will be so full of cock you'll taste me when you breathe."

There was the monster I knew. The arrogant ass who expected his demands be met. This Micha I could handle, or at least I thought I could.

"I've been pretty lenient with you, Mouse, but you keep running your mouth." He leaned in and added in a whisper, "I think it's time you made it up to me."

Chapter 21
Micha

I ALLOWED RILEY HER MODESTY, LET HER KEEP HERSELF HIDDEN, but she had to keep fighting me. I knew she wanted it. She knew she wanted it. She was just too fucking stubborn to admit it. Guess it was a good thing I didn't give a fuck about consent. I wanted her to fight me. Got hard just thinking about it. It would make her moment of surrender that much sweeter.

"I'd be very careful if I were you, I'm barely hanging on here."

I took a second to admire the way she looked, naked, and held against the wall, with my hand wrapped around her neck. She wasn't worried about covering herself now. So I took my time, devouring every inch.

From her little tits with perky pink nipples, down to her tiny waist, over the curve of her hip, and to her smooth pussy. Fuck. That sight alone was enough to make me blow my load. A bare, virgin pussy . . . almost like she did it just for me. At least she fucking better have!

Fiery rage filled Riley's eyes, feeding my need to take her. "You can't do this to me!" she snarled, stomping her foot.

"Oh, I won't be doing anything to you."

The cute little confused look she gave me almost made me chuckle. She was so fucking innocent. It was time to change that.

"You're going to jerk me," I explained, almost losing it when I felt her throat muscles working under my palm to swallow. Fuck, I wanted to feel that around my dick. I'd been picturing those pretty pink lips wrapped around me for months. "Maybe if you do me nice, I'll leave Daddy alone."

Her eyes narrowed into angry slits. "You can't be serious."

My brow arched. "Do I look serious?"

I knew what was coming, and I felt the grin curling my lips before she spoke.

"No."

Bingo.

"Mouth it is."

My mouse was panicked now, struggling to pry my hand off her neck and get away. I was so far past fighting at this point. Riley needed to be taught a lesson, and if that meant I had to hold her mouth open and fuck her face, so be it.

There was no way she'd get out of this one, but my mouse proved me wrong when she reached out and gripped my dick tightly.

"Is this what you want?" she hissed, lightly pumping along my shaft.

Fuck yes!

Her jerky inexperienced movements were doing it for me. One stroke was tentative, the next hard and full of rage. I could see the confusion on her face. How she was angry and hating herself almost as much as me. Yet her eyes sparked when I groaned in pleasure. She wanted to please me, and that was sexy as fuck.

Riley tightened her grip and snarled, "You like this, you sick fuck?"

I was a sick fuck, and I was going to drag her right down the rabbit hole with me.

I growled, fisted her hair, and ran my tongue up the side of her neck. The scent of her fear combined with the taste of her anger was an intoxicating concoction–one that had me tugging roughly on her scalp.

"That's it," I groaned when her tiny hands tightened their hold. "Give me all your rage."

Scared by the primal lust evident in my tone, Riley slowed her movements and whimpered. She tried to shrink back into the shower wall, but we were nowhere near done. She started this shit, and she was going to finish it.

"Don't stop now, Mouse," I taunted in a teasing tone. "I was just starting to reconsider fucking your mouth."

Her eyes gave me those angry fireworks I loved so much while her hands came back to life, jerking roughly along my shaft.

That's more like it.

"Try it and I'll bite it off."

It was so fucked-up that this shit was turning me on. I'd never been harder in my life.

"Harder," I growled, wanting more of her wrath.

"What's wrong?" she snarled, pumping me furiously. "Can't find anyone willing?"

"You seemed pretty willing when you grabbed my dick."

Droplets of water sparkled like diamonds on her lashes as she peeked up at me. "I hate you."

"How wet are you right now?" I leaned in and sucked her earlobe between my teeth. "I bet that hot little pussy is dripping down your thighs."

She did not like that.

I didn't give a fuck. This was the hottest hand-job of my life.

"Do you kiss your mother with that mouth?"

"Do you really want to talk about my mother when your hands are on my cock?" I twisted my fist in her wet locks, enjoying her squeal. "Who's the sick fuck now?"

"Aw," her face twisted in a mocking frown, "Didn't Mommy love you enough?"

Fuck! The gloves were coming off, and her claws were out. Her words struck home, twisting my heart while making my dick harder.

"That's it, baby, get yours before I get mine," I purred. Her ragged breaths and husky tone only spurred me on. "And I will get mine."

Ice shone in those blues eyes. "Arrogant prick."

I ran my tongue up her cheek, loving how her chest heaved, pressing those perfects tits against me. "It's not arrogant if it's true."

"You're sick."

"You like it."

The innocent way her face twisted in confusion threw me over the edge. "No, I don't."

"Yeah?" I groaned, feeling a tingle at the base of my spine as my balls pulled up. "Then why are your hands still on my dick?"

She stilled as my come sprayed on her belly, marking her as mine. I growled and pressed my forehead against the tile wall as my dick twitched, releasing the rest of my load. It took a minute for me to catch my breath. I'd never come so hard in my life.

Listening to the shower spray, I waited for the inevitable backlash. Minutes ticked by and there was nothing but silence. Riley should've hit me by now. Or at least tried to push me away. Confused, I popped an eye open and looked down. She was standing there with a blank stare on her face.

"You look like you just murdered someone, instead of jerking me off."

I had the same look on my face once, but I had killed someone. Still couldn't look Rosy in the eyes.

Riley opened her mouth, but nothing came out. I frowned and pushed off the wall. Maybe my mouse was more fragile than I'd thought? She had nothing to be ashamed of.

One day she'd learn to embrace her desires–I'd teach her. As much as I loved the way she looked covered in my come, right now she needed to be taken care of, and much to my surprise, I wanted to do that.

I steered her into the warm spray, and gently cleaned her. She didn't move. Didn't even twitch as I scrubbed her down. And when I moved on to cleansing myself, she stood there staring blankly at the wall. It wasn't until I sat on the end of the bed, drying her off, that the life started to come back in her eyes.

"Why me?" she asked in a hushed whisper.

I tapped her leg to step in the white lace panties I'd picked out. It was a bit disturbing how easily she complied, lifting her leg and stepping into them without an argument. What was more bother-some was the fact that I was disturbed at all.

I took my time sliding the fabric up her legs, enjoying the feel of her smooth creamy skin, and reminded myself that I shouldn't coddle her. Jerking me off was nothing compared to what I had planned. She needed to toughen up.

She repeated her question, "Why me?"

I sighed and slipped a navy teddy over her head. "Does it matter?"

My dick hardened at the sight of her. When it came to lingerie, Logan knew what he was doing. The silk hugged Riley's curves, and the color brought out her eyes. She looked fucking beautiful.

"Yes it matters."

Fucking chicks, always wanting to talk about their feelings and shit. There was a reason I kicked bitches out when I was done with them. The only thing I felt was satisfied, tired, and fucking annoyed that they were still there. I could've left Riley. I could've gone and slept in another room, but for some fucked up reason, I didn't want to.

Her blue eyes locked with mine, and I could see the desperation in them. "Please tell me."

"Why?" I asked, arching a brow at her.

Why the fuck was this so important to her? Did she expect me to say I loved her or some shit? Because that wasn't happening. That ship sailed the day my mother died. The only thing beating in my chest was a vacant black void.

"Please, Micha," Riley pleaded, "Give me something."

I sighed and sat back, uncomfortable at how the tears brimming in her eyes tugged at the hollow hole in my chest. I'd made Riley cry countless times. She thought I didn't see, but I did. So why the fuck was it bothering me now? I was just exhausted. That's all it was.

"Time for bed," I said, getting up and throwing on a pair of sweats.

"God damn it!" Riley yelled, stamping her foot. "You owe me an explanation!"

"I don't owe you shit."

"Yes, you do!"

Grumbling, I scrubbed a hand down my face. I just wanted to go the fuck to sleep.

"I swear to God, Micha, if you don't give me something I'll–"

"Because I fucking need you!" I ripped the blankets back and glowered at her. "Now get in the fucking bed before I gag you and tie your ass to it!"

Chapter 22
Riley

I hadn't seen Micha since he said that. He was gone the next morning before I woke up, didn't acknowledge me at school, and didn't come over last night. A good thing, right? So why was it that I couldn't fall asleep until I smashed my face in his pillow and soaked up his scent? It was my room, and my pillow.

I kept wondering if I did something wrong? I still felt him in my hands. Hard, smooth, and hot. I don't know why I jerked him off, maybe I wanted to give him a taste of his own medicine, but I did it. Not only that, *I liked it*. Thought he did too, but maybe he didn't? Maybe I did it wrong? Why else would he ignore me?

"He's watching us again." Lana shifted her suspicious gaze to Preston, who was leaning against some lockers down the hall.

Yeah, that was still happening.

Harper glanced warily at him. "He gives me the creeps."

You and me both, Harper.

I was pretty sure he harvested the souls of the innocent for his dark lord. Come to think of it, he was probably the dark lord.

"Parker has a game tonight, right? Maybe he's here for his brother?"

"Maybe?" Lana said, ducking away to hide the pink tinting her mocha skin. "Nan should be here. I'll see you guys tomorrow."

"Bye," Harper said.

I nodded. "See you."

Part of me was dying to meet Lana's grandma. The kid in me was giddy to get a glimpse of the witch we used to whisper about–which only made me feel horrible–I knew what it was like to have people talk about your family.

My nose scrunched up as I closed my locker. Naomi thought it would be super fun to fill my locker with trash today. Mrs. Jones, the vice-principal, had it cleaned out, but there was still a lingering scent. At least they got rid of the *"go home trash"* written on the outside. Naomi definitely lacked originality.

I scowled when Preston looked up at us. "Don't you have something better to do?"

"As a matter of fact, I do," he said, typing something into his phone. "Be good, brat, I'll be back."

I waited until he walked away to stick my tongue out. Only an idiot would taunt Death head on.

"That was, um–"

"You don't have to explain," Harper said. "But I'd be careful what you say around Lana. She'll ask questions."

She was oddly accepting of Preston. I eyed her for a second, wondering if she knew something? Then I remembered that Harper was well versed in Kessler cruelty, maybe more than I was.

I'd slapped Mason and threatened to rip his balls off so many times that it was becoming habit–and that was only the times I'd caught him tormenting her–God knows what he did when I wasn't around. I'd tell Harper to stick up to him, but who was I to talk? I was the one who missed her contractual boyfriend last night.

Talk about self-loathing.

"I have to wait for Logan, so I'm going to go hang out in the library." Something I was informed about this morning. He told me I should come and watch practice. Gotta say, seeing Micha half naked and wet again wasn't really high on my priority list.

"I can come with you. I'm going to be here for awhile. Sean's getting ready for the game," Harper explained. "That is, if y-you want me to?"

This girl broke my heart. She was so unsure about everything. It was like she was waiting for me to wake up and decide that I hated her.

I smiled and threw my arm over her shoulders. "I would love that."

I liked spending time with Harper. She didn't talk my ear off like Shelby or Lana did. She was content to just read her book quietly while I worked on my history assignment. Our teacher dubbed it *The rich and interesting history of Ashen Springs,* and there was nothing rich or interesting about this town. Trust me, I'd been looking for over an hour.

I dropped my forehead in my palm and grumbled, "This is impossible."

"You could write a paper on the founding families," Harper suggested. "Mr. Harris has a bit of an obsession with them. It's a guaranteed good grade."

"The founding families?"

What the hell was she talking about?

She sighed like this was something I should know. "Seven families founded Ashen Springs. Four of them are still here. The Kessler's. The Hudson's. The Whitley's. And the Creswell's."

Huh? Well, I guess that explains why people around here acted like the sun shone out of their asses.

"What happened to the other three?"

"Don't know?" She shrugged. "Moved away or died out, I guess?"

"Well, there's got to be a record somewhere."

"Not that I've found."

Harper must not have looked very hard. Either way, it looked like I found the subject for my paper.

"I'm gonna go look," I said, leaving her at the table to go riffle through the town archives.

It turned out Harper was right. Not only was there no record of the three other families, but their names were blacked out in the archives. I got why some parents didn't want their kids learning about stuff like the Holocaust–which I personally thought was stupid–how can we stop history from repeating if it was hidden from us?

But to wipe family names out of the history books? There was one person I knew who might have some information.

I pulled out my phone and called Marnie. She'd done extensive research into the town for an article in the school paper. If anybody knew anything about this, it was her.

She answered on the third ring. "Hi, Riley. How are things at Ashworth?"

"Is that Riley?" I heard Trina call from the background. "Ask her why she hasn't invited us over yet."

"For Christ's sake, Trina. She's only been there a week. Let her get settled," Marnie growled. "Sorry, Rye."

"It's okay," I said, knowing how her twin could be.

"She's only mad because she wants to nail Logan."

I groaned. Of course she does.

"Hey," Trina yelled.

I could see Marnie giving her sister a sideways glance as she challenged, "Tell me it's not true."

"Well, I want to see Rye too…" Trina conceded.

"Anyway," I rolled my eyes, "I called to ask you about the founding families."

"Let me guess," Marnie said. "You want to know about the three missing families?"

"How did you–" I stopped, remembering that Marnie was a born reporter. Last year, she busted the girl's volleyball coach for sleeping with one of the players. Which, obviously, did not go over well. "You know what? Never mind. Do you know anything about them?"

"I've found a few things, but I'm swamped. Collin has me covering the cheerleading try-outs today, and the football team for the rest of the week."

Bet Marnie loved that. She hated when her parents dragged her to games. Watching her sister jump around with pom-poms was not her idea of fun.

"Why don't we get together this weekend?"

"Okay." I didn't really want Micha around any of my friends, so I added, "We can go for lunch at *Mays*. How's Saturday?"

Mays was a burger joint down by the docks that everyone loved, even the rich kids went there.

"Great, see you then," she said, and hung up.

I sighed at the bookshelf, wishing I didn't have to go to Marnie for information. Then again, I could always do the report on something else. Unfortunately, now I needed to know. Who were these families? Why did the town want to forget them?

I shook my head. "Curiosity killed the cat, Riley."

"Still talking to yourself, *help?*"

I slowly turned my head to glare at the big guy blocking my exit.

What was Lance Peterson doing here? The king of Ashen Springs High shouldn't be at Ashworth. I eyed his letter jacket, remembering there was a game tonight.

Lovely. More assholes in the hall.

I sighed. "I'm flattered that you came down here to find little old me, but it kind of comes off as desperate."

Lance's light eyes raked over my uniform and his lip curled. "Think you're better than me now, Adams?"

"Oh no," I grumbled, rolling my eyes, "I'm sure your superior ball throwing skills will get you far in this world."

"She still has a mouth."

I glanced over my shoulder and saw two more members of Ashen Springs' football team, Evan and Jax.

What, was this asshole day?

Evan and Lance had it out for me since I caught them cornering a girl outside the school last year. They got benched for a week, which was the end of the world to a football player. Guess I should be glad Noah wasn't here. He seemed to take that shit personally.

Evan smirked. "Told you we'd find her in the library."

"Well, this was fun," I said, "But if you don't mind, I have some work to do. Be sure *not* to look for me at the next reunion."

I tried to slip past Lance, but he pushed me back into Evan. "Where do you think you're going?"

"Yeah," Jax snickered. "Didn't you miss us?"

Evan leaned down and whispered, "Because we missed you."

A shiver of disgust raced up my spine. This wasn't good.

"Don't you brush your teeth?" I turned my glare on Evan and grimaced. "I can taste the last girl you had your mouth on."

He reared back and slapped me across the face, twisting my head roughly to the side as I fell on the floor.

"None of your little friends are here to report back to Daddy," Lance seethed down at me. "You're all ours."

Before I had a chance to blink away the tears the sting in my cheek caused, Evan yanked me off the ground and pinned my arms behind my back.

"We've been dying to break in the sheriff's daughter."

Lance pressed in with an unmistakable glint in his eyes. My heart was pounding so hard, I could barely breathe. I struggled to get away from Evan, but what chance did I have? I did the only thing I could. I screamed.

Evan quickly clamped his hand over my mouth. "Quiet down, kitten, we don't want anyone *interrupting us*."

"Come on, guys," Jax argued. "You're taking this too far."

"Don't like it, Jax," Lance growled, "Then fuck off."

I lashed out, kicking my legs, hoping I'd land a strike and make Lance think twice. It didn't work. He grabbed my flailing ankles and held my legs around his waist. I fought, jerking my body around in a desperate attempt to get free, but I couldn't fight one, let alone two.

"I get her first," Lance said, sliding his hand under my skirt.

Their hands were all over me, pawing at places that made me want to vomit. Swallowing the bile rising in my throat, I screamed again as loud as I could behind Evan's palm. I was going to be raped in the library, trapped between their sweaty bodies and mingled breaths. This couldn't be happening. I didn't put up with all of Micha's shit just for this to be my fate.

Suddenly, Lance was gone and I was laying on the floor.

"Mouse, look at me."

"Stop it!" I shrieked, swinging my arms and striking the flesh in front of me. "Get away from me!"

"Mouse!" Micha barked, snapping me out of it.

I blinked my eyes open. "M- Micha?"

"Shh," he hushed, pulling me tightly into his warm embrace. "I got you."

In that moment, I didn't care that he was the enemy. I wanted to stay safe, hiding in his arms… even if he was one of the things I should be hiding from.

"Piece of shit," Logan growled, his green eyes wild with rage.

He looked feral as he kicked Lance, who was curled up on the floor. Mason was on the other side, throwing his fist into Evan's face. I didn't know where Jax was, but I didn't care. I tucked my face into Micha's chest and wrapped my arms around him.

"You came for me."

"Of course I did." He kissed my head and cupped my face. "I'll always come for you. You're mine, remember?"

I tried to hide back in his chest, but flinched when his thumb dug into my cheek. His whole demeanor changed in the matter of a second. Micha's body went stiff and his eyes darkened as they locked on what I was sure was the bright red mark from Evan's hand.

"Who hit you?" He growled low and menacing. "Tell me who the fuck hit you, Mouse!"

I kept my mouth shut. Not because I didn't want Micha to hurt Evan, but because I was scared that he might kill him. I couldn't have that on my conscience.

"God damn it Mouse!" Micha roared. "Why the fuck are you protecting these assholes?"

"Evan hit her." That's when I noticed Jax standing off to the side of a bookshelf. "I'm sorry, Riley I… I didn't think they'd take it that far."

"Don't fucking talk to her," Micha growled, throwing an angry finger Jax's way. "The only reason you're not bleeding on the floor with these two is because you came and got me."

Jax got Micha?

"You so much as look at her again and I'll rip your fucking eyes out! Got it?"

Jax cleared his throat and guiltily turned his gaze to the floor.

"I, however, don't give a fuck if your conscience suddenly kicked in." Logan sauntered up to Jax and grabbed the collar of his letter jacket. "That there is my sister, and if you don't tell me which one of these pricks is Evan, you'll take his place."

Jax audibly swallowed and tipped his chin at Evan. I couldn't blame him. Not only was Lance coughing up blood, but Logan had this elated look on his face, like he enjoyed it and wanted more.

"Don't know if there's much left of this one," Mason said, pushing Evan on his back with his foot. "I fucked him up pretty good."

That was an understatement. Evan's face was somewhere under all that blood.

I looked at Logan, Mason, and Micha, with blood on their hands and rage in their eyes. I was afraid for Evan. These weren't high school boys; they were unhinged creatures full of bloodlust. Not only would they kill Evan, they'd get away with it too. I couldn't let that happen. So, I did the only thing I could think of. I grabbed Micha's face and kissed him.

Chapter 23
Micha

*S**HE** **KISSED** **ME**.*

For some fucking reason, Riley was protecting him. The guy hit her, was going to rape her, and she still tried to save him. But her distraction tactic didn't work—I still fucked him up. I may have gone a little too far; I mean, he was still alive. Fucker could thank Mouse for that.

She was scared enough watching me pound the shit out of him, and I wasn't going to make her watch me gut the fucker, too. He should've known better. Everyone in this town knows not to fuck with mine. And Riley Adams was mine.

Maybe I'll pay him a visit when he gets out of the hospital...

I needed some space after my outburst. *I need you*, what the fuck was that? I didn't need anyone. That's what I thought, until I saw her walk down the hall in that fucking skirt. It was impossible to ignore her, but so fun to watch her squirm.

My mind went back to her kiss. It wasn't an "I want to fuck the shit outta you" kiss, like I would've given her. It was simple and closed mouth. Not quite long enough for me to taste her, but long enough for me to still feel her mouth; soft, sweet, and innocent.

She kissed me.

"What the fuck are you smiling about?" Parker asked, bracing his elbow on my Jeep.

Logan leaned over, looking past me at Parker, and smiled. "He's probably thinking about deflowering my little sister again."

Parker's brow rose. "Deflowering?"

"You know, popping her cherry. Claiming the maidenhood. Skinning the fish. Stamping the V-card. Going where no man has gone before…"

Both Parker and I shook our heads.

"What? I'm just doing my brotherly duty."

"Your brotherly duty is to keep assholes like him," Parker nodded at me, "Away from her."

"Yeah, right?" Logan barked out a laugh. "I bet that shit goes over real well with Ava."

Parker's older sister wasn't some fragile princess. She was a demon sent to punish mankind. Ava and Preston were twins in every aspect, mirroring each other in more ways than one. When someone got on Preston's shit list, he showed them the ninth plane of hell. Ava fucking ruled it.

Speaking of demons sent to punish mankind…

My brow arched at Preston's red BMW pulling into the parking lot.

"What the fuck is my brother doing here?" Parker had the same confused look as me.

"The better question is," Logan crossed his arms and leaned back against the hood of my Jeep, "Why the fuck wasn't he watching Riley today?"

Parker cocked a brow my way. "You put my brother on security detail? Are you trying to get your girl hurt?"

I watched Preston get out of the car and head over to us. "He won't do anything."

"Tell that to my dog," Parker muttered.

"Do I want to know?"

"Probably not," he said, shaking his head. "Poor fucking Max."

"Are you still whining about that dog?" Preston rolled his eyes at his brother. "That was twelve years ago. Let it go."

Parker puffed up, which I found comical. He was a good three inches taller than his brother, yet he still felt the need to make himself bigger. Mase did the same thing. Maybe it was just a little brother thing?

"Shouldn't you be on campus?" Parker challenged. "What if Ava needs you?"

"Since when does our sister need anyone?"

I once saw Ava walk home on a broken foot without shedding a single tear.

"Besides," Preston said, waving his hand through the air, "She has some new boy toy."

Poor fucker.

Parker's light eyes narrowed. "I think I should meet this guy."

We all turned and looked at him. If anything, Parker should make sure the poor sap she was with was okay.

Shaking my head, I turned my attention to Preston. "Where the fuck were you today?"

"Had some shit to do."

"Riley was attacked," I explained.

"I heard." Preston nodded. "She's fine now. Just checked on her at home. She threw some crap at me, so I threatened to cut her arm off and fuck her with it."

Parker looked at his brother. "Just threatened?"

"I may have been playing with my knife when I said it."

I sighed and scrubbed a hand down my face. "So why the fuck are you here, instead of with her?"

If she were going to run, now would be the time. Riley was pretty pissed at me for fucking up that asshole. Slapped me pretty hard.

"Your dad called. It's time."

My eyes snapped up to his. "*Dominare la paura?*"

He nodded.

Well fuck.

All future Kings had to complete the *dominare la paura*. I'd known this shit was coming since I turned eighteen, just didn't think it would be this soon. Preston was halfway to nineteen before he did his.

"Come on," Preston said, walking over to his car.

I sighed and followed him, waving at Parker and Logan.

"Have fun," Logan snickered.

I flipped him off and got in the car.

"What?" I grumbled, noticing the strange look Preston was giving me.

"Nothing," he said, turning the key and bringing the engine to life. "Thought you'd be more anxious is all."

I shrugged. "It's just another test."

"No, it's not."

"I'm sure I can handle it."

Couldn't be any worse than the first time I killed a man. Pulling that trigger was harder than I thought. Back then, life meant something. I didn't have that problem now. All the memories and hard work people put into their lives meant jack shit when they were dead. All they left behind was a pine box six feet down and a headstone no one would visit.

Preston rounded a corner and I sat up, eyes narrowing on Cherry Lake.

"I know you can't tell me anything about this shit," I said glaring at the glistening water, "But can you tell me where we're going?"

"HQ."

Why the fuck were we going this way?

I gritted my teeth at the children playing on the beach.

"Why don't you get a real fucking car?" I growled, rolling my neck.

"What's wrong with my BMW?"

"It's fucking uncomfortable." I slid the seat back and stretched my legs. "What is it with you and Logan and these small fucking cars?"

"You never complained before."

My jaw clenched at the receding lake in the rearview mirror. "I'm usually the one driving."

Fucking cunt!

By the time we pulled into the burnt-out ruins of Manning Keep, I was more than ready to be done with this fucking day. I stepped out into the setting sun and cracked my knuckles. Maybe I'd get lucky and this test would involve pounding the shit out of something or someone?

Manning Keep was once one of the finest houses in Ashen Springs. I should know, my family owned this land, along with half the town. It burnt down over a hundred years ago and nature had taken over.

Green leafy plants covered burnt out husks of wood, and grew up stone pillars. I couldn't help but wonder how Riley would see this place. That dragon she painted, I didn't just see the loneliness in his eyes, I felt it. Could feel it still.

I walked over to the only red marble pillar left standing, brushed the hanging ivy out of the way, and took off my watch, baring the raven tattoo on my wrist for the electronic reader.

The town records said this place burnt down in a freak forest fire, but that wasn't true. Manning Keep was destroyed over a hundred years ago, when the factions of the Order were at war. Though there weren't any wolves left, we kept the name. Sentimental, I guess?

A red panel of marble dropped, and I pressed my hand to the display screen while inserting my key in the slot below. I used to keep it with my other keys, but after what Logan had to go through when he lost his, I decided the safest place was secured around my neck.

A motherfucker would have to kill me to get it from there. The key alone wouldn't do them any good though. They'd have to have a tattoo, and my prints. The tattoo scanner registered body heat and blood vessels, so they couldn't just cut that shit off.

There was a quiet hiss, followed by grinding stone, as a door to my left pressed into the ground and slid out of the way.

"You coming?" I asked Preston, who was leaning against the car with his ankles crossed.

He lit a smoke and said, "You know I can't."

I nodded, and walked down the stone steps that led under Manning Keep. Soft lights lit up the stairwell as the door closed behind me. Some of the Kings argued for HQ to be moved to a more secure location, but I couldn't argue with my father's hide-in-plain-sight logic. Who would think to look for a secret society under ruins? Or a torture chamber under a cop shop?

Once reaching the bottom of the stairs, I looked right, like I did every time I came here. At the end was a large oak door, intricately carved with wolves. Some were howling at the moon, while others hunted prey. I knew what was behind the raven door down the hallway to my right, but I don't think anyone had been on the other side of that one.

The raven door creaked open and my father stepped out. "Good evening, son."

My eyes roamed over the sharp fangs of a howling wolf. "What's in there?"

"No one knows." He shrugged and steered me through the King's meeting room, and down a hallway. "Like us, the wolves had marks to open their doors."

"So copy the mark and open the door."

"A fine idea," he sighed, as if I'd just said something insignificant.

It pissed me off when he dismissed me. I was the next King of Kings and deserved a say in shit. Already had plans for his club. Ava and I were going to get rid of the girls and turn it into a BDSM club with high-priced yearly memberships and all sexual acts consensual.

Already had a few rich pricks interested in purchasing memberships. By the time I was done with it, *Malum* wouldn't be a bar with a brothel underneath. It would be a legit business with a much higher profit margin.

"Tell me, son . . ." my father said. "How do you propose we get through that door, when all the information about it is on the other side?"

We opened our door with a mark added to our raven tattoo that was only visible under certain lights. I'd get mine once I completed the task tonight.

If the door was the problem, then get rid of it. "Knock it down."

"You've read the history on the wolves, correct?"

I nodded.

"Then you know they liked to booby trap things. If we force our way in there, then we could be destroying what's on the other side.

Besides, opening that door in any way other than intended would be… wrong."

And by wrong, he meant sacrilegious. Certain rules in the Order could be bent, but that wasn't one of them.

My father hummed and pushed open a large wooden door. "So you see my dilemma."

That's when I noticed the difference. Instead of photographs hung on the wall, there were paintings. The oldest was a group of seven men standing on the bluffs by the geysers. It wasn't the old-fashioned suits or muskets hanging off their hips that caught my attention. It was one of the three scratched out names on the plaque below the painting. This one was still legible.

Mathers.

How did my father miss that? Maybe he didn't? I thought he had a lot of information on Chase, considering he was just a pawn to use against Riley.

"What was the name of Chase's shop? *Mathers' Tattooing*?"

My father's gaze briefly shifted to the painting in the hall. "Thinking about getting another tattoo, son?"

Yeah, maybe I fucking am.

"I'm afraid your self-mutilation will have to wait," he said, as we entered a room with the other Kings. "You'll be rather busy tonight."

What the fuck was this? The walls were lined with various kegs—which I assumed to be alcohol based on the tinge in the air—there was a large vat that said *Whitley Distilleries* on the side in the middle of the room.

My father passed me a glass of whiskey. "Welcome to your *dominare la paura*."

"Am I supposed to drink myself into a coma?" I asked, taking in the room.

There was a pipe running in the side of the vat, and another on the top, along with what looked like wires. What kind of fucking liquor did Preston's father make in this thing?

"Nothing quite so simple I'm afraid." My father slipped the Order's ceremonial black and purple robes over his shoulders, and then cocked a brow at me. "Shall we begin?"

I shrugged and downed the whiskey, enjoying the way the alcohol burned down my throat and warmed my body.

Dr. Creswell snorted and walked over. "Don't underestimate us, boy," he said, lifting my shirt and taping a small wire on my chest. "We're more capable than you think."

"If you say so." I sighed at the deeply embedded scowl on his face. If Silas didn't learn to lighten up, the same angry lines on his father's face would be permanently etched on his.

"Alright, son," my father said before he ushered me through the open door and into the vat. "You simply have to remain calm for fifteen minutes."

Great, should be done in fifteen minutes then.

He pointed at the wire tapped to my chest. "We'll be monitoring your heart-rate."

I took one last look at the Kings, not sure if I liked the smirk on Dean Whitley's face, and said, "Let's get this shit over with."

"You will appreciate the thought that went into this when it's over."

I highly doubted that. Imagination was one thing the Kings lacked, including my father. It was an interesting choice though. Using a vat as some sort of sensory deprivation tank. Which is what I assumed this was, based on the reinforced metal on the inside, and the hissing click of the airtight door.

I glanced around the dark interior and snickered. Was this the best they could do? Trapping me alone in the dark. Really, I expected more.

"A gentle breeze . . ."

What the fuck!

I pushed off the wall and scoured the dark for the source of the sound.

"It fills the sails of boats . . ."

My pulse picked up and rage boiled through my veins. I hated this fucking song. My mother used to sing this shit to me when she tucked me in at night. She'd stare down, eyes shining with warmth and love. That was, of course, a lie. The selfish cunt wasn't capable of love. She sure as hell was good at faking it though. I fucking fell for it.

"Soon they will fly . . ."

My father said she just wasn't in her right mind. Bullshit!

"Hushabye Mountain."

I kicked the side of the vat. The force of my strike vibrated loudly, and somehow mingled with that infernal fucking voice.

"Shut that shit off!" I yelled, kicking the vat again.

Why the fuck did they have a recording of my mother? My fists clenched as I rolled my shoulders and released a long exhale. *This is just a test. I can do this.*

"Sail far away . . ."

Fuck!

Finally, the song fucking ended. I could breathe. Should've known it wouldn't be that easy. It started up again almost immediately. Only louder this time, so I could hear it over the water rushing in the bottom of the vat.

"What the fuck!" I yelled, throwing my fists against the wall, pounding so hard I felt the skin tear on my knuckles.

The pain didn't bother me, nor did the warm blood dripping off my hand. The vat was filling up with water, lifting my body with it. I needed to get the fuck out of here! I couldn't get trapped in a sinking tin can! Not again.

Mase was getting so heavy. I couldn't keep him above the water...

I pounded furiously on the walls.

We were sinking. Farther down into the darkness...

"Let me out!" I screamed, using all my strength to try to break through the metal roof.

It was so cold, I couldn't stop shivering ...

"Please, just let me out."

"Mase, wake up!" I slapped him and frantically looked around. Everything was black except for the inside of the car. Mase's sleeping face was lit up by the interior lights. What did I do? He wouldn't wake up and the water was coming in fast. "Mom?"

"Shh," she hushed from the driver's seat. "Go to sleep, my sweet boy, and we'll wake up on Hushabye Mountain."

How could she be so calm? Blood was rushing out of her nose and we were sinking into the lake. She drove us in here. Why would she do that? Didn't she love us? Weren't we good sons?

But she didn't do anything. Just laid her head back and started singing, "A gentle breeze..."

The lights flickered and the car creaked. I looked at Mase still asleep in his seat. What was wrong with him? Even the chill of the water wasn't waking him up. I had to keep him warm. Dropping my hands into the cold water, I unbuckled him and hugged him close.

The car was quickly filling up, and I couldn't hear my mother's voice anymore. She just sat there and let herself drown. With Mase tucked under my arm, I tried opening the door. When that didn't work, I tried rolling the window down. Tears rolled down my face as I stared at my little brother.

"I'm sorry, Mase." I was supposed to protect him, but I didn't know what to do.

Light flickered off the trophy I won at the go-cart track.

"Hang on, Mase," I said, propping him up against the back of the passenger seat. "I'll be right back."

It took three times diving under the water to grab it. I swam over to the window and began bashing it.

"I'll get us out."

My arms ached and felt heavy, but I couldn't stop. This would work. It had too…

I pounded on the roof, fists raw and aching.

This wasn't my mother's car. Mase was fine. I smashed that window and pulled him out of the lake, the same time our father and Dr. Creswell showed up. Their headlights were the last thing I remembered seeing.

The Kings succeeded. I was officially freaked the fuck out. Trapped in another tin can full of water, with my mother's god forsaken voice blaring in my ears.

I couldn't help but snicker. If only Riley could see me now. Bet she'd love this shit. The sad fact was, she'd probably be the first to dive in after me. Ever the hero, my mouse.

A week after my mother's funeral–which my father made me attend–Brandon decided to taunt me at the park. Riley came out of nowhere and punched him in the jaw. She still had the cast on her leg from when I pushed her off the swing, but that didn't slow her down. She punched him three more times, and kicked him with her broken leg.

I could still see her blue dress flapping in the breeze as she rained her fury down on him. Watching Brandon get taken down by a little girl was better than anything I could've done. I might've even stopped giving Riley such a hard time, if she hadn't opened her fucking mouth.

"I'm sure your mom loved you very much. You must miss her."

I pushed her down on top of Brandon and threw dirt in her face.

Might've even kicked her a couple of times before I walked away. I hated that sad fucking look in her eyes. I just hated her.

She thought she didn't have to fall in line with everyone else. And I tried to make her. Hurt her, tried to destroy her confidence, and show her there were consequences for her actions, but she was too fucking proud. I hated her. At least… I thought I did?

Now I wasn't so sure. I couldn't stop thinking about the way she looked coming on my fingers. Plump, pink lips parted as she threw her head back and screamed in ecstasy. The way her pussy clenched down on my fingers, along with the sweet yet sinful scent in the air. Fucking perfect.

I was dragged out of my thoughts when a loud click reverberated through the vat and the water began to recede. My chest heaved with heavy breaths as I rode it down. The second my feet touched the ground, I collapsed, and lay in the puddle on the ground listening to the drips coming off my soaked clothes and hair.

I barely had the strength to roll over when my father opened the door. Probably a good thing, considering all I wanted to do was fucking hit him.

"Congratulations, son," he said gazing down at me. "You passed the test." He squatted to my level and cocked his head. "I know you don't want to hear this right now, but it appears Riley may have run. She isn't at home."

Anger surged through me, giving me the energy boost I needed. I peeled myself off the floor and stormed out of the vat. "Fucking find her!"

"And when we do?"

I glared back at my father. "She won't fucking run again."

Words were one thing, now it was time to show my mouse who she belonged to.

Chapter 24
Riley

I DUCKED BEHIND A LARGE FIREBUSH, NARROWLY AVOIDING THE security guard's flashlight. Okay, so maybe sneaking out to paint Ashworth wasn't my best idea. I was just about packed up when some guy came out of nowhere, shining his light in my eyes and yelling at me to stop.

That was a half hour ago. I thought Mr. Kessler had good security, but this guy… he took school safety seriously. I guess that was a good thing, just not necessarily right now. But hey, at least no one would kidnap me from school.

"I know you're out there," the security guard called out, scanning his flashlight across the landscape. "Don't make me call the cops."

Shit.

If my dad saw the south wall, I'd be on house lockdown for the remainder of my teenage life. I peeked over the hedge at the large cheerleader I had painted. Totally worth it! Especially considering Naomi was my muse.

To be fair, I think I did her justice. She looked great. Hourglass figure and manicured nails. I even got the brown highlights in her hair. The reflection in the mirror she was looking at, now that was another story. Something told me Naomi wouldn't appreciate the rotted face with half the jaw showing.

The trash in my locker was bad enough. Then she had to go and flaunt Micha in my face. Hanging off him this afternoon and smiling at me, like she knew he was ignoring me. Not that I was jealous… Okay, I might've been a bit jealous, but that wasn't the point. Naomi walked around here making people's life hell. People like poor little Harper. Someone had to put her in her place.

Now if I could just get the hell out of here.

My chance came when the guard turned the corner. I jumped up and dashed across the field, straight into the forested area bordering the school. Falling back against a large tree, I took a second to catch my breath. This whole thing was oddly exhilarating. My heart was pumping a mile a minute, and I couldn't help but smile.

Unfortunately, I didn't have long to enjoy the moment. The security guard came running back, flashlight lighting up a dark patch between the trees. I groaned. Did this guy have supersonic hearing powers? Pushing off the tree, I darted left. There was one place he'd never find me.

My heart didn't calm down until I saw the outline of a familiar bridge through the tree line. Or what used to be a bridge. Other than a stone arch in the middle of an overgrown field, there wasn't much left. I stepped out into the field and took in the scent of wildflowers.

No one really cared about this place, or they didn't know it was here. Leaving it to us rejects. Some people said this used to be a plantation house and the ghosts of slaves hung from that very bridge haunted the area. I don't know about haunted.

If there was anything here, I'd have seen it. That bridge was covered in graffiti, most of which was mine–had to hone my skills someway–and I hadn't run into Casper yet. We did find some neat stuff though. A few old plates, a doll, and some pictures of a guy named Causgrove, which led us to start calling our little hideout the Causgrove.

I slung my backpack over my shoulder and tromped through the tall grass. The roar of the geysers echoed from the nearby bluffs. The only thing separating the Causgrove from the bluffs was a small forest, and on a clear day the red water could be seen over the treetops.

There was a large cave over there that was a popular party spot for the kids in town. Some of my friends would sneak into the forest and watch them, not me though. Learned that lesson the last time Micha spotted me. They had some sort of mud pit set up for girls to wrestle in, and let's just say, it took forever to wash the mud out of my hair.

The soft glow of a crackling fire caused my lips to tip up. Tico must be here. When things got bad at home–his dad liked to smack him around–he slept on the rundown red couch under the bridge. I hadn't seen him all summer and rushed forward.

"Tico!" I sang excitedly. "You wouldn't believe –"

My words died on my tongue. Tico wasn't sitting on the couch. Micha was. I swallowed my gasp. The soft glow from the firelight cast an eerie shadow over his face, deepening his scowl and blackening his eyes. I referred to him as the devil, but right now, he looked like it.

His commanding presence took over, dwarfing the small rundown couch he sat on, and silencing the roar of the geysers in the distance. He was all I could see, hear, and feel. There was nothing but the king sitting regally on his throne.

"Expecting someone?"

He had the same tone in his voice as he did this afternoon. It was terrifying watching him go off on Evan, yet I couldn't look away. I heard every sickening crunch, and witnessed every blow. I could still hear the squelch of Evan's bloody face when Micha's fists rained down on it.

I shook my head. "No."

"What about Tico?"

Micha's gaze shifted, and that's when I noticed the dark head of hair poking out of a sleeping bag in the corner. I didn't think, I just moved, needing to see if Tico was okay.

"Don't." Micha's words halted me. "If you so much as move in that direction, your friend won't wake up in the morning."

So that meant he was alive, but was he okay. "What did you do to him?"

"I think you should be more worried about yourself right now." He sat forward, resting his elbows on his knees, and glared at me. "You have five seconds to get your ass in my Jeep."

This was different than our normal dance. Micha didn't just look pissed, he was downright murderous. Looking over his shoulder, I glanced at the hood of his black jeep glinting in the firelight, and then back at the field, unsure which to go for.

The deep growl in Micha's voice made the decision for me.

"Don't make me chase you." His dark eyes locked with mine, and I shivered. They were almost black. "I've done enough of that tonight."

Yup, now is definitely not the time to push him.

Without a second thought, I scurried past Micha and hopped in the backseat of his Jeep. The passenger seat wasn't even an option. If I had it my way, the Jeep wouldn't be an option, period. But that clearly wasn't happening. So, instead, I slunk over the other side, flattening against the door when Micha climbed in, putting as much space between us as possible.

"Where are we going?" I whispered when Micha started the Jeep. It was more a question to myself, but he still answered.

"Home."

I looked back at the receding glow of the fire as Micha steered down a tramped-down path in the field other cars had taken.

"Aren't you going to put out the fire?"

His black eyes snapped to mine, glaring at me in the rearview mirror.

Shut the hell up, Riley!

"I'm sure your *friend*, will appreciate the warmth when he wakes up," he growled, pulling out onto a main road.

In this case, I listened to my inner voice and shut the hell up. The way Micha said friend sent a chill up my spine. Something told me if I mentioned Tico one more time, then he might end up in the hospital bed next to Evan. Or the morgue. Tico was a small guy. I didn't think he could take a hit like Evan.

On my left, over the edge of the bluff, was the ocean. In most cases it would be a calming sight, but not today. Tension blanketed the air, and the longer we drove, the worse it got. Anxiety spiked as I nervously chewed on my lip. Whoever said silence was bliss had clearly never been trapped in a car with an enraged Micha.

My heart stopped when we turned down a small road lined with big oak trees. I knew this road. Never been down it before, but there was no mistaking the sign that said Oakleigh Manor. Micha was taking me home alright, just not to mine.

The only thing that gave me comfort was holding onto the small knife tucked in my pocket. Chase said better safe than sorry. At the time, I thought it was silly. I could take care of myself. What the hell did I need a weapon for? Now, I wanted to kiss Chase for giving it to me.

When Micha's house came into view, I forgot about my weapon and sat there with my mouth hung open. I'd joked with my dad about marrying the queen, but I think royalty might actually live here. It was a literal palace. If it wasn't for the garages on either side of the house, I'd think I just stepped through a portal to the Victorian era.

Ivy climbed up red brick faded with age to stone balconies, that even in the moonlight I could see were intricately carved. There were more windows than I could count, some stained glass, and a large three-tiered fountain in the front. Around the fountain was a fenced off courtyard, full of pretty flowers and other plants.

When Trina came to a party at Oakleigh Manor last year, I'd assumed she was exaggerating. Wouldn't be the first time. She'd also tried to convince me that some guy at the party was like twelve inches long. I don't even think that existed in porn. But maybe there was some truth to her outrageous stories?

Micha pulled into one of the garages, and I was too awe-struck to argue when he ordered me to get out. I stepped out, scanning the clean cement floors, beige walls, and expensive vehicles. Weren't garages supposed to be dirty with a bunch of tools laying around?

I could eat off this floor.

"You live here?" I said, as Micha grabbed my elbow and hauled me up some stairs to the right.

"My wing is on the west side of the house."

"You have your own wing?" My brows furrowed. "But you're only eighteen?"

He shrugged. "Mase got his when he was fourteen."

Sure, because all teenagers had their own space, other than their bedroom. Sometimes that wasn't even theirs. Shelby's sister was always snooping around in hers, and her parents walked in whenever they wanted. She complained about it all the time.

I must've looked like I'd just discovered the lost city of Atlantis when he pulled me through a door and into the house. Everywhere I looked there was luxury. Beautiful black marble flooring, furniture that looked both antique and brand new at the same time, and plush Persian rugs.

I would've loved to take a closer look at some of the paintings hung on the walls, but Micha was walking so fast that it took all my attention to not trip. One long stride of his was two of mine.

Tall bastard.

"What about your dad?" I asked him.

"What about him?"

Was that a cannon?

I glanced behind me and said, "Don't you guys have family dinners and stuff?"

"When the occasion calls for it."

I looked up, studying his blank face. Didn't that bother him? Sure families were annoying, but they were always there. I could have the worst day in the world, and I knew that Mom would be at home waiting for me. We may not have had much, but we had each other. Micha had the world at his feet and no one to share it with. Must be incredibly lonely.

We walked into a grand entryway, and I say grand, because when I looked up, I could barely make out the roof. Two staircases on either end of the room curved up the wall, framing a large sundial sitting on a stone table. Above the dial was a skylight.

Shadows of ravens danced across it, cast by a chandelier hung in the middle of the room. Sitting on the top of the front door was a black statue of a raven, with the word "nevermore" engraved in the base.

More of the birds were etched into the railing on the staircases, in paintings on the wall, and a big one with its wings spread wide spanned across the floor. Either there was something to the Order of Ravens and Wolves rumors, or the Kesslers were serious Edgar Allen Poe fans. I was so busy gawking, that I didn't realize Micha's dad was there until he spoke.

"I see you found her."

Micha's grip tightened on my elbow, causing me to wince. "I did."

I sneered at Mr. Kessler's suit. Didn't the guy own any other clothes? Pajamas, perhaps?

Mr. Kessler's dark eyes turned on me. "I believe we had the discussion about running."

My eyes widened. Is that what Micha thought I was doing?

"Oh my God, this is all a huge misunderstanding. I wasn't running–"

"Did you sneak out of the house?"

I may have snuck out, but that wasn't the point.

"Technically, yes. But–"

"And did my son know where you were?"

"Well, no–"

"Sounds like running to me, my dear. Either that, or you have something to hide." Mr. Kessler walked up to me, his footsteps echoing in the vast space. "Do you have something to hide, Riley?"

My thoughts immediately went to The Piper and I quickly shook my head.

Micha's dad hummed and eyed me for a second, before he turned his attention to his son. "I had her things delivered to your room."

I breathed an internal sigh of relief. Sometimes I swore my dad was a living, breathing, lie detector.

Wait...

"Um, what do you mean my things were delivered?"

Neither one of them paid attention to me.

"Did you tell Marco?"

His dad nodded. "Yes, he's been informed. She won't go anywhere without you knowing."

"Hello?" Did I suddenly become invisible?

"Alright," Micha said, and tugged me down a hallway to the left.

"Enjoy your stay at Oakleigh Manor, my dear," his dad called out after us.

What? Oh, hell no.

"I'm not staying here!" I shrieked, fighting to pull my arm out of Micha's grasp.

My back was slammed against the wall before I could blink. It took a second to catch my breath as a dull ache spread across my shoulder blades. By the time my vision cleared, Micha was pressed up against me with his hand around my neck.

"You'll stay where the fuck I tell you to stay."

"But technically, you didn't tell me to stay home, either."

Ah ha!

"Did I say you could leave?"

God damn it, I just couldn't win with him.

"I don't need your permission."

"That's where you're wrong, Mouse." His eyes lit up as a malicious smirk curled his lips.

"Everything you do is mine. Your thoughts, your feelings, even the air you breathe. I own it all. I can leave you to rot in a hole." His arm snaked around my waist and down to my butt. "Or I can make you come so fucking hard you can't see straight."

I squealed as Micha squeezed my ass and pulled me tightly up against him.

"A lesson you'll learn tonight."

And then he kissed me.

My kiss this afternoon was soft and tentative. Not his one. Micha devoured me with his mouth. Feeding me every bit of his hunger, while claiming parts of me I didn't know existed.

I tried to fight it with mumbled arguments. But then he ran his tongue ran along the seam of my lips. It felt so good I groaned. That's when Micha dove in, swirling his tongue along mine. Coaxing me to do the same, and damn it, I did. I couldn't help it. Micha was one hundred percent addictive.

I don't know how my hands got in his hair. Didn't really care. My body was on fire, and I needed more. I growled, yanked roughly on his soft locks and deepened the kiss. Greedily taking what he was offering. The growl he released in response went straight to my clit, sending a spark of pleasure shooting through my body and making me gasp.

"Fuck," he groaned, slamming me harder against the wall.

I had to stop this. Things were going too far. My body wasn't listening to me though. So I fought the only way I could, and vented my frustration by biting his lip until I tasted a coppery tinge. The whimper that escaped me when he pulled away made me hate myself a little more.

"God damn it," Micha grumbled, swiping the blood off his lip with the pad of his thumb.

"Fuck you!" I snarled, chest heaving. But I couldn't let him know the truth. Couldn't let him see how desperately I wanted to lift my head and taste him again.

"You want to play rough, baby?" His breath mingled with mine, warming my skin. "Alright. I'll give you to the count of ten."

I knew I wouldn't like what came next. Still, I asked, "For what?"

His lips tipped up in a crooked smirk. "Your head start."

I gulped. He was staring down at me with a predatory glint in his chocolate eyes. I was about to become the main course in an all-you-can-eat buffet, and a big part of me wanted to give in.

I'm so fucked.

Micha bent down, brushed his cheek against mine, and whispered, "Run, little mouse."

And I did. I dashed down the hall as fast as my legs could carry me. If I ran fast enough, then maybe I could outrun the part that wanted him to catch me?

His deep voice boomed down the hall. "One."

Chapter 25
Micha

I RAN MY TONGUE OVER MY THROBBING LIP AND WATCHED RILEY'S firm ass bounce. My mouse was running full tilt down the hall, and I'd never been harder. The wild eyes of my prey, the chase, and the takedown.

It was a fucking aphrodisiac.

I loved this shit. She did, too. Her fear wasn't the only thing tangible in the air. I sucked in a deep breath. Fear mingled with arousal. I was fucking salivating.

Best fucking foreplay ever.

I followed at a lazy pace. Why end the game early?

"Two."

Riley's panicked footsteps grew heavier, ringing through my ears, and making my dick jump. My lips curled in a sly smirk when she turned right instead of left. She was in my territory now.

Come into my parlor, said the spider to the fly.

"Three!"

I pulled out my phone and clicked on the security app. No one said anything about fighting fair. There she was, heading down the hall in the west wing. Like a lamb to slaughter.

"Four!"

Things got more interesting when the door to my gaming room swung open, and Mase stepped out with a couple games tucked under his arm.

"Five!"

Mase stopped and looked around confused at the same time Riley rounded the corner, and bam! They collided. My mouse flew back, skidding across the floor on her ass. Other than being a little stunned, Mase was unfazed. He was built like a brick shithouse. I'd seen him knock a few fuckers out cold in one hit. It'd take a lot more than a five-foot-two chick running at full speed to take him down.

"Six!"

Riley went from shock to panic in seconds. She sprang off the ground and desperately clung to Mase's shirt. Interesting choice. Did she think my brother would help her? I guess it depended on his mood. Fucker liked to screw with me, so who knew? I could guarantee there was something stuffed in the couch in my game room. Last time it was a used condom—and not his. I burned the fucking couch that day.

I turned my leisurely strides into longer casual ones, and called out, "Seven!"

Mase swung his arm, pointing at a room. Bastard even had the 'oh shit' look on his face. My trusting little mouse didn't hesitate, she rushed right into the lion's den. I think she might've thanked him on her way through.

Mase shut the door, and then slid one of the tables in the hall under the handle, before continuing on his way like normal. I shook my head. Despite how much he annoyed me, I loved that little shit.

"Eight."

There was no need to continue counting. Riley wasn't going anywhere. But there was nothing like a little psychological warfare.

Mase nodded at me when I rounded the corner. "Hey, bro."

"Hey." I nodded back.

"Left something in your room for you," he said as he passed by.

"Thanks." I waved over my shoulder, while grinning at the table propped up on my bedroom door.

I took my time sauntering over to my room. The door handle was jiggling, and Riley called out for Mason.

"Mason, this isn't funny. Let me out. I know you're out there."

Not Mason, baby.

I leaned against the wall and listened to her pound on the door again.

"Nine."

A gasp, and then everything went quiet.

When I pressed my ear to the door, I could hear her scuttling around and cursing. Looking for a place to hide, or a way out, I assumed. She'd be hard pressed to find either. I didn't see the need for a bunch of useless crap in my room, so it was fairly open. She also wouldn't be getting any windows open without security access. Play time was over. Now the fun could begin.

Once everything had gone quiet, I slid the table out of the way and stepped into my room. My eyes immediately went wide. In the corner of the room was Riley's bag, clothes open and obviously rummaged through. But it was my mouse who was wearing a white lace teddy that had my complete attention. I kicked the door shut and took my time taking her in.

Her supple skin wrapped in lace was the best fucking present I'd ever gotten. Over the curve of her breasts pressing against the teddy, her nipples were hard and ready for me to suck. I was drooling. The look on her face, however, had my lips curling.

Riley's lips were pursed in the worst fake pout I'd ever seen, and while she was giving me puppy dog eyes, there was nothing but wrath sparkling in those sapphire depths. My mouse was trying to play me with seduction. *I guess playtime wasn't over after all . . .*

"Upping your pajama game, I see."

"What? This old thing," Riley sang.

I smirked and tossed my keys onto the black dresser to my right. "You sure you want to play this game?"

"I don't know what you mean." She batted her eyes innocently. "I was just getting ready for bed."

"Yeah?" My gaze shifted to my four poster California king bed, and then back to Riley. "So get on the bed then."

She was getting nervous now, swinging her shoulders with her hands behind her back. I loved the way she lit up with embarrassment, the pink tint flowing down her cheeks to fill her chest. My dick liked it too. I was so hard, it bordered on painful.

"I could," she trailed her hand over the swell of her breasts, and my eyes were stuck watching her chest heave, "But you're not ready for bed yet, and I hate to lay in that big bed all by myself." She circled her finger over a pert nipple.

Fuck me.

I cleared my throat and said, "That would be a shame."

She frowned and nodded, and I couldn't stop imagining those pink lips wrapped around my cock. Fuck! She was better at this game than I thought.

Let's see how far she wants to take this.

Riley sucked in a shuddered breath when I peeled off my shirt and tossed it onto the floor. The flush in her face deepened as she tried not to look at me.

I knew I looked good. Chicks checked me out all the time, but when Riley did it, pride swelled in my chest. The shy glances and the way her curious eyes kept falling to my chest only made me want her more.

"You don't have to keep eye-fucking me, Mouse," I said, toeing my shoes off and unbuckling my belt. "You can touch too."

Riley stomped her foot as her face twisted in anger. "I'm not eye-fucking–" She stopped herself, forced a smile on her face and innocently sang, "I mean, it's late. We're just going to sleep."

My gaze swept over her, trailing down from her face to her toes, and back up. It was Christmas morning, and she was the present I wanted to tear into. Looking innocent, while smelling like sin, all wrapped up in lace. There was no way she was making it through the night without getting fucked.

"Oh no, baby, sleeping's not on the schedule for tonight. Unless you're afraid you might like it?"

Cracks started to show in her sweet façade when she rolled her eyes, and snorted, "Doubtful."

"Well then," I said, dropping my jeans, and letting them pool at my feet. "Let's get to it."

Her mouth dropped open at the raging hard on tenting my black boxer briefs. I had to hold back a chuckle when my dick twitched and she jumped back.

I swept my hands toward the bed and called her bluff. "After you."

Chapter 26
Riley

I had no idea what I was doing. After Mason trapped me in what I assumed was Micha's bedroom—only the devil would have black furniture—I tried to find a way out. When I couldn't open the door or windows, I looked for a place to hide.

Most guys had stuff all over their room—games and clothes and crap on the floor—not Micha. It was neat and clean, with so much open space Shelby could run track in here.

Everything was black, except for a blood red accent wall, matching blanket, and throw pillows on the leather wing back chairs. Other than under the massive four poster bed, that looked like it came out of Dracula's castle, there weren't many places to hide. Which kicked that option right out the window. So, I rummaged around. There had to be something in here…

Which was how I came across a black canvas bag full of my clothes. And by my clothes, I mean the new crap from my closet, and a school uniform. I almost tossed the lingerie aside, but then I had an idea. If I could get close enough to Micha, then I could use my pocketknife and maybe get out of here.

It was worth a shot, right?

That's what I did. I tucked the knife in the back of my panties, and put on the lingerie, which was oddly comfortable by the way. It fit me like a glove, and was softer than any of my other jammies. The panties, however, were not comfortable.

This tiny little string thing was riding up my ass crack and my female parts were barely covered. A handkerchief had more fabric. Quite frankly, I was surprised they were still holding up my knife.

My game plan was to try and seduce Micha. Get him to let his guard down, and use the opportunity to turn things to my advantage. Gotta say, I had new respect for those Barbie bimbo girls.

They made it look so easy. A smile here, a touch there, and guys were putty in their hands. It was utterly exhausting, playing cute. My mind wasn't helping any. It turned to goo when Micha took his shirt off, and completely checked out when his jeans followed.

Now, here I was, standing in the beast's room, in nothing more than a white lace teddy with a scrap of fabric covering my nether regions, and I couldn't stop staring at his erection. I touched him, yes, but seeing was a whole lot different. A few things ran through my mind, like there's no way that thing will fit in me, and holy crap, he's going to break me.

"After you."

Oh shit.

I tore my eyes off the instrument of my destruction and looked up into his dark eyes, hooded with desire. Lust was everywhere. Thick in the air, in the husky tone of his voice, and the way he was devouring me with his gaze. It was even rolling through me, making my knees weak and running my throat dry.

"What's wrong, Mouse?" His lips curled in a daring smirk. "Afraid you might lose?"

He was calling my bluff. I knew it, and he knew it. Problem was, I was afraid that if I got in that bed, it would be game over. Because a large part of me really, really wanted to get in that bed.

Come on, Riley, this is what you've been waiting for.

I swallowed my nerves and reached back, brushing my hand over the knife tucked in the waistband of my panties, and sang, "Oh no. After you. I insist."

I had an objective here, and getting naked with Micha wasn't it.

Might be fun though...

I cocked my head and watched Micha when he shrugged and sauntered over to the bed. It should be illegal for someone to look that good in underwear.

"Alright, Mouse, your turn," he said, sitting on the edge of the bed and holding his hand out for me. "Come here."

My nerves got the better of me. I stood there staring at his outstretched arm, afraid that if I got too close, my mind would be lost and my body would take over. I was already having trouble maintaining my sanity.

"Come here, baby," he softly repeated, as if I was an animal he was trying to coax into eating out of his palm.

My feet moved of their own accord, bringing me closer, as my hand reached out to touch the tips of his fingers. That's all Micha needed. Before I could recoil, my wrist was snatched, and I found myself standing between his legs, face to face with the beast himself. So close, I could see the golden flecks glittering in his eyes, and smell his minty breath.

Micha's left hand rose, sweeping my hair over my shoulder, and I stood there, shuddering out anxious breaths, both awed by his beauty and petrified of what was happening. The way he looked at me, like I was something precious, unsettled me the most.

"I know this is your first time." A violent shiver ran down my spine when his fingers traced along my jaw. "And I'm trying to be gentle."

Anxiety coursed through me, settling in the pit of my stomach. But I reminded myself to stick to the plan. "I don't want gentle," I said, crawling on his lap to straddle him.

"Careful what you ask for, baby." Micha's fingers speared in my hair, and he yanked my head to the side. "You might get it."

"Don't make promises you can't keep," I taunted.

Was I scared? Yes. I was terrified.

My next breath was mingled with his. Micha's mouth crashed down on mine, and my mind instantly became a clouded mess. Thoughts of fighting gave way to the hot achy need coursing through my body.

My hands threaded in his hair, and I groaned. I'd dreamed about running my fingers through his soft locks. Thought about what he would feel like all hot and pressed up against me, and it was better than I had imagined.

Maybe addiction really did run in the family. Mom had alcohol, my dad had work, and I had this. The dark beast that tempted me into sin, and I really wanted to take the plunge. I was lost. Didn't argue when Micha grabbed handfuls of my ass and rolled my hips, grinding my clit over his hard cock.

It felt so good, I didn't even care that his hand was less than an inch from my stashed blade. My secret was about to be found out, and all I could do was get more of that delicious pressure. Rolling my hips and soaking through the fabric separating us with each swipe.

"I hate you," I snarled to myself between kisses.

"That's fine, baby," Micha growled against my mouth. "Hate me all you want."

He flipped us, so my back was on the bed with his hard body pressing down on mine.

"Just keep fucking me with that smart mouth."

The rational part of me should be screaming for me to get the hell out of here. But my body was in control now, and all it wanted to do was get closer. Micha's hands worked me expertly, slipping under the teddy and pawing my breast.

"Waited so long to get my hands on these perfect tits." He kissed his way down my neck and flicked his tongue over my nipple. "So long to taste them," he whispered, and closed his hot mouth around my pert nub.

I cried out, arching my back as a spark of electricity shot to my core. It was too much, and not enough. Running purely on instinct, I wrapped my legs around his waist and lifted my hips, grinding against him. Pressure was building and I needed a release.

Micha growled, like full-on wild beast growl, and thrust his hips down to meet mine. After that, we were a ball of pawing hands and hot breaths. It was glorious and primal. I never wanted it to end, and whimpered when he popped my nipple out of his mouth.

"I'm going to fuck you so hard," he groaned, and dove down to claim my mouth.

The spell was broken when his fingers grazed over my scar, tracing the jagged line on my abdomen. The intimacy of that single act snapped me out of it. Logic flooded back, as my mind regained control. I shifted to grab the knife, swept his hand off my scar, and tore my lips away.

"Get off me!" I snarled, pressing the blade to his side.

Micha could claim any part of me, just not that part. I'd give him my virginity before I ever bared my soul. That scar, and the pain that came with it, were mine, and mine alone.

Our chests heaved with heavy breaths, and I couldn't stop staring at Micha's thick lips. But I wasn't backing down. Something like amusement flashed across his face when he glanced down at the knife. That should've been my first warning sign.

"And here I thought you'd given up too easily." The corner of his mouth lifted in a spry smirk. "Gotta say, I was a little disappointed."

Sick fuck was enjoying this!

"I said," I pressed the blade closer to his skin, "Get off me."

"You gonna stab me, baby?"

The thought made me sick. I may hate Micha, but I didn't want to hurt him. I didn't want to hurt anyone.

"If I have to."

"Well, in that case, you should pick a better spot," he said, shifting his gaze once again to his left side. "You might make me bleed, but it's just going to piss me off."

Was he crazy? I was threatening him with a sharp instrument, and he was acting all calm. He was calling my bluff, that was all.

What if he isn't?

I didn't want to do this, but I might have to. But what if I couldn't?

Is he really going to make me do this?

My hand started to tremble.

"You seem to be having trouble, Mouse. Let me help you."

Micha propped himself up on an elbow and seized my wrist with the other hand.

"Stab me here," he said, dragging my hand up to his ribs. "You're going to have to put some force behind it if you want to reach my heart with this tiny pig sticker."

My eyes widened. I may as well have been holding a gun at that point. The implications of what kind of damage my little pocketknife could do weighed down on me. I didn't want it in my hand anymore, and tried to pull away and toss it aside.

Micha wouldn't let me. His fingers tightened around mine, digging the hilt into my palm.

"Of course, you could always go for the kill shot." He lifted his chin and pressed the sharp edge of the knife to his neck, "And slit my throat. It's messy though, so you might want to take a shower after."

I did nothing to stop the tears. Why did I think I could win? This wasn't a dream. I wasn't in some movie. Micha was a real-life monster. The devil incarnate, and once the devil saw your soul, he didn't stop until he devoured it whole.

"Why are you doing this?" I whispered quietly.

"You're the one who pulled the knife." Micha stared down at me calmly. "Not my fault you don't have the balls to use it."

I sucked in a choked sob and steadied myself. If he wanted me to hurt him, fine! I stared at the spot where steel met skin and tried to will myself to do it.

"Come on, Mouse."

Tears leaked out of my eyes, rolling down my face and dropping on the blanket below. Here I was, given the opportunity for freedom, and I couldn't do it. In a twisted way, I needed Micha. He was a monster, but he was my monster. I fell back and let the tears fall.

"Pathetic," Micha scoffed, and snatched the knife out of my hand.

I was pathetic. Sick, twisted, and pathetic. He was saying something to me, but I didn't hear it. I zoned out, imagining the last place I felt normal. At home with Mom. She left me, though. Chose drinking over me.

Now I was alone in this hellish pit of self-hatred. Maybe that's where I belonged. Damned for my sins. After all, who would want someone as broken as me?

"I do, Mouse."

My eyes snapped up to Micha's. We were sitting up now. I was in his lap, with my legs wrapped around him. The way he was looking at me stole my breath. No one had ever looked at me that way before… like I mattered.

"I want every twisted thought in your pretty little head."

All I could say was a weak, "Why?"

His hands slipped under my teddy and slid up my sides. "Because they're mine."

He ripped the teddy off and tossed it onto the floor.

The cool air met my skin and I shivered. "No, they're not."

"When are you going to get it, Mouse?" He pushed me back on the bed, and crawled over me. "You are mine! I own it all. Body, mind, and soul."

Would that really be so bad? Micha saved me from Lance, and went feral on Evan when he found out he hit me. It may have been brutal and wrong, but he protected me. That was more than anyone else had ever given me.

What? No! that's the stupidest thing ever!

"I'll never be yours," I growled.

"Yeah?" He cocked a challenging brow down at me. "Then why aren't you fighting me?"

Why wasn't I fighting him?

When he sat up and hooked his thumbs in my panties, I kicked him in the chest. "Fuck you!"

Though Micha stumbled back, he was quick to recover. Lunging forward, he pinned me down with his weight before I could flip over.

"There's my tough girl." He smiled, and slammed my arms down on the bed above my head. "I was beginning to think I broke you."

"You'll never break me!"

"Oh, I think I will."

Cold metal wrapped around my wrist, followed by a soft click. All the blood drained from my body.

No, no, no!

I fought to free the other arm, but Micha easily secured the cuff around it and sat back to admire his handiwork. I tugged on the chains binding me to the bed and kicked my feet. It was useless. Less than useless… I was trapped.

"You get off on this?" I growled, glaring my hatred at him. "Overpowering girls half your size?"

"I do, Mouse." Micha smiled and flipped open my knife. "It gets my dick hard."

I instantly froze. Oh God, this was it. I was going to die.

"Stay still now." He slid the blade under the thin strap that served as the waistband for my barely-there panties, and cut one side with a flick of his wrist. "I wouldn't want to cut you. Blood's not my thing."

I did. Held my breath and willed my body to remain as still as possible. What else could I do? Mortification burned in my cheeks when the scrap of fabric was cut away, and I was bare before him.

Micha's hands descended, kneading my exposed breasts in a way that had my nipples stiffening into hardened peaks. I managed to contain myself, trapping my moans in my throat, until his mouth closed around me.

Pleasure shot through me, pulling a moan out with it. His tongue swirled over my nipple while his teeth nipped, working me into a frenzy.

"So fucking sweet," Micha grumbled and moved over to give my other breast the same attention.

My legs squeezed together, attempting to quell the aching need in my core. I was so wet, I could feel it on my thighs. I couldn't stop myself from moaning and arching up into his talented mouth.

"Fuck," he growled, popping my nipple out of his mouth with an audible pop. "I need to be inside you right fucking now."

I should've been scared when he stood and striped himself of his boxer briefs. The hot, achy need throbbing between my legs outweighed everything else. I lay on the bed, squishing my thighs together, and hungrily took in his abs and chiseled chest.

Panic stormed back in, slamming down like a barbell, when my eyes locked on the thick head of his cock, glistening with his arousal.

Micha pried my legs apart and settled his hips between my thighs. My fear turned into violent hiccups.

"You're too big!" I cried out, frantically yanking on the handcuffs.

"Shh, you need to calm down, Mouse," Micha shushed. "It's going to hurt more if you don't relax."

I tried to listen to him, I really did. He was the sex expert after all. But the second the smooth head of his cock slid through my slick folds, my muscles tensed.

"You're fucking soaked," he growled, guiding himself along my pussy.

His dick pressed down on my clit and for a second, I forgot about his size. "Please let me touch you."

"You want to touch me, baby?" he groaned, repeating the action.

I felt his cock press against my opening, and I sucked in a staggered breath. If I had my hands free, I might be able to fight him.

Do you really want to fight him?

Of course I do.

Micha slid himself along my pussy, this time circling the smooth head over that traitorous bundle of nerves.

"Oh God," I cried out, arching my back. "Please, I want to touch you."

"No."

His mouth descended on mine, swallowing my gasp as he thrust his hips and pushed in. My muscles stretched, trying to accommodate to the girth forcing its way in. The pressure was both exhilarating and painful. And then he tore through my virginal wall.

The scream that erupted from my lips felt like it was ripped from my very soul. White-hot pain burned its way through me, searing nerves I didn't know I had. I pulled violently on my binds, and fought to pull air into my lungs. But Micha didn't stop. He continued to push inside me, inch by excruciating inch.

I held on to the chains of my handcuffs and furiously shook my head. "It's too much."

"You'll fucking take me." Micha grabbed a handful of my hair and forced my head back on the mattress. "Every goddamn inch."

I almost reveled in the ache spreading across my scalp–anything to take away from the burning ache rocking my system.

"That's it, baby," he growled, pushing in more of his uncompromising hardness.

My body fought back, tightening around him in an effort to push the intrusion out. It felt like my pussy was on fire. My walls were stretched beyond capacity, and I couldn't take any more.

I shook my head as tears streamed down my face. "I can't."

"Yes. You. Can." His neck was corded, and his arms were tense from the strain.

A bead of sweat rolled across his brow, and I realized he was holding back. Micha didn't want to hurt me, so he was containing himself. How pathetic was it that my heart swelled, despite the pain I was in?

"Fuck, you're tight."

With one final snap of his hips, Micha pushed past the last of my resistance. Once he was buried inside me, he nuzzled my neck and released a long, throaty groan. It was one of the sexiest sounds

I'd ever heard. Didn't help the pain I was in, though. I whimpered out a cry and struggled underneath him.

"Shh," Micha soothed, kissing away my tears. "I'll go slow."

I was pathetically thankful that he stuck to his word, starting out with slow light thrusts. It gave me time to adjust, and soon my muscles relaxed, giving way for my pain to subside and something else to take over; a full, almost pleasurable feeling, one that I didn't entirely hate.

Micha must've sensed the change, because he picked up the pace. Drawing himself out in languid strokes before diving back in. Each time the soft ridges of his hard cock scraped along my walls, the coil of tension inside me wound tighter and tighter until I was thrown off that blissful cliff without warning.

My body seized, bowing my back. "Holy fuck."

And that's when Micha fucked me. He growled, hooked my leg over his hip, and pounded into me with the fury of a man possessed.

"This fucking pussy is mine!" We moved farther up the bed with each powerful thrust. "If you so much as shake this shit at someone else, I'll fucking kill him."

His possessiveness shouldn't turn me on, but it did. I loved being wanted like that, even if it was only in the moment. Didn't mean I was about to let him know that.

"Fuck you!" I snarled.

"Oh no, baby, it's me who's fucking you." He thrust in, going deeper than he had before, and hitting some spot that made my toes curl. I couldn't speak. His cock was like a battering ram, beating down the flood gates of ecstasy I didn't know existed. Just when I thought I couldn't take any more, Micha reached down and pinched my clit.

"Please," I whimpered.

My orgasm was right there. I could feel it.

"Eyes on me."

I'd give him whatever he wanted, as long as he kept doing that. My breath hitched when I met his gaze. His eyes were dark with possession and dominance. I smelled it in the air around us. Tasted it with every breath I took, and felt it in the very depths of my soul. In that moment, he truly did own me.

"Do you want to come?"

I furiously nodded my head.

He snapped his hips and stopped. "Ask me nicely."

I whimpered, shifted my hips. "Please–"

He rotated his hips, making my eyes roll into the back of my head.

"Please what?"

There wasn't anything wrong with giving him what he wanted this one time.

"Please make me cum."

He rewarded me with a small thrust.

"Good, now try again with your eyes open."

Shit, my eyes were closed?

I tried to open them, but it was too hard to concentrate on anything other than the way he felt inside me.

"Come on, baby," he purred, giving me another short thrust, but not quite enough to drive me over the edge. "I want to see those pretty fucking eyes when you come."

God damn it! Why did he have to be so infuriating?

"I hate you."

"Nope, try again."

If my body wasn't burning with need, I'd scratch his eyes out. Well, if my hands weren't cuffed to the bed that is. I could always tell him to fuck off and try to take care of myself. Couldn't be that hard. People did it all the time. As if he could sense my anger, Micha gave a few short thrusts, pushing me closer to the edge of ecstasy, and stamping down my desire to rebel. This was worse than torture.

I released a frustrated grunt, and forced my lids to flutter open. "Please make me cum."

"Good girl," he said, moving again and giving me the friction I needed.

With one pinch of my clit, I was sent over the edge, plummeting into nirvana. Micha kept driving into me, building my orgasm higher and higher. It wouldn't end. Ebb after ebb of white-hot bliss, crashing through me like waves on a beach. I screamed for more. Then I screamed for less. I just screamed. Screamed for so long that my throat hurt.

"God. Fucking. Damn it," Micha growled, his face twisted in pleasure as his whole body spasmed.

His fingers dug painfully into my hips, as he rammed into me one last time. I felt his cock twitch as he bathed me with his warm release, and was thrown right back into orgasmic bliss.

By the time he collapsed beside me, sweaty and out of breath, I was spent. I didn't have the energy to keep my eyes open. I heard him get up, felt the warm cloth run over my skin as he cleaned me, but I couldn't move. My body was a puddle, limp, lose, and utterly satisfied.

The last thing I remember before exhaustion took over, was Micha tucking me into the warmth of his body, kissing the top of my head, and saying, "You're mine now, Mouse."

Chapter 27
Micha

Mouse was quiet all morning. The only time she talked to me was to tell me to fuck off, or say how she hated me. Except it wasn't me she hated… it was herself. Riley couldn't stand the fact that hours ago, she was creaming all over my dick, and I was loving every second of it.

Her little angry snorts and sideways glares were making me hard. She's fucking lucky she didn't end up bent over the kitchen table. I didn't give a shit if my brother was there or not.

I couldn't wait to dive back into her tight little pussy. But every time she sat down, or shifted wrong, she'd wince. And for some fucking reason, I cared.

I kept running through shit in my mind that would help. Make her soak in a bath, give her a massage, shit like that. The fucked-up part was that I wanted to do that crap. I wanted to take her pain away. Wanted it to be my arms she sought solace in. Not sure when the fuck that happened.

I was pissed last night when she took off. Not because I thought she ran away. What if someone got their hands on her? Those fuckers from Ashen Springs High didn't seem to have a problem touching my shit. My mind kept picturing her hurt and alone. All I wanted to do was burn the world down. Might've even paid that prick a visit in the hospital.

I was lost; and scared. I didn't know what to do. The last time I felt like that was in that car, sinking in Cherry Lake. Then Riley showed up, calling out that asshole's name, and I wanted to destroy her for ever making me feel that weak.

Instead, I fucked her.

Now she knew who she belonged to, and it sure as fuck wasn't that Tico prick.

Riley shifted in the passenger seat and made a sound that had my inner-self beaming with pride. I wanted her to feel me every time she moved.

"What's wrong, Mouse?" I asked, knowing full well what the issue was.

Fuck you, Tico, that shit is mine.

"I'm fine," she snarled.

My fingers tightened around the steering wheel.

Bet she didn't give Tico the fucking attitude. Scrawny little fuck.

Riley scoffed and rolled her eyes, "Can't you drive any faster? I'd like to get to school today."

"Watch your fucking tone," I barked out, "Or I'll pull over and give you a proper introduction to my cock."

Riley's cheeks flamed and she turned away, but she kept her mouth shut.

That's fucking right.

I couldn't help but notice her hands fidgeting in her lap. She looked more confused than angry. Maybe even a little sad?

"What's wrong, Mouse?"

Why the fuck did I say that?

She sighed. "Nothing."

I could see her out of the corner of my eye, and knew that was bullshit.

She said nothing was wrong, let it go and move the fuck on.

"You can talk to me, you know."

What the hell was I doing? Why was I opening this avenue to her? Chicks liked to talk, and I didn't do emotional crap. Still… I really wanted to know what was up her ass.

Riley latched her glare onto me and spat out, "Go fuck yourself."

That's it! She was keeping something from me, and that I wouldn't stand for. I wanted it all. Everything. And she would goddamn well give it to me!

"Either you tell me what the fuck your problem is, or I'll drag it out of you!"

"Blow me."

She needed to calm down before I hit someone. Fuck it, I might hit someone anyway.

"Oh no, baby, that's your job." I shifted my eyes her way. "And I think it's long overdue."

Riley sighed and turned her gaze back to the window. "Why don't you just leave me alone? You got what you wanted."

Oh, so that was her issue. It all made sense now. She thought this was some fuck and chuck situation. That I was going to ditch her. Not a fucking chance in hell. While I didn't do relationships, I wasn't Logan or Mase. I didn't go dipping my dick in every gaping hole.

"Did you read the contract, Mouse?"

Her furious eyes snapped my way. "Why would I do that?"

"Well, if you had, you'd know this isn't a sex slave thing," I explained. "When you turn eighteen, my ring is going on your finger."

Her eyes widened in surprise and fuck me, if it didn't get me hard. Everything this girl did got me hard. She could breathe on me, and my dick would be ready to go.

"When I said you were mine, I meant it."

"So what! I'm supposed to play pretty little housewife while you're out fucking whoever you want?" She huffed and crossed her arms. "No thanks."

"First off, I wasn't asking for your permission. And secondly, I'm a lot of things, Mouse, disloyal isn't one of them." I pulled up to Ashworth's gates and flashed my student ID. "I told you if you wanted monogamy, you got it."

She looked up at me with a sweet smile on her face. "What if I want to sleep with someone else?"

I damn near punched the security guard.

"If you so much as look at another guy in a way I don't like," I cupped her chin and dug my fingers into her cheeks, so she would know how serious I was. "I'll slit his goddamn throat and fuck you over his corpse."

Her deep swallow was all the answer I needed.

I drove through the gates, and Riley no longer had my attention. Something was up at Ashworth. Students were gathered in little groups, whispering to each other, with a larger crowd at the south side of the building. Teachers were trying to bring back order, but no one was listening. The school was in anarchy.

I watched a bunch of bookworms tell off some cheerleaders, and Eddie, the skinny kid from bio, was poking Sean Callahan in the chest. Eddie ended up with a swollen face stuffed in a garbage can.

Not sure what the kid was thinking. He couldn't weigh much

more than my mouse, and Callahan was the damn quarterback. Harper would put up a better fight for her brother.

The last time I saw this much chaos at Ashworth was freshman year, during the fall out from Ava's broken heart. Not only did Parker beat the shit out of the guy–fucker was in the hospital for a week–but Ava tore his car apart and firebombed it.

I think that was the first time I saw Logan cry… even gave the car a burial. The headstone marking Liam's car sat in his backyard. He had flowers delivered weekly.

Speaking of my best friend…

I cocked my head at Logan. He was standing next to Mase, obviously waiting for me, and based by the look on his face, it wasn't to tell me which chick he banged last night.

I sighed and pulled into my parking spot next to Logan's Mustang. "What now?"

"Oh well, time for school," Riley sang and jumped out of the Jeep.

"Stop!"

She froze.

Riley was a shitty liar and guilt was written all over her face.

"You stay right fucking there," I said, getting out to meet Logan and Mase.

Logan came over to me, while Mase sauntered up to Riley with a shit-eating grin on his face. Riley was less than impressed to see him. If my baby brother got too close, he might lose his balls. I could almost hear her grinding her teeth from here.

"Hey," Logan said, in a hushed tone. "Did you tell anybody about last night?"

"What about last night?" My eyes shifted to Mase and Riley. Unlike him, I didn't broadcast my sexual exploits.

"Not that." Logan rolled his eyes. "The *dominare la paura.*"

"Why the fuck would I tell anyone about that?" Logan knew me better than that. Not only was it forbidden to talk about, but it was my business.

He released a long sigh. "That's what I thought."

"Mind telling me what's going on?"

"As you can see, shit's a little hectic around here."

That was an understatement.

"You're not going to make me attend another car funeral, are you?"

"No." Logan got a far-off look in his eyes and shook his head. "Poor fucking car."

I crossed my arms and waited for his moment of mourning to pass.

"It seems your girlfriend was busy last night."

"Yeah, I know," I grumbled, glaring at Riley. "Meeting some guy named Tico."

Logan's face scrunched up. "Who the fuck is Tico?"

"A dead man, if I ever see him again." Fucker thought he could touch my girl!

"Someone sounds jealous."

"Fuck off."

"Anyways," he said, lips still curled in a sly grin, "Whoever this Tico is, he wasn't in the picture."

That got my attention.

"What fucking picture?"

Logan glanced over at Mase and passed me an envelope. Inside was a picture of Riley at night, with a can of spray paint in her hand. I immediately recognized the Ashworth crest on the wall she was painting. Along with the picture was a note:

Hey diddle diddle,
The mouse is in the middle,

All alone under the moon,
The Piper, he laughed to see her off court,
And the knight, he'll lose her soon.

That explained the backpack full of spray paint in my Jeep. Riley wasn't trying to run away. She snuck out to paint Ashworth. And this fucker watched her.

I looked over at my mouse, watching her black hair blow in the breeze. She was so fucking beautiful; I swear it hurt to look at her. Every inch of her was imprinted in my brain.

The cluster of five freckles on her back, just above the curve of her ass. How her eyes lit up when she was lost in a drawing, and the scar by her belly button that she thought was ugly, but only made her more beautiful. She was flawed, angry, and perfect. And last night, I could've lost her.

"We need to find this guy," I growled, balling the note up in my fist.

Logan didn't get a chance to answer, because Mase sauntered over with his arm over Riley. The second she was within reach, I grabbed her and took those sweet lips. I just needed to touch her, needed to feel her there with me. I slammed her back against my Jeep, and sucked her tongue into my mouth, groaning at her sweet taste.

I didn't give a shit that people were watching. I wanted every asshole in this place to know that she was mine. By the time I came up for air, I'd forgotten about everyone else. There was only my mouse and her gorgeous blue eyes, sparkling like sapphires.

"You have no idea how beautiful you are." My fingers traced the delicate curves of her perfect face. She was so soft and smooth.

Logan cleared his throat, pulling me back to reality. "If you're done molesting my sister, I think you should see what she did."

I took one more look at Riley–since when did I become a pussy–and grabbed her elbow.

"I think I fucking should," I said, hauling her ass across the school yard.

I assumed the large crowd was where we were headed, and I was right. It didn't take long to see what had everybody's attention. Painted on the wall was a large cheerleader, obviously Naomi.

It wasn't the cheerleader I was staring at though. Don't get me wrong, she looked good–shapely legs, hourglass figure, and blonde hair glowing in the light. The reflection in the mirror now, that was another story ... Flesh rotting off the bone, a forked snake like tongue, and blue eyes.

Blue eyes?

The more I looked, the more I saw. Five freckles on the cheerleader's back. A small scar on the right side of her nose, and a black rope bracelet–the same bracelet Riley had been wearing since she was fourteen. Was she saying she hated Naomi, or herself?

"Hey!" Riley called out, her face crinkling in anger. "Someone tagged my painting."

I looked over to what she was scowling at and felt my whole body get stiff. On the corner of the wall, written in black, were the words *Dominare la paura.*

Chapter 28
Riley

Someone tagged my work! I couldn't believe it, that was just so… insulting. I knew a few other artists in the world, and none of them would've done this. It was like a slap in the face. You just didn't do it. Period!

Tico knew most of the people who tagged The Causgrove. He might know who did this, or be able to point me in the right direction. The world needed to know who this tagger was. I pulled out my phone, snapped a pic of the wall, and sent Tico a quick text. He responded a few seconds later.

Tico: *Sorry babe, got no idea. I'll do some digging. We'll find out who it is. The crew won't be happy about someone dissing our queen.*

I smiled, flattered that Tico and his crew called me queen. Only the highest respected street artists got that title, and most of the time it was king. Not a lot of girls in my world, not in Ashen Springs, anyway.

Me: *I don't know about queen.*

Tico: *Are you kidding babe? You tagged Kessler's office.*

That was a good day.

"Who the fuck are you talking to?" Micha's voice barely registered, I'd almost forgotten he was there.

"Tico," I said, typing out a text. The phone was ripped out of my hand before I could hit send. "Hey! Give me that!"

"No."

I scowled at him. "You can't just take my phone."

He tucked my phone into his pocket and glared down at me. "I told you to stay the fuck away from other guys."

"It's not like that," I grumbled, rolling my eyes. "Tico's just a friend."

Besides, I didn't exactly have the right parts. Micha was more Tico's type than I was.

"I don't give a fuck."

Mason nudged me with his elbow, cutting off my argument. "Here comes the welcome wagon," he said, tipping his chin at the crowd.

I groaned. Miss Jones, the vice principal, was headed our way, and based on the deeply imbedded frown on her face, it wasn't to ask me how I was adjusting to Ashworth.

"Miss Adams," she called out, drawing the crowd's attention to me. "Will you come with me please?"

I looked around at all the ogling eyes and sighed. That didn't take long.

Micha's arm shot out, stopping me before I could move.

"What do you want with her?" he said, stepping out in front of me.

Miss Jones glanced back at the painting. "Miss Adams does have a history with this kind of thing."

"Let me get this straight..." Logan strutted up next to Micha, completely blocking my view of the vice-principal. "Someone tagged the school, and you just assume it's my sister?"

Gotta say, I was kind of impressed that Logan knew the proper term. He did have some pretty serious street cred from racing, though, which some of Tico's crew was involved with. So it was possible our worlds had collided.

Logan rolled his jade eyes over to Micha. "Isn't that like discrimination or something?"

Micha crossed his arms and grunted in agreement.

Why the hell were they standing up for me? I eyed Micha. Was this some contract clause, like our supposed marriage? He had to stand up for me or something? Huh? Did that mean if he broke a clause, the contract was null and void? I was seriously going to have to read that thing.

"We have Miss Adams on video."

Video? I didn't see any cameras. A blinking red light drew my attention to the corner of the roof.

Well shit.

Both Logan and Micha grumbled out a sigh.

"Sorry, sis," Logan said, glancing over his shoulder at me. "Can't beat video."

I shrugged. It was my bright idea to paint the school. Not sure why the hell they cared. Micha was the one who got me arrested, for Christ's sake. No one in this town would've known who I was or what I'd done if it wasn't for him. *Dick.*

"If you would've paid attention to your surroundings," Micha growled, "You would've seen the damn camera!"

What the hell was he so mad about?

I crossed my arms and returned his scowl. "Just testing out the next location for our porn shoot."

"Miss Adams!" the vice-principal scolded. "We don't stand for that kind of talk here."

"Oh relax, it's not like I'm going to suck him off right here."

Not sure where my boldness came from. I usually stayed in the background, out of others' attention—something I had a lot of right now. The crowd gasped.

A few people looked impressed, and other's snickered, especially Logan and Mason, who were practically bent over. The only person who didn't react was Micha. Other than a brief flare in his eyes, there was nothing. Not sure if that was a good thing or not, but I was guessing not.

"Alright people, show's over," Miss Jones said, clapping and ushering me through the crowd.

"It's about time you started clearing the trash out of this place," a voice called out.

"Hey!" I heard Mason yell before a couple girls shrieked.

The crowd quickly dispersed after that, and I could see why. On the ground at Mason's feet was a guy I'd seen in my English class. My hand flew over my mouth, covering my gasp as I noticed the blood gushing out of his nose. I'd witnessed Mason's violence first-hand, and this guy was getting off easy.

What they did to Evan still turned my stomach, which was why I was worried about Tico. He wouldn't stand a chance against Micha. Talking to him gave me some relief. If Micha had hurt him, he would've said something. Like, who the fuck was that crazy guy looking for you last night?

Miss Jones sighed heavily. "You too, Mr. Kessler. Come on."

"Great." Mason flashed the vice-principal a big smile. "I'm sure Edith is utterly heartbroken with my absence."

Based on Miss Jones' reaction, I was going to say Edith was

perfectly fine with Mason's absence.

"Who's Edith?" I whispered.

"My one and only true love."

Miss Jones muttered under her breath and nodded at the office doors. "I believe you know the way, Mr. Kessler."

"Don't worry," Mason said, opening the door and making a grand gesture of sweeping his hand through the air. "I'll give her the grand tour."

Mrs. Grier's cold, steely eyes rolled up when we walked in. "Mr. Kessler," she said with a sigh, "What did you do now?"

"I'm insulted." Mason threw his hand over his chest. "And here I brought you a new recruit."

I shrank back when Mrs. Grier's soul sucking glare penetrated Mason. He didn't seem bothered by it, though. If anything, he brightened up.

"Oh, Edith, don't be jealous," he said, batting his thick lashes. "You know I only have eyes for you."

I was beginning to think Mason spent more time here than in actual school, because the hard-nosed receptionist didn't bat an eye at his comment. She looked over her square-framed glasses at me.

"Miss Adams. Why am I not surprised?"

"Well, I'd hate to disappoint," I replied.

She turned her attention back to the computer screen on her desk and said, "Have a seat. Mr. Sampson will be with you shortly."

I slumped down in one of the hard chairs, while Mason took the other. There'd be no getting out of this one. Why the hell did a school have cameras anyway? It wasn't friggin' Fort Knox. There was no gold in here, just teenage assholes, and nobody wanted those, including their parents.

"Hey," Mason whispered. "How much you wanna bet she's looking at porn over there?"

I couldn't help but snort out a chuckle. Mrs. Grier's stoic stare was glued to the computer screen. If it was porn, it was the world's most boring porn ever.

"I bet she likes the weird stuff," he continued. "You know, like golden showers and shit."

My nose scrunched up in confusion. "What's a golden shower?"

"That's when you take out your dick and piss on someone. Well, I guess chicks could do it, too. Though they'd have to squat or something. Not sure how well that would work."

"Eww." Did he have to be so descriptive? "Why would anyone like that?"

He shrugged. "Different strokes for different folks. Why do people like dressing up like animals or pretending they're little kids? My personal favorite are the dakimakura people. Those crazy sons of bitches treat their pillow better than they do their wife."

I stared at him with my lip curled. Did people really like that stuff? Did Micha? I mean, it seemed like normal sex last night, but it wasn't like I had a lot of experience to go from.

Mason chuckled and threw his arm over my shoulder. "I know that look. Don't worry, my brother's not going to make you piss on him. That's not his thing."

"What is his thing?"

"And here I thought you were still mad at me for last night."

My eyes narrowed. *"Quick, he'll never find you in here."* Asshole!

"I am still mad at you. You locked me in his bedroom."

He gave me a sly look. "But you liked it."

"No, I didn't."

"Yes, you did, or you wouldn't be asking me what my brother's thing was."

"If you don't mind," I huffed and crossed my arms. I wasn't prepared to broach that topic yet. "I'm going to mentally prepare for my dad's *what were you thinking* speech."

"Yeah," Mason muttered, "I've heard that one."

I rolled my eyes. "Oh, please. I'm sure you're the golden boy of your family."

He barked out a laugh. "That's a good one." The amusement dropped off his face as his brows furrowed. "That's Micha. I'm just his little brother, a wingless bird who can't fly. But hey, at least you got the good brother, right?"

I frowned at the deep-set crease on his forehead. I knew that look. The one that came with the pain of knowing you'll never be good enough. I'd never seen this side of Mason.

Then again, I guess I never really looked. But why would I? He was a Kessler, and everything was perfect in their world. Who'd have thought they'd turn out to be people, just like the rest of us?

I don't know how long we sat there before Mason's face lit back up, and he nodded at the door. "Please tell me he's here for you."

I groaned when Chase strutted into the office. Why would they call him? Chase was the last person the distinguished staff of Ashworth wanted in their school.

He was dressed in dark jeans and a black shirt he probably grabbed off the floor. Didn't stop girls from openly eye-fucking him, though. One of the teachers popped her head in just to say hi, while a group of cheerleaders giggled and waved from the hall.

Even Mrs. Grier gave him a quick scan. Shouldn't the proper girls of Ashworth be looking for someone a little more upstanding?

Chase probably rode his bike here, and if it wasn't for the black beanie on his head, his brown hair would be wild, which he wouldn't have taken the time to brush before walking in.

Add in his numerous tattoos and giant size, and Chase was closer to the criminal side of the social scale. I knew him, and still wouldn't be surprised if he was caught in a dark alley doing some shady deal. He just had that look.

"Why did they call you?"

"Your dad was busy at work, and they wouldn't have *had* to call me at all if you didn't tag the princess academy!" he bellowed loud enough for half the school to hear.

Mrs. Grier gasped like that was the most offensive thing she'd heard.

"But you're always telling me to embrace my artistic side," I said with a smile.

As if things couldn't get worse, my dad chose that moment to enter. I rolled my eyes at his uniform. *Typical!*

"And that's the kind of shit I'm talking about!" he growled, pointing at Chase. "You need to stop encouraging her."

"Fuck off, Derek! You don't know shit about your daughter."

My dad puffed up and got right in Chase's face. "That's right, she's *my* fucking daughter!"

"Well, *I* was the one taking care of *your* fucking daughter when you left her with your drunk ex-wife!"

I cringed. Mom was gone and I was still the drunk's daughter.

"Listen here you biker piece of shit…"

Their voices drowned out as I looked around. People were staring. The windows to the hallway had become viewing portals with faces pressed up against them.

The principal was peeking out of his office like he wasn't sure if he wanted to get between the sheriff and this big burly man, and I was pretty sure Mason would love a bowl of popcorn right now.

"Guys," I called out, grabbing their attention. "In case you haven't noticed, we're kind of in a school?"

Chase and my dad both stopped and looked around.

My dad cleared his throat.

Chase straightened up.

"Aw man, why'd you stop them?" Mason whined. "It was just getting interesting."

I cocked my head and gave him a dirty look. My dad held his

own against criminals, but Chase was a big guy, and I didn't particularly feel like watching my dad get beat down—no matter how mad I was at him.

"You promised me you'd try, baby girl," Chase said, giving me that disappointed look that ate my insides up. "You've got a good thing going here. Don't fuck it up."

"Those are good words of advice, son," Mr. Kessler said, walking into the office to join us. He nodded at my dad and Chase. "Chase. Derek."

Mason rolled his eyes and slumped back. "I'll be sure to remember that."

A minute later, the principal finally came out. The danger was over now, and as much as Mr. Sampson tried to fit in with the students, he was really more of a joke. I kind of felt bad for him. It was nice to have a principal who cared for a change. Watching the four of them huddled up talking was like being in a live action bad joke.

A biker, a cop, and a businessman walk into a bar . . .

I snorted out a chuckle.

"What's so funny?" Mason whispered.

"Look at them," I said, waving at the group discussing our punishment. "They're like the worst A-team ever."

"I love that show," Mason said. "Didn't think anybody still watched it."

"I've got the whole series on DVD."

"We're definitely going to have to do a marathon."

Though I wasn't Mason's biggest fan, I was kind of excited to have someone to watch my cheesy shows with. Shelby wouldn't do it anymore. "Deal."

"Are you two paying attention?"

I looked up at Mr. Sampson and nodded. "Uh, yeah."

"Heard every word," Mason added with a big smile.

Mr. Sampson sighed and shook his head. "As I was saying, I think three days suspension is fitting."

"I don't know if we should go that far," Mr. Kessler said. "I'm sure the girl can clean the wall, and my son and I are working on his anger issues."

"If you say so," Mason grumbled.

"I think it's great you're working with your son, sir, but you have to understand where I'm coming from. This isn't Mason's first offence, and we're only into the first week of the school year." Mr. Sampson glanced over at Mason with a disappointed frown. "And Riley is lucky the school isn't pressing charges."

"Thank you for that," my dad said, shooting a glare my way.

"Great," Mason said, stretching his arms over his head. "I could use a break."

Time away from Micha and Ashworth? That didn't sound so bad. There had to be a way out of this contract, and Micha couldn't stop me from digging around if he wasn't there.

Chase frowned at the look on my face. "Don't get any ideas, baby girl. You'll spend that time doing the shit work at the parlor."

"What?" I liked working at the tattoo parlor, but I knew what Chase's idea of shit work was, and shit was a nice way of putting it.

My dad nodded in agreement. "I think that's a great idea."

Since when did they agree? This sucked. I wanted them to go back to fighting.

Mason burst out in laughter. "Enjoy your time off, spit fire. I'll be thinking of you while I'm poolside."

Mr. Kessler's dark eyes zeroed in on his son. "How would you feel about another set of hands?"

I smiled at the shocked look on Mason's face.

Welcome to hell, asshole!

My hands gripped the steering wheel, as I glared through the windshield. I hated fucking hospitals. The only people here were sick or dying, and it smelled like chemicals. All those stark white walls reminded me of waking up in that stiff fucking bed, body aching and exhausted, with no idea if my little brother was alive.

The doctors wouldn't tell me shit, of course. Who listens to a kid? I didn't find out Mase was okay until my father arrived.

"Gonna have to go in, you know?" Logan said. "Can't stare at it all day."

I tightened my grip on the steering wheel, whitening my knuckles. Fucking Julia! This was the third time in as many months that I had to come help Junior out. I'd think the druggie bitch would stop overdosing. She'd stuck enough needles in her arm to know what her damn limit was by now!

Logan slapped a hand on my back. "Come on. You can do this."

Of course I could fucking do this. I just didn't want to.

"Fuck!" I yelled, throwing open the door and charging across the parking lot. That sterile chemical smell was already filling my nostrils.

This day was fucked. Riley and Mase got suspended. Mase I understood, but Riley? What the fuck was she thinking? To top it all off, after practice, I got a call from the hospital.

"Julia better be fucking dead this time."

I might kill her myself. Junior would get over it.

"You know how this shit goes." Logan sighed. "She'll refuse treatment, and Junior will be home with her by the end of the night."

Unfortunately, that was true. I don't know how many times I'd threatened Julia. She didn't give a fuck.

"Not this time," I said, cringing at the ding of the sliding hospital doors.

"That's what you said last time."

I walked through the waiting room and shook my head at the amount of people sitting in chairs. More than half of them looked perfectly fine. People came to the hospital for the stupidest shit. *"My arm feels funny." "There's a tickle in my throat."* Go to the fucking doctor. Hospitals were where people came to die.

"Dad, where's Mase?"

Taking a deep breath, I headed toward the administration desk.

"Yeah, but this time," I explained, tipping my head at my father who was waiting for us, "I called in backup."

There were a few advantages to having Louis Kessler for a father. Since he was the head chair of the hospital board, Junior and his mother didn't have to pay for treatment.

Though I didn't really give a fuck if Julia got treated for shit. A common flu could kill her, for all I cared. Would save me the trouble. But it was my father's Masters in Psychiatry that made me call him today. Whether she fucking wanted to or not, Junior's mother was going to rehab.

"Did you get it?"

"Of course." My father nodded and held up what I assumed to be Julia's comitial papers.

"Good. I can get Junior, and we can get the fuck out of here." I let out a sigh of relief and turned down the hall for Julia's room.

"Junior's not down there, son. He wasn't the one who called 9-1-1; his neighbor did. Your young charge is in pediatrics."

I stopped dead in my tracks. The blood in my veins boiled as I slowly turned around. It took every ounce of my strength not to scream my words. "Why the fuck is he in pediatrics?"

"First off, I want you to know Junior's going to be fine. From what we can tell, he only has a few bumps and bruises, and maybe a mild concussion. They'll probably want to keep him for a couple of days for observation. He's been through quite an ordeal."

"What do you mean, from what we can tell? Don't you have doctors in this place. Isn't it their job to assess injuries and prescribe treatment?"

"Junior won't let the doctors give him a thorough exam. He won't even let me go near him," my father explained. "I was hoping you could help with that."

I swore under my breath. Junior was a tough kid. He didn't like to accept help and had a hard time trusting anyone. I don't think he even trusted me fully yet. With his past, I couldn't blame him. The only adults he saw wanted to do fucked up shit to him.

"Yeah, I'll talk to him."

My father nodded. "When done on Peds, come see me in my office. I have a few questions about the man who attacked Junior and his mother."

"I wasn't there," I pointed out.

But I'll find out who it was.

In true psychiatrist fashion, my father didn't answer my question. He simply looked at Logan and said, "I expect you there, too. This involves you as well."

"How the hell does this involve Logan?" I argued. The only reason my best friend tolerated Junior was because of me.

"No offence, Lou," Logan piped in, "But the kid and I aren't exactly on friendly terms. I kind of hate the little shit."

My father's next words stunned us both into silence.

"Who's The Piper, son?"

The look on our faces must've been enough for him, because the next second, my father walked away.

Logan and I didn't say a word on the way to Junior's room, or after I'd convinced him to let the doctors give him an exam. We stood in the hall watching various tests be run on the stubborn little fucker and didn't say a damn thing… We didn't have to. We both knew what the other was thinking. How the fuck did my father find out, and what else did he know?

The fact that Logan didn't respond when Junior sneered at him and said, "Why'd you bring pretty boy?" told me just how scared my best friend was.

"It'll be okay." I said.

The Knights were my brothers, my family. I'd die for any one of them, but Logan… I'd walk through hell for that bastard. We'd been through too much shit together, and I wouldn't let it end this way. Even if it meant taking on my father.

He killed his for me, and I'd do the same for him. It would hurt like a bitch–I really did love my father–but I owed my life to Logan, and so much more. He didn't just save me, he saved my mouse and Mase. You can't pay someone back for that kind of shit.

"Will it?" Logan's green eyes openly displayed his concern. "We don't even know how he found out about The Piper."

"The guy who broke in called himself The Piper." We both

turned and looked at Junior. "He told me to give you this," he added, holding out a piece of paper.

I recognized it immediately. Every note left by The Piper was on the same white card stock. Unfortunately, it was sold everywhere and too common to trace. I took the note from Junior and held it up.

Little Boy Blue couldn't bow his horn.
Forced to watch the woman from who he was born.
Where was the Knight who watches him sleep?
He was at school, commanding his sheep.
One by one, they will all fall.
Mouse, Little Boy Blue, and King on the Wall.

Come play with me,
The Piper

"This guy's really starting to piss me off," Logan grumbled.

Me too.

I frowned at Junior. His left eye was swollen, and there were bruises on his wrists and ankles. The bastard tied him and up and forced him to watch his mother's rape. Which, from Junior's reaction, was nothing short of brutal. I may not give a fuck about Julia—this probably wasn't the worst thing to happen to her—but Junior was mine.

The Piper didn't rape and torture Julia to get his rocks off. He did it to fuck with Junior. and, in turn, me. Julia was nothing more than a casualty of war. Because that's exactly what this was-- war.

This motherfucker was drawing a line in the sand and daring me to cross.

"Did you show this to my father?"

"Yes," Junior said, confirming my suspicions. "But I wouldn't give it to him. That guy told me to give it to you, with a message."

My brow rose, along with Logan's. "What message?"

"You can't keep your mouse in a cage forever."

"Fuck!" Logan muttered. "Where is she right now?"

"Her father took her home. I think Mase is with her."

Why didn't that make me feel any better?

"Where the fuck is Preston?"

That was a good question. I'd been trying to get ahold of the asshole all day. "I don't know."

Logan pulled out his phone. "I'm gonna send Parker and Silas over there."

I looked at him. How was he going to explain the sudden need for security detail, without telling them what was going on?

"I know you're trying to protect Mase, but your dad knows. This shit's already out in the open."

"Yeah, but…" I said, as my eyes locked onto a scar that blended in with one of his tattoos.

It was one of the many times Ryker burned him with a cigarette. *"Toughening him up to be a real man,"* he called it. I didn't have to say anything more. Neither one of us wanted Mason to connect the dots and find out who his biological father was.

Logan sighed. "All we have to tell them is that someone threatened her. She was attacked the other day."

That reminded me, I was already in the hospital. I should pay that asshole another visit.

"Alright." I nodded for him to make the call.

"Besides," he shot me a sly smirk as he walked out of the room,

"After the way you looked at her this morning, you'd probably kill us all if anything happened to her."

I scrubbed my hand down my face. That was a fuck up. I don't even know why I did it. Next thing, she'd be thinking I had feelings for her and using it as leverage. I'd remedy that shit when I saw her tonight.

She called me the Antichrist, said I was a monster, but she was about find out just how much of a monster I was. It was time to remind my little mouse who was in charge. First, I had to deal with my father.

"Micha?" Junior called out before I could leave the room.

"Yeah?"

"You're gonna kill him, right?"

Junior looked so small in that hospital bed with an IV in his arm.

"Yeah, I'm gonna kill him."

"Good." His eyes grew darker with his next words. "Make sure he suffers."

"He will," I said and walked out, grabbing Logan on my way.

My father's office was on the third floor in the professional wing of the hospital. It wasn't his regular office, which was in a building downtown, and one of Riley's targets when she started painting shit. This office was just as well-decorated, though, with dark cherry-wood bookshelves and a matching desk that took up half the room. Sitting in one of the black leather chairs, enjoying a drink when we walked in, was Preston.

"Welcome to the shit show," he said, holding up his glass.

"What are you doing here?"

Preston pulled out a pack of cigarettes and offered one to Logan. "You didn't think he'd bust you two and not me, did you?"

Logan eyed the smokes for a second, before taking one. He normally only smoked when he drank. Given the situation, I was tempted to take one, and I'd never smoked in my life.

"So, he went for Junior?" Preston lit his cigarette and took a long pull. "Didn't see that one coming."

I sat in the last empty chair and sighed. "Me either."

The Order had enemies, and I should've known Junior was a target. Should've protected him. I wouldn't make that mistake again.

"This is a hospital," my father said, marching in the room. "Put those out."

Preston rolled his eyes and dropped his smoke in the glass of scotch, while Logan continued to puff away.

"What?" He shrugged when I looked at him. "I'm fucked anyway, may as well enjoy my last few minutes of life."

My father sat down behind the desk, making the leather chair creak. "No one will be dying today, son, now put that out."

I'd like to think that the entirety of my father's knowledge was on the note Junior had. But I knew him. He would've started digging around the second he knew something was up. According to the doctors, Junior had been here since this morning. Since I wasn't called until about an hour ago, my father had hours. He wouldn't have told them to call me at all unless he'd found something. The question was, what?

My father sat forward and steepled his fingers under his chin. "So, who wants to start?"

The key to handling this situation was finding out what he knew, before giving away any information. Unfortunately, Logan was with us.

"That depends," Logan said, eyeing him suspiciously, "If you know anything about the tape?"

I sighed and pinched the bridge of my nose, while Preston declared he needed something stronger to drink.

"That's what I love about you, my boy. I could sit here with Preston and my son for hours, and we'd be no further than we are right now." My father chuckled. "But you… your impulsiveness will get you every time. The fact that you've managed to keep this secret for so many years is nothing short of impressive."

"So, you know?" I wasn't going to give specifics. I'd leave that up to him.

My father looked at me, insulted. "Of course I know. You boys didn't think you could kill a King, and I wouldn't find out, did you? We all know. Have this whole time."

Okay, I'm officially confused.

"Not that I'm arguing Logan's life, but killing a King is punishable by death."

Logan shot me a dirty look, and I gave him an apologetic shrug.

"Did either of you actually read the Charter?" My father tsk-ed. "It's forbidden for another King to kill another King, and you boys aren't kings yet."

When we just stared at him, he continued, "Ryker was a problem, one we couldn't take care of ourselves. So, I arranged for him to pay a visit to the sheriff, because I knew my son wouldn't be able to sit back, knowing that man was alone with his girl. Just like I knew Ryker would get the sheriff to sign the contract. Two problems solved at once. What neither of us expected was for Logan to be the one to pull the trigger. Well done, son."

I was stunned. Not only did the Kings know we killed Ryker, but they'd planned that shit? "And you just let us think that Logan was going to die if anyone found out?"

My father shrugged. "I thought it would help bond you boys."

Logan shook his head. "That's fucked up."

"I gotta admit," Preston said, "It's kind of brilliant."

My friends were taking this much better than I was.

"Riley's mother was tortured!"

"Yes," my father nodded, "That was unfortunate. But I did make sure the girl wasn't home that night, and kept her mother employed all these years, despite her lack of job performance."

I didn't know what to say. While I was impressed at how flawlessly he pulled this shit off, I was contemplating testing the non-king, killing a King rule myself.

"I'm confused," Logan said. "What does this have to do with what happened to Junior?"

"Ah, yes, that." My father slid open his desk drawer. "After I read the note the boy had, I pulled some images off the security camera at a gas station across the street from his apartment."

He slapped a picture down, and my heart stopped.

Fuck!

"It seems you boys didn't do a very good job killing Ryker after all."

Chapter 30
Riley

It's funny how two people who don't like each other can suddenly band together. I thought, when my dad brought me home, it would be the end of it. Nope. Chase not only followed us back, but he helped my dad give me the third degree. I definitely liked it better when they didn't get along. The only thing that got me through it was thinking about Mason's face.

I was in for another surprise when Shelby decided to show up with her little sister in tow. I could never deny Maggie. Her big eyes met mine, and any excuse I had to go somewhere else went out the window. Maggie was nine now, but I still saw that blonde little girl, in a pink dress with red sneakers. Shelby knew it too. Just like she knew something was wrong.

"Are you going to tell me why you've been avoiding me?" Shelby said, rummaging through my closet.

"I haven't been avoiding you."

She peeked her head out and gave me a, *"do you think I'm stupid"* look. "You know we're happy for you, right? After everything you went through with your mom, you deserve a little luxury. You don't have to shut us out."

"I'm not shutting you out."

Unable to look her in the eyes, I continued shading the phoenix's wings. Because she was right, and Micha wasn't the only reason. It was this house and all this stuff. I didn't want people looking at me differently.

"Uh huh?" she murmured unconvinced. "Trina says you haven't been taking her calls."

I rolled my eyes up, glancing over my sketchbook. "When do I ever answer her calls?"

While I liked Marnie, Trina annoyed me almost as much as Logan, and I spent most of my time with Logan looking for something to throw at him.

"Fair enough," Shelby said, disappearing back in my closet. "Tell me something, Rye? You have a closet full of brand-new clothes, so why are you still wearing this crap?"

"I happen to like my clothes," I argued. "Besides, I didn't ask for any of that fancy stuff."

"Ah! So it's a matter of principle then?"

"Exactly."

"You know how stupid that sounds right?"

"It's not stupid," I huffed.

"No, no, you're totally right. I wouldn't want to wear these Chucks, either."

Chucks?

I looked up, eyeing the closet carefully. "What color?"

Knowing Paisley, they were probably pink.

"Which pair?"

Just because Paisley got one thing right didn't mean anything.

The rest of the closet was probably full of ballgowns and sparkly princess shirts. Then again, she did get me Chucks… I slipped off the bed and took a few steps closer.

"Why is there a present in here?"

I stopped.

"Riley?" Shelby said, walking out with the pink box I'd stuffed in the back of my closet. "This is from your mom. Why haven't you opened it?"

I gritted my teeth at the perfectly tied red ribbon. That present was nothing more than another lie wrapped up in a pretty package.

"You should open it."

"I don't want to," I grumbled, returning to my sketchbook on the bed.

"Riley—"

"Don't."

Whatever was in the box labeled "for my precious daughter," could stay in there, because it obviously wasn't for me. People didn't leave precious things behind.

Shelby frowned. "Alright."

The room grew quiet as my pencil furiously moved across the paper. Why didn't I leave that present in our apartment? Shelby wasn't going to let it go, because that's what Shelby did. She tried to fix me.

Been doing it our whole lives. Telling me things would get better. That I was a survivor. But she was wrong. I wasn't a survivor, because only the strong survived, and I wasn't strong. A strong person could control their body. They wouldn't be mesmerized by a pair of chocolate eyes.

"You have no idea how beautiful you are."

No, I wasn't strong. I was broken and pathetic.

"I'm a princess," Maggie sang, waltzing out of the closet in a blue dress too big for her with jewelry draped around her neck and wrists.

I knew there were dresses in there.

"Yes, you are," I said, giving her the biggest smile I could muster.

Maggie giggled and did a little curtsey. Even at her young age, there was no denying she'd be a knockout like her sister. She had the same pretty face, golden hair, and big brown eyes as Shelby. And Shelby could give Naomi a run for her money. In fact, I'd be willing to bet if a guy had a choice between my best friend, and Naomi, they'd pick Shelby.

The only reason she wasn't queen bee of Ashen Springs High was because she didn't fit the stereotype. My best friend was a conundrum. She did the typical girly things, getting her nails done, doing her hair, and dressing up. Shelby also didn't hesitate to dive headfirst into a greasy engine.

Maggie jumped up on the bed next to me. "I like your house."

"She's got a pool, too," Shelby called out.

Maggie shrieked excitedly. "Can I go swimming?"

"Uh, sure," I muttered, staring at the necklace around her neck.

My eyes ran over the rose pendant, pausing on the small chip on the farthest left petal. It couldn't be? My grandma had one just like it, but I hadn't seen it in years. Mom sold it to pay bills. Still…

I reached out tenderly, lifting the pendant. "Where did you get this?"

"In the jewelry box," Maggie said, pointing at the closet. "There's all kinds of neat stuff in there. See?" She held up her arm, displaying a bracelet. The charms on it had me stunned–a ballet slipper, a wine glass, a puppy, and a flute . . . *Just like Mom's.*

I was too focused on the jewelry to notice Shelby had joined us until she said, "Is that your Mom's…"

"I think so?"

Shelby and I looked at each other, and then promptly walked into the closet and dumped out the jewelry box. I couldn't believe it! Everything was there. Grandma's sapphire earrings, Mom's pearl necklace. Even my grandpa's old pocket watch. All the things that I'd thought were lost forever were, sitting in a pile on my closet floor.

Shelby held up a small silver chain. "How did your dad do this?"

With tears in my eyes, I slipped on Mom's engagement ring. One thing I knew for sure, this wasn't my dad. He was completely daft when it came to jewelry. When Mom was wearing Grandma's necklace, he thought it was the one he bought her for Christmas.

"This wasn't my dad."

Shelby's brows furrowed. "Who else could it be?"

There was only one person who could pull this off. But why would he do this? I swallowed the lump in my throat and stared down at the pile.

"Swimming, swimming, swimming," Maggie chanted while dancing around.

This was just another mind game. Humiliating me wasn't enough anymore, now Micha wanted to break me. He wouldn't be happy until my heart was shattered into a hundred tattered pieces. Because the only thing Micha Kessler needed from me was my suffering.

Then why didn't he tell you about it?

I shook the thoughts out of my head and scooped the jewelry back into the box.

"Rye."

"I'm fine," I said, giving Shelby a look that told her to drop it. "Come on, let's go throw this kid in the water before she annoys us to death."

Maggie jumped up and ran out of the room. "Yay!" Her long, drawn out screech could be heard in my room.

I clamped my hands over my ears to drown out the noise. "You got a volume remote for her?"

"I told my parents we needed a shock collar, but they wouldn't go for it."

Maggie was still screaming when we got out in the hall.

"Tell them I second the shock collar motion."

Thankfully, when we reached the bottom of the stairs, Maggie was quiet. Either her voice had died, or she found something more interesting. I swear that kid had ADD. Apparently, cupcakes was the cure for a screaming child. Maggie had a mouthful of chocolate cupcake when we entered the kitchen.

Paisley was standing on the other side of the island, talking to her. "You sure like chocolate."

Maggie nodded and stuffed more inside her already full mouth. "And I get to go swimming."

"Swimming, huh?" Paisley said. "You know, I think I saw a mermaid bathing suit about your size in the pool house."

Maggie's mouth dropped open.

"I can take you to see if it fits… if it's okay with Riley and your sister?"

As much as Paisley annoyed me, I had to admit she was great with kids. When Shelby and Maggie first got here, Paisley patiently listened to Maggie ramble off all her stuffed animal's names. And there were a lot.

"Please, take her," Shelby groaned.

"Come on, Megan." Paisley said, holding her hand out for her. "We can make some milkshakes while we're out there."

"You have a kitchen outside?" Maggie was utterly shocked by this.

You'd be amazed at what this place has, Mags.

Once we were left alone, Shelby turned to me with big wide eyes. "Alright, lady, spill."

"Spill what?"

"You and Micha Kessler? When? Where? How?"

I wasn't about to go into the brutal details of my fucked-up relationship. So, I went with the short, honest approach. "In the kitchen, about a week ago."

Has it only been that long? It felt longer. Oh God, was I getting used to him being around? Crap, I think I was. I even missed the bastard when he wasn't here.

"Details, Rye." Shelby rolled her eyes. "How did it happen? Did he sweet talk you, or woo you into his embrace?"

Woo me into his embrace? Did Shelby have me confused with an eighteenth-century romance novel?

"Oh, has he kissed you yet? I went out with Sebastian Moore last week. You remember him? He was that creepy guy in science class. Well, let me tell you, the summer treated him well because… Oh, my, God. Unfortunately, it didn't do anything for his kissing skills. He smelled like Tabasco sauce, and his tongue did this weird snaky thing … you know, like curved up and to the left. I seriously thought he was eating my face. I told Trina about it, and she said he did the same thing to her. Seriously it was weird like…"

I zoned out, watching Shelby use not only her words, but her hands, to demonstrate the apparently very sloppy kiss of Sebastian Moore. Her hand wrapped around her lower jaw as she continued to ramble on.

Micha didn't just kiss me. He owned me. How he tasted, the way he smelled, and the electric feel of his soft lips on my skin was addictive. This morning it was different. It was like he was pouring part of himself inside me, and taking part of me in him. Using our souls to fill some void in the other. And I let him. I wanted to feel him with me.

"Ugh," Shelby gagged. "And you know how I hate tuna. I swear Liam eats that every day at lunch. I don't even know why I let him kiss me. I mean, he's kind of cute, but his lips were like around my nose..."

When did she start talking about Liam?

"Good God, I hope you didn't suck his dick."

I openly groaned. Great, Mason. Can this day get any better? As if Karma had heard my silent complaint, English class creeper, AKA Silas, stepped in wearing his usual scowl, followed by Parker, who sauntered over and snatched a cupcake.

"You should allow me to demonstrate a proper kiss." Mason's green eyes raked over Shelby. "You know, as an apology on behalf of all mankind."

I almost hurled.

Shelby actually blushed as she leaned over to whisper, "He's cute."

This was so not happening.

"He's really not."

"I happen to think I'm adorable," Mason argued.

Gag.

I rolled my eyes his way. "No, puppies and kittens are adorable. You're a walking hard-on, and she is off limits."

He waggled his brows at me. "Can I at least know her name?"

"I'm Shelby." Shelby smiled warmly and held up her hand.

I slapped her arm back down and gave her a dirty look. Which she returned.

"You should listen to your friend," Parker said, tossing the last piece of cupcake into his mouth. "This one will have you on your back in thirty seconds."

Mason's face lit up with a big smile. "My record's twenty-seven."

"See," I said, shifting my eyes Shelby's way. "Asshole."

She grunted in agreement, while studying Silas. "What's his problem?"

"I'm guessing life." I didn't have to see the deep frown on Silas's face to know what she was talking about. Though I had to admit, I was kind of curious. There had to be a reason someone was so angry all the time. I'd never even heard him speak. "I think he's mute, too."

Shelby didn't hesitate. She clapped her hands and called out, "Hey! Grumpy! Can you talk, cause you're kind of coming off as a serious perv right now!"

And that was why I loved my best friend.

Mason burst out laughing. Even Parker chuckled a little. Silas, however, was not amused. His cold glare turned on Shelby. What he didn't know was that would only spur her on.

She slipped off the stool and sauntered over to him, swinging her hips the whole way. After which she grabbed his face and planted a firm kiss on his lips.

"What the fuck?" Silas grumbled, pushing Shelby away.

I gotta admit, I was surprised. Silas came off as one of those guys that would have a deep, gravelly voice. Instead, it was smooth, with a melodic undertone. He could give guys like Justin Bieber a run for their money.

"See," Shelby sang with a sweet smile, "I knew you could talk."

"These bitches are crazy," Silas muttered, and stormed out the patio doors to the pool.

Little did he know, there was a mini Shelby out there.

"Oh man," Mason choked out. "My brother is gonna love you."

I instantly straightened up. "What do you mean he's going to love her?"

"He should be here any minute."

"Oh yay!" Shelby declared with a clap. "I get to meet the boyfriend."

Yeah... Yay.

My heart picked up as I tried to think of a reasonable excuse to get Shelby out of here. Not an easy task, considering my so-called boyfriend was showing up. Not to mention the way she was smiling at the boys in the room.

She was like a kid in a candy store. There was a higher chance of me convincing Micha to leave me alone, than there was of prying Shelby out of this room. Most of her visual attention seemed to be aimed at Parker. So, there was that, I guess.

He was either completely unaware of my best friend's attention, or didn't care. I cocked my head at Parker. Maybe he didn't like blondes? Besides, if he was anything like his crazy brother, I didn't want him near any of my friends, including Lana. Preston was definitely not boyfriend material.

Parker sighed and looked my way. "Did my brother hurt you?"

"No." I shook my head, and then stopped and studied his vivid crystal eyes. His at least had life in them. "He wouldn't *really* hurt me, would he?"

He remained silent and stared blankly at me.

I'll take that as a yes.

"You have a brother?" Shelby propped her elbow on the island, and rested her hand under her chin. "Is he as cute as you?"

For the first time, Parker took note of Shelby, his eyes twinkling as they raked over her body. "You don't want to go out with my brother."

"Why's that?" Shelby purred.

"Well, for starters, he's fucking crazy." Parker licked his lips, bent over the island and continued in a hushed voice, "Besides, my dick's bigger."

I felt like throwing up when Shelby blushed and batted her eyelashes.

"Careful there, princess," Mason said, "Parker's the caring and sharing type. You might find yourself with two dicks to service instead of one."

Shelby's mouth dropped open with mine, and we stared at Parker wide-eyed. He simply smiled, shot us a wink, and sauntered outside to join Silas.

"He's not gay, is he?" Shelby whispered, like it was a big secret.

I guess it could be. Tico hadn't come out to his dad yet, but to be fair, his dad already used him as a punching bag.

Mason laughed. "Let's just say, Parker's not picky. Tits and pussy, or dick and balls… sometimes both."

Huh? I wonder if Lana knew. Was that part of the reason why she liked him? Did she want two guys? I could barely handle one. I know I'd only had sex once, but Micha was a lot to handle. My fingers absently ran over my lips. He kissed me in front of the whole school.

In all the years I'd known Micha, I'd never seen him do more then put his arm around a girl. Well, other than that girl at the ice cream shop. He gave her a smoldering smile and grazed his knuckles down her face. It wasn't the milkshake said girl dumped on my head that I remembered the most… It was the way he touched her.

"Earth to Riley."

"Huh?"

A sly smirk spread across Shelby's face. "Thinking about your boyfriend?"

"What? No, of course not. Pfft!"

She wasn't buying it. "Uh huh."

"I wasn't."

"Whatever you say."

I sighed.

"Anywho," she crooned. "My dad wants us to come home. Can you get Mags ready?"

"Why can't you do it?"

"I'll have to fight with her forever, and she listens so much better to you." She pouted and gave me her puppy dog eyes. "Please."

"Fine. But you are coming with me," I added, pointing at Mason.

"Why do I have to come?" he whined.

"Because the second I leave, you'll be all over Shelby."

She smiled like this was a good thing.

Mason sucked in a shocked gasp. "I would never!"

I just looked at him.

"Yeah, okay, let's go." He nodded and headed out to the pool. "See you later, legs."

Shelby scoffed at me, "You're no fun."

"Love you, too," I sang, skipping after Mason.

Chapter 31
Micha

"Do you see what I see?"

I exhaled loudly at Logan's question. "Yeah, I fucking see it."

Parked in the driveway, next to Logan's Mustang, was a pink Camaro. The same Pink Camaro that cost him a race this summer.

"What the fuck is that bubblegum piece of shit doing in my driveway?"

Should I tell him that the owner of said "bubblegum piece of shit" was Riley's best friend? Logan didn't get pissed at cars; they were innocents in his eyes. Yet he was glaring at this one, green eyes wild with vengeance and wrath.

If I handed him a blow torch right now, he'd probably burn the fucker down. I could try to calm him down, but fuck it. I could use a little entertainment.

I got out of the Jeep and walked toward the house. "Let's go find out."

"Yeah," Logan grumbled, "I'd like to give this bitch a piece of my mind."

This should be interesting.

When I walked inside the house, I heard someone moving around in the kitchen. So that's where I went, with Logan in tow. Two steps in and he froze. Riley's friend Shelby was bent over, scooping crap back into her purse.

I looked over at my best friend. He looked stunned as his gaze slowly rolled over Shelby's blonde hair, long legs, and pert ass pointed directly at us. His throat bobbed as he forced down a swallow. I smirked.

Definitely going to be interesting.

"Way to go, Shell," Riley's friend quietly cursed. "Just throw your stuff everywhere, why don't you?"

"Need some help?" I asked, sauntering over to the fridge for a bottle of water.

"Shit." Shelby jumped back, clutching her chest. "I didn't hear you come in."

I heard Logan suck in a breath, and I held back my chuckle. Fucker looked like he just got hit by a Mack truck.

"Hi," she smiled sweetly at me and held out her hand, "I'm Shelby."

"Micha."

"So you're the boyfriend?"

"I am."

"I met you once." Her eyes narrowed, as she skeptically took me in. "You were telling Rye that she should go home and make sure her mom had enough vodka for the night."

Did she expect me to feel bad for that shit? My mouse needed a wake-up call, and I was more than happy to give it to her.

I leaned back and twisted the cap off the water. "Did she?"

"Did she what?"

"Have enough vodka for the night?"

Shelby reared back, her mouth hung open. "Boyfriends are supposed to be nice, you know."

I almost choked on my water.

"Are they?" Bracing my elbows on the island, I leaned in a little closer, and said, "Let me guess, I should bring her flowers and take her for walks on the beach?"

"Yes," she insisted with a little nod. "You should also be polite and say nice things to her."

My brow rose. Did Riley's friend know her at all?

Shelby had been so focused on me, that she squeaked a little when Logan's voice rang out.

"Who are you fucking? A goddamn Care Bear?"

Most times when chicks were embarrassed, they shied away. Not this girl. Shelby's cheeks were as bright as a tomato, yet she held her glare firmly on Logan.

"I don't think it's any business of yours who I am, or am not, sleeping with."

"Sleeping with?" He sighed and shook his head. "Jesus Christ, she can't even fucking say it."

Shelby's eyes narrowed. "Do you have a problem with me?"

"I have a problem with that bubblegum piece of shit in my driveway. Who the fuck paints their car that color?"

"Hey!" she shrieked. "Don't talk about Suzie Q like that."

Logan looked over at me. "She named her car *Suzie Q*?"

I don't know what his problem was. He called his Mustang 'Betty.' Know what I called my Jeep? Jeep. I'll never understand car people.

"You know what I think?" Shelby's lips curled in a half smirk. "I think maybe it's not my car that intimidates you."

Logan barked out a laugh. "Sweetheart, you couldn't handle my dick if you had an instruction manual and ten other chicks to help out."

Shelby's mouth dropped.

"I'll tell you what, cherry pie." He shot her a wink. "Why don't you pick your jaw up off the floor, get rid of the stuffed animals I'm sure are crowding your room, and come back to see me when you graduate from the Mickey Mouse Club." With that, he strutted out of the room, smiling in pride.

"Can you believe him?" Shelby scoffed and turned to face me.

I rolled my eyes over her jean shorts and pink "girl power" T-shirt. "How many of those stuffed animals are unicorns?"

"Just because I have…" She stomped her foot and marched to the patio doors. "Come on Mags, these guys are–" She stopped mid-sentence and broke into laughter. "What happened to you?"

A blonde little girl came skipping through the kitchen as Riley appeared in the doorway. "Take a wild guess."

I heard the little girl say something, but I didn't care. My eyes were stuck on Riley, who was dripping, her wet clothes clinging to her tight little body. I watched a drop roll down her neck, disappearing into her cleavage, and licked my lips.

"Um, yeah, I'm meeting Marnie on Saturday." Riley's face flushed when she looked over at me. "Why are you staring at me? Think this is funny?"

My eyes dropped to her breasts. Her nipples were pressing against the wet fabric of her white T-shirt; red bra visible underneath. My dick twitched. Was she still sore? Because I was half a heartbeat away from fucking her right here.

Shelby giggled. "I think hungry is more like it."

Riley's eyes widened as she shyly whispered, "Oh."

Fuck it!

I charged across the room and heaved Riley over my shoulder.

"Micha, what the hell are you doing?" she cried out, slapping my back. "Put me down."

I smacked my hand down on her ass and grabbed a fistful. Stepping through the patio doors, I ignored the hoots and hollers of my brother and friends and headed for the pool house. It'd take too long to get to her room.

"Say goodbye to your friend, Mouse. You're about to get fucked stupid."

Riley dropped her head and buried her face in my back. "You can't say shit like that."

Shelby giggled and said something. What, I don't know. Didn't fucking care.

I barged into the pool house, kicked the door shut, dropped her on her feet, and crushed my lips to hers. Wetness seeped in, soaking my clothes, but I just squeezed her shivering body into mine. Her nipples were so fucking hard, I could feel them through the layers of clothing separating us.

Riley fought at first, but gave in. She threw the same passion I saw burning in her every day into our kiss. Sweet lips slamming back on mine and greedy tongue swirling. When she was like this–lost in that feral world where need took over logic–she dropped her walls.

I couldn't just see her heart, I fucking felt it. The way her hands desperately clutched onto me, fingers digging into my flesh, as her hot breath mingled with mine. And because I was a selfish prick, I took it. Not just the taste she was offering, I took it all. Every single fucking ounce.

I was obsessed before, but now that I'd had her… There'd be no escape. No running away. I'd hunt her to the ends of the Earth and burn the world down around me, until there wasn't another motherfucker left on this planet but her and me. She was mine.

Fucking mine.

"Off," I growled, between kisses, while tugging on her shirt and pulling mine over my head.

When she didn't move fast enough, I did it for her, tearing our clothes off like they were on fire. Riley argued. She tried pushing my hands away and clinging to her wet clothes.

All that did was make me harder. She liked it too, got wet when I manhandled her. I could smell her pussy, felt it calling out to me. Once I had her striped to her panties–blue little virgin panties–she wasn't complaining anymore.

Last night she pulled a knife on me, so I tied her up. But when her hot little hand raked down my sides and cupped my ass, I vowed to never fucking tie her up again! Knife be damned. She could flay me alive as long as touched me while doing it.

With my hands full of the greatest ass on the planet, I hoisted Riley up and set her on the counter. "Gonna fuck you so hard."

"Micha," she breathed. "Everyone's out there."

"Good," I muttered, peppering kisses down her neck and across her collarbone. "I want them to hear you scream."

I took her mouth, cutting her arguments off, and fucked her with my tongue. And fuck me if she didn't fuck me right back.

It was hot.

Mind-blowing.

Perfect.

Riley reached down, palming my cock through my boxer briefs, and I damn near blew my load. All this girl had to do was touch me and it was like I was fucking twelve again, getting my first boob and praying I don't come in my pants.

I made quick work of the rest of our clothes, dropping my briefs and tearing her panties off. Riley made a grunt of disagreement. She could scold me later.

If I had it my way, she'd never wear them again. Panties just got in the way. I sighed when we were finally skin on skin. Her soft body felt like coming home. Her sweet scent was better than the morning air after rain.

I broke away and gazed down at my panting beauty, not sure if this was real. I'd dreamt about it a thousand times. Jerked off to every filthy image of Riley my mind could conjure. I tormented her. Made her life hell in any way I could. Riley could do better than me. Hell, she deserved better than me. Yet here she was, with her legs wrapped around me, eyes filled with the same need I felt every damn day.

What the fuck was wrong with her?

I looked down at her glistening pink pussy–my pussy–and slid my fingers through her slit. My mouth watered. She was so fucking wet already, juices coating my fingers as I dipped them in her.

I needed to taste her.

She tried to jump back when I knelt down, burying my face between her legs. I clamped my hand down on her hip and held her in place. No one was taking this away from me.

"Micha, what are you–Oh shit!"

Her back arched, and she threw her head back as I licked her from clit to ass, and back up again. I groaned; she was so much sweeter than I'd imagined. If this was the last thing I ever tasted, I'd die a happy man.

"Micha... we can't..." She was struggling to hold back her moans. "They're all out there."

I pumped my finger inside her tight channel, hitting that spot that made her toes curl. "We could let them watch," I said, and sucked on her clit.

Riley moaned and pulled on my hair.

She liked that.

"Maybe we should invite one of them in to join us?"

She shook her head as her pussy clamped down on my finger. "I wish I was normal."

"Normal is nothing more than a white picket fence to hide an unhappy marriage. You don't want normal." I flattened my tongue on her clit, while pushing another finger in her tight walls. "Normal sucks," I softly growled, before sucking the sensitive nerve between my teeth.

Riley tugged my hair harder and threw her head back. She was close, and I wanted it. Wanted to feel her come on my face.

My cock was aching, and if I didn't get inside her soon, my balls were going to explode. But it was worth it when she screamed out my name. There was nothing more beautiful than my girl's mouth twisted in pleasure. When the devil dragged me to hell, that was the image I wanted to take with me.

"This is my fucking pussy," I growled, standing up to take her mouth again. "Fucking mine."

I fisted my cock, guiding my shaft home. Riley made me pause.

"Did I do it right last time?"

"Did you do what right?" I asked, watching her pert nipples rise and fall with her quick breaths.

There wasn't enough blood in my brain for a conversation right now.

"Sex," she whispered shyly. "Did I do it right."

With cock in hand, I arched a brow down at her, not quite sure what to say. "Uh, baby, I came. Fucking hard."

"But did you enjoy it?"

I hunted her like an animal, tied her up, and took what I wanted. Would I change it if I could? Fuck no. And here she was, worried that I didn't like it. My chest tightened. This girl was going to kill me with her innocent eyes.

I think I fucking love her.

Fuck!

I couldn't think about that right now. My dick was aching. I needed to be inside her.

"Baby," I said, pressing a kiss on her soft lips, "There's no way I could not enjoy it."

With that, I lined my cock up, and sank deep inside in one long thrust. My eyes rolled into the back of my head.

Tight.

Hot.

Wet.

Perfect.

I grabbed a fistful of her wet hair and pumped into her, watching her moan and come undone. When her second orgasm hit, she let go. Walls fluttering around my dick as she clawed at my skin and moved her hips to fuck me back. I couldn't take it. *I need to be deeper.* I needed to hit every nerve she had, until I didn't know where I started and she ended.

I pulled out long enough to flip her over, bend her over the counter, and slammed back into her from behind. Fucking her furiously. Pumping into her with everything I had. Sweat dripped down my brow, and my balls were screaming for release. But I wasn't ready to stop. Not now, not ever. This was as close to heaven as I'd ever get, and I was going to enjoy it. Every damn day!

"So." *Thrust* "Fucking." *Thrust* "Good." *Thrust.*

I couldn't hold back anymore when Riley's cunt clamped down, and she screamed into the counter with her hands fisting.

"Fuuuck!" I roared, slamming into her has hard as I could, as my balls pulled up and I shot my load.

My body spasmed with the greatest orgasm of my life. When my dick finally stopped twitching, I collapsed on her back, out of breath. It felt like I'd just been hit by a wrecking ball.

As I lay there listening to our heavy breaths, I realized I was content. For the first time in my life, I didn't have shit to deal with. No father, no cunt of a mother, or Order. It was just me, and my mouse.

"We didn't use a condom."

"What?"

Riley twisted her neck and looked back at me. "We didn't use a condom."

I couldn't help but shake my head. She was gorgeous right now, with her face all flushed and her hair stuck to her forehead. "I know."

"What if I get pregnant?"

I chuckled. My sweet little mouse. Did she really think I didn't know?

"You won't," I said, running my nose up her neck. I loved the way she smelled right now, like sex and me. "You're on the shot."

She released a shocked gasp, which, if I wasn't already starting to get hard inside her, might've made me laugh. I ran my thumb over her lips, tugging on the bottom one and coaxing her mouth open. Fuck, I wanted to see those lips wrapped around my dick.

"I can't take any more," Riley whined when I gave her a short thrust.

I ground my hips against her ass, pressing my cock in deep. "I think you can."

And I was right. She could take more.

Twice.

Chapter 32
Riley

THE TATTOO PARLOR WAS QUIET FOR MOST OF THE DAY, WHICH WAS pretty normal considering it was Friday and most people would be at work. Unfortunately, that gave me too much time in my head, and right now it was a complete mess. I was almost happy when Mason pestered me.

"How many ink wells can two guys use?" Mason whined.

"Some of these haven't been cleaned for months," I explained.

Mathers' Tattooing only had three employees–Chase, Tanner, and Mia, who booked appointments. There wasn't always time to take care of the little things, and since this was a punishment, we got all that crap. I could tell Mason that Chase used cartridges now instead of ink wells, but it was more amusing this way. Besides, I had to do it too.

"Look, pink," Mason said, holding a stained finger in front of my face. "Guys should not be pink."

"I told you to wear gloves."

"The gloves are uncomfortable," he whined. "They're all tight and shit."

I snickered. "Now you look like you jacked-off a unicorn."

"Unicorn, huh?" Mason got a mischievous glimmer in his green eyes. "Chicks like unicorns."

I rolled my eyes and shook my head. "Only you would turn dyed skin into a pick-up line."

"You think I'm good? I once saw Logan convince a girl that his dick was a lucky charm. Every time that bitch had a test, she'd go running to him, and the fucker would get a hassle-free blow job."

Why did that not surprise me?

"The fucked-up thing," Mason continued, "Was the chick actually started acing her tests. Fucker had a line of girls begging to suck his dick that whole year." He shook his head. "I may be good, but that asshole is a master."

Over the years, I'd seen Logan in action, and every time he smooth-talked some poor unsuspecting girl, I lost a little more faith in the female species. Then again, was I really any better? I slept with Micha, my arch nemesis. More than once, I might add. I should be filled with shame and self-hatred, not worried that he was done with me.

"What about Micha?"

"What about him?"

I dug my fingers in the ink well, acting cool as I furiously scrubbed the dye. "Does he sleep around?"

The corner of Mason's mouth tipped up. "My, my, firecracker… it sounds like you're starting to like my brother."

"I am not," I growled, scrubbing the ink well harder. Fuck Micha! He was an asshole. I hated him. Only, I wasn't so sure about that anymore. I sighed and slumped back. "It doesn't matter."

"If it's any consolation, I think he's just as confused as you."

I highly doubted that.

"He doesn't trust women, and he cares about you. Just don't hurt him."

"You do realize I didn't have a choice, right?" I pointed out. Considering Mason was Micha's brother, he probably knew about the contract.

Mason sighed and slid his eyes over to me. "Would you have gone out with him if he asked?"

No. Well, maybe? I don't know?

"See."

I rolled my eyes. "He can't just take what he wants."

"In case you haven't noticed, firecracker, we're all crazy."

Trust me, I noticed.

"We'd die to protect the people we care about, though, and whether you like it or not, you're on that list," he said, and picked up another ink well to clean. "Always have been."

"Yeah, right." I snorted. "Cause your brother's been so nice to me over the years."

Mason cocked his head at me. "Why do you think you were never hassled walking down the street at night, or why your apartment was never broken into? Can any of your neighbors say that?"

I stared at him, shocked. Never really thought about it before. Everyone in my neighborhood had problems, except me. Was Micha protecting me all these years? I thought he was going to kill Evan, and after Naomi filled my locker with trash, a rather embarrassing video of her went around the school. I thought it was karmic retribution. What if it was Micha this whole time?

I glanced down at Mom's engagement ring and felt a twang of guilt. The glass I collected for The Piper this morning… I still had to get the key. What if this guy did something bad to him? Could I live with myself? My chest hurt just thinking about it. I know it was pretty much my only way to get out of this contract, but did I really want to?

"Whatever it is you're hiding," Mason said, as if he could read my thoughts, "Tell him."

Chase's booming voice rang out, cutting me off before I could respond. "You two get out here!"

Mason and I rolled our eyes at each other and groaned. We dropped our tedious cleaning projects and walked out of the backroom.

"Sooner or later," Mason said, glancing back at me, "You're going to have to admit you love him."

I stared at him, listening to the soft buzzing of a tattoo machine. I didn't love Micha. Did I?

Chase stood by the front counter, tapping his foot impatiently. "Took you long enough."

"Sorry, my super speed powers are on the fritz," I grumbled, peeking around the corner to catch a glimpse at the piece Tanner was working on.

Chase and Tanner had used a few of my designs, and the thought that someone would want something I drew was exhilarating. It made me want to do it myself. Chase had even started giving me lessons. I hadn't done anything on actual skin yet, but there were a couple of grapefruits in the fridge that looked pretty kick ass.

"We have back to back appointments and Mia's sick," Chase said. "I need you to take care of the front."

"Okay," I nodded. Answering calls and showing customers in was better than being stuck in the back cleaning.

He started to walk away, and then stopped to eye Mason. "Let him answer the phone. Last thing I need is some little boy hitting on my customers."

"Scared of the competition, old man?" Mason smirked.

Chase's brow rose as he gave Mason a quick scan. "Have your balls even dropped yet?"

I snickered, while Mason puffed up. Chase was thirty-four, barely old enough to be my father. Still, he had this look in his hazel eyes that told me he'd seen enough shit for two lifetimes.

"Keep talking like that old man and I'll show you how much of a boy I am."

The room suddenly got tense as I glanced from one to the other. Mason was ready to go, muscles flexed and shoulders rolled back. Chase, on the other hand, was smirking, with his arms folded over his chest.

I honestly didn't know who would win–nor did I want to find out. Having two massive walls of muscle go at it in the middle of the parlor was not my idea of a good time. Thankfully Tanner sauntered out and defused the situation.

"You gonna bend my boy over and fuck him?" he said, pulling his glove off with a snap. "Cause I'd pay to see that shit."

I breathed a sigh of relief when they relaxed, and the testosterone level dropped.

"Get to work," Chase growled, and disappeared around the corner.

Tanner shot me a knowing wink. His lighthearted attitude was great for bad situations. He had the same scruffy appearance as Chase–a wardrobe of jeans and t-shirts, with a face full of stubble– but other than that, they were complete opposites.

Half the girls that came in here ended up in bed with Tanner, and I don't remember Chase ever going on a date. It wasn't that he didn't have the opportunity, I think he just wasn't interested. His wife's death broke him.

"Don't worry," Tanner said. "He'll lay off in a couple days."

I groaned, "I hope so."

"Ashworth, huh?" He smiled, face beaming with pride. "My girl's got balls."

Mason chuckled. "Not according to my brother."

Tanner's face instantly dropped. "Tell me you're still a virgin," he said, eyes pleading with me.

I looked away guiltily.

"Oh my God. Baby girl's been getting dick." Tanner pulled me in for a hug, squishing my face against his hard chest.

"Can't breathe," I coughed out, but his arms only tightened around me.

"It's okay. It's alright. You're still my innocent baby girl. Just a sweet little girl in pigtails. Wait… you haven't had a dick in your mouth, have you?"

I didn't get a chance to answer, because he threw his arms up in the air and stormed away.

"Chase," he called out, walking around the corner. "Come here, I need to hit your ugly face!"

I closed my eyes and prayed to whatever god was listening that he wouldn't tell Chase.

"Huh?" Mason muttered. "Something tells me that guy is not going to like my brother very much."

"Yeah," I cringed when I heard something crash against the wall. "He's a little protective."

They both were. The trick would be making sure Tanner wasn't armed when he met Micha, because I was pretty sure he'd shoot him. I'd seen him do it before; he shot some guy that hit Mia in the leg. Don't know how he stayed out of jail for that one.

Thankfully, the rush allowed me to forget about Tanner, and Micha's impending death. I was content working the books and taking care of customers. Other than Mason answering the phone, "Mathers' Tattooing, ugly, fat, thin and tall, we tat 'em all," the day was pretty good.

It moved quickly and the customers left happy–some of Tanner's left a little happier than they should've–I did not need to hear those sounds coming out of his room. Before I knew it, the sun was setting and we were getting ready to close up.

The bell above the door rang and I groaned.

Scratch that, this day sucks.

Naomi sauntered in with her lip curled. "Why are we here?"

"Wanna check it out," Logan said, following her through the door. "My sister," he glanced over at me, "Neglected to tell me she works at a tattoo parlor."

"A tattoo parlor that's only been here for six years. Excuse me for assuming you knew it existed."

"You're excused." He shot me a smile and walked over to the photos displayed on the wall.

I rolled my eyes.

Dick!

"Fucking finally," Mason grumbled. "I thought this day would never end."

He'd been a grouchy pain in the ass for the last hour. I chalked it up to the fact that he had to actually do some work, but now that I thought about it... I cocked my head at the empty soda bottles in the trash. His mood started to drop right around the same time he polished off the last one. I shook my head. I really needed to stop overthinking things.

Tanner walked out and stopped, locking his glare on Logan. "Did he do this to you?"

My lips curled. Logan was hot and all, and I may have thought about it a couple times... "No."

"You sure?" Tanner asked, eyeing Logan skeptically. "Cause he looks like he should get shot for something."

Well, I couldn't argue that.

"In case you haven't noticed," I waved my hand over Logan's torso, "He has a thing for tattoos."

Tanner shrugged and sauntered over to him. "You looking to get some ink?"

"Depends," Logan said, peeling his eyes off the wall. "You any good?"

"Better than whoever did those." Tanner's gaze rolled over the ink covering Logan's skin. "Come on, I'll show you some of my work."

"Alright," Logan nodded, and rounded the corner with Tanner.

"Hey!" Naomi called out, throwing her hand in my direction. "You can't leave me here with them."

"Oh, come on, Barbie. I don't know about you, but I'm excited to spend some quality time together." I dropped my chin in my hands and leaned across the counter. "What should we do first? Braid each other's hair, paint our nails, or should we get right down to the girly talk? You can tell me about your boyfriend…"

I paused and gave her a fake grimace. "Oh sorry. I meant boyfriends."

"At least I know how to satisfy my men," she shot back.

"Do you though? It seems to me, if you knew how to satisfy a man, you wouldn't bounce around so many of them."

Naomi grumbled under her breath and rolled her eyes.

"Riley, have you seen the–" Chase strolled out to the front of the parlor and stopped dead in his tracks.

"Seen what?" I asked.

He didn't answer. His eyes were stuck on Naomi.

"Hello?" I called out with a snap of my fingers.

That seemed to work. Chase cleared his throat and said, "Have you seen my coils?"

"They're in the back, in the supply cabinet."

He didn't move, just continued to stand there staring at Naomi. I knew she was pretty, but come on! I turned to roll my eyes at Mason. He wasn't paying attention, either. He was bent over, digging through his bag. My eyes narrowed when he sighed and pulled out another soda bottle.

Naomi sneered at Chase, "Can I help you?"

"Sorry." Chase shook his head. "Don't get many girls like you in here."

Naomi, with her red designer dress and diamonds, screamed high-class. Guess I'd be surprised if someone like her walked in my store, too.

"That's because it stinks of sweat." Naomi shrugged uncomfortably. "I feel dirty just being in here."

Chase's brow rose. "Not much for manners, are you?"

"Not when it comes to docksider trash."

"Watch it, princess. I don't put up with mouthy bitches."

Naomi's jaw dropped and her light eyes went wide. "What did you call me? Listen to me, you little–"

I watched in utter fascination as Naomi went on to lecture Chase, waving her manicured finger in his face. Other than Tanner and my dad, I'd never seen anyone stand up to him before, and especially not a girl. They were usually batting their lashes trying to get his attention.

It was kind of like seeing a mythical creature in real life. A unicorn tromping through my backyard, or the Loch Ness monster diving off the docks.

In the blink of an eye, Chase had Naomi bent over the counter, her face pressed down not more than a foot away from where I sat. Even when I heard his hand hit her ass, I couldn't believe what was happening. I sat there in shock, listening to his strike vibrate around the room.

"What the hell do you think you're doing?!" Naomi squealed.

Chase grunted and delivered another swat. "What your daddy should've done."

I couldn't look away. I barely noticed Mason standing beside me, with the soda bottle held in front of his open lips. When his assault stopped, Naomi shot up and spun around, arm in the air ready to strike. Chase caught it and glared down at her with a look I'd never seen on his face.

"The next time you come in my shop running your mouth, you'll get my belt."

Naomi ripped her arm out of his grip. "When my father hears about this—"

"You're running your mouth again."

Her lips pursed, before she stomped her foot. "Screw this," she said, heading for the door. "I'm calling an Uber."

"That's right, princess, go running home to daddy," Chase called and rounded the corner.

I glanced at the doorway, and then the hallway Chase disappeared down. "Um, what just happened?"

"I think Naomi just got a daddy," Mason snickered, and took a drink of his soda.

Chapter 33
Riley

Mason and Chase left shortly after Naomi, leaving Tanner, Logan and me in the shop. I didn't mind the quiet. It gave me time to draw, which I was more than happy to have. I sat out in the front, listening to the soft buzz of Tanner's tattoo machine, while shading my phoenix. Soon I found myself lost in my project. So much so that I jumped at the sound of Tanner's voice.

"Hey, baby girl."

My hand flew up to my chest. "Oh Jesus!"

"The son of God. I've been called worse." Tanner chuckled and snapped off his gloves.

I grumbled, "I know, I heard." And rolled my eyes.

I'd heard women call him sir, God, and daddy. Among other things.

He tossed his gloves and walked over. "Whatcha working on?"

"A phoenix."

"Can I see?"

I shrugged and laid my sketchbook open on the counter. His eyes poured over the page while I anxiously waited. Both Chase and Tanner were amazing artists. I valued their opinion.

"I like how you added just a touch of blue here," he said, fingers drifting over the bird's wings. "You gonna let me tat it when you're done?"

"On me?"

He winked. "Gotta break that virgin skin sometime."

My heart fluttered. I really wanted a tattoo…

"Chase said I had to wait until I was eighteen."

"He's taking this responsible adult crap too far," Tanner scoffed, rolling his eyes to the roof. "Ask him how old he was when he got his first ink."

Most of the time, Chase was on my side. He encouraged my art. Told me not to live up to societies' expectations, and didn't jump down my throat if I had a drink. He was the first person to give me alcohol. It was a beer, and tasted horrible.

Unsurprisingly, I didn't drink much. Maybe had four in my whole life? While Chase was easy-going on some things, he was like a friggin' Nazi with others. That's where Tanner came in. Except when it came to boys. As far as they were both concerned, I should walk around wearing a chastity belt and stay a virgin until I was thirty.

"I want to catch the end of the game with Rico. Mind cleaning up your boy?"

I nodded and got up to grab the antiseptic and plastic wrap. Rico was Tanner's roommate, and Mia's brother. When Rico lost his place to a fire, Tanner insisted he move in with him, despite the fact they didn't get along. Some people might say he did it for Mia, but as Tanner always claimed, they were "just friends."

"Oh, and tell Logan, I'll tat him any time," Tanner added as he opened the front door. "Fucker fell asleep on me twice and didn't even twitch when I went over his ribs."

I learned a few things working here. Girls were partial to flowers. Never get your breasts tatted. After pregnancy, that stuff did not look like it should. And even the toughest man could be a secret wimp. I'd seen big burly men cry when those needles pierced their skin, especially over the bone.

"Later, baby girl," Tanner said, stepping out just as Micha came in.

I'd never been more thankful for soccer. Otherwise, Tanner might've done more than give Micha a dirty look.

Micha cocked a brow at Tanner and then looked at me. "Why's Logan's car out front?"

"He decided to get a tattoo." I held up my hands, displaying the supplies. "Gotta clean him up before we can go."

He shrugged and followed.

In the back, Logan was laying casually on the tattoo bed, shirtless, with his arms over his head and jeans open. I was kind of scared to go near him. He looked like some sculpted god, sprawled out for my viewing pleasure. I got, now, why girls dropped to their knees for him. Logan was really nice to look at.

He looked over, his lips twisting in a lazy smile. "I don't bite, sis... unless, of course, you want me to."

I cleared my throat, which was suddenly dry, walked over to him, and set my supplies on the table. Micha didn't say anything, just glared at me from the corner of the room.

Wonderful.

"This might sting a little," I explained, before stopping and cocking my head at his new tattoo.

An hourglass, with a skull on the bottom, and blood dripping from the top. I knew the image well. I drew it while in the hospital recovering from a car accident—the same accident that caused my scar. My eyes roamed over the black frame of the hourglass and down the cracked glass at the bottom. Tanner blended it perfectly into a twisted and dead tree across Logan's chest.

"Like it?" Logan asked.

I sprayed the image and gently wiped it clean. "I drew it."

"I know," he said, watching me carefully spread the medicated cream. "Made Tanner burn it after."

I didn't know whether to be flattered or pissed off. While my drawing was burned, it was immortalized on Logan's skin.

"She's my girl," Micha grumbled, making my heart flutter.

"And she's my sister," Logan smirked. "I have just as much claim to her as you do."

"It's my dick she's gonna ride in the morning, asshole, not yours."

"That's it! You're not invited to family dinners," Logan said, "And Christmas is definitely off the table."

Are they seriously having this argument?

I sighed and shook my head, preferring to concentrate on my work rather than join their stupidity. The tattoo bed was high up. I had to stand on my tip toes, and bend over Logan to attach the final piece of tape, securing the plastic over his tattoo. Which was the only reason I noticed the scar blended into one of the tree branches.

It looked like a small circular burn, something someone might get from a cigarette. The more I looked, the more I saw. Cuts, scrapes, and more burns. They were everywhere, hidden among the black ink. Like a road map of pain and torture.

I looked up and whispered, "What happened to you?"

Micha answered for him, "Being tossed in jail for a night isn't the worst thing a dad can do to their kid, Mouse."

His dad did this?

My heart broke a little when pain flashed across Logan's green eyes.

"Thanks," he growled, shooting Micha a dirty look.

"Is that why you got all the tattoos?" I asked, glancing at the grisly images inked on his skin. "To hide it?"

Logan shifted uncomfortably.

"Leave it alone, Mouse," Micha warned when I opened my mouth.

But I couldn't unsee the shame in Logan's eyes. He didn't spend all that time primping himself because he was conceited. He thought he was ugly? This beautiful man didn't see himself that way. It made my chest ache to think what he must've gone through to feel that way. I wanted to heal him. Make Logan see himself as others did.

"You're beautiful," I whispered, pressing my lips to one of his scars.

Logan sucked in a shocked gasp, and I could feel Micha watching me as I did it again and again. Planting hot kisses across his chest and down hard abs while I whispered, "You're beautiful."

Logan's muscles flexed under my palms as I slid my hands over his tanned skin. His clean, cool scent filled my nostrils, making me want to taste him. When my tongue darted out, Micha pushed off the wall and inched closer.

He watched me intently, chest lifting with his heavy breaths. In that moment, none of us were broken and flawed. We didn't have to hide alone in the dark. We were desired.

Wanted.

Needed.

Completely free.

I stared into Micha's hooded chocolate eyes, and swept my tongue over Logan's hard abs. The salty taste of his sweat, along with the wrongness of the situation, was a heady concoction. My clit throbbed watching Micha watch me put my mouth on my step-brother. Something this wrong shouldn't feel this good.

"Fuck," Logan growled, fisting the arms of the chair. "Get her off me before I do something you're going to punch me for."

Micha's voice came out deep and husky. "Do it again."

"You like this?" I purred, slipping the tips of my fingers into Logan's open jeans. "Maybe I should do more?"

Logan shot up when my thumb brushed over the head of his cock. He speared his fingers in my hair and yanked my head back. "You sure you want this?"

Did I want this? Them?

But Logan wasn't talking to me.

I felt a wall of muscle behind me, and the next thing I knew, my shirt was being lifted over my head.

"I'm not as nice as your boyfriend." Logan's piercing green eyes followed his finger, trailing along my jaw and across my bottom lip. "I'll fuck you hard."

God, yes!

"She doesn't like nice." Micha slid his warm palms down my back and around my hips. "Do you, Mouse?" he said, pulling my ass back into him.

Logan's lips came down on mine, swallowing my words. My nervous movements weren't enough for him, because he tightened his grip on my hair, making my scalp burn, and swept his tongue in my mouth when I gasped. I moaned and sunk into him. His kiss didn't have the mind-numbing effect Micha's did, but he tasted sweet and sinful. I wanted more.

Micha popped open my jeans and pushed them over my hips, while Logan dropped his on the floor. Seconds later, I was naked and sandwiched between two hard, sweaty bodies.

Logan's finger slid through my slick folds. He pressed down on my throbbing clit and breathed, "Do you taste as good here, sis?"

"Do you have to call me that?" I groaned and arched my back, pulling Micha's mouth down to mine.

As soon as I felt his lips, fireworks exploded down my body, pushing away my nervousness and making me moan.

"We're both going to fuck you, Mouse." Micha slid his palm down my ass, and around to my pussy. "And we're not going to stop, even if you beg."

Pleasure poured through me, heating my body up, as Micha pumped his fingers in my pussy, while Logan worked my clit. It was too much and not enough at the same time.

"Please," I whimpered, needing more.

"Don't worry, baby," Micha breathed, sliding his finger back and pressing against my back entrance. "Logan's gonna make you come so hard you'll be seeing stars."

He pushed the tip of his finger past the tight ring of muscles, making me tense at the burn. If he thought he was going in there, he was crazy! I didn't get a chance to argue, because Logan gripped my chin, and twisted my head to look at him.

"Hang on, sis," he said, shoving his fingers deep inside me, "I'm about to rock your world."

He pumped his fingers in me hard and fast. I don't know what he was hitting, but all I could do was hang onto Micha and ride it. My nerves were on fire, and my pussy clenched, filled with a need so intense, I thought my heart might give out.

And then I snapped; my vision blurred, and my back seized in a cloud of euphoria. I don't know how long I was trapped in Nirvana, but when I floated back down, Micha had two fingers in my ass, and the floor was wet.

I looked down at the arousal literally dripping down my thighs and muttered, "I'm sorry."

"That's cute," Logan chuckled.

Micha drug my earlobe between his teeth and said, "You just squirted, baby."

"Oh." I glanced down at the wet floor, chest still heaving from my orgasm. "Holy shit."

Logan shot me a smirk and winked. "My pleasure."

Cocky bastard.

They didn't give me any time to think about it. Micha growled and pressed in, letting me feel his hard cock, while Logan's jutted out hard and proud. His dick was longer, but not as thick. I licked my lips and swallowed. Both of them were big. Could I even do this?

"Nervous yet, sis?" Logan asked, ripping a foil packet open with his teeth, and rolling the condom along his shaft.

"No," I lied.

"Hurry the fuck up," Micha growled, yanking my head back so he could claim my lips. "I need to fuck her now."

Logan lifted me up, wrapping my legs around his waist, and the three of us shifted. Micha's lips never left mine, nor did his fingers. He continued to scissor in and out, stretching my tight hole, as Logan sat down on the tattoo bed, and pulled me to straddle him. The thick head of his cock pressed against my entrance, making my pussy squeeze.

I gasped in Micha's mouth when he sunk into me in one thrust.

"Fuck," Logan groaned, pulling my lips away from Micha and taking them for himself.

"You need to relax, baby." Micha squeezed my ass and pulled my cheeks apart.

The second I felt something impossibly large press against my back hole, I shot up.

No fucking way!

Micha simply pushed down on my back, pressing my chest into Logan's. With a grunt, he forced his way past my tight muscles. Tears sprang from my eyes, as a burn unlike any I'd felt shook my thighs.

"Hey," Logan said, cupping my face and resting my forehead on his. "Look at me. Look in my eyes, and just breathe."

I tried to listen to him. I stared into those deep green depths and tried to forget about the pain. Every time Micha inched forward, I winced, which caused Logan's dick to twitch inside me. Almost as if he liked this. Enjoyed my pain. His face twisted in pleasure, while mine twisted in pain.

"Do you… Are you enjoying this?"

"Pain gets me hard, sis," Logan said with a smile. "But don't worry, I won't hurt you. Micha would kill me if I did."

Micha's fingers were just above Logan's and tightened around my hips. "You bet your fucking ass I will," he growled, and forced another inch inside me.

I gritted my teeth and asked, "You like pain?"

Logan nodded.

"Then use it." I winced. "Fuck me, please."

He didn't need to be told twice. Logan lifted my hips, sliding out of me, only to slam back in. Fucking me hard and fast.

It was a weird concoction. Pain and pleasure. My body wasn't sure what to do. Roll my hips and fuck Logan back, or rock back into Micha. Because despite the pain, I needed to feel him.

I ended up doing both, and soon pain was outweighed by the pleasurable sensation of them moving inside me, filling me in a way I didn't know was possible.

"Oh God," I moaned, arching back into Micha, while Logan wrapped his mouth around my tight nipple.

"Fuck, Mouse," Micha wrapped his hand around my neck and drug his tongue up my cheek. "I love your tight little ass."

They slid in and out. One filled me up when the other pulled away. Sparks of ecstasy shot though me, spreading from the tips of my toes to the top of my head. Logan groaned and Micha grunted. It was dirty, wrong, and utterly perfect.

I went first. My body bowed and muscles seizing as the most intense orgasm I'd experienced rocked through me. Logan was next, slamming up into me with a grunt. Followed by Micha, who growled and bit down on my shoulder.

Afterward we lay there spent, in a content heap of sweat and panting breaths. That is, until Logan chuckled.

"If Mom and Dad could see us now."

I groaned and slapped his chest.

"Asshole," Micha muttered, and slowly slid out of me, making me wince.

"Way to ruin the moment," I said and jumped down to find my clothes.

I had my shirt and panties on when a thought occurred to me.

"You're not going to be mad at me for this later, are you?" I asked, looking up at Micha, who was holding my jeans out for me.

"No." He wrapped his arms tightly around me and placed a tender kiss on my forehead. "I wanted it as much as you did. Did you like it?"

"Did you?"

"If he was anyone else, I'd have killed him." His hard glare turned on Logan, who was busy pulling up his jeans. "Still might."

Nestled up against Micha's warm chest, breathing in his intoxicating scent, I realized that Mason was right. I did love him. Yes, he was cruel and unrepentant. He'd never be sorry for what he did to me, but he'd also never let anyone hurt me. Because I was his. Always had been.

I had to tell him about The Piper.

"Micha—"

A couple of soft clicks stopped me dead. We all turned and looked at Tanner, who was holding two guns, cocked and aimed at the guys.

"You boys done fucked up."

Micha immediately pushed me behind his back, shielding me with his body. While it was a sweet gesture, I was probably the only thing standing between him and a bullet. Logan, however, seemed completely unphased by the threat of impending death.

He casually slipped his shirt over his head and said, "Hey, Tanner."

"Who the fuck is this guy," Micha growled loudly and passed me my jeans, which I quickly put on.

"That's just Tanner," I said, trying to slip out from behind him, but I'd take a step and he'd push me back. "For the love of God," I grumbled, "He's not going to shoot me."

"He's got a fucking gun," Micha barked out angrily. "That's good enough for me."

"Her, you don't have to worry about." Tanner said, confirming my statement, "You on the other hand …"

"How'd you know?" Logan asked, looking around. "What, do you have cameras in this place?"

"I live upstairs, dickhead."

I groaned and pressed my face into Micha's back. Tanner probably heard everything.

"I told you what would happen if you touched her." I assumed he was talking to Logan. I couldn't tell, because I couldn't friggin' see.

"Yeah, yeah. You're gonna cut my dick off," Logan sang. "She started it, by the way."

"That's because *he* tainted her."

"Jealous?" Micha responded smugly.

Yup, it was definitely time to defuse this situation.

"He didn't taint me, Tanner. Micha's my boyfriend," I snarled, managing to slip past Micha to face Tanner. "And if you hurt him, I swear to God, I'll tell every girl that walks in here that you have syphilis."

"Aw, come on, baby girl. That's just playing dirty."

"Well, I did learn from the best."

He looked at me and the guys, and then sighed. "Fine." He dropped his arms and holstered the guns. "But if he hurts you, I'm putting a bullet between his eyes."

"That's fair."

Micha grumbled behind me, and I smirked.

"And I'm telling Chase," Tanner added, and spun around.

"What! No!" I shrieked, running after him.

Thankfully, I managed to catch him and convince him not to tell Chase. Tanner was bad enough. If Chase found out, one of two things would happen. Micha would disappear, or I'd end up locked in the basement until I was thirty.

Tanner left and I cleaned up while the guys took their sweet time getting dressed. By the time they came around the corner, I had everything but the front door locked up. Neither one looked too impressed when they came out from the back.

Logan wouldn't even look at me. He just said, "See you at my house," to Micha and walked out.

"Ready to go?" I asked, smiling up at Micha.

He coldly glared down at me.

"Forgot your phone," he said, tossing it to me, before marching out the door.

What crawled up his butt?

Chapter 34
Micha

Betrayal stings like a bitch.

It burns its way down your throat and rots your insides out. The festering cesspool inside me started the day my mother tried to drag me and my brother to hell with her. I lived in that pit. Reveled in the dark abyss of my dead heart for so long I didn't even notice it was beating again. My mouse had breathed life back into me. Life that was tramped down the second I read the text message that came in on her phone.

The Piper: *Have you got what I asked for?*

Not only did she name the contact, but she didn't erase the message history properly. All a person had to do to read deleted texts was know where to look, which I did. Ryker wanted my fingerprint and key, meaning he wanted access to the Order.

When he died, my father took him out of the system. The only thing he couldn't remove was the tattoo, and Ryker had that covered. I might've done the same thing in Riley's shoes. Only difference is, I would've pulled that knife across my throat.

I didn't think she could get any more perfect, and then she started that shit with Logan. She didn't want to fuck him because she fell for his shit or thought he was attractive. It was the pain inside him. She wanted to heal him, and maybe I did too.

I'd do anything to take away his nightmare past. When her eyes met mine, silently seeking permission, my heart damn near burst out of my chest. I could picture a future with her. Marriage, kids, and not just out of reproductive obligations. An actual happy family. But it was all just a play. She was only bidding her time until she could strike back.

Touché, Mouse, touché.

Unfortunately, this was chess, and she'd merely moved her pawn in check. Problem was, I couldn't make myself do what I should. I wanted to wrap my hands around her pretty little neck and strangle the life out of her. At least then I wouldn't have to feel this goddamn ache in the pit of my stomach. Wouldn't have to worry about losing her, because I'd be the one to take her away, and this shit would be over.

But what did I do when we got to Logan's? Nothing. We walked in the house, Riley turned those sapphire eyes my way, and I just stood there. Let her walk up the stairs without doing a mother-fucking thing. Why? Because as much as I hated her, I still fucking wanted her.

Fuck!

Mase walked into the kitchen and slapped his hand on my back. "You look like you need a drink."

"Got one right here," I said, holding up the beer in my hand.

"Party?" Logan asked. He knew the reason for my mood. He read the messages with me. Though he was more scared for Riley, than pissed. But she wasn't betraying him. "Derek took Mom out of town for the weekend, so we got the house to ourselves."

I shrugged. Why the fuck not? I was already well into my third drink.

Logan pulled out his phone and walked away, making calls to set shit up.

"You think Riley dances?" Mason sighed longingly. "I've been staring at that ass all day, and I'd love to see it shaking around."

Great, now I was thinking about it. Her hips swaying as she ground against me. My fist tightened around the glass neck, and I quickly swallowed the rest of my beer, washing away the images with the bubbles gliding down my throat.

"No offence bro, but I'd tap that shit in a hot minute."

"You want her?" I said, grabbing another beer out the fridge and twisting the top off. "She's all fucking yours." I marched past my brother and slipped out the patio doors to the pool. "Have fucking fun."

* * *

An hour later, the party was in full swing. "Teeth" by 5 Seconds of Summer blared from in the house. A couple groups were spread out pool side, while a few others splashed in the water. My eyes landed on Mase, who was sitting by the fire with a blonde in his lap. Silas was on the other side of the fire, looking as bored as I was.

Across the pool, under a canopy of string lights, Parker was engaged in an active game of beer pong with Ivy and Dunkin. He'd probably have both of them in bed by the end of the night.

Though, based on the way Dunkin had his arm around Ivy, it'd take some convincing to get him on his knees. Parker would do it though. It was amazing what people were willing to do once you got a few drinks in them. Speaking of drinks…

I looked in my cup and frowned.

"Here," Logan said, holding out a fresh drink.

My fucking savior.

I tossed the empty Solo cup and took the full one.

"You gonna to tell me what's up?" He flopped down on the chair beside me.

I brought the cup to my mouth and swallowed half the contents. This wasn't beer, it was real alcohol burning my throat on the way down. Just what I needed.

"Mase said you gave him the go ahead to bang Riley?"

I rolled my eyes Logan's way and sighed.

Can't a guy drink in peace?

"She really pissed you off, huh?"

"Nope," I said, sloshing my cup in his direction. "Don't give a fuck."

"Uh huh?" Logan hummed. "Is that why you're out here watching Mase, because you don't give a fuck?"

I glared over at my brother and gritted my teeth. "He can do whatever the fuck he wants."

"So I can fuck her again?"

"Go for it," I growled, gulping down the rest of my drink and crunching the empty cup in my fist, rather than punching my best friend.

Logan flopped his head back on the chair and said, "When I walked past her room earlier, I heard her crying."

My eyes snapped over to him. *Why the fuck was she crying?*

"I think she thinks you hate her because of what happened."

It was so fucking hot watching her touch Logan. The thought of her crying over it made my chest ache. It also made me hate her more because fuck her for ever making me feel this way.

"So?" I sighed, scrubbing a hand down my face. "Why the fuck should I care?"

"Look, I get that you're pissed, but you know my dad." Logan's green eyes rolled my way. "He'd have gotten Riley to cooperate one way or another. If anything, she bought herself some time."

Couldn't argue that. When Paisley's family wouldn't sign the contract, he killed every single man, woman, and child, until she was all that was left.

"She could've told me about it."

"Would you have?"

I wasn't nearly drunk enough for this conversation. I pushed myself up off the chair, which was harder than it should've been, and grumbled, "Doesn't matter." Then I made my way to the house.

What I wanted was a stiff drink, not a fucking heart to heart. Pushing a few assholes out of my way, I made my way to the cupboard above the fridge–that's where Rosy hid the premium shit. She'd kick my ass if she saw me drinking like this. Her husband lost his life trying to break up a fight I started, but fuck it, right?

"Micha?"

When I turned around, I was met with Riley's stormy eyes, red rimmed from shed tears. Logan was right, she had been crying.

Good.

"What do you want?" I said, pouring myself a glass of scotch.

"Can we talk?"

Her big blue eyes met mine, and I felt my breath hitch. My hands itched to touch her, and I couldn't stop myself from breathing in her sweet coconut scent.

Fuck my life.

"I don't see what we have to talk about." My dick didn't agree. It wanted to talk all night long.

Guilt flashed across her face. "I need to tell you something."

"I've got a better idea." I bent over the counter. *Fuck, she smelled good.* I ran the tip of my nose up her neck and whispered, "Why don't you come over here and suck my dick."

She reared back, eyes wide with shock.

"No?" I frowned, looking at a brunette in the corner. She was a poor substitute for my mouse, but not bad. Decent ass and tits. "Guess I'll have to find someone else then."

My plan was to lose myself in the brunette. Pussy was pussy, right? Riley stopped that when she grabbed my arm.

"Please, Micha, it's important."

Maybe it was sheer morbid curiosity that had me following her in an unoccupied room, because it sure as hell wasn't the unshed tears shining in her eyes. I wanted those to fall. At least, that's what I told myself.

I gritted my teeth at the large desk and filled bookshelves. Did she have to pick Ryker's old office? I swear she was trying to punish me.

"What the fuck was so important that you had to drag me away from a party?" I growled, running my hand over the smooth oak desk.

"You don't strike me as much of a partier."

I'm not, but there's alcohol out there, and you're in here.

"What do you want, Riley?" I sighed, and stared at a painting on the wall, pulling my eyes over the white sails of a boat in the raging water. It was easier than looking at her.

"I think someone's trying to hurt you."

I snorted.

Too late for that, Mouse.

"I don't know who he is. He calls himself The Piper."

I spun around, brows knit together. Was this a trick?

"How'd you meet him?"

"He messaged me one day, saying he could help me get out of the contract."

"And you accepted?" I folded my arms across my chest and leaned back against the desk.

She nodded and shifted her guilty eyes away. "I didn't give him anything though."

At first, I thought maybe Riley knew that I knew, until she passed me her phone, explaining that she'd erased most of the messages, but he sent one tonight. She even gave me the key mold she hadn't used yet, and glass with my fingerprints.

"I'm sorry. I know you hate me for what happened with Logan," she whispered in a cracked voice, "But I thought you should know."

Every fiber of my being wanted to grab her. Wipe away her tears, and tell her I wanted what happened as much as she did. Instead, I gazed down at the stuff she'd given me and said, "Why are you telling me this?"

"I think I love you."

My heart jumped. "What?"

Riley's sapphire eyes rolled up, emotion glimmering under those thick lashes. "I love you, Micha."

How long had I waited to hear those words?

This is the part where I declared my love for her. We run into each other's arms and live happily ever after. That didn't happen. I didn't hold her. Didn't tell her I loved her back. Didn't even take a step closer.

I looked into those beautiful eyes, eyes I wanted to see every day for the rest of my life, and said, "Congratulations. You want a fucking cookie?"

I watched her heart break. Saw it tear apart in front of my eyes, feeling sick about it, but doing nothing.

"Right," she whispered. A single tear rolled down her cheek, staining her perfect skin like my cruelty stained her soul. "Sorry I bothered you."

She turned and walked away, looking so broken, with her head hung and feet shuffling across the floor. I did that to her. I took this beautiful thing and snapped it in half.

Stop her! Grab her! Kiss her! Do something! Don't let her walk away!

"Riley."

She stopped, hand on the doorknob. "Yeah?"

God, she was beautiful. Even now, heartbroken and utterly destroyed, she was a goddess. Perfect in every way that mattered.

I swallowed my pain, said, "Nothing."

I let her leave.

Because I was a fucking coward.

Chapter 35
Riley

THE FIRST THING I FELT WAS A SHARP BURN SEARING THROUGH MY skull, followed by the cold hard surface under me, and how heavy my limbs were. It took a lot of effort to reach up and rub my temples. Even that didn't dull the pounding ache throbbing in my ears.

I didn't drink anything, did I? My mouth was so dry my tongue stuck to it, and when I swallowed, it felt like my throat was lined with sandpaper. Maybe I did drink? After Micha tore my heart out and stomped on it, I ran outside. Couldn't breathe in the house. I remember standing by the fountain…

I shot up and immediately cried out, clutching my head. I was grabbed from behind and someone put a wet cloth over my face. Not just anyone. The Piper. I knew this, because right before I passed out, he said, *"I told you we'd meet soon, little one."*

Shit! Was I really kidnapped?

One look at the stone walls told me, that yes, yes, I was indeed kidnapped.

And placed in a dungeon, by the looks of it.

A torch burned on the wall in the far corner. I could hear water dripping, and there was a musty smell in the air. In the middle of the room was a stone slab with restraints, and on the other side, against the farthest wall, was a long table.

Wait… I'd seen that table before. Except for the iron-barred gate across it, I knew that stone staircase, too. I gasped when a familiar whistle flowed down the dark tunnel.

This was the room Micha branded me in!

Since I had the dream, which Micha confirmed, I hadn't really thought about it. My mind was so caught up on other things, I'd completely forgotten about it.

A groan to my left drew my attention to a darkened corner of the room. A crumpled-up form shifted. "Fuck. I didn't think I drank that much."

"Mason?"

I watched him push himself up to sit, and then glance around the room, brows furrowing in confusion. "Are we being punked?"

"More like kidnapped." I stood and forced my heavy legs to move. Maybe the gate was unlocked?

"Really? You sure we're not being punked, cause this seems like some sick shit Preston would do."

"I'm sure." I tugged on the gate, making the chain locked on the other side rattle. "Ever heard of someone called The Piper?"

"No."

Guess I pissed him off when I told him yesterday to find another lackey. Wasn't sure why he took Mason though.

"Well, that's who took us." I peeked through the metal bars. Nothing but more stairs.

Jesus, how far down are we?

"I wish I knew where we were." I muttered to myself.

Mason grunted and jumped to his feet. "We're in the basement."

"So, everyone's just up there?" My heart leapt with joy and I started yelling. Someone had to hear me.

"Oh God, stop yelling," Mason groaned, pinching the bridge of his nose. "Not the basement of the house. Just… the basement."

"What? I don't understand?"

"It's where–" He paused to sigh. "You know what? Let's just say good things don't happen down here, okay?"

"Alright then, oh wizard of basement knowledge," I said. "How do we get out then?"

His green eyes rolled up to meet mine. "We don't."

"So, we're just stuck here?"

"Pretty much."

I couldn't accept that. Mason could stand there if he wanted to, but I was going to find a way out. Or, at the very least, a weapon.

My search began in the part of the room lit by the torch. I thought about using that–fire was a good weapon–but it was too high for me to reach. The rest of the room didn't offer much more than a couple of small rocks and a brittle branch.

"You're wasting your time," Mason said as I felt around the last corner of the room. "This room hasn't been used in years. You're not going to find anything."

"You don't know that."

"I do, actually. I was the last one to use this room."

I stopped and glared over at him. "What did you use it for?"

"Come on Riley… you know what I used it for."

Images of being tied to that stone slab flashed through my mind. I touched the back of my neck, wishing I could feel a mark. A bump, a scratch, anything to remind me that if even for a fleeting second, someone wanted me.

He broke me, just like he said he would.

I lurched forward and hurled, throwing up what little contents my stomach had left on the floor.

"Who?" I whispered, whipping my mouth with the back of my hand.

"It doesn't–"

"Who, Mason?"

"It doesn't matter."

"God damn it, who?" I demanded.

"The person I loved is dead, okay," he barked out angrily, "So just drop it."

"Oh, Mason," I said, feeling like a complete ass. "I'm sorry."

He brushed his hand down his face, smoothing out the scowl. "It's fine."

"It's not fine," I said, tears springing from my eyes as I slid down the wall to the cold floor. "No one should feel that kind of pain."

"Micha?"

I remained silent, preferring to chew on my lip versus deal with the hollow ache in my chest.

Mason sighed, and slumped down beside me. "You told him you loved him, and he threw it back in your face, didn't he?"

It hurt like hell to hear, but what did I expect? I knew not to give the devil my soul, yet somehow, he still took it. And he ripped it apart. My chin quivered as hot droplets dripped down my face. I didn't stop Mason from wrapping his arms around me. I'd take the comfort. I needed the illusion. It was an empty comparison to what I craved, but it was better than nothing.

"He's just afraid, you know," Mason said in a soft voice. "He'll come around."

"Micha's not afraid of anything," I grumbled into his chest. The devil doesn't feel fear, he causes it.

"Do you know how our mom died?"

Everybody knew that.

"She drove into Cherry Lake."

"Yeah," he sighed, and then quietly added, "With Micha and me in the backseat."

What?

I looked up at Mason with my mouth hung open. Their mother tried to kill them? Oh my God! What kind of mother would do that? My chest ached when I thought about the look on Micha's face as I walked out. It looked like he wanted to stop me, but he didn't. Maybe he was afraid, and who could blame him? The first woman he'd loved, betrayed him in the worst possible way.

And then I betrayed him with The Piper.

"Mason, I'm so sorry. Parents are supposed to take care of you and love you."

"Doesn't mean they do." He shrugged. "Besides, I barely remember it."

I wanted to cry for him, and for Micha, and Logan, and all the other kids who went through hell.

"It's okay," he said, tucking me under his arm. "And don't worry about Micha. It might take him a bit to figure it out, but he does love you."

"Indeed he does." We both sat up straight, suddenly alert at the sound of a new voice. A tall man with short blond hair and bright green eyes swung the gate open and stepped into the room. "I have to hand it to you, little one. I thought it would take longer for him to fall, but it seems the boy was halfway there before the game even started."

I scanned his black jeans and white shirt. Though his face was cloaked in shadows, he seemed oddly familiar. "There was no game."

He tipped his head, and I could make out a smirk tugging on the corner of his mouth. "There's always a game."

He stepped into the light and Mason swore under his breath. "Ryker."

My nose crinkled. Who was Ryker? Should I know that name? Mason sure didn't seem to like him. His arm tensed around me as he pulled us both off the floor and onto our feet. I recognized the stance he took. It was defensive, which considering Mason was the attack first type, didn't exactly bode well for us.

I leaned over and whispered, "Who is he?"

"I'm disappointed. We are practically family, after all," Ryker said, giving me a small frown. "Your father did marry *my wife*."

It was then that I saw the similarities. The way his jade eyes sharpened. How his mouth tipped up just a bit on the right. Ryker was Logan's dad, the same man that gave him all those scars.

"You're a piece of shit," I growled loudly. "What kind of man beats his own son. What's the matter, don't have the stones to pick on someone your own size? You have to target a little boy."

"Riley, don't." Mason tried to stop me when I stomped forward.

I should've been scared, maybe kept my cool. But all I could see was that look in Logan's eyes. I wanted to punch his dad. Hell, if I could, I'd dig up Micha's mom and punch her, too. My mom was a drunk, and my dad signed that contract. They weren't winning parent of the year, but they would never do something like that.

"You don't deserve the title of father." Ryker cocked his head and watched me march closer. The amusement in his eyes only fueled the fire raging through me. "I'm not afraid of you. You're pathetic. A nobody. A cow–."

His fist shot out, hitting me in the gut and knocking all the air out of my body. I crumpled over, gasping through the pain climbing my ribs to suck in more oxygen.

"You son of a–"

The sound of a gun cocking shut Mason up. "Sit down, boy."

"Fuck you," I growled through my coughs.

"Such a big mouth for such a little girl." Ryker crouched and swept away the hair stuck on my forehead. "My son would still be standing right now."

I couldn't have fought if I wanted to when Ryker hefted me over his shoulder. Pain had rendered my body useless.

"Why are you doing this?" I squeaked out.

"I have many different reasons," Ryker answered. "Betrayal, revenge, things like that."

He dropped me on the stone slab, and I cried out as a hot slice of pain shot up my spine.

"The Kings wanted me gone, and they used my son to do it."

Who are the Kings?

Before I could ask, or catch my breath, cuffs were clipped around my wrists.

"My own flesh and blood. Can you imagine?" He grabbed my leg and paused to look off into the distance. "I think that was the only time I was proud of the boy, but he couldn't even do that properly." After securing my ankle, Ryker moved to my last free limb. "I suppose I can't say much more for my other son, either."

I tried to kick out of his grasp, but it was no use. Once the metal cuff was clipped around my ankle, completely securing me to the slab, Ryker sauntered around and looked down at me. "Isn't that right, Mason?"

Oh my God! The eyes!

Both Mason and Logan had the same deep green color eyes as their father.

I looked over at Mason, who didn't seem surprised. "You knew?"

"He knew," Ryker answered for him. "Should've seen his face when he read the paternity papers. Instead of doing something about it, he buried himself in a mountain of drugs and alcohol. Sad really, I had hope for the boy."

I looked over, wishing I could comfort Mason. He swallowed and turned guiltily away. This man didn't just drive his own son to become an addict, he watched it happen. I'd have done anything to stop Mom.

"So that's why you're doing this? Because Mason's a Kessler?" I lifted my head as far as the binds would let me. "Good. He's better off. You. Don't. Deserve him."

Ryker barked out a laugh. "I like you. You've got spunk."

"Why don't you uncuff me, and I'll show you how much spunk I have," I growled, tugging on my binds.

"As much fun as that would be, it would accomplish nothing. It's the keys to the kingdom that I want, and you and Mason are my ticket to that."

I rolled my eyes. "I don't know who you think you kidnapped, but Mason and I don't have the keys to anything."

Mason's dad was a shrink, and mine was a cop. What was he after? Some therapy sessions and a little prison time?

"As you so willingly pointed out, Mason is a Kessler, and you, little one," Ryker's green eyes locked with mine, "Are the golden boy's finest prize."

This wasn't about Mason or me. He was doing this to get to– "Micha."

"Close, but my aim is higher. It's Louis I want, and what better way to eliminate the King, than to destroy his son?"

My heart picked up, pounding in my chest. I couldn't let him hurt Micha, I wouldn't. "I don't care what you do to me, I won't play your sick games."

Ryker's gaze narrowed. "I believe you."

My cheeks puffed out with my exhale. Unfortunately, my relief didn't last long.

"Mason," Ryker called, "Come here, son."

When Mason didn't move, he pressed the gun against my temple.

Mason pushed off the wall and cautiously walked over. We looked at each other, not needing to say anything. Whatever happened now, it was just us. We were all the other had, and that would have to be enough.

Nothing could've prepared either of us for what Ryker said next.

"I'm going to give you a choice, son. You can climb on top of your brother's girlfriend and fuck her, or I'll do it." He held up the gun, "With this. You have thirty seconds to decide."

My chest heaved as I glanced back and forth between Mason's wide eyes and the gun in Ryker's hand.

"You're bigger. You can take him," I tried desperately.

"I can't." Mason apologized with his eyes. "He's a Navy Seal. He'd shoot us both before I got the gun away from him."

"He's right." Ryker nodded at me, while tapping his watch. "Tick tock, Mason."

Mason pressed his forehead down on mine and released a shuddered breath. "I'll be quick, I promise."

Ryker wanted to hurt me, Mason didn't, and we were all out of options. Ryker could make us do this, he could try and rip us apart with his fucked-up games. But maybe, I could make this one hurt a little less for Mason.

I tipped my chin to give him a gentle kiss and whispered, "I trust you."

"Micha, wake up!"

Didn't know who was yelling at me, just that they were too fucking loud.

"Fuck off," I grumbled, throwing my arm over my face.

I wasn't ready to get up yet, because when I did, I'd have to see that look in Riley's eyes.

"Alright, that's it. You brought this on yourself, son."

What the fuck was my father doing here?

My head was pounding and my body ached. I spent most of last night punching the wall, and was not in the mood to deal with him. Guess he didn't agree, because next thing I knew, the couch was tipped, flopping me on the floor with a thud.

"What the fuck!" I growled, sitting up to glare at my father.

Logan was with him. The scowl on their faces told me I wasn't going to like what they had to say.

Too fucking bad.

"Do you know where your brother and your girlfriend are?" my father asked.

Fuck!

Mase did it. He actually fucked Riley. I knew I should've watched the prick. "I'm gonna fucking kill him."

"It's worse than that," Logan said, throwing me my father's phone.

I looked down at the cued-up video.

"Press play."

I cocked a brow at Logan and did as he said.

Ryker's face appeared, looking as smug as ever.

"Hello, Louis. I hadn't planned on having this conversation so soon, but Riley refused to cooperate so I had to speed things up. You and the Kings thought you had me, but you seem to forget I'm always one step ahead. Though, I gotta say, using my own son was pretty genius. I'm a little impressed that the boy had it in him."

My stomach churned. Ryker wasn't reckless. He had eight years to plan his revenge. If he came out of the shadows and contacted my father, it was because he wanted us all to know he was alive. Which meant he thought he had the upper hand.

"You and the Kings played me and now it's my turn. I only have one question for you, old friend. Do you know where your kids are?"

The video cut off.

Dread settled heavy in my gut. "Where's Mase?"

"We can't find him." Logan gave me a worried look. "Can't find Riley, either."

"What? No," I shook my head, knowing the words were a lie

before they left my mouth. "He wouldn't take Riley. She's nothing to him."

And everything to me.

"Where's your phone, son?" my father asked. "If Ryker did take your girl, he'd want you to know."

I was up on my feet searching the room before my father finished speaking. Time slowed down as I tossed the couch cushions and flipped over furniture. I eventually found my phone on the floor under the couch. My muscles tensed when I saw the red light blinking with a missed message.

There was a text. ***It's time to pay the piper, boy***, along with a picture from an unknown number. That single image was enough to make my entire world collapse. The photo was of Mase and Riley lying on a cement floor in a dark room.

This was all my fault. I should've stopped her last night. If I wasn't such a fucking coward.

"Fuck!" I yelled, throwing my fist into the wall over and over again.

Logan and my father remained silent, letting me vent my anger until the skin on my knuckles tore and blood dripped down my hand.

I tossed my phone to Logan. "He's got them both."

Pain flashed across my father's face when he gazed down at the image. He may be a hard man, but he loved his children. Knowing Mase was in the hands of a sick fuck like Ryker was killing him.

"We'll find them, son."

"How? He's had eight years to plan this shit." My father was trying to reassure me, but he had to face the hard facts. "They could be anywhere."

"No, he's still here," Logan said. "He'd want to stay close so he could watch you suffer."

"That he would," my father agreed. "I'll call Derek. The sheriff's department can help us search. We'll have to spread out in small groups. If Ryker sees us coming, he's likely to kill them. That man does not like to lose."

I knew something else he didn't like.

"Come on, Logan," I walked to the door and waved for him to follow. "We're going to talk to Chase Mathers."

My father's unsure eyes rolled my way. "Are you sure that's a good idea, son?"

"The only thing Ryker values more than winning, is his own life," I explained. "If there's a bunch of bikers riding around town looking for Riley, he's not going to get rid of his only leverage."

"Clever," my father said, cocking a brow at me. "One problem though…. Mathers' boys think he's dead."

"Won't be a problem," I said, walking out of the room with Logan in tow.

Chase Mathers would want to find Riley as much as I did, and I was willing to bet he'd come back from the grave to do it.

* * *

Preston met us outside Mathers' tattoo parlor. I called him just in case that crazy motherfucker tried to shoot us again. Riley thought he was overreacting, but I'd seen that look before. Tanner would've pulled that trigger. The only reason he didn't was because she was there.

"What's your plan?" Preston leaned back against my Jeep and lit a smoke. "I don't think Mathers will be too inclined to talk to you. You are fucking his niece."

I eyed the doors to *Mathers' Tattooing*. "Tell him the truth."

Logan and I filled Preston in when he arrived. Considering what Ryker did to his brother and sister, he was more than willing to help–all my boys were. Silas and Parker were out looking right now.

"So, you're just going to walk in there and tell him this asshole's dad," He nodded at Logan, "Kidnapped Mase and Riley, and is doing God knows what to them?"

"Yup."

"Huh?" Preston grunted, and flicked his cigarette on the ground. "Well, let's go. I can't wait to see this shit."

My eyes narrowed. "What's that supposed to mean?"

"There's a reason your old man's never bothered this guy. Mathers has a higher body count than Bundy, and you're bringing the son of the man who has his niece right to him."

Well shit, I didn't think about that. While this would help Mase and Riley, it could put Logan in serious danger. I sighed and shook my head. We didn't have a choice.

"You don't have to come," I said to Logan.

"Yeah I do. Wouldn't be in this situation if I killed him right the first time." He blew out a breath, puffing his cheeks out. "Let's get this shit over with before Tanner shoots us in the parking lot."

We all pushed off my Jeep and sauntered through the door to the parlor. The little bell rang over our heads like a death chime.

Chase was sitting behind the front counter doing paperwork, with Tanner standing behind him.

"I was wondering how long it would take you come in," Chase said, not even bothering to look up.

Tanner tipped his chin at us. "You boys back for round two?"

We could bullshit, give them some small talk, but there wasn't time for that.

"We need your help."

Chase was a big motherfucker. The chair he sat in squeaked when he leaned back and crossed his arms. "And why would I help you?"

"You wouldn't," I said, tossing my phone with the image of Riley and Mase displayed on the counter, "But you'd help her."

I don't know what scared me more, the lack of emotion on Chase's face when he saw the picture, or the look he and Tanner exchanged.

"Who has her?"

"My piece of shit father," Logan answered Chase. "We thought he was dead. I shot him years ago."

"Something tells me that one wouldn't have made the same mistake." Tanner's eyes landed on Preston, who'd been watching him from the second we walked in. "You want a shot at the title, big boy?"

I had a sudden understanding of what a gazelle felt like trapped between two hungry lions. Luckily, the tension was cut when the little bell above the door rang, and a small brunette walked in.

"Hey Chase, have you seen Riley?" she said, sparing us a glance. "We were supposed to meet at Mays, and she's not answering her phone. Thought maybe she was working?"

"Sorry, Marnie," Chase said, rolling his eyes my way, silently telling me to keep my mouth shut. A bit insulting. I wasn't a fucking child. "Haven't seen her."

Marnie pushed her glasses up her nose and clinched her brows together. "Are you sure? Cause I'm a little worried about her."

None of us missed the look she gave us when she spoke.

Especially Preston, who narrowed his eyes on her. "He said he hasn't seen her. Now fuck off."

The girl may look frumpy—no makeup, glasses and shapeless clothes—but the expression set in her face was hard.

"I know who you are, Preston Whitley," she growled. "I know who all of you are, and if I find out you did something to her, I'll make you pay. And there'll be nothing your Order can do to stop me."

All our brows arched.

Who the fuck is this chick?

Chase snickered. "If I see her, I'll tell her to call you."

"Thank you," Marnie said, and walked out, pausing long enough to shoot us a dirty look.

Once she was gone, I turned my attention back to Chase. I'd deal with the girl's knowledge on The Order later. "So, will you help?"

"You know what you're asking me to do, right?"

I nodded. "I do."

"I don't think you do. My boys don't play well with others, and you're inviting them into your playground. Not to mention the danger it puts Riley in. If I come back, it paints a bullseye on her back. Families are only sacred to the club, to everyone else they're an opportunity."

"I'll protect her."

And I would. Once I got Riley back, I wasn't letting go.

"You better." Chase gave me a stern look. "Tanner, call the boys. I've just been resurrected."

I released the breath I was holding, and silently thanked God, or fate, or whatever was up there. We may not know where Mase and Riley were, but at least they'd be alive when we found them. I scooped up my phone and stared down at my mouse's beautiful face.

"Keep her safe, Mase, we're coming."

"Hang on." Preston grabbed my arm and stared down at the image. "I think I know where they are."

Chapter 37
Riley

After what felt like the hundredth swipe of Ryker's whip, I passed out. Mason apparently wasn't rough enough with me, so Ryker decided I needed some extra pain. And pain is what I got. My back was on fire, and it hurt to breathe. I groaned and rolled over, both wincing, and sighing in relief, when my back met the cold hard floor.

"Riley," Mason's voice cracked as if he'd been crying, "Are you okay?"

Was I okay? Not by a long shot. Honestly, I was surprised I was still alive, but I couldn't let Mason know that. He did what he had to do and it broke him. I watched the light go out of his eyes.

"I've been better," I said while looking around.

We were still in the same room, except instead of being strapped down to a stone slab, I was on the floor with my ankle chained to the wall. I looked over at Mason, who was across the room in the same predicament.

"Is he gone?"

He swallowed and looked away with a grimace of disgust. "How can even you look at me? I- I–"

I didn't just hear his pain, I felt it, and it broke my heart.

"You did what you had to."

"I raped you, Riley!" he yelled, smashing his fist against the floor.

"You saved my life, Mason." I could say it a hundred times, and he'd probably never see it that way. He was taking it all on himself, instead of realizing that I wasn't the one raped. We both were.

I thought Micha was a monster–and in a way he was–but Ryker was a whole new level of evil. With one single act, he destroyed both Mason and Micha. Mason would never be able to look at himself, and Micha would never be able to look at me. A hot tear dripped from the corner of my eye onto the floor. He destroyed all three of us.

"I'm sorry," Mason whispered while his hand clawed at the floor. "Maybe if I was rougher, he wouldn't have–"

"He would've done it anyway, Mason." I licked my lips, hoping to pull some moisture down my parched throat.

I stared up at the roof and let my gaze follow the lines of stone. All the torches were lit in the room now, probably so we could watch each other. Ryker wanted us to see the pain he caused. He made Mason watch me get whipped, and every time he looked away, a punch was added to my torment.

"Did I hurt you?"

Ryker didn't need to torture him. Mason was doing that all on his own.

"No." I rolled my head Mason's way and forced myself to smile. "You didn't hurt me."

"I'm glad to see you two are bonding," Ryker snickered, and strutted through the open gate.

There was no need to lock it now. We weren't going anywhere. Even if I wasn't chained to this wall, I could barely move.

"Stay the fuck away from her," Mason growled loudly, yanking on his chain and making it clatter.

Ryker tsk-ed. "Now, now, Mason, calm down. I come bearing gifts."

Dread filled my gut at the way Ryker's lips curled.

Venom dripped from every word, as Mason said, "I don't want shit from you."

"Oh, I think you'll want this," Ryker sang and pulled a cloth off the tray in his hand.

My eyes widened at the needle, spoon, and other ingredients.

No.

He set it down on the floor, and Mason's eyes locked on the drugs. I knew addiction well, lived with it for years, and Mason was lost to it.

"Don't," I pleaded when Mason licked his lips and lifted the spoon. "You don't know what he did to it."

"I'll have you know," Ryker said, "That is grade-A, premium cut heroin and nothing else."

I tried to stop Mason. Called out, begged, and pleaded. My body screamed in pain when I fought my binds to crawl closer. Mason ignored it all.

"Just a taste," he said simply, and cooked the drugs like I wasn't even there.

Tears welled up in my eyes, clouding my vision. I couldn't watch someone else destroy themselves. Not again.

"Mason, please. Think about your dad and Micha. They love you."

"Yes, Mason, think about the people who lied to you your entire life." Ryker cocked his head down at him. "Doesn't sound like love to me."

The muscles in Mason's jaw clenched, as he filled the needle with what I was sure was a lot more than he should.

"Don't listen to him. You know your brother loves you. Would Micha want you to do this?" My voice cracked as memories of Mom and that horrible night came flooding back to me. "This won't just hurt you, it'll destroy him."

Mason held the needle up and pressed the sharp point to his arm, but he paused. I could see him fighting with himself. His brows furrowed, and his face twisted.

"Don't," I whispered, seeing hope on the horizon, "Don't let him win."

Ryker's green eyes narrowed in on me. "Tell me, boy, what do you plan on telling your brother about what you did to sweet little Riley?"

Mason's arm started to shake. He wanted to push that needle in, and I couldn't let Ryker win. Not like that.

"Are you going to tell him how you held her down and forced your cock inside her?" Ryker looked at me, a slow smirk spreading across his face. "Or are you going to lie and say you didn't like it?"

"Shut up, you sick fuck!" I screamed.

"You've never come so hard in your life, isn't that right, boy? A part of you wants to do it again."

"Don't listen to him, Mason. Put that down. It could kill you."

Mason's eyes rolled up, locking with mine. "Let's hope so," he said, and plunged the needle in his arm.

"No!" I cried out, "Don't leave me alone."

It was too late.

Just like with Mom, all I could do was watch Mason's eyes roll into the back of his head.

I can't save anyone.

"Good boy," Ryker said, petting his head.

Tears rolled down my face, warming my cheek with their hot streaks. I welcomed the pain radiating through my body. I wanted it to rip me apart, because it was better than lying there, watching Mason die.

"Just kill me," I whispered.

"Now, what fun would that be?"

I closed my eyes, shutting the monster in the corner out. He could do what he wanted. Beat me, rape me, torment me, I wouldn't give him a reaction. I didn't care enough to.

"Micha's had you for years and couldn't break you." I stayed still and listened to his footsteps fall closer. "I expected more. I've only had you for seventeen hours. Where's this spark of stubbornness I've heard so much about?"

It was gone. Just like my hopes and dreams. What was the point in fighting? Mom left me. My dad gave me away. Micha didn't want me. Even Mason checked out.

Ryker hummed. He was next to me now. I could felt those evil eyes and heard his breaths fill the air. I just didn't care.

I listened to him shuffle around, and heard a phone ring, but it was the voice that barked out on the other line that made my heart flip and eyes fly open.

"Ryker, you sick fuck."

Micha!

Ryker looked down at me and grinned. "I must admit, Micha, calling in the bikers… that was a clever tactic."

Bikers? Did Micha go to Chase? That's when I heard it. The loud rumbles rolling over the street above me. They were faint, but they were there.

While Micha may be done with me, he could still make it in time to save his brother. I looked over at Mason, who was seizing on the ground. If he made it out alive, then nothing else mattered. I could do one good thing with my life.

"Mason called it the base–" I called out, and was cut off when Ryker slapped me, sending my face twisting to the side and causing blood to fill my mouth.

"Don't fucking touch her!" Micha growled so loudly I could feel his anger. "We're already here, asshole."

I heard pops for gunfire ring in the background.

"Your girlfriend has such pretty eyes," Ryker said, running his finger down my face.

Though I didn't have much strength left, I managed to slap him and twist my head out of the way. That only seemed to amuse him. Ryker's lips curled in a sinister smile as he crawled over me, and straddled my prone form.

"Did you know it takes four minutes to strangle someone?"

My blood ran cold. I struggled to get out from under his heavy weight, but my body was so weak.

Micha grunted and swore as another round of gunfire went off. "If you kill her, you'll never get out of there in one piece."

"Neither will you," Ryker said, "Oh, and Micha, I'd hurry. Poor Mason is frothing at the mouth."

He tossed the phone and wrapped his hands around my neck. I fought, swinging my arms, slapping his face. The pressure mounted, weighing down on me, pounding in my ears, and drowning out the loud pops growing closer.

I gasped, fighting to suck in air, and clawed desperately at the hands constricting my airway. Blackness seeped in at the edge of my vision, darkening the world around me.

The last thing I heard was Micha's voice.

"I'll fucking kill you!"

Chapter 38
Micha

It was a good thing Preston tackled Ryker because I would've killed him, and my father wanted him alive. Tanner and Chase agreed to it, as long as they got to pay him a couple visits. I saw what Chase and his boys did to Ryker's men. They were ruthless sons of bitches. Whatever was left of Ryker's miserable life wouldn't be pleasant.

"Has she woken up yet?" Shelby asked, walking into Riley's hospital room.

I gazed down at my mouse and grazed my fingers along her jaw. "No."

It'd been two days now, and she hadn't woken up. At least she was breathing on her own. No more tube down her throat. But why wouldn't she wake up?

Mase did. One shot of epinephrine and he was alert as a motherfucker. A minute later and he wouldn't have woken up at all. I almost lost them both.

Come on, baby, wake up. Let me see those beautiful blue eyes.

"You should go get some sleep." Shelby laid her hand on my shoulder. "I'll stay with her."

"No." I lifted Riley's hand, pressing it to my lips and kissing each tiny finger. "I'm not leaving her."

"Micha, you haven't taken a break. You have to sleep." Shelby sighed. "Even those gruff bastards out there take shifts."

The hospital staff wasn't too happy about being taken over by a bunch of rowdy bikers, but they didn't really have a choice.

"Her father seems fine," I grumbled, glaring back at Derek asleep in the chair.

"He went home yesterday, now it's your turn." Shelby frowned at me. "Seeing you like this isn't going to help her any. Go get some rest… just a couple hours."

I huffed out a sigh. Shelby was right.

"Fine," I growled, taking one more look at my mouse before standing up. "I'll be back in two hours."

I should visit Mase anyway.

"Fine. Go," Shelby said, ushering me out.

Tanner was leaning against the wall outside Riley's room. "Got kicked out?"

"She told me to get some sleep," I grumbled, glaring at the now closed door.

"You should, you look like shit."

"Thanks."

I started walking away, but Tanner called out, stopping me.

"We commandeered a room down the hall. You can crash there if you don't want to leave."

"Yeah," I said, a little shocked. "Thanks."

"If you give me your address, I'll send someone to pick up some clothes."

I cocked my head at Tanner. "You wanted to shoot me the other day... why help me now?"

"I watched you run through a hail of gunfire for that girl, and since then you've done nothing but sit at her bedside." His chest rose with a long sigh. "I'd say that earns you some points."

Huh? Looks like the psycho was coming around.

"Doesn't mean I like you," he pointed out, "I just won't shoot you."

"Fair enough," I snickered. "I can accept that."

"Good, now go get some sleep," he said, and walked away, leaving me to do just that.

* * *

A shower and some sleep did me a world of good. I felt like a whole new man. I even stopped in to visit Mase on my way to Riley. He was leaving for rehab in a couple days, and I wanted to see him before he went. Mase told us everything.

About the paternity papers, how he remembered what our mother did, and the drugs. It was happening right under my nose, and I didn't see the signs. Part of me wanted to blame myself, but as Mase pointed out, I had to let him grow up sometime. As much as it hurt to do, I'd have to start letting him make his own mistakes.

"You're gonna have to tell her, you know?" Mase said.

"Tell her what?"

"It's not that hard to tell someone you love them." He sighed and rolled his eyes. "Come on, you can practice on me. I love you, Mase."

I cocked my brow at my brother, sitting in a hospital bed, grinning like an idiot.

"See, I almost died and you still can't say it."

"I can say it," I argued.

Mase looked me right in the eyes and said, "You've never said it to me."

I opened my mouth and closed it again, because I knew he was right. Why was it so fucking hard?

"I gotta go see Riley."

He didn't say anything. I knew what Ryker made him do, and though I didn't blame him for it, he blamed himself. He asked not to see her when she woke up.

I paused at the door and looked back at him. "I do, you know."

"I know." He nodded. "Now go see your girl."

I gave him a smile and left, walking two doors down to Riley's room. I froze outside the open door. My mouse was awake, sitting up in the bed talking to Shelby. I stood there, staring at her bright eyes, thinking I was dreaming. I wanted to rush in there, but my feet wouldn't move.

"If you love her, you'll let her go," Chase said from behind me, "Tanner was right, she doesn't belong in our world."

I should listen to him. Turn around and walk away, leaving Riley to live a happy life, while taking the dangers of mine with me.

"I can't."

Chase released a long sigh. "Yeah, I know. Just promise me something,"

"What?"

"Promise me that she will always come first. That no matter what, you'll pick her. Don't make the same mistake I did."

I looked back, seeing the pain in his eyes and promised, "Always her."

He didn't say anything else. Just nodded and walked away.

When I turned back, Riley's eyes were locked on me.

"Hi."

She sounded so small.

"Hi," I said, and stepped in.

"I'm going to go find your dad in the cafeteria." Shelby kissed Riley on the head and left, closing the door behind her.

"How's Mason?"

"He's good." I inched closer, afraid that if I touched her, she'd disappear. "Going to rehab in a couple of days."

"I know," Riley said. "Shelby told me."

"Oh."

I stood there watching as her eyes shifted around the room, looking at anything other than me. She was right there, awake, and I couldn't think of a fucking thing to say.

"She also said that she had to pry you away from my bedside." Her watery eyes rolled up and met mine.

Open your fucking mouth! Say something!

"Why are you here, Micha? You made it pretty clear that you didn't want me."

Finally, my feet fucking moved.

"I don't want you," I said, reaching out to touch her face. "I need you." I sat on the bed and cupped her face, holding her forehead against mine so I could feel her breath. "I love you, baby. I should've fucking told you that night, and I'm so fucking sorry I didn't, but I'll never leave you again. You're going to hate me sometimes, probably even want to kill me…"

I kissed her forehead. "But I'll always be there." I kissed her cheek. "To kiss you." I kissed her nose. "To fuck you." I kissed her quivering chin. "To hold you." And I kissed her lips, wet with her tears. "It won't be the normal life you want, but it'll be ours, and perfect."

She looked at me with so much emotion shining in her sapphire orbs, I couldn't breathe.

"Someone once told me, normal sucks."

I smiled down at her. "Sounds like a smart man."

"Actually, he's kind of an asshole." A smirked pulled at her perfect pink lips. "But I love him."

"I love you too, baby," I said and took those perfect lips to show her just how much I needed her.

"Pass me the socket wrench."

I scrunched my nose at the tools, trying to determine what tool Shelby was asking for.

"Here you go," I said, passing her something I thought matched the name.

She grumbled out a sigh and shook her head. "I don't know why you didn't just get a new car," she said, reaching past me to grab the correct tool. "God knows you can afford it."

I rolled my eyes. I had the same argument with my dad. It had been two months since the Ryker incident, and one of the first things I did was get my license, which entailed taking Logan's insane driving lessons. He was worse than my dad—who I was talking to now. Our relationship wasn't great, but we were getting there.

"First cars are supposed to be junkers," I pointed out.

"They're also supposed to run." Shelby shifted her eyes my way. "You could've picked something else."

I liked the yellow bug. It was sitting all alone in the back of the lot. I knew how that felt. Before Micha, I was alone, drifting through life happy to be invisible and afraid to open up to anyone. I still didn't like attention, and Micha was still an arrogant, demanding asshole, but I never felt more loved.

"How about I go get us something to drink?" Hydration was definitely where I would shine in the car fixing category.

"Got any beer?" Shelby asked, "I'm gonna need a drink after fighting with this thing. I think your car hates me."

"She's just temperamental."

"Just like her owner," Shelby muttered.

I smiled and skipped inside the house. Rosy'd made some cookies and I wanted to get some before Logan got home and ate them all. I don't know where he put it all, but holy crap could that guy eat.

Sometimes all this was a little surreal. Less than three months ago, I was living in a rundown apartment, praying Mom wouldn't drink that night. Now all I had to worry about was school and grades, almost like a normal teenager.

Well, that and Chase. He left town a month ago. Said it was time he faced his brother and took control back. Though I didn't want to see him go, I got it. He'd been hiding, just like me, and as safe as that was, it felt so much better when you came out in the sun. He was still protecting me hours away in Miami. He called every day, just so I'd know he was okay.

Mason was also taking control of his life. He wouldn't see me before he left for rehab, but I wrote him every week, and he wrote back. He was working with the counselors and opening up. Micha was a pissed that I wouldn't let him read our letters. I think he was just worried about his brother, but he had to let Mason learn how to take care of himself.

My heart warmed when Micha walked in the kitchen, looking good in a pair of dark jeans and white shirt. One look at his raw knuckles and I knew where he'd been. Every time I had a nightmare, the next day he'd go visit Ryker. I didn't know why they didn't turn him over to the police, but I didn't ask.

Micha told me The Order of Ravens and Wolves was real, and I understood that he had to do things, but I didn't ever want to know about that part of his life. Yes, he was a monster, but he was my monster.

"Want a cookie?" I asked, taking a bite out of one and moaning when the chocolate chips melted in my mouth.

Micha scooped me up in his arms and said, "I think I'd rather taste yours," before he slammed his lips down on mine.

I moaned and swirled my tongue around his. He growled, lifted me up on the counter, and pushed his way between my thighs, making my clit throb. This was definitely better than a cookie.

"Where's Logan?"

"Fuck Logan," he growled against my mouth and popped my jeans open. "You're all mine, and I'm fucking hungry."

He always was after he vented his anger. The last time he went to see Ryker, he fucked me for eight hours straight. I had other plans. Micha hadn't let me go down on him yet. I don't know if my threat to bite it off detoured him, or if we were always in too much of a hurry for me to do it, but this time I was going to get my taste.

"Tell me again," I said, slipping my hand inside his jeans to fist his hard cock. "What happens if I say no."

"I'll fuck that smart mouth of yours," he purred, while sliding his tongue down my neck.

I leaned in, nipped on his earlobe and whispered, "No."

He kissed the sensitive spot behind my ear and I felt him smile. "Get on your knees."

I obeyed and hopped off the counter to lower to my knees. Once I was down there, I wasn't so sure about this anymore. Staring at the large bulge, I licked my lips and looked into his chocolate eyes for reassurance.

"Do you have any idea," he said, swiping the pad of his thumb over my bottom lip and tugging my mouth open, "How many times I've pictured those perfect lips wrapped around me?"

"Well, don't let me stop you," Logan strutted into the room, ruining our moment.

Micha grumbled and pulled me up to my feet. "Asshole."

Logan smiled and blew a bubble with the gum he was chewing.

Since when does he chew gum?

Micha arched a brow at Logan and asked, "Are you chewing gum?"

"Yup," Logan said, shifting his gaze to Shelby as she walked in the room. "Cherry… my favorite flavor."

Shelby rolled her eyes and groaned. "Well, I got it running," she said to me. "Don't know for how long though."

"Thanks," I said, backing up into Micha, so I could stroke him through his jeans. His fingers tightened around my hip, making me smile. "You still coming over Saturday?"

"Can't." Shelby shook her head. "I've got a date."

Did Logan just growl?

"Okay, how about Sunday then?" I asked, as I continued to stroke Micha through his jeans.

He groaned and whispered, "You're about to get fucked in front of your friend, Mouse."

"Sure. I gotta go. I'm on babysitting duty tonight." Shelby said goodbye and left.

Logan watched her go, eyes narrowed, and then walked out

himself. Once we were alone, I jumped away from Micha, before he could rip my clothes off.

"Ah, ah, ah," I sang, smiling sweetly at him. I liked our games and was in the mood to play. "I want a ten second head start."

"Fuck that!" he growled, tearing his shirt off. "You get five."

I spun on my heels and ran.

"One."

Dear Mason

I know things can get lonely in there, and I'm glad to hear you made some friends. Things around here haven't really changed much. You brother's still an ass. Logan's still a slut, and Parker is still playing football. Okay, I know I should actually make an effort to get to know him. Silas is cranky as ever, I think a little more since you're not here. But don't worry I've been keeping him company for you. You were right, he really doesn't like talking about feminine hygine.

I haven't heard from Chase in a couple of days. Tanner did send me a few texts though, and i'm sure he'd let me know if something was wrong. I'm using that to not freak out. The tattoo parlor is doing okay, but the guy running it is an idiot. I might have to run him off.

Shelby's parents are getting divorced, so she's been kind of down in the dumps. I've been trying to be there for her, but there's only so many times I can watch The Notebook. Don't forget you owe me an A-Team marathon. I might throw Airwolf in there too.

Ashworth isn':t the same without you. Classes are boring, and I'm trying to keep Mrs. Grier company, but I just don't have your charming smile. Plus, I'm pretty sure she survives on a diet of souls.

Anyway, we all miss you, and are proud of all your hard work. Keep it up. I promise when you get home, I'll help you nut punch Silas.

Riley

AFTERWORD

Thank you for reading Aftereffect.
If you enjoyed this book please consider leaving a review. Reviews are always appreciated by authors.

If you'd like to be among the first to know about new releases and get an inside look into my world join my Facebook group T.L. Hodel's Murder Of Ravens.

The next book in the series is Scartissue

Also by T.L. Hodel

The Order Of Ravens And Wolves:
Aftereffect
Scartissue
Happenstance
Accident-Prone
Relapse
Panic-Button (coming soon)

Deviant House:
Innocence
Innocence corrupted (coming soon)

The Lost Souls:
Adversaries
Frenemies

Brothers Of Shadow And Death:
Backfire (coming soon)

The Seven Sins Series:
Pride

Logan

The two most prominent horsemen visited this field today.

Death and war.

They hung in the air with the taint of blood and whimpering cries. I couldn't see them, but I heard their silent call. I'd felt it tugging at the darkest parts of my soul since I was a kid. They were the monsters in my closet. The things under my bed that demanded to feed, and I answered. Because that's what all it boiled down to, in the end. There was nothing else.

Just death and war.

I rode out the last spikes of my adrenaline surge and sucked in a deep breath. Minutes ago, this place was anarchy, filled with roaring bikes and a hail of bullets. Now, there was only a soft breeze blowing through the grass. Calm, like the eye of a storm. Except my old man wasn't just any storm. He was a motherfucking hurricane. I could still hear his voice in the back of my head.

'It's time to pay the piper, boy.'

The Order of Ravens and Wolves thought they were infallible. That no one could touch the Kings. They ruled from behind their wall of secrets and golden towers. They seemed to forget one important fact. My old man was a King. There was no way he'd have started this shit if he wasn't prepared.

While everyone else was patting themselves on the back, I waited for the punchline. The second-rate guns for hire we took out were nothing more than cannon fodder. There was a bigger picture here. That much I knew. My old man always told me, the best way to catch someone off guard was to let them think they won. Whatever his endgame was, this shit was part of it.

Lou wanted my old man taken alive. Micha's dad was an idiot.

The only way we'd have captured mine, was if he wanted us to. Otherwise, he wouldn't have wasted his time taking Mase and Riley. He would've put a bullet in their heads from a thousand yards away. If Lou wasn't so busy playing King of Kings, he'd see that.

I looked at two bikers lounging on their Harleys and scanned the scythe on the back of their leather jackets. Above were the words *'Lost Souls, Miami, Chapter 11'*. Gotta say, I'd thought Micha lost his damn mind when he asked their president for help.

Chase Mathers was Riley's uncle—though he acted more like her dad—and according to Preston, the guy had a higher body count than Bundy. When Preston is sketchy about someone, that's when you need to worry. I half expected him to slit our fucking throats when we walked into his tattoo parlor. We were the reason Riley was in danger, after all.

Instead of painting the walls with our blood, Chase came back from the dead and called his boys in. Not sure why he let people think he was offed with his wife and kid, and I didn't really care. We all had the same agenda: rescue my stepsister, Riley, and my brother, Mason. My endgame was different, though. Eight years ago, I shot my old man and dumped his body in the ocean, thinking that was it. The boogeyman was dead. Saving Mase and Riley was a bonus. I came here for one reason. To finish what I started.

All this shit, the hired guns, taking Mase and Riley, was just my old man's way of saying *'surprise motherfuckers'*. Riley was to make Micha suffer—he never did like him—but Mase… that shit was all for me. Another one of his twisted lessons. Like when he made me kill my puppy. I loved that fucking dog.

One shot of epinephrine and Mase woke up. Riley was still unconscious when the ambulance took off. I'd never seen Micha cry before. Not even the first time he had to kill a man, and most of us at least shed a tear for that test. My old man had finally broken the one person I never thought he could.

My eyes locked on the open wing doors and the staircase leading into the dark.

He's down there right now.

"Shit kid," Chase's vice president, Tanner, pointed at the seeping wound in the left side of my abdomen. "You're hit."

I glanced down at one of my old man's men groaning on the ground and popped one in his skull.

"I'm fine," I said, shrugging off the dull ache crawling up my spine with the recoil.

Lou wanted to keep my dad alive, and the King of Kings word was law. Fucking Order hierarchy. Except Lou wasn't my King. Micha was, and he'd want the son of a bitch dead.

Fuck the King of Kings, and fuck the Order.

ABOUT THE AUTHOR

T.L Hodel is a Canadian author, poet and artist. Though coming from a difficult childhood she excelled at writing, having her first poetry published in junior high school. When she's not writing she occupies her self with numerous crafts, hobbies and is an avid gamer. She lives in Calgary with her kids and cat, and may have a slight weakness for horror movies. (Okay, that's a lie, she's probably seen them all)